Dear Reader,

I love nothing [more than the special] [...intimacy]
between a dark, anguished man and the very special
woman who makes him feel safe enough—human
enough—to love.

Not Just the Boss's Plaything and *A Devil in Disguise*
feature two of my hardest, most dangerous heroes
yet—and the women who love them when it seems no
one else can.

In *Not Just the Boss's Plaything,* grim ex-soldier Nikolai
Korovin (who first appears in *No More Sweet Surrender,*
February 2013) has given up on the world. But when he
meets Alicia Teller with her joyful smile, he can't quite
keep himself as cold and removed as he'd like—as he
knows he should....

In *A Devil in Disguise,* Cayo Vila prides himself on
being a ferocious machine of a businessman. When
his perfect personal assistant Drusilla throws him off
balance by quitting, he reacts the only way he knows
how: ruthlessly and decisively. But Dru knows him too
well, and now that she's thrown him for a loop, anything
can happen—even something as unthinkable as love....

I hope you'll enjoy both of these stories. I certainly had
a great time writing them!

Happy reading!

Caitlin

All about the author...
Caitlin Crews

CAITLIN CREWS discovered her first romance novel at the age of twelve. It involved swashbuckling pirates, grand adventures, a heroine with rustling skirts and a mind of her own, and a seriously mouthwatering and masterful hero. The book (the title of which remains lost in the mists of time) made a serious impression. Caitlin was immediately smitten with romances and romance heroes, to the detriment of her middle-school social life. And so began her lifelong love affair with romance novels, many of which she insists on keeping near her at all times.

Caitlin has made her home in places as far-flung as York, England, and Atlanta, Georgia. She was raised near New York City, and fell in love with London on her first visit when she was a teenager. She has backpacked in Zimbabwe, been on safari in Botswana and visited tiny villages in Namibia. She has, while visiting the place in question, declared her intention to live in Prague, Dublin, Paris, Athens, Nice, the Greek Islands, Rome, Venice, and/or any of the Hawaiian islands. Writing about exotic places seems like the next best thing to moving there.

She currently lives in California with her animator/comic-book-artist husband and their menagerie of ridiculous animals.

Other titles by Caitlin Crews available in ebook:

A SCANDAL IN THE HEADLINES *(Sicily's Corretti Dynasty)*
A ROYAL WITHOUT RULES *(Royal & Ruthless)*
NO MORE SWEET SURRENDER *(Scandal in the Spotlight)*
HEIRESS BEHIND THE HEADLINES *(Scandal in the Spotlight)*

Caitlin Crews

—

Not Just the Boss's Plaything

HARLEQUIN PRESENTS®

Recycling programs
for this product may
not exist in your area.

ISBN-13: 978-0-373-13202-7

First North American Publication 2013

NOT JUST THE BOSS'S PLAYTHING
Copyright © 2013 by Caitlin Crews

A DEVIL IN DISGUISE
Copyright © 2012 by Caitlin Crews

Printed in U.S.A.

CONTENTS

Not Just the Boss's Playth**i**ng

To the fabulous Sharon Kendrick, who sorted out what was wrong with an early draft of this book on a long, rainy, Irish drive to and from Sligo town (and an atmospheric tour of Yeats country)—both of which amounted to a master class in writing for the Harlequin Presents line.

And to Abby Green, Heidi Rice, Fiona Harper and Chantelle Shaw, for our inspiring days in Delphi.

And to all the readers who wrote me to ask for Nikolai's story. This is for you most of all!

CHAPTER ONE

TORTURE WOULD BE preferable to this.

Nikolai Korovin moved through the crowd ruthlessly, with a deep distaste for his surroundings he made no effort to hide. The club was one of London's sleekest and hottest, according to his assistants, and was therefore teeming with the famous, the trendy and the stylish.

All of whom appeared to have turned up tonight. In their slick, hectic glory, such as it was. It meant Veronika, with all her aspirations to grandeur, couldn't be far behind.

"Fancy a drink?" a blank-eyed creature with masses of shiny black hair and plumped-up lips lisped at him, slumping against him in a manner he imagined was designed to entice him. It failed. "Or anything else? Anything at all?"

Nikolai waited impatiently for her to stop that insipid giggling, to look away from his chest and find her way to his face—and when she did, as expected, she paled. As if she'd grabbed hold of the devil himself.

She had.

He didn't have to say a word. She dropped her hold on him immediately, and he forgot her the moment she slunk from his sight.

After a circuit or two around the loud and heaving

club, his eyes moving from one person to the next as they propped up the shiny bar or clustered around the leather seating areas, cataloging each and dismissing them, Nikolai stood with his back to one of the giant speakers and simply waited. The music, if it could be called that, blasted out a bass line he could feel reverberate low in his spine as if he was under sustained attack by a series of concussion grenades. He almost wished he was.

He muttered something baleful in his native Russian, but it was swept away in the deep, hard thump and roll of that terrible bass. *Torture.*

Nikolai hated this place, and all the places like it he'd visited since he'd started this tiresome little quest of his. He hated the spectacle. He hated the waste. Veronika, of course, would love it—that she'd be *seen* in such a place, in such company.

Veronika. His ex-wife's name slithered in his head like the snake she'd always been, reminding him why he was subjecting himself to this.

Nikolai wanted the truth, finally. She was the one loose end he had left, and he wanted nothing more than to cut it off, once and for all. Then she could fall from the face of the planet for all he cared.

"I never loved you," Veronika had said, a long cigarette in her hand, her lips painted red like blood and all of her bags already packed. "I've never been faithful to you except by accident." Then she'd smiled, to remind him that she'd always been the same as him, one way or another: a weapon hidden in plain sight. "Needless to say, Stefan isn't yours. What sane woman would have *your* child?"

Nikolai had eventually sobered up and understood that whatever pain he'd felt had come from the surprise of Veronika's departure, not the content of her farewell speech. Because he knew who he was. He knew *what* he was.

And he knew her.

These days, his avaricious ex-wife's tastes ran to lavish Eurotrash parties wherever they were thrown, from Berlin to Mauritius, and the well-manicured, smooth-handed rich men who attended such events in droves—but Nikolai knew she was in London now. His time in the Russian Special Forces had taught him many things, much of which remained etched deep into that cold, hard stone where his heart had never been, and finding a woman with high ambitions and very low standards like Veronika? Child's play.

It had taken very little effort to discover that she was shacking up with her usual type in what amounted to a fortress in Mayfair: some dissipated son of a too-wealthy sheikh with an extensive and deeply bored security force, the dismantling of which would no doubt be as easy for Nikolai as it was entertaining—but would also, regrettably, cause an international incident.

Because Nikolai wasn't a soldier any longer. He was no longer the Spetsnaz operative who could do whatever it took to achieve his goals—with a deadly accuracy that had won him a healthy respect that bordered on fear from peers and enemies alike. He'd shed those skins, if not what lay beneath them like sinew fused to steel, seven years ago now.

And yet because his life was nothing but an exercise in irony, he'd since become a philanthropist, an internationally renowned wolf in the ill-fitting clothes of a very soft, very fluffy sheep. He ran the Korovin Foundation, the charity he and his brother, Ivan, had begun after Ivan's retirement from Hollywood action films.

Nikolai tended to Ivan's fortune and had amassed one of his own thanks to his innate facility with investment strategies. And he was lauded far and near as a man of great compassion and caring, despite the obvious ruthlessness he did nothing to hide.

People believed what they wanted to believe. Nikolai knew that better than most.

He'd grown up hard in post-Soviet Russia, where brutal oligarchs were thick on the ground and warlords fought over territory like starving dogs—making him particularly good at targeting excessively wealthy men and the corporations they loved more than their own families, then talking them out of their money. He knew them. He understood them. They called it a kind of magic, his ability to wrest huge donations from the most reluctant and wealthiest of donors, but Nikolai saw it as simply one more form of warfare.

And he had always been so very good at war. It was his one true art.

But his regrettably high profile these days meant he was no longer the kind of man who could break into a sheikh's son's London stronghold and expect that to fly beneath the radar. Billionaire philanthropists with celebrity brothers, it turned out, had to follow rules that elite, highly trained soldiers did not. They were expected to use diplomacy and charm.

And if such things were too much of a reach when it concerned an ex-wife rather than a large donation, they were forced to subject themselves to London's gauntlet of "hot spots" and *wait*.

Nikolai checked an impatient sigh, ignoring the squealing trio of underdressed teenagers who leaped up and down in front of him, their eyes dulled with drink, drugs and their own craven self-importance.

Lights flashed frenetically, the awful music howled and he monitored the crowd from his strategic position in the shadows of the dance floor.

He simply had to wait for Veronika to show herself, as he knew she would.

Then he would find out how much of what she'd said seven years ago had been spite, designed to hurt him as much as possible, and how much had been truth. Nikolai knew that on some level, he'd never wanted to know. If he never pressed the issue, then it was always possible that Stefan really *was* his, as Veronika had made him believe for the first five years of the boy's life. That somewhere out there, he had a son. That he had done something right, even if it was by accident.

But such fantasies made him weak, he knew, and he could no longer tolerate it. He wanted a DNA test to prove that Stefan wasn't his. Then he would be done with his weaknesses, once and for all.

"You need to go and fix your life," his brother, Ivan, the only person alive that Nikolai still cared about, the only one who knew what they'd suffered at their uncle's hands in those grim years after their parents had died in a factory fire, had told him just over two years ago. Then he'd stared at Nikolai as if he was a stranger and walked away from him as if he was even less than that.

It was the last time they'd spoken in person, or about anything other than the Korovin Foundation.

Nikolai didn't blame his older brother for this betrayal. He'd watched Ivan's slide into his inevitable madness as it happened. He knew that Ivan was sadly deluded—blinded by sex and emotion, desperate to believe in things that didn't exist because it was far better than the grim alternative of reality. How could he blame Ivan for preferring the delusion? Most people did.

Nikolai didn't have that luxury.

Emotions were liabilities. Lies. Nikolai believed in sex and money. No ties, no temptations. No relationships now his brother had turned his back on him. No possibility that any of the women he took to his bed—always nameless, faceless and only permitted near him if they agreed to adhere to a very strict set of requirements—would ever reach him.

In order to be betrayed, one first had to trust.

And the only person Nikolai had trusted in his life was Ivan and even then, only in a very qualified way once that woman had sunk her claws in him.

But ultimately, this was a gift. It freed him, finally, from his last remaining emotional prison. It made everything simple. Because he had never known how to tell Ivan—who had built a life out of playing the hero in the fighting ring and on the screen, who was able to embody those fights he'd won and the roles he'd played with all the self-righteous fury of the untainted, the unbroken, the *good*—that there were some things that couldn't be fixed.

Nikolai wished he was something so simple as *broken.*

He acted like a man, but was never at risk of becoming one. He'd need flesh and blood, heat and heart for that, and those were the things he'd sold off years ago to make himself into the perfect monster. A killing machine.

Nikolai knew exactly what he was: a bright and shining piece of ice with no hope of warmth, frozen too solid for any sun to penetrate the chill. A hard and deadly weapon, honed to lethal perfection beneath his uncle's fists, then sharpened anew in the bloody Spetsnaz brotherhood. To say nothing of the dark war games he'd learned he could make into his own kind of terrible poetry, despite what it took from him in return.

He was empty where it counted, down to his bones. Empty all the way through. It was why he was so good at what he did.

And it was safer, Nikolai thought now, his eyes on the heedless, hedonistic crowd. There was too much to lose should he relinquish that deep freeze, give up that iron control. What he remembered of his drinking years appalled him—the blurred nights, the scraps and pieces of too much frustrated emotion turned too quickly into violence, making him far too much like the brutal uncle he'd so despised.

Never again.

It was better by far to stay empty. Cold. Frozen straight through.

He had never been anything but alone. Nikolai understood that now. The truth was, he preferred it that way. And once he dealt with Veronika, once he confirmed the truth about Stefan's paternity, he would never have to be anything else.

Alicia Teller ran out of patience with a sudden jolt, a wave of exhaustion and irritation nearly taking her from her feet in the midst of the jostling crowd. Or possibly that was the laddish group to her left, all of them obviously deep into the night's drinking and therefore flailing around the dance floor.

I'm much too old for this, she told herself as she moved out of their way for the tenth time, feeling ancient and decrepit at her extraordinarily advanced age of twenty-nine.

She couldn't remember the last time she'd spent a Saturday night anywhere more exciting than a quiet restaurant with friends, much less in a slick, pretentious club that had recently been dubbed *the* place to be seen in London. But then again, she also didn't like to look a gift horse in the mouth—said gift horse, in this case, being her ever-exuberant best friend and flatmate Rosie, who'd presented the guest passes to this velvet-roped circus with a grand flourish over dinner.

"It's the coolest place in London right now," she'd confidently assured Alicia over plates of *saag paneer* in their favorite Indian restaurant not far from Brick Lane. "Dripping with celebrities and therefore every attractive man in London."

"I am not cool, Rosie," Alicia had reminded her gently. "You've said so yourself for years. Every single time you try to drag me to yet another club you claim will change my life, if memory serves. It might be time for you to accept the possibility that this is who I am."

"Never!" Rosie had cried at once, feigning shock and outrage. "I remember when you were *fun,* Alicia. I've made a solemn vow to corrupt you, no matter how long it takes!"

"I'm incorruptible," Alicia had assured her. Because she also remembered when she'd been *fun,* and she had no desire to repeat those terrible mistakes, thank you, much less that descent into shame and heartache. "I'm also very likely to embarrass you. Can you handle the shame?"

Rosie had rolled her extravagantly mascaraed and shimmery-purple shadowed eyes while tossing the last of the poppadoms into her mouth.

"I can handle it," she'd said. "Anything to remind you that you're in your twenties, not your sixties. I consider it a public service."

"You say that," Alicia had teased her, "but you should

be prepared for me to request 'Dancing Queen' as if we're at a wedding disco. From the no doubt world-renowned and tragically hip DJ who will faint dead away at the insult."

"Trust me, Alicia," Rosie had said then, very seriously. "This is going to be the best night of our lives."

Now Alicia watched her best friend shake her hips in a sultry come-on to the investment banker she'd been flirting with all night, and blamed the jet lag. Nothing else could have made her forget for even a moment that sparkly, dramatic still Rosie viewed it as her sacred obligation to pull on a weekend night, the way they both had when they were younger and infinitely wilder, and that meant the exorbitant taxi fare back home from the wilds of this part of East London to the flat they shared on the outskirts of Hammersmith would be Alicia's to cough up. Alone.

"You know what you need?" Rosie had asked on the chilly trek over from the Tube, right on cue. "Desperately, I might add?"

"I know what *you* think I need, yes," Alicia had replied dryly. "But for some reason, the fantasy of sloppy and unsatisfying sex with some stranger from a club pales in comparison to the idea of getting a good night's sleep all alone in my own bed. Call me crazy. Or, barring that, *a grown-up.*"

"You're never going to find anyone, you know," Rosie had told her then, frowning. "Not if you keep this up. What's next, a nunnery?"

But Alicia knew exactly what kind of people it was possible to meet in the clubs Rosie preferred. She'd met too many of them. She'd *been* one of them throughout her university years. And she'd vowed that she would never, ever let herself get so out of control again. It wasn't worth the price—and sooner or later, there was always a price. In her case, all the years it had taken her to get her father to look at her again.

Alicia had been every inch a Daddy's girl until that terrible night the summer she'd been twenty-one. She'd been indulged and spoiled and adored beyond measure, the light of his life, and she'd lost that forever on a single night she still couldn't piece together in her head. But she knew the details almost as if she could remember it herself, because she'd had to sit and listen to her own father tell them to her the next morning while her head had pounded and her stomach had heaved: she'd been so drunk she'd been practically paralytic when she'd come home that night, but at some point she'd apparently wandered out into the back garden—which was where her father had found her, having sex with Mr. Reddick from next door.

Married Mr. Reddick, with three kids Alicia had babysat over the years, who'd been good mates with her dad until that night. The shame of it was still scarlet in her, bright and horrid, all these years later. How could she have done such a vile, despicable thing? She still didn't know.

Afterward, she'd decided that she'd had more than enough *fun* for one lifetime.

"Sorry," Alicia had said to Rosie then, smiling the painful memories away. "Are you talking about love? I was certain we were talking about the particular desperation of a Saturday night shag...."

"I have a radical idea, Saint Alicia," Rosie had said then with another roll of her eyes toward the dark sky above. "Why don't you put the halo aside for the night? It won't kill you, I promise. You might even find you like a little debauchery on a Saturday night the way you used to do."

Because Rosie didn't know, of course. Nobody knew. Alicia had been too embarrassed, too ashamed, too *disgusted* with herself to tell her friend—to tell anyone— why she'd abruptly stopped going out at the weekend, why she'd thrown herself into the job she hadn't taken seriously until then and turned it into a career she took a great deal of pride in now. Even her mother and sisters didn't know why there had been that sudden deep chill between Alicia and her dad, that had now, years later, only marginally improved into a polite distance.

"I'm not wearing my halo tonight, actually," Alicia had replied primly, patting at her riot of curls as if feeling for one anyway. "It clashed with these shoes you made me wear."

"Idiot," Rosie had said fondly, and then she'd brandished those guest passes and swept them past the crowd outside on the pavement, straight into the clutches of London's hottest club of the moment.

And Alicia had enjoyed herself—more than she'd expected she would, in fact. She'd missed dancing. She'd missed the excitement in the air, the buzz of such a big crowd. The particular, sensual seduction of a good beat. But Rosie's version of fun went on long into the night, the way it always had, and Alicia grew tired too easily. Especially when she'd only flown back into the country the day before, and her body still believed it was in another time zone altogether.

And more, when she wasn't sure she could trust herself. She didn't know what had made her do what she'd done that terrible night eight years ago; she couldn't remember much of it. So she'd opted to avoid anything and everything that might lead down that road—which was easier to do when she wasn't standing in the midst of so much cheerful abandon. Because she didn't have a halo—God knows, she'd proved that with her whorish behavior—she only wished she did.

You knew what this would be like, she thought briskly now, not bothering to fight the banker for Rosie's attention when a text from the backseat of a taxi headed home would do, and would furthermore not cause any interruption to Rosie's obvious plans for the evening. *You could have gone straight home after the curry and sorted out your laundry—*

And then she couldn't help but laugh at herself: Miss Misery Guts acting exactly like the bitter old maid Rosie often darkly intimated she was well on her way to becoming. Rosie was right, clearly. Had she really started thinking about her *laundry?* After midnight on a dance floor in a trendy London club while music even she could tell was fantastic swelled all around her?

Still laughing as she imagined the appalled look Rosie would give her when she told her about this, Alicia turned and began fighting her way out of the wild crowd and off the heaving dance floor. She laughed even harder as she was forced to leap out of the way of a particularly energetic couple flinging themselves here and there.

Alicia overbalanced because she was laughing too hard to pay attention to where she was going, and then, moving too fast to stop herself, she slipped in a puddle of spilled drink on the edge of the dance floor—

And crashed into the dark column of a man that she'd thought, before she hurtled into him, was nothing more than an extension of the speaker behind him. A still, watchful shadow.

He wasn't.

He was hard and male, impossibly muscled, sleek and

hot. Alicia's first thought, with her face a scant breath from the most stunning male chest she'd ever beheld in real life and her palms actually *touching* it, was that he smelled like winter—fresh and clean and something deliciously smoky beneath.

She was aware of his hands on her upper arms, holding her fast, and only as she absorbed the fact that he *was* holding her did she also fully comprehend the fact that somehow, despite the press of the crowd and the flashing lights and how quickly she'd been on her way toward taking an undignified header into the floor, he'd managed to catch her at all.

She tilted her head back to thank him for his quick reflexes, still smiling—

And everything stopped.

It simply—*disappeared.*

Alicia felt her heart thud, hard enough to bruise. She felt her mouth drop open.

But she saw nothing at all but his eyes.

Blue like no blue she'd ever seen in another pair of eyes before. Blue like the sky on a crystal cold winter day, so bright it almost hurt to look at him. Blue so intense it seemed to fill her up, expanding inside of her, making her feel swollen with it. As if the slightest thing might make her burst wide-open, and some mad part of her wanted that, desperately.

A touch. A smile. Anything at all.

He was beautiful. Dark and forbidding and still, the most beautiful thing she'd ever seen. Something electric sizzled in the air between them as they gazed at each other, charging through her, making her skin prickle. Making her feel heavy and restless, all at once, as if she was a snow globe he'd picked up and shaken hard, and everything inside of her was still floating drowsily in the air, looking for a place to land.

It scared her, down deep inside in a place she hadn't known was there until this moment—and yet she didn't pull away.

He blinked, as if he felt it too, this terrible, impossible, beautiful thing that crackled between them. She was sure that if she could tear her eyes from his she'd be able to see it there in the air, connecting their bodies, arcing between them and around them and through them, the voltage turned high. The faintest hint of a frown etched between his dark brows, and he moved as if to set her away from him, but then he stopped and all he'd done was shift them both even farther back into the shadows.

And still they stood there, caught. Snared. As if the world around them, the raucous club, the pounding music, the wild and crazy dancing, had simply evaporated the moment they'd touched.

At last, Alicia thought, in a rush of chaotic sensation and dizzy emotion she didn't understand at all, all of it falling through her with a certain inevitability, like a heavy stone into a terrifyingly deep well.

"My God," she said, gazing up at him. "You look like a wolf."

Was that a smile? His mouth was lush and grim at once, impossibly fascinating to her, and it tugged in one hard corner. Nothing more, and yet she smiled back at him as if he'd beamed at her.

"Is that why you've dressed in red, like a Shoreditch fairy tale?" he asked, his words touched with the faint, velvet caress of an accent she didn't recognize immediately. "I should warn you, it will end with teeth."

"I think you mean tears." She searched his hard face,

looking for more evidence of that smile. "It will end in *tears,* surely."

"That, too." Another small tug in the corner of that mouth. "But the teeth usually come first, and hurt more."

"I'll be very disappointed now if you don't have fangs," she told him, and his hands changed their steely grip on her arms, or perhaps she only then became aware of the heat of his palms and how the way he was holding her was so much like a caress.

Another tug on that austere mouth, and an answering one low in her belly, which should have terrified her, given what she knew about herself and sex. On some level, it did.

But she still didn't move away from him.

"It is, of course, my goal in life to keep strange British women who crash into me in crowded clubs from the jaws of disappointment," he said, a new light in his lovely eyes, and a different, more aware tilt to the way he held his head, the way he angled his big body toward her.

As if he might lean in close and swallow her whole.

Staring back at him then, his strong hands hard and hot on her arms and her palms still pressed flat against his taut chest, Alicia wanted nothing more than for him to do exactly that.

She should have turned away then and bolted for the door. Tried to locate whatever was left of her sanity, wherever she'd misplaced it. But she'd never felt this kind of raw, shimmering excitement before, this blistering heat weighing down her limbs so deliciously, this man so primal and powerful she found it hard to breathe.

"Even if the jaws in question are yours?" she asked, and she didn't recognize that teasing lilt in her voice, the way she tilted her head to look up at him, the liquid sort of feeling that moved in her then.

"Especially if they're mine," he replied, his bright winter gaze on her mouth, though there was a darkness there too, a shadow across his intriguing blade of a face that she nearly got lost in. *Jaws,* she reminded herself. *Fangs. He's telling me what a wolf he is, big and bad.* Surely she should feel more alarmed than she did— surely she shouldn't have the strangest urge to soothe him, instead? "You should know there are none sharper or more dangerous."

"In all of London?" She couldn't seem to keep herself from smiling again, or that sparkling cascade of something like light from rushing in her, making her stomach tighten and her breasts pull tight. *Alive. At last.* "Have you measured them, then? Is there some kind of competition you can enter to prove yours are the longest? The sharpest in all the land?"

Alicia felt completely outside herself. Some part of her wanted to lie down in it, in this mad feeling, in *him*—and exult in it. Bask in it as if it was sunshine. As if *he* was, despite the air of casual menace he wore so easily, like an extra layer of skin. Was that visible to everyone, or only to her? She didn't care. She wanted to roll around in this moment, in him, like it was the first snow of the season and she could make it all into angels.

Her breath caught at the image, and somehow, he heard it. She felt his reaction in the sudden tension of his powerful frame above her and around her, in the flex of his fingers high on her arms, in the tightening of that connection that wound between them, bright and electric, and made her feel like a stranger in her own body.

His blue eyes lifted to meet hers and gleamed bright. "I don't need to measure them, *solnyshka.*" He shifted closer, and his attention returned to her mouth. "I know."

He was an arctic wolf turned man, every inch of him

a predator—lean and hard as he stood over her despite the heels Rosie had coerced her into wearing. He wore all black, a tight black T-shirt beneath a perfectly tailored black jacket, dark trousers and boots, and his wide, hard shoulders made her skin feel tight. His dark hair was short and inky black. It made his blue eyes seem like smoke over his sculpted jaw and cheekbones, and yet all of it, all of *him,* was hard and male and so dangerous she could feel it hum beneath her skin, some part of her desperate to fight, to flee. He looked intriguingly uncivilized. Something like feral.

And yet Alicia wasn't afraid, as that still-alarmed, still-vigilant part of her knew she should have been. Not when he was looking at her like that. Not when she followed a half-formed instinct and moved closer to him, pressing her hands flatter against the magnificently formed planes of his chest while his arms went around her to hold her like a lover might. She tilted her head back even farther and watched his eyes turn to arctic fire.

She didn't understand it, but she burned.

This isn't right, a small voice cautioned her in the back of her mind. *This isn't you.*

But he was so beautiful she couldn't seem to keep track of who she was supposed to be, and her heart hurt her where it thundered in her chest. She felt something bright and demanding knot into an insistent ache deep in her belly, and she found she couldn't think of a good reason to step away from him.

In a minute, she promised herself. *I'll walk away in a minute.*

"You should run," he told her then, his voice dark and low, and she could see he was serious. That he meant it. But one of his hands moved to trace a lazy pattern on her cheek as he said it, his palm a rough velvet against her skin, and she shivered. His blue gaze seemed to sharpen. "As far away from me as you can get."

He looked so grim then, so sure, and it hurt her, somehow. She wanted to see him smile with that hard, dangerous mouth. She wanted that with every single part of her and she didn't even know his name.

None of this made any sense.

Alicia had been so good for so long. She'd paid and paid and paid for that single night eight years ago. She'd been so vigilant, so careful, ever since. She was never spontaneous. She was never reckless. And yet this beautiful shadow of a man had the bluest eyes she'd ever seen, and the saddest mouth, and the way he touched her made her shake and burn and glow.

And she thought that maybe this once, for a moment or two, she could let down her guard. Just the smallest, tiniest bit. It didn't have to mean anything she didn't want it to mean. It didn't have to mean anything at all.

So she ignored that voice inside of her, and she ignored his warning, too.

Alicia leaned her face into his hard palm as if it was the easiest thing in the world, and smiled when he pulled in a breath like it was a fire in him, too. Like he felt the same burn.

She stretched up against his hard, tough body and told herself this was about that grim mouth of his, not the wild, impossible things she knew she shouldn't let herself feel or want or, God help her, *do*. And they were in the shadows of a crowded club where nobody could see her and no one would ever know what she did in the dark. It wasn't as if it counted.

She could go back to her regularly scheduled quiet life in a moment.

It would only be a moment. One small moment outside all the rules she'd made for herself, the rules she'd lived by so carefully for so long, and then she would go straight back home to her neat, orderly, virtuous life.

She would. She had to. *She would.*

But first Alicia obeyed that surge of wild demand inside of her, leaned closer and fitted her mouth to his.

CHAPTER TWO

HE TASTED LIKE the night. Better even than she'd imagined.

He paused for the barest instant when Alicia's lips touched his. Half a heartbeat. Less.

A scant second while the taste of him seared through her, deep and dark and wild. She thought that was enough, that small taste of his fascinating mouth. That would do, and now she could go back to her quiet—

But then he angled his head to one side, used the hand at her cheek to guide her mouth where he wanted it and took over.

Devouring her like the wolf she understood he was. *He really was,* and the realization swirled inside of her like heat. His mouth was impossibly carnal, opening over hers to taste her, to claim her.

Dark and deep, hot and sure.

Alicia simply…exploded. It was like a long flash of light, shuddering and bright, searing everything away in the white hot burn of it. It was perfect. It was beautiful.

It was too much.

She shivered against him, overloaded with his bold taste, the scrape of his jaw, his talented fingers moving her mouth where he wanted it in a silent, searing command she was happy to obey. Then his hands were in her hair, buried in her thick curls. Her arms went around his neck of their own volition, and then she was plastered against the tall, hard length of him. It was like pressing into the surface of the sun and still, she couldn't seem to get close enough.

As if there was no *close enough*.

And he kissed her, again and again, with a ruthless intensity that made her feel weak and beautiful all at once, until she was mindless with need. Until she forgot her own name. Until she forgot she didn't know his. Until she forgot how dangerous *forgetting* was for her.

Until she forgot everything but him.

When he pulled back, she didn't understand. He put an inch, maybe two, between them, and then he muttered something harsh and incomprehensible while he stared at her as if he thought she was some kind of ghost.

It took her a long, confused moment to realize that she couldn't understand him because he wasn't speaking in English, not because she'd forgotten her own language, too.

Alicia blinked, the world rushing back as she did. She was still standing in that club. Music still pounded all around them, lights still flashed, well-dressed patrons still shouted over the din, and somewhere out in the middle of the dance floor, Rosie was no doubt still playing her favorite game with her latest conquest.

Everything was as it had been before she'd stumbled into this man, before he'd caught her. Before she'd kissed him.

Before he'd kissed her back.

Everything was exactly the same. Except Alicia.

He was searching her face as if he was looking for something. He shook his head slightly, then reached down and ran a lazy finger over the ridge of her collarbone, as if testing its shape. Even that made her shudder, that simple slide of skin against skin. Even so innocuous a touch seemed directly connected to that pulsing heat between her legs, the heavy ache in her breasts, the hectic spin inside of her.

She didn't have to speak his language to know whatever he muttered then was a curse.

If she were smart, the way she'd tried to be for years now, she would pull her hand away and run. Just as he'd told her she should. Just as she'd promised herself she would. Everything about this was too extreme, too intense, as if he wasn't only a strange man in a club but the kind of drug that usually went with this kind of rolling, wildly out-of-control feeling. As if she was much too close to being high on *him*.

"Last chance," he said then, as if he could read her mind.

He was giving her a warning. Again.

In her head, she listened. She smiled politely and extricated herself. She marched herself to the nearest exit, hailed a taxi, then headed straight home to the comfort of her bloody laundry. Because she knew she couldn't be trusted outside the confines of the rules she'd made for herself. She'd been living the consequences of having no rules for a long, long time.

But here, now, in this loud place surrounded by so many people and all of that pounding music, she didn't feel like the person she'd been when she'd arrived. Everything she knew about herself had twisted inside out. Turned into something else entirely in that electric blue of his challenging gaze.

As if this really was a Shoreditch fairy tale, after all.

"What big eyes you have," she teased him.

His hard mouth curved then, and she felt it like a

burst of heat, like sunlight. She couldn't do anything but smile back at him.

"So be it," he said, as if he despaired of them both.

Alicia laughed, then laughed again at the startled look in his eyes.

"The dourness is a lovely touch," she told him. "You must be beating them off with a stick. A very grim stick."

"No stick," he said, in an odd tone. "A look at me is usually sufficient."

"A wolf," she said, and grinned. "Just as I suspected."

He blinked, and again looked at her in that strange way of his, as if she was an apparition he couldn't quite believe was standing there before him.

Then he moved with the same decisiveness he'd used when he'd taken control of that kiss, tucking her into his side as he navigated his way through the dense crowd. She tried not to think about how well she fitted there, under his heavy arm, tight against the powerful length of his torso as he cut through the crowd. She tried not to drift away in the scent of him, the heat and the power, all of it surrounding her and pouring into that ache already inside of her, making it bloom and stretch and grow.

Until it took over everything.

Maybe she was under some kind of spell, Alicia thought with the small part of her that wasn't consumed with the feel of his tall, lean frame as he guided her so protectively through the crowd. It should have been impossible to move through the club so quickly, so confidently. Not in a place like this at the height of a Saturday night. But he did it.

And then they were outside, in the cold and the damp November night, and he was still moving in that same breathtaking way, like quicksilver. Like he knew exactly where they were headed—away from the club and the people still milling about in front of it. He led her down the dark street, deeper into the shadows, and it was then Alicia's sense of self-preservation finally kicked itself into gear.

Better late than never, she thought, annoyed with herself, but it actually *hurt* her to pull away from the magnificent shelter of his body, from all of that intense heat and strength. It felt like she'd ripped her skin off when she stepped away from him, as if they'd been fused together.

He regarded her calmly, making her want to trust him when she knew she shouldn't. She couldn't.

"I'm sorry, but…" She wrapped her arms around her own waist in an attempt to make up for the heat she'd lost when she'd stepped away from him. "I don't know a single thing about you."

"You know several things, I think."

He sounded even more delicious now that they were alone and she could hear him properly. *Russian*, she thought, as pleased as if she'd learned his deepest, darkest secrets.

"Yes," she agreed, thinking of the things she knew. Most of them to do with that insistent ache in her belly, and lower. His mouth. His clever hands. "All lovely things. But none of them worth risking my personal safety for, I'm sure you'll agree."

Something like a smile moved in his eyes, but didn't make it to his hard mouth. Still, it echoed in her, sweet and light, making her feel far more buoyant than she should have on a dark East London street with a strange man even she could see was dangerous, no matter how much she wanted him.

Had she ever wanted anything this much? Had anyone?

"A wolf is never without risk," he told her, that voice of his like whiskey, smooth and scratchy at once, heating her up from the inside out. "That's the point of wolves. Or you'd simply get a dog, pat it on the head." His eyes gleamed. "Teach it tricks."

Alicia wasn't sure she wanted to know the tricks this man had up his sleeve. Or, more to the point, she wasn't sure she'd survive them. She wasn't certain she'd survive this as it was.

"You could be very bad in bed," she said, conversationally, as if she picked up strange men all the time. She hardly recognized her own light, easy, flirtatious tone. She hadn't heard it since before that night in her parents' back garden. "That's a terrible risk to take with any stranger, and awkward besides."

That smile in his eyes intensified, got even bluer. "I'm not."

She believed him.

"You could be the sort who gets very, very drunk and weeps loudly about his broken heart until dawn." She gave a mock shudder. "So tedious, especially if poetry is involved. Or worse, *singing*."

"I don't drink," he countered at once. His dark brows arched over those eyes of his, challenging her. Daring her. "I never sing, I don't write poems and I certainly do not weep." He paused. "More to the point, I don't have a heart."

"Handy, that," she replied easily. She eyed him. "You could be a killer, of course. That would be unfortunate."

She smiled at that. He didn't.

"And if I am?"

"There you go," she said, and nodded sagely. Light,

airy. Enchanted, despite herself. "I can't possibly go off into the night with you now, can I?"

But it was terrifying how much she *wanted* to go off with him, wherever he'd take her, and instead of reacting to that as she should, she couldn't stop smiling at him. As if she already knew him, this strange man dressed all in black, his blue eyes the only spot of color on the cold pavement as he stared at her as if she'd stunned him somehow.

"My name is Nikolai," he said, and she had the oddest impression he hadn't meant to speak at all. He shifted, then reached over and traced her lips with his thumb, his expression so fierce, so intent, it made her feel hollowed out inside, everything scraped away except that wild, wondrous heat he stirred in her. "Text someone my name and address. Have them ring every fifteen minutes if you like. Send the police. Whatever you want."

"All those safeguards are very thoughtful," she pointed out, but her eyes felt too wide and her voice sounded insubstantial. Wispy. "Though not exactly wolfish, it has to be said."

His mouth moved into his understated version of a smile

"I want you." His eyes were on fire. Every inch of him that wolf. "What will it take?"

She swayed back into him as if they were magnets and she'd simply succumbed to the pull. And then she had no choice but to put her hand to his abdomen, to feel all that blasting heat right there beneath her palm.

Even that didn't scare her the way it should.

"What big teeth you have," she whispered, too on edge to laugh, too filled with that pulsing ache inside of her to smile.

"The biting part comes later." His eyes gleamed

again, with the kind of sheer male confidence that made it difficult to breathe. Alicia stopped trying. "If you ask nicely."

He picked up her hand and lifted it to his mouth, tracing a dark heat over the back of it. He didn't look away.

"If you're sure," she said piously, trying desperately to pretend she wasn't shaking, and that he couldn't feel it. That he didn't know exactly what he was doing to her when she could see full well that he did. "I was promised a wolf, not a dog."

"I eat dogs for breakfast."

She laughed then. "That's not particularly comforting."

"I can't be what I'm not, *solnyshka*." He turned her hand over, then kissed her palm in a way that made her hiss in a sharp breath. His eyes were smiling again, so bright and blue. "But I'm very good at what I am."

And she'd been lost since she'd set eyes on him, hadn't she? What use was there in pretending otherwise? She wasn't drunk. It wasn't like that terrible night, because she knew what she was doing. Didn't she?

"Note to self," Alicia managed to say, breathless and dizzy and unable to remember why she'd tried to stop this in the first place, when surrendering to it—to him—felt so much like triumph. Like fate. "Never eat breakfast with a wolf. The sausages are likely the family dog."

He shrugged. "Not *your* family dog," he said with that fierce mouth of his, though she was sure his blue eyes laughed. "If that helps."

And this time, when she smiled at him, the negotiation was over.

The address he gave her in his clipped, direct way was in an extraordinarily posh part of town Alicia could hardly afford to visit, much less live in. She dutifully texted it to Rosie, hoping that her friend was far too busy to check it until morning. And then she tucked her phone away and forgot about Rosie altogether.

Because he still moved like magic, tucking her against him again as if there was a crowd he needed to part when there was only the late-night street and what surged between them like heat lightning. As if he liked the way she fitted there as much as she did. And her heart began to pound all over again, excitement and anticipation and a certain astonishment at her own behavior pouring through her with every hard thump.

At the corner, he lifted his free hand almost languidly toward the empty street, and for a second Alicia truly believed that he was so powerful that taxis simply materialized before him at his whim—until a nearby engine turned over and a powerful black SUV slid out of the shadows and pulled to a stop right there before them.

More magic, when she was enchanted already.

Nikolai, she whispered to herself as she climbed inside the SUV, as if the name was a song. Or a spell. *His name is Nikolai.*

He swung in behind her on the soft leather backseat, exchanged a few words in curt Russian with the driver and then pressed a button that raised a privacy shield, secluding them. Then he settled back against the seat, near her but not touching her, stretching out his long, lean body and making the spacious vehicle seem tight. Close.

And then he simply looked at her.

As if he was trying to puzzle her out. Or giving her one last chance to bolt.

But Alicia knew she wasn't going to do that.

"More talk of dogs?" he asked mildly, yet all she heard was the hunger beneath. She could see it in his eyes, his face. She could feel the echo of it in her, new and huge and almost more than she could bear. "More clever little character assessments couched as potential objections?"

"I got in your car," she pointed out, hardly recognizing her own voice. The thick heat in it. "I think I'm done."

He smiled. She was sure of it, though his mouth didn't move. But she could see the stamp of satisfaction on his hard face, the flare of a deep male approval.

"Not yet, *solnyshka,*" he murmured, his voice a low rasp. "Not quite yet."

And she melted. It was a shivery thing, hot and desperate, like she couldn't quite catch her breath against the heat of it.

"Come here," he said.

They were cocooned in the darkness, light spilling here and there as the car sped through the city, and still his blue gaze was brilliant. Compelling. And so knowing—so certain of himself, of her, of what was about to happen—it made her blood run hot in her veins.

Alicia didn't move fast enough and he made a low noise. *A growl*—like the wolf he so resembled. The rough sound made her shake apart and then melt down into nothing but need, alive with that crazy heat she couldn't seem to control any longer.

He simply picked her up and pulled her into his lap, his mouth finding hers and claiming her all over again with an impatience that delighted her. She met him with the same urgency. His hands marveled down the length of her back, explored the shape of her hips, and Alicia's mind blanked out into a red-hot burst of that consuming, impossible fire. Into pure and simple *need*.

It had been so long. *So long,* and yet her body knew exactly what to do, thrilling to the taste of him, the feel of his hard, capable hands first over and then underneath her bright red shirt. His hands on her stomach, her waist, her breasts. So perfect she wanted to die. And not nearly enough.

He leaned back to peel off his jacket and the tight black T-shirt beneath, and her eyes glazed over at the sight of all of that raw male beauty. She pressed herself against the hard planes of his perfect chest, tracing the large, colorful tattoos that stretched over his skin with trembling fingers, with her lips and her tongue, tasting art etched across art.

Intense. Hot. Intoxicating.

And that scent of his—of the darkest winter, smoke and ice—surrounded her. Licked into her. Claimed her as surely as he did.

One moment she was fully clothed, the next her shirt and the bra beneath it were swept away, while his hard mouth took hers again and again until she thought she might die if he stopped. Then he did stop, and she moaned out her distress, her desperation. That needy ache so deep in the core of her. But he only laughed softly, before he fastened his hot mouth to the tight peak of one breast and sucked on it, not quite gently, until she thought she really *had* died.

The noises she heard herself making were impossible. Nothing could really feel this good. This perfect. This wild or this *right*.

Nikolai shifted, lifting her, and Alicia helped him peel her trousers down from her hips, kicking one leg free and not caring what happened to the other. She felt outside herself and yet more fully *in* herself than she had been in as long as she could remember. She explored the expanse of his gorgeous shoulders, the distractingly ten der spot behind his ear, the play of his stunning muscles, perfectly honed beneath her.

He twisted them both around, coming down over her on the seat and pulling her legs around his hips with an urgency that made her breath desert her. She hadn't even been aware that he'd undressed. It was more magic—and then he was finally naked against her, the steel length of him a hot brand against her belly.

Alicia shuddered and melted, then melted again, and he moved even closer, one of his hands moving to her bottom and lifting her against him with that devastating skill, that easy mastery, that made her belly tighten.

He was muttering in Russian, that same word he'd used before like a curse or a prayer or even both at once, and the sound of it made her moan again. It was harsh like him, and tender, too. It made her feel as if she might come out of her own skin. He teased her breasts, licking his way from one proud nipple to the other as if he might lose himself there, then moved to her neck, making her shiver against him before he took her mouth again in a hard, deep kiss.

As raw as she was. As undone.

He pulled back slightly to press something into her hand, and she blinked at it, taking much longer than she should have to recognize it was the condom she hadn't thought about for even an instant.

A trickle of unease snaked down the back of her neck, but she pushed it away, too far gone for shame. Not when his blue eyes glittered with sensual intent and his long fingers moved between them, feeling her damp heat and then stroking deep into her molten center, making her clench him hard.

"Hurry," he told her.

"I'm hurrying. You're distracting me."

He played his fingers in and out of her, slick and hot, then pressed the heel of his hand into her neediest part, laughing softly when she bucked against him.

"Concentrate, *solnyshka*."

She ripped open the foil packet, then took her time rolling it down his velvety length, until he cursed beneath his breath.

Alicia liked the evidence of his own pressing need. She liked that she could make his breath catch, too. And then he stopped, braced over her, his face close to hers and the hardest part of him poised at her entrance but not *quite*—

He groaned. He sounded as tortured as she felt. She liked that, too.

"Your name."

She blinked at the short command, so gruff and harsh. His arms were hard around her, his big body pressed her back into the soft leather seat, and she felt delicate and powerful all at once.

"Tell me your name," he said, nipping at her jaw, making her head fall back to give him any access he desired, anything he wanted.

Alive, she thought again. *At last.*

"Alicia," she whispered.

He muttered it like a fierce prayer, and then he thrust into her—hot and hard and so perfect, so beautiful, that tears spilled from her eyes even as she shattered around him.

"Again," he said.

It was another command, arrogant and darkly certain. Nikolai was hard and dangerous and between her legs, his eyes bright and hot and much too intense on

hers. She turned her head away but he caught her mouth
with his, taking her over, conquering her.

"I don't think I can—" she tried to say against his
mouth, even while the flames still licked through her,
even as she still shuddered helplessly around him, aware
of the steel length of him inside her, filling her.

Waiting.

That hard smile like a burst of heat inside her. "You
will."

And then he started to move.

It was perfect. More than perfect. It was sleek and
hot, impossibly good. He simply claimed her, took her,
and Alicia met him. She arched into him, lost in the slide
and the heat, the glory of it. Of him.

Slick. Wild.

Perfect.

He moved in her, over her, his mouth at her neck and
his hands roaming from her bottom to the center of her
shuddering need as he set the wild, intense pace. She
felt it rage inside her again, this mad fire she'd never felt
before and worried would destroy her even as she hun-
gered for more. And more. *And more.*

She met every deep thrust. She gloried in it.

"Say my name," he said, gruff against her ear, his
voice washing through her and sending her higher, making her glow. "Now, Alicia. Say it."

When she obeyed he shuddered, then let out another
low, sexy growl that moved over her like a newer, better fire. He reached between them and pressed down
hard against the heart of her hunger, hurtling her right
over the edge again.

And smiled, she was sure of it, with his warrior's

mouth as well as those winter-bright eyes, right before he followed her into bliss.

Nikolai came back to himself with a vicious, jarring thud.

He couldn't move. He wasn't sure he breathed. Alicia quivered sweetly beneath him, his mouth was pressed against the tender junction of her neck and shoulder, and he was still deep inside her lovely body.

What the hell was that?

He shifted her carefully into the seat beside him, ignoring the way her long, inky-black lashes looked against the creamy brown of her skin, the way her perfect, lush mouth was so soft now. He ignored the tiny noise she made in the back of her throat, as if distressed to lose contact with him, which made him grit his teeth. But she didn't open her eyes.

He dealt with the condom swiftly, then he found his trousers in the tangle of clothes on the floor of the car and jerked them on. He had no idea what had happened to his T-shirt, and decided it didn't matter. And then he simply sat there as if he was winded.

He, Nikolai Korovin, *winded.* By a woman.

By *this* woman.

What moved in him then was like a rush of too many colors, brilliant and wild, when he knew the only safety lay in gray. It surged in his veins, it pounded in his temples, it scraped along his sex. He told himself it was temper, but he knew better. It was everything he'd locked away for all these years, and he didn't want it. He wouldn't allow it. It made him feel like an animal again, wrong and violent and insane and drunk....

That was it.

It rang like a bell in him, low and urgent, swelling

into everything. Echoing everywhere. No wonder he felt so off-kilter, so dangerously unbalanced. This woman made him feel *drunk*.

Nikolai forced a breath, then another.

Everything that had happened since she'd tripped in front of him flashed through his head, in the same random snatches of color and sound and scent he remembered from a thousand morning-afters. Her laughter, that sounded the way he thought joy must, though he'd no basis for comparison. The way she'd tripped and then fallen, straight into him, and hadn't had the sense to roll herself as he would have done, to break her fall. Her brilliant smile that cracked over her face so easily. Too easily.

No one had ever smiled at him like that. As if he was a real man. Even a good one.

But he knew what he was. He'd always known. His uncle's fists, worse after Ivan had left to fight their way to freedom one championship at a time. The things he'd done in the army. Veronika's calculated deception, even Ivan's more recent betrayal—these had only confirmed what Nikolai had always understood to be true about himself down deep into his core.

To think differently now, when he'd lost everything he had to lose and wanted nothing more than to shut himself off for good, was the worst kind of lie. Damaging. Dangerous. And he knew what happened when he allowed himself to become intoxicated. How many times would he have to prove that to himself? How many people would he hurt?

He was better off blank. Ice cold and gray, all the way through.

The day after Veronika left him, Nikolai had woken bruised and battered from another fight—or *fights*—he couldn't recall. He'd been shaky. Sick from the alcohol and sicker still with himself. Disgusted with the holes in his memory and worse, with all the things he *did* remember. The things that slid without context through his head, oily and barbed.

His fists against flesh. His bellow of rage. The crunch of wood beneath his foot, the shattering of pottery against the stone floor. Faces of strangers on the street, wary. Worried. Then angry. Alarmed.

Blood on a fist—and only some of it his. *Fear in those eyes*—never his. Nikolai was what grown men feared, what they crossed streets to avoid, but he hadn't felt fear himself in years. Not since he'd been a child.

Fear meant there was something left to lose.

That was the last time Nikolai had drunk a drop of alcohol and it was the last time he'd let himself lose control.

Until now.

He didn't understand this. He was not an impulsive man. He didn't pick up women, he *picked* them, carefully—and only when he was certain that whatever else they were, they were obedient and disposable.

When they posed no threat to him at all. Nikolai breathed in, out.

He'd survived wars. This was only a woman.

Nikolai looked at her then, memorizing her, like she was a code he needed to crack, instead of the bomb itself, poised to detonate.

She wore her dark black hair in a cloud of tight curls around her head, a tempting halo around her lovely, clever face, and he didn't want any part of this near-overpowering desire that surged in him, to bury his hands in the heavy thickness of it, to start the wild rush all over again. Her body was lithe and ripe with warm, mouthwatering curves that he'd already touched and tasted, so why did he feel as if it had all been rushed, as if it wasn't nearly enough?

He shouldn't have this longing to take his time, to really explore her. He shouldn't hunger for that lush, full mouth of hers again, or want to taste his way along that elegant neck for the simple pleasure of making her shiver. He shouldn't find it so impossible to look at her without imagining himself tracing lazy patterns across every square inch of the sweet brown perfection of her skin. With his mouth and then his hands, again and again until he *knew* her.

He'd asked her name, as if he'd needed it. He'd wanted her that much, and Nikolai knew better than to want. It could only bring him pain.

Vodka had been his one true love, and it had ruined him. It had let loose that monster in him, let it run amok. It had taken everything that his childhood and the army hadn't already divided between them and picked down to the bone. He'd known it in his sober moments, but he hadn't cared. Because vodka had warmed him, lent color and volume to the dark, silent prison of his life, made him imagine he could be something other than a six-foot-two column of glacial ice.

But he knew better than that now. He knew better than this.

Alicia's eyes fluttered open then, dark brown shot through with amber, almost too pretty to bear. He hated that he noticed, that he couldn't look away. She glanced around as if she'd forgotten where they were. Then she looked at him.

She didn't smile that outrageously beautiful smile of hers, and it made something hitch inside him, like a stitch in his side. As if he'd lost that, too.

She lifted one foot, shaking her head at the trousers that were still attached to her ankle, and the shoe she'd never removed. She reached down, picked up the tangle of her bright red shirt and lacy pink bra from the pile on the floor of the car, and sighed.

And Nikolai relaxed, because he was back on familiar ground.

Now came the demands, the negotiations, he thought cynically. The endless manipulations, which were the reason he'd started making any woman who wanted him agree to his rules before he touched her. Sign the appropriate documents, understand exactly how this would go before it started. Nikolai knew this particular dance well. It was why he normally didn't pick up women, let them into the sleek, muscular SUV that told them too much about his net worth, much less give them his address....

But instead of pouting prettily and pointedly, almost always the first transparent step in these situations, Alicia looked at him, let her head fall back and laughed.

CHAPTER THREE

THAT DAMNED LAUGH.

Nikolai would rather be shot again, he decided in that electric moment as her laughter filled the car. He would rather take another knife or two to the gut. He didn't know what on earth he was supposed to do with laughter like that, when it sparkled in the air all around him and fell indiscriminately here and there, like a thousand unwelcome caresses all over his skin and something worse—much worse—deep beneath it.

He scowled.

"Never let it be said this wasn't classy," Alicia said, her lovely voice wry. "I suppose we'll always have that going for us."

There was no we. There was no *us*. Neither of those words were *disposable*. Alarms shrieked like air raid sirens inside of him, mixing with the aftereffects of that laugh.

"I thought you understood," he said abruptly, at his coldest and most cutting. "I don't—"

"Relax, Tin Man." Laughter still lurked in her voice. She tugged her trousers back up over her hips, then pulled her bra free of her shirt, shooting him a breezy smile that felt not unlike a blade to the stomach as she clipped it back into place. "I heard you the first time. No heart."

And then she ignored him, as if he wasn't vibrating beside her with all of that darkness and icy intent. As if he wasn't Nikolai Korovin, feared and respected in equal measure all across the planet, in a thousand corporate boardrooms as well as the grim theaters of too many violent conflicts. As if he was the kind of man someone could simply *pick up* in a London club and then dismiss...

Except, of course, he was. Because she had. She'd done exactly that.

He'd let her.

Alicia fussed with her shirt before pulling it over her head, her black curls springing out of the opening in a joyful froth that made him actually ache to touch them. *Her.* He glared down at his hands as if they'd betrayed him.

When she looked at him again, her dark eyes were soft, undoing him as surely as if she really had eviscerated him with a hunting knife. He would have preferred the latter. She made it incalculably worse by reaching over and smoothing her warm hand over his cheek, offering him...comfort?

"You look like you've swallowed broken glass," she said.

Kindly.

Very much as if she cared.

Nikolai didn't want what he couldn't have. It had been beaten out of him long ago. It was a simple, unassailable fact, like gravity. Like air.

Like light.

But he couldn't seem to stop himself from lifting his

hand, tracing that tempting mouth of hers once more, watching the heat bloom again in her eyes.

Just one night, he told himself then. He couldn't help it. That smile of hers made him realize he was so tired of the cold, the dark. That he felt haunted by the things he'd lost, the wars he'd won, the battles he'd been fighting all his life. Just once, he *wanted.*

One night to explore this light of hers she shone so indiscriminately, he thought. Just one night to pretend he was something more than ice. A wise man didn't step onto a land mine when he could see it lying there in front of him, waiting to blow. But Nikolai had been through more hells than he could count. He could handle anything for a night. Even this. Even her.

Just one night.

"You should hold on," he heard himself say. He slid his hand around to cup the nape of her neck, and exulted in the shiver that moved over her at even so small a touch. As if she was his. That could never happen, he knew. But he'd allowed himself the night. He had every intention of making it a long one. "I'm only getting started."

If only he really had been a wolf.

Alicia scowled down at the desk in her office on Monday and tried valiantly to think of something—*anything*—other than Nikolai. And failed, as she'd been doing with alarming regularity since she'd sneaked away from his palatial penthouse in South Kensington early on Sunday morning.

If he'd really been a wolf, she'd likely be in hospital right now, recovering from being bitten in a lovely quiet coma or restful medicated haze, which would mean she'd be enjoying a much-needed holiday from the self-recriminating clamor inside her head.

At least I wasn't drunk....

Though if she was honest, some part of her almost wished she had been. *Almost.* As if that would be some kind of excuse when she knew from bitter experience that it wasn't.

The real problem was, she'd been perfectly aware of what she was doing on Saturday. She'd gone ahead and done it precisely *because* she hadn't been drunk. For no other reason than that she'd wanted him.

From her parents' back garden to a stranger in a car. She hadn't learned much of anything in all these years, had she? Given the chance, she'd gleefully act the promiscuous whore—drunk *or* sober.

That turned inside of her like bile, acidic and thick at the back of her throat.

"I think you must be a witch," he'd said at some point in those long, sleepless hours of too much pleasure, too hot and too addicting. He'd been sprawled out next to her, his rough voice no more than a growl in the dark of his cavernous bedroom.

A girl could get lost in a room like that, she'd thought. In a bed so wide. In a man like Nikolai, who had taken her over and over with a skill and a thoroughness and a sheer masculine prowess that made her wonder how she'd ever recover from it. *If* she would. But she hadn't wanted to think those things, not then. Not while it was still dark outside and they were cocooned on those soft sheets together, the world held at bay. There'd be time enough to work on forgetting, she'd thought. When it was over.

When it was morning.

She'd propped herself up on an elbow and looked

down at him, his bold, hard face in shadows but those eyes of his as intense as ever.

"I'm not the driving force in this fairy tale," she'd said quietly. Then she'd dropped her gaze lower, past that hard mouth of his she now knew was a terrible, electric torment when he chose, and down to that astonishing torso of his laid out before her like a feast. "Red Riding Hood is a hapless little fool, isn't she? Always in the wrong place at the wrong time."

Alicia had meant that to come out light and breezy, but it hadn't. It had felt intimate instead, somehow. Darker and deeper, and a different kind of ache inside. Not at all what she'd intended.

She'd felt the blue of his gaze like a touch.

Instead of losing herself there, she'd traced a lazy finger over the steel plates of his harshly honed chest. Devastatingly perfect. She moved from this scar to that tattoo, tracing each pucker of flesh, each white strip of long-ago agony, then smoothing her fingertip over the bright colors and Cyrillic letters that flowed everywhere else. Two kinds of marks, stamped permanently into his flesh. She'd been uncertain if she was fascinated or something else, something that made her mourn for all his body had suffered.

But it wasn't her place to ask.

"Bullet," he'd said quietly, when her fingers moved over a slightly raised and shiny patch of skin below his shoulder, as if she had asked after all. "I was in the army."

"For how long?"

"Too long."

She'd flicked a look at him, but had kept going, finding a long, narrow white scar that slashed across his taut abdomen and following the length of it, back and forth. So much violence boiled down to a thin white line etched into his hard, smooth flesh. It had made her hurt for him, but she still hadn't asked.

"Kitchen knife. My uncle." His voice had been little more than a rasp against the dark. She'd gone still, her fingers splayed across the scar in question. "He took his role as our guardian seriously," Nikolai had said, and his gruff voice had sounded almost amused, as if what he'd said was something other than awful. Alicia had chanced a glance at him, and saw a different truth in that wintry gaze, more vulnerable in the clasp of the dark than she'd imagined he knew. "He didn't like how I'd washed the dishes."

"Nikolai—" she'd begun, not knowing what she could possibly say, but spurred on by that torn look in his eyes.

He'd blinked, then frowned. "It was nothing."

But she'd known he was lying. And the fact that she'd had no choice but to let it pass, that this man wasn't hers to care for no matter how it felt as if he should have been, had rippled through her like actual, physical pain.

Alicia had moved on then to the tattoo of a wild beast rendered in a shocking sweep of bold color and dark black lines that wrapped around the left side of his body, from his shoulder all the way down to an inch or so above his sex. It was fierce and furious, all ferocious teeth and wicked claws, poised there as if ready to devour him.

As if, she'd thought, it already had.

"All of my sins," he'd said then, his voice far darker and rougher than before.

There'd been an almost-guarded look in his winter gaze when she'd glanced up at him, but she'd thought that was that same vulnerability again. And then he'd sucked in a harsh breath when she'd leaned over and pressed a kiss to the fearsome head of this creature that claimed him, as if she could wash away the things that had hurt him—uncles who wielded kitchen knives, whatever battles he'd fought in the army that had got him shot, all those shadows that lay heavy on his hard face. One kiss, then another, and she'd felt the coiling tension in him, the heat.

"Your sins are pretty," she'd whispered.

He'd muttered something ferocious in Russian as he'd hauled her mouth to his, then he'd pulled her astride him and surged into her with a dark fury and a deep hunger that had thrilled her all the way through, and she'd been lost in him all over again.

She was still lost.

"For God's sake, Alicia," she bit out, tired of the endless cycle of her own thoughts, and her own appalling weakness. Her voice sounded loud in her small office. "You have work to do."

She had to snap out of this. Her desk was piled high after her two weeks abroad, her in-box was overflowing and she had a towering stack of messages indicating calls she needed to return now that she was back in the country. To say nothing of the report on the Latin American offices she'd visited while away that she had yet to put together, that Charlotte, her supervisor, expected her to present to the team later this week.

But she couldn't sink into her work the way she wanted, the way she usually could. There was that deep current of shame that flared inside of her, bright like some kind of cramp, reminding her of the last night she'd abandoned herself so completely.…

At least this time, she remembered every last second of what she'd done. What *they'd* done. Surely that counted for something.

Her body still prickled now, here, as if electrified, every time she thought of him—and she couldn't seem to stop. Her nipples went hard and between her legs, she ran so hot it almost hurt, and it was such a deep betrayal of who she'd thought she'd become that it made her feel shaky.

Her thighs were still tender from the scrape of his hard jaw. There was a mark on the underside of one breast that he'd left deliberately, reminding her in that harsh, beautiful voice that *wolves bite, solnyshka*, making her laugh and squirm in reckless delight beneath him on that wide, masculine bed where she'd obviously *lost her mind*. Even her hips held memories of what she'd done, reminding her of her overwhelming response to him every now and again with a low, almost-pleasant ache that made her hate herself more every time she felt it.

She'd been hung over before. Ashamed of herself come the dawn. Sometimes that feeling had lingered for days as she'd promised herself that she'd stop partying so hard, knowing deep down that she wouldn't, and hadn't, until that last night in the back garden. But this wasn't *that*. This was worse.

She felt out of control. Knocked flat. Changed, utterly.

A stranger to herself.

Alicia had been so sure the new identity she'd built over these past eight years was a fortress, completely impenetrable, impervious to attack. Hadn't she held Rosie at bay for ages? But one night with Nikolai had showed her that she was nothing but a glass house, precarious and fragile, and a single stone could bring it all crashing down. A single touch.

Not to mention, she hadn't even *thought* about protection that first time. He'd had to *put it in her hand*. Of all her many betrayals of herself that night, she thought that one was by far the most appalling. It made the shame that lived in her that much worse.

The only bright spot in all of this recrimination and regret was that her text to Rosie hadn't gone through. There'd been a big X next to it when she'd looked at her mobile that next morning. And when she'd arrived back at their flat on Sunday morning, Rosie had still been out.

Which meant that no one had any idea what Alicia had done.

"I wish I'd gone home when you did," Rosie had said with a sigh while they sat in their usual Sunday-afternoon café, paging lazily through the Sunday paper and poking at their plates of a traditional full English breakfast. "That place turned *absolutely mental* after hours, and I have to stop getting off with bankers who talk about the flipping property ladder like it's the most thrilling thing on the planet." Then she'd grinned that big grin of hers that meant she didn't regret a single thing, no matter what she said. "Maybe someday I'll actually follow your example."

"What fun would that be?" Alicia had asked lightly, any guilt she'd felt at lying by giant, glaring omission to her best friend drowned out by the sheer relief pouring through her.

Because if Rosie didn't know what she'd done, Alicia could pretend it had never happened.

There would be no discussing Nikolai, that SUV of his or what had happened in it, or that astonishing penthouse that she'd been entirely too gauche not to gape at, openly, when he'd brought her home. There would be no play-by-play description of those things he could do with such ease, that Alicia hadn't known could feel like that. There would certainly be no conversations about all of these confusing and pointless things she felt sloshing around inside of her when she thought about those moments he'd showed her his vulnerable side, as if a man whose last name she didn't know and hadn't asked was something more than a one-night stand.

And if there was no one to talk about it with, all of this urgency, this driving sense of loss, would disappear. *It had to.* Alicia would remain, outwardly, as solid and reliable and predictably boring as she'd become in these past years. An example. The same old Saint Alicia, polishing her halo.

And maybe someday, if she was well-behaved and lucky, she'd believe it again herself.

"Are you ready for the big meeting?"

Her supervisor's dry voice from the open doorway made Alicia jump guiltily in her chair, and it was much harder than it should have been to smile at Charlotte the way she usually did. She was sure what she'd done over her weekend was plastered all over her face. That Charlotte could *see* how filthy she really was, the way her father had. All her sins at a single glance, like that furious creature that bristled on Nikolai's chest.

"Meeting?" she echoed weakly.

"The new celebrity partnership?" Charlotte prompted her. At Alicia's blank look, she laughed. "We all have to show our faces in the conference hall in exactly five minutes, and Daniel delivered a new version of his official presidential lecture on tardiness last week. I wouldn't be late."

"I'll be right along," Alicia promised, and this time, managed a bit of a better smile.

She sighed heavily when Charlotte withdrew, feeling much too fragile. Hollow and raw, as if she was still fighting off that hangover she hadn't had. But she knew it was him. Nikolai. That much fire, that much wild heat, had to have a backlash. She shouldn't be surprised.

This will fade, she told herself, and she should know, shouldn't she? She'd had other things to forget. *It always does, eventually.*

But the current of self-loathing that wound through her then suggested otherwise.

This was not the end of the world. This was no more than a bit of backsliding into shameful behavior, and she wasn't very happy with herself for doing it, but it wouldn't happen again.

No one had walked in on her doing it. No one even knew. Everything was going to be fine.

Alicia blew out a shaky breath, closed down her computer, then made her way toward the big conference hall on the second floor, surprised to find the office already deserted. That could only mean that the celebrity charity in question was a particularly thrilling one. She racked her brain as she climbed the stairs, but she couldn't remember what the last memo had said about it or even if she'd read it.

She hated these meetings, always compulsory and always about standard-waving, a little bit of morale-building, and most of all, PR. They were a waste of her time. Her duties involved the financial planning and off-site management of the charity's regional offices scattered across Latin America. Partnering with much bigger, much more well-known celebrity charities was more of a fundraising and publicity endeavor, which always made Daniel, their president, ecstatic—but didn't do much for Alicia.

She was glad she was a bit late, she thought as she hurried down the gleaming hallway on the second level.

She could slip in, stand at the back, applaud loudly at something to catch Daniel's eye and prove she'd attended, then slip back out again and return to all that work on her messy desk.

Alicia silently eased open the heavy door at the rear of the hall. Down at the front, a man was talking confidently to the quiet, rapt room as she slipped inside.

At first she thought she was imagining it, given where her head had been all day.

And then it hit her. Hard.

She wasn't hearing things.

She knew that voice.

She'd know it anywhere. Her body certainly did.

Rough velvet. Russian. That scratch of whiskey, dark and powerful, commanding and sure.

Nikolai.

Her whole body went numb, nerveless. The door handle slipped from her hand, she jerked her head up to confirm what couldn't possibly be true, couldn't possibly be happening—

The heavy door slammed shut behind her with a terrific crash.

Every single head in the room swiveled toward her, as if she'd made her entrance in the glare of a bright, hot spotlight and to the tune of a boisterous marching band, complete with clashing cymbals.

But she only saw him.

Him. Nikolai. *Here.*

Once again, everything disappeared. There was only the fearsome blue of his beautiful eyes as they nailed her to the door behind her, slamming into her so hard she didn't know how she withstood it, how she wasn't on her knees from the force of it.

He was even more devastating than she'd let herself remember.

Still dressed all in black, today he wore an understated, elegant suit that made his lethal frame look consummately powerful rather than raw and dangerous, a clever distinction. And one that could only be made by expert tailoring to the tune of thousands upon thousands of pounds. The brutal force of him filled the room, filled her, and her body reacted as if they were still naked, still sprawled across his bed in a tangle of sheets and limbs. She felt too hot, almost feverish. His mouth was a harsh line, but she knew how it tasted and what it could do, and there was something dark and predatory in his eyes that made her tremble deep inside.

And remember. Dear God, what she remembered. What he'd done, how she'd screamed, what he'd promised and how he'd delivered, again and again and again....

It took her much too long to recollect where she was *now*.

Not in a club in Shoreditch this time, filled with drunken idiots who wouldn't recall what they did, much less what she did, but *in her office*. Surrounded by every single person she worked with, all of whom were staring at her.

Nikolai's gaze was so blue. So relentlessly, impossibly, mercilessly blue.

"I'm so sorry to interrupt," Alicia managed to murmur, hoping she sounded appropriately embarrassed and apologetic, the way anyone would after slamming that door—and not as utterly rocked to the core, as lit up with shock and horror, as she felt.

It took a superhuman effort to wrench her gaze away from the man who stood there glaring at her—who wasn't a figment of her overheated imagination, who had the same terrifying power over her from across a crowded room as he'd had in his bed, whom she'd never thought she'd see again, *ever*—and slink to an empty seat in the back row.

She would never know how she did it.

Down in the front of the room, a phalanx of assistants behind him and the screen above him announcing who he was in no uncertain terms, NIKOLAI KOROVIN OF THE KOROVIN FOUNDATION, she saw Nikolai blink. Once.

And then he kept talking as if Alicia hadn't interrupted him. As if he hadn't recognized her—as if Saturday night was no more than the product of her feverish imagination.

As if she didn't exist.

She'd never wished so fervently that she didn't. That she could simply disappear into the ether as if she'd never been, or sink into the hole in the ground she was sure his icy glare had dug beneath her.

What had she been thinking, to touch this man? To give herself to him so completely? Had she been drunk after all? Because today, here and now, he looked like nothing so much as a sharpened blade. Gorgeous and mesmerizing, but terrifying. That dark, ruthless power came off him in waves the way it had in the club, even stronger without the commotion of the music and the crowd, and this time, Alicia understood it.

This was who he was.

She *knew* who he was.

He was Nikolai Korovin. His brother was one of the most famous actors on the planet, which made Nikolai famous by virtue of his surname alone. Alicia knew his name like every other person in her field, thanks to his brilliant, inspired management of the Korovin Foundation since its creation two years ago. People whispered he was a harsh and demanding boss, but always fair, and the amount of money he'd already raised for the good causes the Korovin Foundation supported was staggering.

He was *Nikolai Korovin*, and he'd explored every part of her body with that hard, fascinating mouth. He'd held her in his arms and made her feel impossibly beautiful, and then he'd driven into her so hard, so deep, filling her so perfectly and driving her so out of her mind with pleasure, she had to bear down now to keep from reacting to the memory. He'd made her feel so wild with lust, so deliciously addicted to him, that she'd sobbed the last time she'd shattered into pieces all around him. *She knew how he tasted.* His mouth, his neck, the length of his proud sex. That angry, tattooed monster crouched on his chest. She knew what made him groan, fist his hands into her hair.

More than all of that, she knew how those bright eyes looked when he told her things she had the sense he didn't normally speak of to anyone. She knew too much.

He was Nikolai Korovin, and she didn't have to look over at Daniel's beaming face to understand what it meant that he was here. For Daniel as president, for making this happen. For the charity itself. A partnership with the Korovin Foundation was more than a publicity opportunity—it was a coup. It would take their relatively small charity with global ambitions and slam it straight into the big time, once and for all. And it went without saying that Nikolai Korovin, the legendary CEO of the Korovin Foundation and the person responsible for all its business decisions, needed to be kept happy for that to happen.

That look on his face when he'd seen her had been anything but happy.

Alicia had to force herself to sit still as the implications of this washed through her. She had betrayed herself completely and had a tawdry one-night stand. That was bad enough. But it turned out she'd done it with a man who could end her career.

Eight years ago she'd lost her father's respect and her own self-respect in the blur of a long night she couldn't even recall. Now she could lose her job.

Today. At the end of this meeting. Whenever Nikolai liked.

When you decide to mess up your life, you really go for it, she told herself, fighting back the panic, the prick of tears. *No simple messes for Alicia Teller! Better to go with total devastation!*

Alicia sat through the meeting in agony, expecting something to happen the moment it ended—lightning to strike, the world to come crashing to a halt, Nikolai to summon her to the front of the room and demand her termination at once—but nothing did. Nikolai didn't glance in her direction again. He and his many assistants merely swept from the hall like a sleek black cloud, followed by the still-beaming Daniel and all the rest of the upper level directors and managers.

Alicia told herself she was relieved. This had to be relief, this sharp thing in the pit of her stomach that made it hard to breathe, because nothing else made sense. She'd known he was dangerous the moment she'd met him, not that it had stopped her.

Now she knew exactly *how* dangerous.

She was an idiot. A soon-to-be-sacked idiot.

Her colleagues all grimaced in sympathy as they trooped back downstairs. They thought the fact she'd slammed that door was embarrassing enough. Little did they know.

"Can't imagine having a man like that look at me the way he did you," one said in an undertone. "I think I'd have nightmares!"

"I believe I will," Alicia agreed.

She spent the rest of the afternoon torn between panic and dread. She attacked all the work on her desk, like a drowning woman grasping for something to hold. Every time her phone rang, her heart leaped in her chest. Every time she heard a noise outside her office door, she tensed, thinking she was finished.

Any minute now, she'd be called up to Daniel's office. She could see it spool out before her like a horror film. Daniel's secretary would message the salacious news to half the office even as Alicia walked to her doom. So not only would Alicia be dismissed from her job because of a tawdry one-night stand with a man most people would have recognized and she certainly should have—but everyone she worked with and respected would know it.

It would be as it had been that morning her father had woken her up and told her what he'd seen, what she'd done—but this time, far more people would know what kind of trollop she was. People she'd impressed with her work ethic over the years would now sit about imagining her naked. *Having sex. With Nikolai.* She felt sick even thinking about it.

"I warned you!" Charlotte said as she stuck her head through the doorway, making Alicia jump again. A quick, terrified glance told her that her supervisor looked...sympathetic. Not horribly embarrassed. Not scandalized in the least. "I told Daniel you were on a call that ran a bit long, so no worries there."

"Thank you." Alicia's voice sounded strained, but Charlotte didn't seem to notice.

"Nikolai Korovin is very intense, isn't he?" Charlotte shook her head. "The man has eyes like a laser beam!"

"I expect he doesn't get interrupted very often," Alicia said, fighting for calm. "I don't think he cares for it."

"Clearly not," Charlotte agreed. And then laughed.

And that was it. No request that Alicia pack up her things or don a scarlet letter. No summons to present herself in Daniel's office to be summarily dismissed for her sexually permissive behavior with the fiercely all-business CEO of their new celebrity partner foundation. Not even the faintest hint of a judgmental look.

But Alicia knew it was coming. She'd not only seen the way Nikolai had looked at her, but now that she knew that he was Nikolai *Korovin,* she was afraid she knew exactly what it meant.

He was utterly ruthless. About everything. The entire internet agreed.

It was only a matter of time until all hell broke loose, so she simply put her head down, kept off the internet because it only served to panic her more, and worked. She stayed long after everyone else had left. She stayed until she'd cleared her desk, because that way, when they tittered behind their hands and talked about how they'd never imagined her acting *that way,* at least they wouldn't be able to say she hadn't done her job.

Small comfort, indeed.

It was almost nine o'clock when she finished, and Alicia was completely drained. She shrugged into her coat and wrapped her scarf around her neck, wishing there was a suit of armor she could put on instead, some way to ward off what she was certain was coming. Dread sat heavy in her stomach, leaden and full, and there was nothing she could do about it but wait to see what Nikolai did. Go home, hole up on the couch with a takeaway and Rosie's usual happy chatter, try to ease this terrible anxiety with bad American television and wait to see what he'd do to her. Because he was Nikolai Korovin, and he could do whatever he liked.

And would. Of that, she had no doubt.

Alicia made her way out of the building, deciding the moment she stepped out into the cold, clear night that she should walk home instead of catching the bus. It was only thirty-five minutes or so at a brisk pace, and it might sort out her head. Tire her out. Maybe even allow her to sleep.

She tucked her hands into her pockets and started off, but had only made it down the front stairs to the pavement when she realized that the big black SUV pulled up to the curb wasn't parked there, but was idling.

A whisper of premonition tingled through her as she drew closer, then turned into a tumult when the back door cracked open before her.

Nikolai Korovin appeared from within the way she should have known he would, tall and thunderous and broadcasting that dark, brooding intensity of his. He didn't have to block her path. He simply closed the door behind him and stood there, taking over the whole neighborhood, darker than the sky above, and Alicia was as unable to move as if he'd pinned her to the ground himself.

She was caught securely in his too-knowing, too-blue gaze all over again, as if he held her in his hands, and the shiver of hungry need that teased down the length of her spine only added insult to injury. She despaired of herself.

If she respected herself at all, Alicia knew with that

same old kick of shame in her gut, she wouldn't feel even that tiny little spark of something far too much like satisfaction that he was here. That he'd come for her. As if maybe he was as thrown by what had happened between them as she was…

"Hello, Alicia," Nikolai said, a dark lash in that rough voice of his, velvet and warning and so very Russian, smooth power and all of that danger in every taut line of his beautiful body. He looked fierce. Cold and furious. "Obviously, we need to talk."

CHAPTER FOUR

FOR A MOMENT, Alicia wanted nothing more than to run.

To bolt down the dark street like some desperate animal of prey and hope that this particular predator had better things to do than follow.

Something passed between them then, a shimmer in the dark, and Alicia understood that he knew exactly what she was thinking. That he was picturing the same thing. The chase, the inevitable capture, and *then*...

Nikolai's eyes gleamed dangerously.

Alicia tilted up her chin, settled back on her heels and faced him, calling on every bit of courage and stamina at her disposal. She wasn't going to run. She might have done something she was ashamed of, but she hadn't done it alone. And this time she had to face it—she couldn't skulk off back to university and limit her time back home as she'd done for years until the Reddicks moved to the north.

"Well," she said briskly. "This is awkward."

His cold eyes blazed. He was so different tonight, she thought. A blade of a man gone near incandescent with that icy rage, a far cry from the man she'd thought she'd seen in those quieter moments—the one who had told her things that still lodged in her heart. The change should have terrified her. Instead, perversely, she felt that hunger shiver deeper into her, settling into a hard knot low in her belly, turning into a thick, sweet heat.

"This is not awkward," he replied, his voice deceptively mild. Alicia could see that ferocious look in his eyes, however, and wasn't fooled. "This is a quiet conversation on a deserted street."

"Perhaps the word loses something in translation?" she suggested, perhaps a shade too brightly, as if that was some defense against the chill of him.

"Awkward," he bit out, his accent more pronounced than before and a fascinating pulse of temper in the hinge of his tight jaw, "was looking up in the middle of a business meeting today to see a woman I last laid eyes upon while I was making her come stare right back at me."

Alicia didn't want to think about the last time he'd made her come. She'd thought they were finished after all those long, heated hours. He'd taken that as a challenge. And he'd held her hips between his hands and licked into her with lazy intent, making her writhe against him and sob....

She swallowed, and wished he wasn't watching her. He saw far too much.

"You're looking at me as if I engineered this. I didn't." She eyed him warily, her hands deep in the pockets of her coat and curled into fists, which he couldn't possibly scc. Though she had the strangest notion he could. "I thought the point of a one-night stand with no surnames exchanged was that this would never happen."

"Have you had a great many of them, then?"

Alicia pretended that question didn't hit her precisely where she was the most raw, and with a ringing blow.

"If you mean as many as you've had, certainly not." She shrugged when his dark brows rose in a kind of affronted astonishment. "There are no secrets on the internet. Surely you, of all people, must know that. And it's a bit late to tally up our numbers and draw unflattering conclusions, don't you think? The damage is well and truly done."

"That damage," Nikolai said, that rough voice of his too tough, too cold, and that look on his hard face merciless, "is what I'm here to discuss."

Alicia didn't want to lose her job. She didn't want to know what kind of pressure Nikolai was prepared to put on her, what threats he was about to issue. She wanted this to go away again—to be the deep, dark secret that no one ever knew but her.

And it still could be, no matter how pitiless he looked in that moment.

"Why don't we simply blank each other?" she asked, once again a touch too brightly—which she could see didn't fool him at all. If anything, it called attention to her nervousness. "Isn't that the traditional method of handling situations like this?"

He shook his head, his eyes looking smoky in the dark, his mouth a resolute line.

"I do not mix business and pleasure," he said, with a finality that felt like a kick in the stomach. "I do not *mix* at all. The women I sleep with do not infiltrate my life. They appear in carefully orchestrated places of my choosing. They do not ambush me at work. Ever."

Alicia decided that later—much later, when she knew how this ended and could breathe without thinking she might burst into panicked, frustrated tears—she would think about the fact that a man like Nikolai had so many women that he'd developed *policies* to handle them all. *Later.* Right now, she had to fight back, or surrender here and now and lose everything.

"I assure you," she said, as if she had her own set of violated policies and was considering them as she met his gaze, "I feel the same way."

Nikolai shifted, and then suddenly there was no distance between them at all. His hands were on her neck, his thumbs at her jaw, tipping her head back to look up at him. Alicia should have felt attacked, threatened. She should have leaped for safety. Screamed. *Something*.

But instead, everything inside of her went still. And hot.

"I am not here to concern myself with your feelings," he told her in that rough velvet whisper. That fascinating mouth was grim again, but she could almost touch it with hers, if she dared. She didn't. "I am here to eliminate this problem as swiftly and as painlessly as possible."

But his hands were on her. Just as they'd been in the club when he'd told her to run. And she wondered if he was as conflicted as she was, and as deeply. What it would take to see that guarded look on his face again, that vulnerable cast to his beautiful mouth.

"You really are the gift that keeps on giving, Nikolai," she managed to say, retreating to a sarcastic tone, hoping the bite of it might protect her. She even smiled, thinly. "I've never felt happier about my reckless, irresponsible choices."

He let out a short laugh, and whatever expression that was on his hard face then—oddly taut and expectant, dark and hot—was like a flame inside of her. His hands were strong and like brands against her skin. His thumbs moved gently, lazily, as if stroking her jaw of their own accord.

"I don't like sharp women with smart mouths, Alicia," he told her, harsh and low, and every word was a caress against her skin, her sex, as if he was using those long fingers deep in her heat. "I like them sweet. Soft. Yielding and obedient and easily dismissed."

That same electricity crackled between them even here on the cold street, a bright coil that wound tight inside of her, making her feel mad with it. Too close to an explosion she knew she couldn't allow.

"What luck," she said, sharp and smart and nothing like soft at all. "I believe there's a sex shop in the next street, filled with exactly the kind of plastic dolls you prefer. Shall I point you in the right direction?"

He let go of her as if she'd burned him. And she recognized that dark heat in his gaze, the way it changed his expression, the things it did to that mouth.

"Get in the car, Alicia," he ordered her darkly. "I have an aversion to discussing my private life on a public street, deserted or not."

It was her turn to laugh, in disbelief.

"You have to be crazy if you think I'm getting back in that thing," she told him. "I'd rather get down on my hands and knees and crawl across a bed of nails, thank you."

She knew it was a mistake almost before the words left her mouth, and that sudden wolfish look on his face nearly undid her. It was impossible, then, not to picture herself down on her hands and knees, crawling toward that ravenous heat in his winter eyes she could remember too well, and could see right there before her now.

"I wasn't thinking about sex at present," he said coolly, and even though she could see from that fire in his gaze that he'd imagined much the same thing she had, she felt slapped. Shamed anew. "Why? Were you?"

It was time to go, Alicia realized then. It had been time to go the moment she'd seen that SUV idling at the curb. Before this thing got any worse—and she had no doubt at all that it would.

"It was lovely to finally meet you properly, Mr. Korovin," she said crisply. She put a faint emphasis on the word *properly,* and he blinked, looking almost... abashed? But that was impossible. "I'm sure your partnership with the charity will be a huge boost for us, and I'm as grateful as anyone else. And now I'm going home, where I will continue to actively pretend none of this ever happened. I can only hope you'll do the same."

"You didn't tell me you worked for a children's charity."

She didn't know what she'd expected him to say, but it wasn't that, with that sting of accusation. She eyed him warily. "Neither did you."

"Did you know who I was, Alicia?" Nikolai's face was so hard, his gaze so cold. She felt the chill suddenly, cutting into her. "You stumbled into my arms. Then you stumbled into that conference room today. Convenient." His eyes raked over her, as if looking for evidence that she'd planned this nightmare. "Your next stumble had best not involve any tabloid magazines or tell-all interviews. You won't like how I respond."

But she couldn't believe he truly thought that, she realized when the initial shock of it passed. She'd been in that bed with him. She knew better. Which meant he was lashing out, seeing what would hurt her. *Eliminating problems,* as he'd said he would.

"There's no need to draw out this torture," she told him, proud of how calm she sounded. "If you want me sacked, we both know you can do it easily. Daniel would have the entire staff turn cartwheels down the length of the Mall if he thought that would please you. Firing me will be a snap." She squared her shoulders as if she might have to sustain a blow. As if she already had. "If that's what you plan to do, I certainly can't stop you."

He stared at her for a long moment. A car raced past on the street beside them and in the distance she could hear the rush of traffic on the main road. Her breath was coming hard and fast, like she was fighting whole battles in her head while he only stood there, still and watchful.

"You're a distraction, Alicia," he told her then, something like regret in his voice. "I can't pretend otherwise."

"Of course you can," she retorted, fighting to keep calm. "All people do is pretend. I pretended to be the sort of woman—" She didn't want to announce exactly what she'd been pretending for eight years, not to him, so she frowned instead. "Just ignore me and I'll return the favor. It will be easy."

"I am not the actor in the family."

"I didn't ask you to play *King Lear*," she threw at him, panicked and exasperated in equal measure. "I only asked you to ignore me. How difficult can that possibly be? A man like you must have that down to a science."

"What an impression you have of me," Nikolai said after a moment, his voice silken, his eyes narrow. "I treated you very well, Alicia. Have you forgot so soon? You wept out your gratitude, when you weren't screaming my name."

She didn't need the reminder. She didn't need the heat of it, the wild pulse in her chest, between her legs.

"I was referring to your wealth and status," Alicia said, very distinctly. "Your position. The fact you have armies of assistants to make sure no one can approach you without your permission. Not your..."

"Particular talents?" His voice was mild enough as he finished the thought for her. The effect his words had on her, inside her, was not.

But then he leaned back against the side of his car, as if he was perfectly relaxed. Even his face changed, and she went still again, because there was something far more predatory about him in this moment than there had been before. It scraped the air thin.

"I have a better solution," he said, in the confident and commanding tone she recognized from the conference room. "I don't need to fire you, necessarily. It will serve my purposes far better to use this situation to my advantage."

Alicia could only shake her head, looking for clues on that face of his that gave nothing away. "I don't know what that means."

"It means, Alicia," he said almost softly, a wolf's dangerous smile in those winter eyes if not on that hard mouth, "that I need a date."

He could use this, Nikolai thought, while Alicia stared up at him as if he'd said that last sentence in Russian instead of English. He could use her.

A problem well managed could become a tool. And every tool could be a weapon, in the right hands. Why not Alicia?

He'd expected her to want more than Saturday night—they always did. And the sex they'd had had been…troubling. He'd known it while it was happening. He'd known it in between, when he'd found himself talking of things he never, ever talked about. He'd known it when he'd opened his eyes to watch her tiptoe from his room on Sunday morning, and had discovered he wanted her to stay.

He knew it now, remembering her sweet, hot mouth against his tattoo as if she'd blessed that snarling representation of the monster in him. As if she'd made it sacred, somehow. The moment he'd seen her, he'd expected she would try to leverage that, take it from him somehow. He'd planned to make it clear to her she had to go—before she could try.

But she claimed she wanted to ignore him. He should have been thrilled.

He told himself he was.

"I'm sorry." Her voice was carefully blank when she finally spoke, to match the expression on her face. "Did you say you needed a *date?*"

"I did." It occurred to him that he was enjoying himself, for the first time since he'd looked up and seen her standing in that conference room, in clear violation of all his rules. "There is a Christmas ball in Prague that I must attend in a few weeks, and it will go much more smoothly with a woman on my arm."

These things were always better with a date, it was true. It didn't matter who it was. The presence of any date at his side would repel most of the vulturelike women who always circled him like he was fresh meat laid out in the hot sun, allowing Nikolai to concentrate on business. And in the case of this particular charity ball, on Veronika—who had only this morning confirmed that she and her lover would attend.

Because Nikolai had realized, as he looked at her in the light of the streetlamps and thought strategy instead of containment, that Alicia could very well turn out to be the best weapon yet in his dirty little war.

"I'm certain there are hordes of women who would love nothing more than to fill that opening for you," she said, with none of the deference or courtesy he was used to from his subordinates and dates alike. There was no reason on earth he should find that intriguing. "Perhaps one of your many assistants has a sign-up sheet? A call list? Maybe even an audition process to weed out the lucky winner from the multitudes?"

He'd told her he liked sweet and biddable, and he did. But he liked this, too. He liked the way she talked to him, as if it hadn't occurred to her that she should fear him like everyone else did. It made him want to lick her until all of that tartness melted all over him, and he didn't want to examine that particular urge any closer.

"Something like that," he said. "But it's all very tedious. All I want is a pretty dress, a polite smile. I don't have time for the games."

"Or the person, apparently," she said, her voice dry. "I'm sure that's very rewarding for whichever pretty dress you choose. But what does this have to do with me?"

Nikolai smiled, adrenaline moving through him the way it always did before a tactical strike. Before another win.

"You want nothing to do with me." His voice was a silken threat in the cold night. "Or so you claim."

"You're right," she said, but her voice caught. "I don't."

"Then it's perfect," he said. "It's only a handful of weeks until the ball. We'll allow ourselves to be photographed on a few dates. The world will think I'm smitten, as I am very rarely seen with the same woman more than once. More specifically, my ex-wife will think the same. And as she has always greatly enjoyed her fantasy that she is the only woman to have any power over me, and has never been one to resist a confrontation, it will put her right where I want her."

She stared at him. "And where is that, exactly?"

"Veronika and I need to have a conversation," Nikolai

said with cool dismissal. "Hopefully, our last. The idea that I might have moved on will expedite that, I think."

"How tempting," she said after a moment, her voice as arid as that look in her eyes. "I've always aspired to be cold-bloodedly used to make another woman jealous, of course. It's truly every girl's dream. But I think I'll pass."

"This has nothing to do with jealousy," he said impatiently. "The only thing left between Veronika and me is spite. If that. I'm sure you'll see it yourself at the ball."

"Even more appealing. But still—no."

"Your whole office saw me stare at you today." He shrugged when her eyes narrowed. "They could hardly miss it. How much of a leap will it be for them to imagine that was the beginning of an infatuation?"

"But they won't have to make that leap." Her eyes were glittering again. "I've declined your lovely offer and we're going to ignore each other."

"I don't think so." He watched her take that in. Knew she didn't like it. Found he didn't much care if she was happy about it, so long as she did it. "I'm going to take an interest in you, Alicia. Didn't you know? Everybody loves a romance."

"They won't believe it." Her voice sounded thick, as if the idea of it horrified her, and he was perverse enough to take that as a challenge. "They won't believe someone like you could get infatuated at all, much less with me."

He smiled. "They will. And more to the point, so will Veronika."

And he could kill two birds with one stone. He could dig into this attraction, the unacceptable intoxication this woman made him feel, and in so doing, strip away its power over him. Make certain he never again felt the need to unburden himself in such a shockingly uncharacteristic manner to a total stranger. At the same time, he could use Veronika's smug certainty about her place in his life against her. It was perfect.

Alicia stared back at him, so hard he thought he could hear her mind racing.

"Why bring any of this into the office at all?" she asked, sounding frustrated. Panicked, even. "If you want me to go to this ball, fine. I'll do it, but I don't see why anyone needs to know about it but us. No unlikely romance necessary."

"And how will that work?" he asked mildly. "When pictures of us at that ball show up in all the papers, and they will, it will look as if we were keeping our relationship a secret. As if we were hiding something. Think of the gossip then."

"You said you're not an actor," she said. "Yet this seems like a very elaborate bit of theater."

"I told you, you're a distraction," he replied, almost gently. He wanted to show her what he meant. To bury his face in that crook of her neck. To make her quiver for him the way he knew he could. Only the fact he wanted it too much kept him from it. "I don't allow distractions, Alicia. I neutralize them or I use them for my own ends."

"I don't want to be in any papers." Her voice was low, her eyes intense on his. It took him a moment to realize she was panicked. A better man might not have enjoyed that. "I don't want *pictures* of me out there, and certainly not with you."

"There's a certain liberty in having no choices, Alicia," he told her, not sure why it bothered him that she was so opposed to a picture *with him*. It made his voice harsher. "It makes life very simple. Do what I tell you to do, or look for a new job."

Nikolai didn't think that was the first moment it had occurred to her that he held all the power here, but it was no doubt when she realized he had every intention of using it as he pleased. He saw it on her face. In her remarkable eyes.

And he couldn't help but touch her again then, sliding his hand over her cheek as he'd done before. He felt the sweet heat of her where his fingertips touched her hairline, the chill of her soft skin beneath his palm. And that wild heat that was only theirs, sparking wild, charging through him.

Making him almost wish he was a different man.

She wore a thick black coat against the cold, a bright red scarf looped around her elegant neck. Her ink-black curls were pulled back from her face with a scrap of brightly patterned fabric, and he knew that beneath it she was dressed in even more colors, bright colors. Emerald greens and chocolate browns. She was so bright it made his head spin, even here in the dark. It made him achingly hard.

She is nothing more than an instrument, he told himself. *Another weapon for your arsenal. And soon enough, this intoxication will fade into nothing.*

"Please," she whispered, and he wished he were the kind of man who could care. Who could soothe her. But he wasn't, no matter what he told her in the dark. "You don't understand. I don't want to lose my job, but I can't do this."

"You can," Nikolai told her. "And you will." He felt more in control than he had since she'd slammed into him at the edge of that dance floor, and he refused to give that up again. He wouldn't. "I'll be the one infatuated, Alicia. You need only surrender."

She shook her head, but she didn't pull her face from his grasp, and he knew what that meant even if she didn't. He knew what surrender looked like, and he smiled.

"Feel free to refuse me at first," he told Alicia then, his voice the only soft thing about him, as if he was a sweet and gentle lover and these words were the poetry he'd told her he didn't write. As if he was someone else. Maybe it would help her to think so. "Resist me, if you can. That will only make it look better."

"I won't do it," Alicia told him, hearing how unsteady her voice was and hating that he heard it, too. Hating all of this. "I won't play along."

"You will," he said in that implacable way that made something inside her turn over and shiver, while that half smile played with the corner of his hard mouth as if he knew something she didn't. "Or I'll have you sacked so fast it will make your head spin. And don't mistake sexual attraction for mercy, Alicia. I don't have any."

"Of course not," she bit out, as afraid that she would burst into tears right there as she was that she would nestle further into his hand, both impulses terrible and overwhelming at once. "You're the big, bad wolf. Fangs and teeth. I get the picture. I still won't do it."

She wrenched herself away from the terrible beguilement of his touch then, and ran down the street the way she should have at the start, panic biting at her heels as if she thought he might chase her.

He didn't—but then, he didn't have to chase her personally. His words did that for him. They haunted her as she tossed and turned in her sleepless bed that night. They moved over her like an itch she couldn't scratch. Like a lash against her skin, leaving the kind of scars he wore in their wake. Kitchen knives and bullets.

Do what I tell you to do.

Alicia was appalled at herself. He could say terrible things, propose to use her in some sick battle with his ex-wife, and still, she wanted him. He was mean and surly and perfectly happy to threaten her—and she wanted him. She lay awake in her bed and shivered when she thought about that last, simple touch, his hand hot despite the chill of the night air, holding her face so gently, making everything inside her run together and turn into honey.

Because that fool inside of her wanted that touch to mean something more. Wanted this attraction between them to have more to do with that vulnerability he'd shown her than the sex they'd had.

Wanted Saturday night to be different from that terrible night eight years ago.

He wants to use you, nothing more, she reminded herself for the millionth time, punching at her pillow in exhausted despair. *It means nothing more than that.*

But Alicia couldn't have pictures of herself in the tabloids. Not at all, and certainly not in the company of a man who might have been called a playboy, had he been less formidable. Not that it mattered what they called him—her father would know exactly what he was. Too wealthy, too hard. Too obvious. A man like that wanted women for one thing only, and her father would know it.

He would think she was back to old tricks. She knew he would.

Alicia shuddered, her face pressed into her pillow. She could *see* that awful look on her father's face that hideous morning as if he stood in front of her the way he'd done then.

"He is a *married man.* You know his wife, his children," her father had whispered, looking as deeply horrified as Alicia had felt.

"Dad," she'd managed to say, though her head had pounded and her mouth had been like sand. "Dad, I don't know what happened.... It's all—I don't remember—"

"I know what happened," he'd retorted, disgust plain in his voice and all across his face. "I saw you, spread-eagled on the grass with a *married man,* our *neighbor*—"

"Dad—" she'd tried again, tears in her voice and her eyes, afraid she might be sick.

"The way you dress, the way you flaunt yourself." He'd shaken his head, condemnation and that deep disgust written all over him. "I knew you dressed like a common whore, Alicia, but I never thought you'd *act* like one."

She couldn't go through that again, she thought then, staring in mute despair at her ceiling. She wouldn't go through it again, no matter how *infatuated* Nikolai pretended he was. No matter what.

He was going to have to fire her, she decided. She would call his bluff.

"No," she said, very firmly, when a coworker ran up to her the following day as she fixed herself a midmorning cup of tea and breathlessly asked if she'd *heard.* "Heard what?"

But she had a terrible suspicion she could guess. Ruthless and efficient, that was Nikolai.

"Nikolai Korovin *expressly* asked after you at the meeting this morning!" the excitable Melanie from the PR team whispered in that way of hers that alerted the entire office and most of the surrounding neighborhood, her eyes wide and pale cheeks red with the thrill of it all. "He *grilled* the team about you! Do you think that means he…?"

She couldn't finish that sentence, Alicia noted darkly.

It was too much for Melanie. The very idea of Nikolai Korovin's interest—his *infatuation*—made the girl practically crumple into a shivering heap at Alicia's feet.

"I imagine he's the kind of man who keeps an annotated enemies list within arm's reach and several elaborate revenge plots at the ready," Alicia said as calmly as possible, dumping as much cold water on this fire of his as she could, even though she suspected it wouldn't do any good. "He certainly doesn't *like* me, Melanie."

The other woman didn't looked particularly convinced, no doubt because Alicia's explanation flew in the face of the grand romance she'd already concocted in her head. Just as Nikolai had predicted.

"No, thank you," Alicia told the emissary from his army of assistants two days after that, who walked up to Alicia as she stood in the open plan part of the office with every eye trained on her and asked if she might want to join them all for a meal after work?

"Mr. Korovin wanted me to tell you that it's a restaurant in Soho he thinks you'd quite enjoy," the woman persisted, her smile never dropping from her lips. "One of his favorites in London. And his treat, of course."

Alicia's heart hammered in her chest so hard she wondered for a panicked moment if she was having some kind of heart attack. Then she remembered how many people were watching her, much too avidly, and forced a polite smile in return.

"I'm still catching up from my trip," she lied. "I'll have to work late again, I'm afraid. But please do thank Mr. Korovin for thinking of me."

Somehow, that last part didn't choke her.

By the end of that week, the fact that ruthless and somewhat terrifying billionaire Nikolai Korovin had *taken an interest* in Alicia was the only thing anyone in the office seemed able to talk about, and he'd accomplished it without lowering himself to speak to her directly. She felt hunted, trapped, and she hadn't even seen him since that night on the street.

He was diabolical.

"I believe Nikolai Korovin wants to *date* you, Alicia," Charlotte said as they sat in her office on Friday morning, going over the presentation for their team meeting later that afternoon. She grinned widely when Alicia looked at her. "I don't know whether to be excited or a bit overwhelmed at the idea of someone like him dating a normal person."

"This is so embarrassing," Alicia said weakly, which was perhaps the first honest thing she'd said on the topic all week. "I honestly don't know why he's doing this."

"Love works in mysterious ways," Charlotte sing-songed, making Alicia groan.

Everybody loves a romance, he'd said in that cold, cynical voice of his. Damn him.

"This is a man who could date anyone in the world, and has done," Alicia said, trying to sound lighter, breezier, than she felt. "Why on earth should a man like that want to date *me?*"

"You didn't drop at his feet on command, obviously," Charlotte said with a shrug. Only because he hadn't issued that particular command that night, Alicia thought sourly, fighting to keep her expression neutral. "Men like Nikolai Korovin are used to having anything they desire the moment they desire it. Ergo, they desire most what they can't have."

Alicia hadn't been so happy to see the end of a work week in years. She hated him, she told herself that weekend, again and again and again, until she could almost pretend that she really did. That it was that simple.

"I hate him," she told Rosie, taking out her feelings on the sad little boil-in-the-bag chicken curry they'd made for Sunday dinner with a violent jab of her fork. It had been two blessed Nikolai-free days. She couldn't bear the thought of what tomorrow might bring. "He's incredibly unprofessional. He's made the whole office into a circus! Nothing but gossip about him and me, all day every day!"

Rosie eyed Alicia from her side of the sofa, her knees pulled up beneath her and her blond hair piled haphazardly on her head.

"Maybe he likes you."

"No. He does not. This is some kind of sick game he's playing for his own amusement. That's the kind of man he is."

"No kind of man goes to all that trouble," her friend said slowly. "Not for a game. He really could simply like you, Alicia. In his own terrifyingly wealthy sort of way, I mean."

"He doesn't like *me*, Rosie," Alicia retorted, with too much heat, but she couldn't stop it. "The women he likes come with their own *Vogue* covers."

But she could see that Rosie was conjuring up Cinderella stories in her head, like everyone else, as Nikolai had known they would. Alicia felt so furious, so desperate and so trapped, that she shook with it. She felt his manipulation like a touch, like he was sitting right there next to her, that big body of his deceptively lazy, running his amused fingers up and down her spine.

You wish you were anything as uncomplicated as furious, a little voice taunted her, deep inside.

"Maybe you should play along," Rosie said then, and

she grinned wide. "It's not going to be a drink down at
the pub on a date with the likes of him, is it? He's the
sort who has *mistresses,* not *girlfriends.* He could fly
you to Paris for dinner. He could whisk you off to some
private island. Or one of those great hulking yachts they
always have."

"He could ruin my reputation," Alicia countered, and
yet despite herself, wondered what being Nikolai's *mistress* would entail—what sort of lover he would be, what
kind of sensual demands he would make if he had more
than one night to make them. All of that lethal heat and
all the time in the world... How could anyone survive
it? She shoved the treacherous thoughts aside. "He could
make things very difficult for me at work."

"Only because they'll all be seething with jealousy,"
Rosie said with a dismissive sniff. "And your reputation
could use a little ruining."

Because she couldn't imagine what it was like to *actually* be ruined, Alicia knew. To have gone and ruined
herself so carelessly, so irrevocably. She couldn't know
what it was like to see that disgust in her own father's
eyes whenever he looked at her. To feel it in her own
gut, like a cancer.

Rosie smiled again, wickedly. "And I think Nikolai
Korovin sounds like the kind of man who knows his
way around a ruining."

Alicia only stabbed her chicken again. Harder. And
then scowled at the television as if she saw anything at
all but Nikolai, wherever she looked.

CHAPTER FIVE

ALICIA WAS RUNNING a file up to Charlotte's office the following week when she finally ran into him, larger than life, sauntering down the stairs in the otherwise-empty stairwell as if he hadn't a care in the world.

The shock of it—the force and clamor that was Nikolai—hit her as hard as it had at the club. As it had outside the office building that night. Making her feel restless in her own skin. Electric.

Furious, she told herself sternly.

He saw her instantly and smiled, that tug in the corner of his hard mouth that made her insides turn to water no matter how much she wished it didn't. No matter how much she wanted to be immune to it. To him.

Because whatever she was, whatever this *thing* was that made her so aware of him, she certainly wasn't immune.

And Nikolai knew it.

He moved like water, smooth and inexorable. He seemed bigger than he actually was, as if he was so powerful he couldn't be contained and so expanded to fit—and to effortlessly dominate—any and all available space. Even an ordinary stairwell. Today he wore another absurdly well-fitting suit in his usual black, this one a rapturous love letter to his lean, muscled, dangerous form. He looked sinfully handsome, ruthless and cool, wealthy beyond imagining, and it infuriated her. So deeply it hurt.

Alicia told herself that was all it did.

"This is harassment," she informed him as she marched up the stairs, her heels clicking hard against each step, her tone as brisk as her spine was straight.

"No," he said, his gaze on hers. "It isn't."

Alicia stopped moving only when she'd reached the step above him, enjoying the fact it put her on eye level with him, for once. Even if those eyes were far too blue, bright and laughing at her, that winter cold moving in her, heating her from within.

She hated him.

God, how she wished she could hate him.

"It most certainly is," she corrected him with a bit of his own frostiness. "And I hate to break this to you when you've gone ahead and made your pretend infatuation so public, but it's actually quite easy to resist you."

"Is it?" He shouldn't sound so amused. So indulgent.

She would have scowled at him, but thought he would read that as weakness. Instead, she tilted up her chin and tried to project the kind of tough, cool competence she wished she felt as she called his bluff to his face.

"I'm not going to take part in your little bit of revenge theater no matter how much time you spend feeding the office gossip mill," she told him. Tough. Calm. Cool. "If you want to have me fired because you took me home from a club of your own free will, go right ahead." She let that sit there for a moment, then angled her head ever so slightly closer to his, for emphasis. "I didn't do anything wrong, I'm not afraid of you and I'd advise you try to communicate with your ex-wife through more traditional channels."

Nikolai simply…shifted position.

He moved with a primal grace that robbed her of speech, pivoting without seeming to do so much as breathe. All Alicia knew was that she was facing him one moment and the next her back was up against the wall. As if he'd *willed* her to let him cage her there, his hands flat against the smooth wall on either side of her face.

He hadn't laid so much as a single finger upon her. He didn't now. He leaned in.

Much too close, and her body reacted as if he'd plugged her into the nearest socket. The white-hot light of this shocking heat between them pulsed through her, making her gasp. Her body betrayed her in a shivering flush, sensation scraping through her, making her skin pull taut, her breasts feel suddenly full and that wet, hot hunger punch its way into her belly before settling down between her legs. Where it stayed, a wild and greedy need, and all of it his. *His.*

As if she was, too.

"What the hell are you doing?" But it was no more than a whisper, and it gave her away as surely as that treacherous ache inside of her that Alicia was sure he could sense, somehow.

"I am a man possessed," Nikolai murmured, his mouth so close to hers she felt the pull of it, the ache, roll through her like a flash of pain, despite the hint of laughter she could hear in his voice. "Infatuated. Just as I promised you."

"I can see why your brother is the famous actor while you storm about, growling at other rich men and demanding their money." But her voice was little more than a breath, completely insubstantial, and she had to dig her fingers into the folder she carried to keep from touching that glorious chest that was right there in front of her, taunting her. "Because you're not terribly convincing, and by the way, I'm fairly certain this counts as stalking."

"Those are very strong words, Alicia." He didn't sound concerned. Nikolai rested his considerable, sleek weight on his hands and surrounded her. Hemmed her in. Let his body remind her of all those things she wanted to forget. *Needed* to forget. "Harassment. Stalking."

"Strong, yes." She could feel her pulse in her throat, a frantic staccato. "And also accurate."

Alicia felt more than heard his small laugh against the tender skin of her neck, and she knew he saw the goose bumps that prickled there when he lifted that knowing gaze to hers.

"This is the first time I've seen you inside this office since you walked into the conference hall." Nikolai didn't move back. He gave her no room to breathe. If she tried to twist away, to escape him the way she wanted to do, she would have to brush up against him—and she didn't dare do that. She couldn't trust herself. Not when he smelled like winter. Not when she had the alarming urge to bury her face in his chest. "I haven't followed you around making suggestive comments. I extended a single invitation to you, Alicia. I didn't even do it myself. And you declined it without any repercussions at all."

"Says the man who has me pinned up against a wall."

"I'm not touching you," Nikolai pointed out, that dangerously lazy gleam in his bright gaze. "I'm not restraining you in any way. I could, of course." That gleam grew hotter, making her toes curl inside her shoes, making that need inside her rage into a wildfire. Making her despair of herself. "All you have to do is ask."

"I want you to stop this," she managed to get out,

desperate to fight off the maelstrom he'd unleashed in her, the images carnal and tempting that chased through her head and made her much too aware of how weak she was.

How perilously close to compounding the error she'd already made with this man, right here in her office. In the *stairwell.* Every inch of her the whore her father had called her.

"Which *this?*" He sounded impossibly male, then. Insufferably smug, as if he knew exactly how close she was to capitulation. "Be specific."

She shifted then, and it was agonizing. He was *right there,* and she knew she couldn't allow herself to touch him, not even by accident—but she was terribly afraid she wasn't going to be able to help herself. How could she fight herself *and* him?

"I'd rather be sacked right now than have to put up with this," she whispered fiercely.

He laughed again then, and she wished that sound didn't get to her. She wished she could simply ignore it and him along with it. But it made him that much more beautiful, like a perfect sunset over a rugged mountain, and it made something inside of her ignite no matter how much she wished it didn't.

"You and I both know I could prove you a liar." He dropped his head slightly, and inhaled, as if pulling the scent of her skin deep into his lungs, and that fire in her began to pulse, greedy and insistent. Her nipples pressed against the soft fabric of her dress, and she was terrified he'd see it. Terrified he'd *know.* "How long do you think it would take, *solnyshka?* One second? Two? How long before you wrap yourself around me and beg?"

Of course he knew. Hadn't that long night with him taught her anything?

Alicia stiffened, panic like a drumbeat inside of her, but it only seemed to make that fire in her burn hotter. Nikolai moved even closer, somehow, though that shouldn't have been possible, and he was so big, so powerful, that it was as if nothing existed except the breadth of his shoulders. He surrounded her, and there was a part of her way down deep that wasn't at all conflicted. That simply exulted in it. In him.

But that was the part that had started all this. The part that had looked up into his face in that dark club and surrendered, there and then. She couldn't succumb to his version of dark magic again. She had too much to lose.

"You don't understand," she said hurriedly, almost desperately. "This is—you are—" She pulled in a breath. "I'm afraid—"

But she couldn't tell Nikolai Korovin the things she feared. She couldn't say them out loud, and anyway, this was only a bitter little game to him. The ways she hated herself, the ways she'd let herself down, the way she'd destroyed her relationship with her father—he didn't need to know about any of that.

She couldn't understand why she had the strange urge to tell him anyway, when she'd never told a soul.

It seemed to take him a very long time to pull his head back far enough to look her in the eyes, to study her too-hot face. Even through her agitation, she could see him grow somber as he watched her. Darker. He pushed back from the wall, letting his hands drop to his sides, and Alicia told herself that was exactly what she'd wanted.

"Good," he said quietly, an expression she couldn't read on his hard face. "You should be afraid of me. You should have been afraid that night."

She scowled at him, not caring anymore what he read into it.

"For God's sake," she snapped, not liking that look on his face and not at all sure why it bothered her so much and so deeply. "I'm not afraid of *you*."

That sat there between them, telling him things she should have kept to herself, and the expression on his face made her think of that moment in his bed, suddenly. When he'd talked of kitchen knives and sins and she'd kissed his tattoo, as if she could kiss it all away. As if he was wounded.

"I thought you liked the fact that I *don't* want you," she said after a moment, when all he did was stare at her, in a manner she might have called haunted if it was someone other than Nikolai. "Why are you so determined to prove otherwise?"

"You mistake me." His voice was silky then, but there was a dark kick beneath it, and it shivered over her skin like a caress. "I know you want me. I still want you. I told you this was a distraction." He stuck his hands in his pockets, shifting back on his heels, and his expression grew cooler. More distant. Assessing her. "It's your disinterest in having any kind of connection to me, your horror at the very idea, that makes the rest of this possible."

"And by that do you mean keeping my job?" she asked, ignoring his talk of who wanted who, because she didn't dare let herself think about it. She couldn't go there, or who knew what would become of her? "Or the twisted game you feel you need to play with your ex-wife?"

Nikolai only stared back at her, his face a study in ice. Impassive and cool.

"Let me guess," she said tightly. "You only want what you can't have."

"But you don't qualify, Alicia," he said, in that dangerously soft way of his that was like a seismic event inside of her, and she had to fight to hide the aftershocks. "I've already had you."

"That was a mistake," she retorted, and she wanted to play it down. Laugh, smile. But his eyes flashed and she knew she'd sounded too dark. Too close to *hurt*. "There won't be a repeat."

"You don't want to challenge me to prove you wrong." His winter eyes probed hers, moved over her face, saw things she didn't want to share. "Or perhaps you do."

That last was a low growl. Wolf again, not man, and she wasn't sure she could survive it without imploding. Without betraying herself all over again, and there was no *wild night* to lose herself in, not here in this chilly stairwell. No pounding music, no shouting crowd. She felt the danger in him, the profound sensual threat, like heat all around her, seducing her without a single word or touch. She could smell that scent that was only his, the faint smoke and crisp slap of winter. She felt the strength of him, that lethal power, and her fingers ached to explore it again, every last lean muscle, until he groaned beneath her hands.

And she *wanted*.

Suddenly, and with every last cell in her body, Alicia wanted to be someone else. Someone free of her past, free to throw herself heedlessly into all of this wondrous fire and not care if it swallowed her whole. Someone who could do what she liked with this man without bringing her whole world down around her all over again.

Someone very much like the person she'd seemed to think she was the night she'd met him.

But she couldn't. And Nikolai still didn't touch her, which almost made it worse.

"It's time to move into the public phase of this arrangement," he told her in that distant way again, as if this was a planned meeting in the stairwell to calmly discuss the calendar of events that would lead to her downfall. "We'll start with dinner tomorrow night. There are things we need to discuss."

"What a lovely invitation—"

"It's not a request."

She studied him for a moment, all that ice and steel. "I'm otherwise engaged."

"Cancel."

"And if I refuse?"

Nikolai's smile turned dangerous. Her stomach contracted hard at the sight, and the ache of it sank low, turning molten and making her despair of herself anew.

It was that easy. *She* was that easy.

"You can try to run from me if you like." He looked intrigued at the prospect, and something dark and sensual twisted through her, leaving marks. "But I should give you fair warning—I'll find you. And you might not like the mood I'm in when I do."

"Fine," she made herself say, because she couldn't think of an alternate plan, certainly not while he stood there in front of her with a look on his face that told her he'd love to spend more time convincing her. She couldn't have that. And she certainly didn't want him to pursue her through the streets of London, to run her to ground like some mutinous fox, which she had no doubt he would do…. Did she? "Tomorrow night we'll suffer through the date from hell. That sounds delightful. Where do you want me to meet you?"

He reached out then and she braced herself, but he only wrapped a sprig of her curls around his finger, gave them a tug that was very nearly gentle, then let his hand drop, an odd cast to his fierce, proud mouth as he did it.

There was no reason at all that should pierce her heart.

"Don't try to top from the bottom, Alicia," he said, laughter in his brilliant gaze for a moment before it chilled into something much harder. More ruthless. "I'll let you know what I want tomorrow. And you'll do it. Because I really will have you fired if you don't, and despite this entertaining display of bravado, I think you know it."

And there it was.

She didn't want to lose her job—which meant she'd have to figure out how to survive losing her father all over again, once there were pictures to prove once more that she was nothing but a whore. And if there was a tiny spark inside of her, because some foolish part of her wished this wasn't all a game, that it wasn't all for show, that she was the kind of person men didn't use, she did her best to ignore it.

"I don't want to do this." Her voice was small, but still firm, and she thought she'd be proud, later, that she kept her head high. Even in defeat. "Any of it."

"I know you don't," Nikolai said, whole winters in his voice, in his beautiful eyes, so blue she wanted to cry. And there was a flash of something there, bright for a moment and then gone, as if this was more of a struggle for him than it seemed. It scared her, how much she wanted to believe that. "But you will."

Alicia sat where Nikolai had put her, at the corner of the dark wood table that stretched across a significant length of the great two-story room that was the center of his apartment, all low-slung modern couches and soaring windows. Nikolai could read her stiff tension in the way she sat, the way she held her lips too tight, the precise, angry movements of her hands.

His staff had served a five-star dinner that she'd barely touched. Nikolai hadn't spoken a word, and she hadn't broken the silence. Now she was pushing her dessert around on her plate, and he was well aware that her agitation level had skyrocketed even higher than before.

Bastard that he was, that amused him. He lounged in his seat, at the head of the table with her at his right, and studied her. He would figure her out. He would solve the mystery of this woman and when he did, lose interest in her. It was inevitable.

But he hadn't anticipated he would enjoy the process quite this much.

"You're a terrible date," he told her, and her dark eyes flashed when they met his. Then, after a moment, she rolled them. *At* him.

No one else would dare.

"Thank you," she said in that dry way that made him want her beneath him, right there on the table. He had to yank himself back under control, and it was significantly harder than it should have been. *Focus,* he ordered himself. "I can see why you're considered such a catch."

"This is an excellent opportunity to discuss my expectations," Nikolai said, as if her fearless defiance didn't make him want to lick his way into the heat of her, to make her writhe and sob in his hands. And he would, he promised himself, as soon as they came to an understanding. "Dating me comes with a number of requirements, Alicia. Making appropriate dinner conversation is only one of them."

"You're perfectly capable of making conversation," she pointed out in the same dry tone. "In fact, you're doing it right now, though I don't know if it qualifies as 'appropriate.'" She considered him for a moment, a small smile that he didn't like, yet found he wanted to taste, flirting with her full lips. "I suspected there must be some kind of application process and I'm delighted I'm right, but I'm not dating you. This isn't real." Her gaze turned hard on his. "This is blackmail."

"Call it whatever you like," he said, with a careless shrug. "The result is the same."

"Blackmail," she repeated, very distinctly. "I think you'll find that's what it's called when you force someone into doing something they don't want to do by holding something else over their head."

Nikolai could see all of that temper in her dark gaze, the flash of it when she couldn't hide her feelings. She wore a sleeveless wool top tonight in a deep aubergine shade, with a neck that drooped down low and left her smooth, toned arms on display, looking soft and sweet in the candlelight. But most important, he could see every time she tensed, every time she forced herself to relax, written up and down the lean, elegant shape of those arms and all across her slender frame. Like now, when she forced her shoulders back and down, then smiled at him as if she wasn't agitated at all.

She didn't know, yet, that he could read her body the way others read words on a page. But she would learn, and he would greatly enjoy teaching her. First, though, they had business to take care of. If it alarmed him that he had to remind himself of business before pleasure for the first time in living memory, he ignored it.

"There is a confidentiality agreement that you'll need to sign," he told her, dismissing her talk of blackmail, which he could see she didn't like. "Beyond that, I have only standard expectations. Don't venture out into public unless you're prepared to be photographed, as terrible pictures of you could lead to negative coverage of me, which is unacceptable. I'll let you know what pleases me—"

"If you mention a single thing about altering my appearance to suit your tastes, whatever those might be," she said almost conversationally, though there was murder in her eyes, "I will stab you with this fork. I'm not dating you, Nikolai. I'm acquiescing to your bizarre demands because I want to keep my job, but we're not re-enacting some sick little version *My Fair Lady.* I don't care about pleasing you."

Nikolai was definitely enjoying himself. Especially when he saw that little shiver move through her, and knew they were both thinking about all the ways she could please him. All the ways she had. He smiled slightly.

"Is that a passive-aggressive demand that I compliment your looks?" he asked silkily. "I had no idea you were so insecure, Alicia. I'd have thought the fact that I had my mouth on every inch of that gorgeous body of yours would have told you my feelings on that topic in no uncertain terms. Though I'm happy to repeat myself."

"I may stab you with this fork anyway." She met his gaze then and smiled. But he could see that her breathing had quickened. He knew arousal when he saw it. When he'd already tasted it. All of that heat and need, sweet against her dark skin. "Fair warning."

"You can always try."

She considered that for a moment, then sat back against her chair, inclining her head slightly as if she held the power here and was granting him permission to carry on.

"Don't ever keep me waiting," Nikolai said, continuing as if she hadn't interrupted him. "Anywhere. For any reason. My time is more valuable than yours."

Her eyes narrowed at that, but she didn't speak. Perhaps she was learning, he thought—but he hoped not. He really hoped not. He wanted her conquered, not coerced. He wanted to do it himself, step by delectable step.

"Don't challenge my authority. In your case, I'll allow some leeway because I find that smart mouth of yours amusing, but only a little leeway, Alicia, and never in public. Your role is as an ornament. I won't tolerate disrespect or disobedience. And I will tell you what you are to me, explicitly—never imagine yourself anything else. I can't stress that enough."

The silence between them then felt tighter. Hotter. Breathless, as if the great room had shrunk down until there was nothing but the two of them and the gently flickering candles. And her eyes were big and dark and he realized he could no longer read the way she looked at him.

"You're aware that this is a conversation about dating you *for show,* not working for you as one of your many interchangeable subordinates at the Korovin Foundation," she said after a moment. "Aren't you?"

"The roles aren't dissimilar."

He stretched his legs out in front of him and lounged even lower in the chair.

"Is this your usual first date checklist, then?"

Her gaze swept over him, and he had no idea what she saw. It surprised him how much he wanted to know.

He nodded, never taking his gaze from hers. "More or less."

"You actually ask a woman to dinner and then present her with this list." She sounded dubious, and something else he wasn't sure he recognized. "Before or after you order starters? And what if she says no? Do you stand up and walk out? Leave her with the bill for her temerity?"

"No one has ever said no." He felt that fire between them reach higher, pull tighter. He could see it on her face. "And I don't take women to dinner without a signed confidentiality agreement. Or anywhere else."

Alicia tapped a finger against her lips for a moment, and he wanted to suck that finger into his own mouth almost more than he wanted his next breath. Need raked through him, raw and hungry.

"You brought me here that night," she pointed out, her tone light, as if there was no tension between them at all. "I certainly didn't sign anything."

Nikolai almost smiled. "You are an anomaly."

"Lucky me," she murmured, faint and dry, and there was no reason that should have worked through him like a match against flint. He didn't like anomalies. He shouldn't have to keep telling himself that.

"If you've absorbed the initial requirements," he said, watching her intently now, "we can move on."

"There are more? The mind boggles."

She was mocking him, he was sure of it. He could see the light of it bright in her eyes and in that wicked twist of her lips, and for some reason, he didn't mind it.

"Sex," he said, and liked the way she froze, for the slightest instant, before concealing her reaction. He had to shift in his seat to hide his.

"You don't really have rules for sex with your girl-friends, Nikolai," she said softly. Imploring him. "Please tell me you're joking."

"I think of this as setting clear boundaries," he told her, leaning forward and smiling when she shivered and sat back. "It prevents undue confusion down the line."

"Undue confusion is what relationships are all about,"

Alicia said, shaking her head. Her dark eyes searched his, then dropped to her lap. "I rather think that might be the whole point."

"I don't have relationships." He waited until her eyes were on him again, until that tension between them pulled taut and that electric charge was on high, humming through them both. "I have sex. A lot of it. I'll make you come so many times your head will spin, which you already know is no idle boast, but in return, I require two things."

Nikolai watched her swallow almost convulsively, but she didn't look away. She didn't even blink. And he didn't quite know why he felt that like a victory.

"Access and obedience," he said, very distinctly, and was rewarded with the faintest tremor across those lips, down that slender frame. "When I want you, I want you—I don't want a negotiation. Just do what I tell you to do."

He could hear every shift in her breathing. The catch, the slow release. It took every bit of self-control he possessed to wait. To keep his distance. To let her look away for a moment and collect herself, then turn that dark gaze back on him.

"I want to be very clear." She leaned forward, putting her elbows on the table and keeping her eyes trained on him. "What you're telling me, Nikolai, is that every woman pictured on your arm in every single photograph of you online has agreed to all of these *requirements*. All of them."

He wanted to taste her, a violent cut of need, but he didn't. He waited.

"Of course," he said.

And Alicia laughed.

Silvery and musical, just as he remembered. It poured

out of her and deep into him, and for a moment he was stunned by it. As if everything disappeared into the sound of it, the way she tipped back her head and let it light up the room. As if she'd hit him from behind and taken him down to the ground without his feeling a single blow.

That laughter rolled into places frozen so solid he'd forgotten they existed at all. It pierced him straight through to a core he hadn't known he had. And it was worse now than it had been that first night. It cut deeper. He was terribly afraid it had made him bleed.

"Laugh as much as you like," he said stiffly when she subsided, and was sitting back in her chair, wiping at her too-bright eyes. "But none of this is negotiable."

"Nikolai," she said, and that clutched at him too, because he'd never heard anyone speak his name like that. So warm, with all of that laughter still moving through her voice. It was almost as if she spoke to someone else entirely, as if it wasn't his name at all—but she looked directly at him, those dark eyes dancing, and he felt as if she'd shot him. He wished she had. He knew how to handle a bullet wound. "I'll play this game of yours. But I'm not going to do any of that."

He was so tense he thought he might simply snap into pieces, but he couldn't seem to move. Her laughter sneaked inside him, messing him up and making even his breathing feel impossibly changed. He hated it.

So he couldn't imagine why he wanted to hear it again, with an intensity that very nearly hurt.

"That's not one of your options," he told her, his voice the roughest he'd ever heard it.

But she was smiling at him, gently, and looked wholly uncowed by his tone.

"If I were you, Nikolai," she said, "I'd start asking

myself why I'm so incapable of interacting with other people that I come up with ridiculous rules and regulations to govern things that are supposed to come naturally. That are *better* when they do."

"Because I am a monster," he said. He didn't plan it. It simply came out of his mouth and he did nothing to prevent it. She stopped smiling. Even the brightness in her eyes dimmed. "I've never been anything else. These rules and regulations aren't ridiculous, Alicia. They're necessary."

"Do they make you feel safe?" she asked with a certain quiet kindness he found deeply alarming, as if she knew things she couldn't possibly guess at, much less *know*.

But this was familiar ground even so. He'd had this same conversation with his brother, time and again. He recognized the happy, delusional world she'd come from that let her ask a question like that, and he knew the real world, cynical and bleak. He recognized himself again.

It was a relief, cold and sharp.

"Safety is a delusion," he told her curtly, "and not one I've ever shared. Some of us live our whole lives without succumbing to that particular opiate."

She frowned at him. "Surely when you were a child—"

"I was never a child." He pushed back from the table and rose to his feet. "Not in the way you mean."

She only watched him, still frowning, as he crossed his arms over his chest, and she didn't move so much as a muscle when he glared down at her. She didn't shrink back the way she should. She looked at him as if he didn't scare her at all, and it ate at him. It made him want to show her how bad he really was—but he couldn't start down that road. He had no idea where it would lead.

"Why do you think my uncle tried to keep me in line with a kitchen knife? It wasn't an accident. He knew what I was."

"Your parents—"

"Died in a fire with seventy others when I was barely five years old," he told her coldly. "I don't remember them. But I doubt they would have liked what I've become. This isn't a bid for sympathy." He shrugged. "It's a truth I accepted a long time ago. Even my own brother believes it, and this after years of being the only one alive who thought I could be any different. I can't." He couldn't look away from her dark eyes, that frown, from the odd and wholly novel notion that she wanted to fight *for* him that opened up a hollow in his chest. "I won't."

"Your brother is an idiot." Her voice was fierce, as if she was prepared to defend him against Ivan—and even against himself, and he had no idea what to do with that. "Because while families always have some kind of tension, Nikolai, monsters do not exist. No matter what an uncle who holds a knife on a child tells you. No matter what we like to tell ourselves."

"I'm glad you think so." Nikolai wasn't sure he could handle the way she looked at him then, as if she hurt for him. He wasn't sure he knew how. "Soft, breakable creatures like you *should* believe there's nothing terrible out there in the dark. But I know better."

CHAPTER SIX

That was *pain* on his face.

In those searing eyes of his. In the rough scrape of his voice. It was like a dark stain that spilled out from deep inside of him, as if he was torn apart far beneath his strong, icy surface. *Ravaged*, it dawned on her, as surely as if that ferocious thing on his chest rent him to pieces where he stood.

Alicia felt it claw at her, too.

"I'm neither soft nor breakable, Nikolai." She kept her voice steady and her gaze on his, because she thought he needed to see that he hadn't rocked her with that heartbreakingly stark confession, even if he had. "Or as naive as you seem to believe."

"There are four or five ways I could kill you from here." His voice was like gravel. "With my thumb."

Alicia believed him, the way she'd believed he'd be good in bed when he'd told her he was, with a very similar matter-of-fact certainty. It occurred to her that there were any number of ways a man could be talented with his body—with his clever hands for pleasure, with his thumb for something more violent—and Nikolai Korovin clearly knew every one of them. She thought she ought to be frightened by that.

What was wrong with her that she wasn't?

"Please don't," she said briskly, as if she couldn't feel the sting of those claws, as if she didn't see that thick blackness all around him.

Nikolai stared at her. He stood so still, as if he expected he might need to bolt in any direction, and he held himself as if he expected an attack at any moment. As if he expected *she* might be the attacker.

Alicia thought of his coldness tonight, that bone-deep chill that should have hurt, so much harsher than the gruff, darkly amusing man she'd taken by surprise in that club. Who'd surprised her in return. She thought about what little he'd told her of his uncle meant for the boy he must have been—what he must have had to live through. She thought about a man who believed his own brother thought so little of him, and who accepted it as his due. She thought of his lists of rules that he obviously took very seriously indeed, designed to keep even the most intimate people in his life at bay.

I am a monster, he'd said, and she could see that he believed it.

But she didn't. She couldn't.

She ached for him. In a way she was very much afraid—with that little thrill of dark foreboding that prodded at her no matter how she tried to ignore it— would be the end of her. But she couldn't seem to make it stop.

"Nikolai," she said when she couldn't stand it any longer—when she wanted to reach over and touch him, soothe him, and knew she couldn't let herself do that, that *he* wouldn't let her do that anyway, "if you were truly a monster, you would simply *be* one. You wouldn't announce it. You wouldn't know how."

A different expression moved across his face then, the way it had once before in the dark, and tonight it broke her heart. That flash of a vulnerability so deep, so intense. And then she watched him pack it away, cover it in ice, turn it hard and cold.

"There are other things I could do with my thumb," he said, his voice the rough velvet she knew best. Seductive. Demanding. "That wouldn't kill you, necessarily, though you might beg for it before I was done."

But she knew what he was doing. She understood it, and it made her chest hurt.

"Sex is easier to accept than comfort," she said quietly, watching his face as she said it. He looked glacial. Remote. And yet that heat inside of him burned, she could feel it. "You can pretend it's not comfort at all. Just sex."

"I like sex, Alicia." His voice was a harsh lash through the room, so vicious she almost flinched. "I thought I made that clear our first night together. Over and over again."

He wanted to prove he was the monster he said he was. He wanted to prove that he was exactly as bad, as terrifying, as he claimed he was. Capable of killing with nothing more than his thumb. She looked at that cold, set face of his and she could see that he believed it. More— that he simply accepted that this was who he was.

And she found that so terribly sad it almost crippled her.

She got up and went to him without consciously deciding to move. He didn't appear to react, and yet she had the impression he steeled himself at her approach, as if she was as dangerous to him as he was to her. But she couldn't let herself think about that stunning possibility.

Nikolai watched her draw near, his expression even colder. Harder. Alicia tilted her head back and looked into his extraordinary eyes, darker now than usual as he stared back at her with a kind of defiance, as if he was prepared to fight her until she saw him as he saw himself.

Until she called him a monster, too.

"Do you want to know what I think?" she asked.

"I'm certain I don't."

It was a rough scrape of sound, grim and low, but she thought she saw a kind of hunger in his eyes that had nothing to do with his sexual prowess and everything to do with that flash of vulnerability she almost thought she'd imagined, and she kept going.

"I think you hide behind all these rules and boundaries, Nikolai." She felt the air in the room go electric, but she couldn't seem to stop herself. "If you tell yourself you're a monster, if you insist upon it and act upon it, you make it true. It's a self-fulfilling prophecy."

And she would know all about that, wouldn't she? Hadn't she spent eight long years doing exactly that herself? That unexpected insight was like a kick in the stomach, but she ignored it, pushing it aside to look at later.

"Believe me," she said then, more fiercely than she'd intended. "I know."

His hands shot out and took her by the shoulders, then pulled her toward him, toward his hard face that was even more lethal, even more fierce than usual. His touch against her bare arms burned, and made her want nothing more than to melt into him. It was too hot. Too dark.

And he was close then, so powerful and furious. *So close.* Winter and need, fire and longing. The air was thick with it. It made her lungs ache.

"Why don't you have the good sense to be afraid of me?" he said in an undertone, as if the words were torn from that deep, black part of him. "What is the matter with you? Why do you *laugh* when anyone else would cry?"

"I don't see any monsters when I look at you, Nikolai," she replied, winning the fight to keep her tone light, her gaze on his, no matter how ravaged he looked. How undone. Or how churned up she felt inside. "I only see a man. I see you."

His hands tightened around her shoulders for a brief instant, and then he let her go. Abruptly, as if he'd wanted to do the opposite.

As if he couldn't trust himself any more than she could.

"You don't want to play with this particular fire," he warned her, his expression fierce and dark, his gaze drilling holes into her. "It won't simply burn you—it will swallow you whole. That's not a self-fulfilling prophecy. It's an inevitability."

Alicia didn't know what seared through her then, shocking and dark, thrilling to the idea of it. Of truly losing herself in him, in that fire neither one of them could control, despite the fact there was still that panicked part of her—that part of her that wished she'd gone home and done her laundry that night and never met him—that wanted anything but that. And he saw it. All of it.

She had no idea what was happening to her, or how to stop it, or why she had the breathless sense that it was already much too late.

"Get your coat," he growled at her. "I'll take you home."

Alicia blinked, surprised to find that she was unsteady on her own feet. And Nikolai was dark and menacing, watching her as if no detail was too small to escape his notice. As if he could see all those things inside of her, the fire and the need. That dark urge to demand he throw whatever he had at her, that she could take it, that she understood him—

Of course you don't understand him, she chided herself. *How could you?*

"That's unnecessary," she said into the tense silence, stiffly, and had to clear the roughness from her voice with a cough.

She straightened her top, smoothed her hands down the sides of her trousers, then stopped when she realized she was fidgeting and he'd no doubt read the anxiety that betrayed the way he did everything else.

"You don't have to take me home," she said when he didn't respond. When he only watched her, his expression brooding and his blue eyes cold. She frowned at him. "This night has been intense enough, I think. I'll get a taxi."

The ride across London—in the backseat of Nikolai's SUV with him taking up too much of the seat beside her because he'd informed her a taxi was not an option— was much like sitting on simmering coals, waiting for the fire to burst free.

Not exactly comfortable, Alicia thought crossly. And as the fever of what had happened between them in his penthouse faded with every mile they traveled, she realized he'd been right to warn her.

She felt scorched through. Blackened around the edges and much too close to simply going up in flames herself, until she very much feared there'd be nothing left of her. A few ashes, scattered here and there.

Had she really stood there thinking she wanted more of this? Anything he had to give, in fact? What *was* the matter with her?

But then she thought of that bleak look in his beautiful eyes, that terrible certainty in his voice when he'd told her what a monster he was, and she was afraid she knew all too well what was wrong with her.

"You can go," she told him, not bothering to hide the tension in her voice as they stood outside the door that led into her building in a narrow alcove stuck between two darkened shops.

Nikolai had walked her to the door without a word, that winter fire roaring all around them both, and now stood close beside her in the chilly December night. Too close beside her. Alicia needed to get inside, lock her doors, take a very long soak in the bath—*something* to sort her head out before she lost whatever remained of her sanity, if not something far worse than that. *She needed him to go.* She dug for her keys in her bag without looking at him, not trusting herself to look away again if she did.

"I'm fine from here. I don't need an escort."

He didn't respond. He plucked the keys from her hand when she pulled them out, and then opened the door with no hesitation whatsoever, waving her inside with a hint of edgy impatience.

It would not be wise to let him in. That was perfectly clear to her.

"Nikolai," she began, and his gaze slammed into her, making her gulp down whatever she might have said.

"I understand that you need to fight me on everything," he said, his accent thicker than usual. "If I wanted to psychoanalyze you the way you did me, I'd say I suspect it makes you feel powerful to poke at me. But I wouldn't get too comfortable with that if I were you."

"I wasn't psychoanalyzing you!" she cried, but he brushed it off as if she hadn't spoken.

"But you should ask yourself something," He put his

hand on her arm and hauled her into the building, sent the door slamming shut with the back of his shoulder and then held her there in the narrow hall. "Exactly what do you think might happen if you get what you seem to want and I lose control?"

"I don't want—"

"There are reasons men control themselves," he told her, his face in hers, and she should have been intimidated. She should have been terrified. And instead, all she felt was that greedy pulse of need roll through her. That impossible kick of this jagged-edged joy he brought out in her no matter what she thought she *ought* to feel. "Especially men like me, who stand like wolves in the dark corners of more than just London clubs. You should think about what those reasons are. There are far worse things than a list of demands."

"Like your attempts to intimidate me?" she countered, trying to find her footing when she was so off balance she suspected she might have toppled over without him there to hold her up.

"Why don't you laugh it off?" he asked softly, more a taunt than a question, and she had the wild thought that this might be Nikolai at his most dangerous. Soft and deadly and much too close. His gaze brushed over her face, leaving ice and fire wherever it touched. "No? Is this not funny anymore?"

"Nikolai." His name felt unwieldy against her tongue, or perhaps that was the look in his eyes, spelling out her sure doom in all of that ferocious blue. "I'm not trying to make you lose control."

"Oh, I think you are." He smiled, though it was almost feral and it scraped over her, through her. "But you should make very, very sure that you're prepared to handle the consequences if you succeed. Do you think you are? Right here in this hallway, with a draft under the door and the street a step away? Do you think you're ready for that?"

"Stop threatening me," she bit out at him, but it was a ragged whisper, and he could see into her too easily.

"I don't make threats, Alicia." He leaned in closer and nipped at her neck, shocking her. Making her go up in flames. And flinch—or was that simply an electric charge? "You should think of that, too."

And then he stepped away and jerked his head in an unspoken demand that she lead him up the stairs. And Alicia was so unsteady, so chaotic inside, so unable to process all the things that had happened tonight—what he'd said, what she'd felt, that deep ache inside of her, that fire that never did anything but burn hotter—that she simply marched up the stairs to the flat she shared with Rosie on the top floor without a word of protest.

He didn't ask if she wanted him inside when they reached her door, he simply strode in behind her as if he owned the place, and the insanity of it—of *Nikolai Korovin* standing there *in her home*—was so excruciating it was like pain.

"I don't want you here," she told him as he shut her door behind him, the sound of the latch engaging and locking him inside with her too loud in her ears. "I didn't invite you in."

"I didn't ask."

He was still dressed in black, and that very darkness made him seem bigger and more lethal as he walked inside, his cold gaze moving over the cheerful clutter that was everywhere. Bright paperbacks shoved haphazardly onto groaning shelves, photographs in colorful frames littering every surface, walls painted happy colors and filled with framed prints of famous art from around the world. Alicia tensed, expecting Rosie to pad into view at any moment, but the continuing stretch of silence suggested she was out. *Thank God.*

"It's messy," she said, aware she sounded defensive. "We never quite get around to cleaning it as we should. Of course, we also don't have a household staff."

"It looks like real people live here," he replied, frowning at one of Rosie's abandoned knitting projects, and it took her a moment to understand that this, too, was a terribly sad thing to say.

That ache in her deepened. Expanded. Hurt.

Alicia tossed her keys on the table in the hall, her coat over the chair, and then followed Nikolai warily as he melted in and out of the rooms of the flat like a shadow.

"What are you looking for?" she asked after a few minutes of this.

"There must be a reason you're suicidally incapable of recognizing your own peril when you see it," he said, his eyes moving from place to place, object to object, taking everything in. Cataloging it, she thought. Examining every photograph the way he did every dish left in the sink, every pair of shoes kicked aside in the hall, and the spine of every book piled on the overstuffed bookshelves. "Perhaps there are environmental factors at play."

He moved past the kitchen off to the right and stood at the far end of the hall that cut down the middle of the flat, where the bedrooms were.

"And what would those be, do you think?" she asked, her voice tart—which felt like a vast improvement. Or was perhaps a response to what had sounded like the faintest hint of that dark humor of his. It was absurd how much she craved more of it. "Fearlessness tucked away in the walls like asbestos?"

Nikolai didn't answer her, he only sent one of those simmering looks arrowing her way down the hallway, as effective from a few feet away as it was up close. And almost as devastating.

Alicia blew out a breath when he opened the door to her bedroom, the aftershocks of that winter-blue look shifting into something else again. A kind of nervous anticipation. He looked inside for a long moment, and her heart raced. She wished, suddenly, that she'd had the presence of mind to prevent this. She didn't like the fact that he knew, now, that she favored all those silly, self-indulgent throw pillows, piled so high on her bed, shouting out how soft and breakable she really was. They felt like proof, somehow—and when he looked back at her it was hard to stand still. To keep from offering some kind of explanation.

"A four-poster bed." It could have been an innocent comment. An observation. But the way he looked at her made her knees feel weak. "Intriguing."

Alicia thought she understood then, and somehow, that eased the relentless pulse of panic inside.

"Let me guess." She leaned her hip against the wall and watched him. "The faster you puzzle me out, the less you think you'll have to worry about losing this control of yours."

"I don't like mysteries."

"Will it make you feel safe to solve whatever mystery you think I am, Nikolai? Is that what this is?"

The look he gave her then did more than simply *hurt*. It ripped straight down into the center of her, tearing everything she was in two, and there was nothing she could do but stand there and take it.

"I'm not the one who believes in safety, Alicia," he said softly, "It's nothing more than a fairy tale to me.

I never had it. I wouldn't recognize it." His expression was hard and bleak. Almost challenging. "The next time you tally up my scars, keep a special count of those I got when I was under the age of twelve. That knife was only one among many that drew my blood. My uncle used the back of his hand if I was lucky." His beautiful mouth twisted, and her heart dropped to her feet. "But I was never very lucky."

He stood taller then. Almost defiant. And it tore at her. She felt her eyes heat in a way that spelled imminent tears and knew she couldn't let herself cry for this hard, damaged man. Not where he could see it. She knew somehow that he would never forgive her.

"Don't waste your pity on me." His voice was cold, telling her she'd been right. No sympathy allowed. No compassion. He sounded almost insulted when he continued, as if whatever he saw on her face was a slap. "Eventually, I learned how to fight back, and I became more of a monster than my uncle ever could have been."

"We're all monsters," she told him, her voice harsh because she knew he wouldn't accept anything softer. Hoping against hope he'd never know about that great tear inside of her that she could feel with every breath she took, rending her further and further apart. "Some of us actually behave like monsters, in fact, rather than suffer through the monstrous actions of others. No one escapes their past unscathed."

"What would you know about it, Alicia?" His gaze was cold, his tone a stinging lash. "What past misdeeds could possibly haunt while you're tucked up in your virginal little bedroom, laughing your way through your cheery, happy life? What blood do you imagine is on your hands?"

And so she told him.

Alicia had never told a soul before, and yet she told Nikolai as easily as if she'd shared the story a thousand times. Every detail she could remember and all the ones she couldn't, that her father had filled in for her that awful morning. All of her shame, her despicable actions, her unforgivable behavior, without garnishment or pretense. As if that tear in her turned her inside out, splayed there before him.

And when she was finished, she was so light-headed she thought she might sag straight down to the floor, or double over where she stood.

"Everyone has ghosts," she managed to say, crossing her arms over her chest to keep herself upright.

Nikolai turned away from her bedroom door and moved toward her, thrusting his hands into the pockets of his trousers as he did. It made him look more dangerous, not less. It drew her attention to the wide strength of his shoulders, the long, lethal lines of his powerful frame. It made her wonder how anyone could have hurt him so badly when he'd been small that he'd felt he needed to transform himself into so sharp, so deadly a weapon. It made her feel bruised to the core that he'd no doubt look at her now the way her father had....

His eyes burned as they bored into hers, and he let out one of those low laughs that made her stomach tense.

"That doesn't sound like any ghost," he said, his voice dark and sure. "It sounds like an older man who took advantage of a young girl too drunk to fight him off."

Alicia jolted cold, then flashed hot, as he turned her entire life on end that easily. She swayed where she stood.

"No," she said, feeling desperate, as some great wave of terror or emotion or *something* rolled toward her. "My father said—"

"Your father should have known better than to speak to you like that." Nikolai scowled at her. "News flash, Alicia. Men who aren't predators prefer to have sex with women who are capable of participating."

Her head was spinning. Her stomach twisted, and for a panicked moment she thought she might be sick. She felt his words—so matter-of-fact, as if there could be no other interpretation of that night, much less the one that she'd held so close all these years—wash through her, like a quiet and devastating tsunami right there in her own hallway.

"What's his name?" Nikolai asked, in that soft, lethal way of his that lifted the hairs at the back of her neck. "The man who did these things to you? Does he still live next door to your parents?"

He was the first person she'd told. And the only one to defend her.

Alicia couldn't understand how she was still standing upright.

"That doesn't sound like a question a monster would ask," she whispered.

"You don't know what I'd do to him," he replied, that dark gleam in his gaze.

And he looked at her like she was important, not filthy. Not a whore. Like what had happened had been done to *her,* and hadn't been something *she'd* done.

Like it wasn't her fault after all.

She couldn't breathe.

His gaze shifted from hers to a spot down at the other end of the flat behind her, and she heard the jingling of keys in the hall outside. She felt as if she moved through sticky syrup, as if her body didn't understand what to do any longer, and turned around just as Rosie pushed her way inside.

Rosie sang out her usual hello, slinging her bags to the floor. Nikolai stepped closer to Alicia's back, then reached around to flatten his hand against the waist-band of her trousers before pulling her into his bold heat. Holding her to his chest as if they were lovers. Claiming her.

"What...?" Alicia whispered, the sizzle of that un-expected touch combining with the hard punch of the revolution he'd caused inside of her, making her knees feel weak.

"I told you we were taking this public," he replied, his voice a low rumble pitched only to her that made her shiver helplessly against him. "Now we have."

Rosie's head snapped up at the sound of his voice. Her mouth made a perfect, round O as if the devil him-self stood there behind Alicia in the hall, no doubt star-ing her down with those cold winter eyes of his. And then she dropped the bottle of wine she'd been holding in her free hand, smashing it into a thousand pieces all over the hall floor.

Which was precisely how Alicia felt.

Nikolai stared out at the wet and blustery London night on the other side of his penthouse's windows while he waited for the video conference with Los Angeles to begin. His office was reflected in the glass, done in imposing blacks and burgundies, every part of it care-fully calculated to trumpet his wealth and power with-out him having to say a word to whoever walked in. The expensive view out of all the windows said it for him. The modern masterpieces on the walls repeated it, even louder.

It was the sort of thing he'd used to take such plea-sure in. The application of his wealth and power to the most innocuous of interactions, the leverage it always afforded him. War games without a body count. It had been his favorite sport for years.

But now he thought only of the one person who seemed as unimpressed with these trappings of wealth and fame as she did with the danger he was well aware he represented. Hell, *exuded.* And instead of regaining his equilibrium the more time he spent with Alicia, instead of losing this intense and distracting interest in her the more he learned about her, he was getting worse.

Much worse. Incomprehensibly worse. And Nikolai knew too well what it felt like to spiral. He knew what obsession tasted like. *He knew.*

She was a latter-day version of his favorite drink, sharp and deadly. And he was still nothing but a drunk where she was concerned.

He'd ordered himself not to hunt down the man who had violated her, though he knew it would be easy. Too easy. The work of a single phone call, an internet search.

You are not her protector, he told himself over and over. *This is not your vengeance to take.*

He'd sparred for hours with his security team in his private gym, throwing them to the floor one after the next, punching and kicking and flipping. He'd swum endless laps in his pool. He'd run through the streets of London in the darkest hours of the night, the slap of the December weather harsh against his face, until his lungs burned and his legs shook.

Nothing made the slightest bit of difference. Nothing helped.

She'd all but pushed him out her front door that night, past her gaping flatmate and the wine soaking into her floorboards, her eyes stormy and dark, and he'd let her.

"Rosie calls me *Saint Alicia* and I *like* it," she'd whis-

pered fiercely to him, shoving him into the narrow hall
outside her flat. She'd been scolding him, he'd realized.
He wasn't sure he'd ever experienced it before. His uncle
had preferred to use his belt. "It's better than some other
things I've been called. But you looming around the flat
will be the end of that."

"Why?" he'd asked lazily, those broken, jagged things
moving around inside of him, making him want things
he couldn't name. Making him want to hurt anyone
who'd dared hurt her, like she was his. "I like saints.
I'm Russian."

"Please," she'd scoffed. "You have 'corruptor of in-
nocents' written all over you."

"Then we are both lucky, are we not, that neither one
of us is innocent," he'd said, and had enjoyed the heat
that had flashed through her eyes, chasing out the dark.

But by the next morning, she'd built her walls back
up, and higher than before. He hadn't liked that at all,
though he'd told himself it didn't matter. It shouldn't
matter. He told himself that again, now.

It was the end result he needed to focus on: Veronika. The truth about Stefan at long last, and the loose
thread she represented snipped off for good. Whatever
he suffered on the way to that goal would be worth it,
and in any case, Alicia would soon be nothing but a
memory. One more instrument he'd use as he needed,
then set aside.

He needed to remember that. There was only a week
left before the ball. Nikolai could handle anything for
one last week, surely. He'd certainly handled worse.

But she was under his skin, he knew, no matter how
many times he told himself otherwise. No matter how
fervently he pretended she wasn't.

And she kept clawing her way deeper, like a wound

that wouldn't scar over and become one more thing he'd survived.

He'd picked her up to take her to the Tate Modern on the opening night of some desperately chic exhibit, which he'd known would be teeming with London's snooty art world devotees and their assorted parasites and photographers. It wasn't the kind of place a man took a woman he kept around only for sex. Taking a woman to a highly intellectual and conceptual art exhibit suggested he might actually have an interest in her thoughts.

It was a perfect place for them to be "accidentally spotted," in other words. Nikolai hadn't wanted to dig too deeply into his actual level of interest in what went on inside her head. He hadn't wanted to confront himself.

Alicia had swung open the door to her flat and taken his breath that easily. She'd worn a skimpy red dress that showed off her perfect breasts and clung to her curves in mouthwatering ways he would have enjoyed on any woman, and deeply appreciated on her—and yet he'd had the foreign urge to demand she hide all of her lush beauty away from the undeserving public. That she keep it for him alone. He'd been so startled—and appalled—at his line of thought that he'd merely stood there, silent and grim, and stared at her as if she'd gone for his jugular with one of her wickedly high shoes.

Alicia had taken in the black sweater with the high collar he wore over dark trousers that, he'd been aware, made him look more like a commando than an appropriately urbane date to a highly anticipated London art exhibit.

Not that commandos wore cashmere, in his experience.

"Have you become some kind of spy?" she'd asked

him, in that dry way that might as well have been her
hands on his sex. His body hadn't been at all conflicted
about how he should figure her out. It had known exactly what it wanted.

When it came to Alicia, he'd realized, it always did.

"You must be confusing me for the character my
brother plays in movies," he'd told her dismissively,
and had fought to keep himself from simply leaning
forward and pressing his mouth to that tempting hollow between her breasts, then licking his way over each
creamy brown swell until he'd made them both delirious
and hot. He'd almost been able to taste her from where
he stood in the doorway.

Alicia had pulled on her coat from the nearby chair
and swept her bag into her hand. She hadn't even been
looking at him as she stepped out into the hall and turned
to lock her door behind her.

"Your brother plays you in his Jonas Dark films,"
she'd replied in that crisp way of hers that made his
skin feel tight against his bones. "A disaffected kind of
James Bond character, stretched too thin on the edge
of what's left of his humanity, yet called to act the hero
despite himself."

Nikolai had stared at her when she'd turned to face
him, and she'd stared back, that awareness and a wary
need moving across her expressive face, no doubt re-
flecting his own. Making him wish—

But he'd known he had to stop. He'd known better
from the first with her, hadn't he? He should have let
her fall to the floor in that club. He'd known it even as
he'd caught her.

"I'm no hero, Alicia," he'd said, sounding like sand-
paper and furious that she'd pushed him off balance
again. Hadn't he warned her what would happen? Was

that what she wanted? She didn't know what she was asking—but he did. "Surely you know this better than anyone."

She'd looked at him for a long moment, her dark gaze shrewd, seeing things he'd always wanted nothing more than to hide.

"Maybe not," she'd said. "But what do you think would happen if you found out you were wrong?"

And then she'd turned and started down the stairs toward the street, as if she hadn't left the shell of him behind her, hollow and unsettled.

Again.

Nikolai saw his own reflection in his office windows now, and it was like he was someone else. He was losing control and he couldn't seem to stop it. He was as edgy and paranoid and dark as he'd been in those brutal days after he'd quit drinking. Worse, perhaps.

Because these things that raged in him, massive and uncontrollable and hot like acid, were symptoms of a great thaw he knew he couldn't allow. A thaw she was making hotter by the day, risking everything. Oceans rose when glaciers melted; mountains fell.

He'd destroy her, he knew. It was only a matter of time.

If he was the man she seemed to think he was, the man he sometimes wished he was when she looked at him with all of those things he couldn't name in her lovely dark eyes, he'd leave her alone. Play the hero she'd suggested he could be and put her out of harm's way.

But Nikolai knew he'd never been any kind of hero. Not even by mistake.

CHAPTER SEVEN

NIKOLAI HADN'T HEARD his family nickname in such a long time that when he did, he assumed he'd imagined it.

He frowned at the sleek and oversize computer display in front of him, realizing that he'd barely paid attention to the video conference, which was unlike him. Stranger still, no one remained on his screen but his brother.

Nikolai wasn't sure which was more troubling, his inattention during a business meeting or the fact he'd imagined he'd heard Ivan speak his—

"Kolya?"

That time there was no mistaking it. Ivan was the only person alive who had ever used that name, very rarely at that, and Nikolai was looking right at him as he said it from the comfort of his Malibu house a world away.

It was the first time he'd spoken directly to Nikolai in more than two years.

Nikolai stared. Ivan was still Ivan. Dark eyes narrowed beneath the dark hair they shared, the battered face he'd earned in all of those mixed martial arts rings, clothes that quietly proclaimed him Hollywood royalty, every inch of him the action hero at his ease.

Nikolai would have preferred it if Ivan had fallen

into obvious disrepair after turning his back on his only brother so cavalierly. Instead, it appeared that betrayal and delusion suited him.

That, Nikolai reflected darkly, and the woman who'd caused this rift between them in the first place, no doubt.

"What's the matter with you?" Ivan asked in Russian, frowning into his camera. "You've been staring off into space for the past fifteen minutes."

Nikolai chose not to investigate the things that churned in him, dark and heavy, at the way Ivan managed to convey the worry, the disappointment and that particular wariness that had always characterized the way he looked at Nikolai, talked to him, in two simple sentences after so much silence. And yet there was a part of him that wanted nothing more than to simply take this as a gift, take his brother back in whatever way Ivan was offering himself....

But he couldn't let himself go there. Ivan's silence had been a favor to him, surely. He knew where it led, and he wanted nothing to do with that particular prison any longer.

"I'm reeling from shock," he said. "The mighty Ivan Korovin has condescended to address me directly. I imagine I ought to feel festive on such a momentous occasion." He eyed Ivan coolly, and without the faintest hint of *festive*. "I appreciate the show of concern, of course."

Nikolai could have modified his tone, the sardonic slap of it. Instead, he kept his face expressionless, his gaze trained on his brother through the screen. *Your brother is an idiot,* Alicia had said, so emphatically. It felt like encouragement, like her kind hand against his cheek even when she wasn't in the room.

But he didn't want to think about Alicia. She didn't

know what he'd done to deserve the things his brother thought of him. And unlike her confession of the sins of others, Nikolai really had done each and every thing Ivan thought he had.

Ivan's mouth flattened and his dark eyes flashed with his familiar temper.

"Two years," he said in that gruff way of his, his long-suffering older brother voice, "and that's what you have to say to me, Nikolai? Why am I not surprised that you've learned nothing in all this time?"

"That's an excellent question," Nikolai replied, his voice so cold he could feel the chill of it in his own chest. "If you wanted me to learn something you should have provided some kind of lesson plan. Picked out the appropriate hair shirts for me to wear, outlined the confessions you expected me to make and at what intervals. But you chose instead to disappear, the way you always do." He shrugged, only spurred on by the flash of guilt and fury he knew too well on his brother's face. "Forgive me if I am not weeping with joy that you've remembered I exist, with as much warning as when you decided to forget it." He paused, then if possible, got icier. *"Brother."*

"Nikolai—"

"You come and you go, Vanya," he said then, giving that darkness in him free rein. Letting it take him over. Not caring that it wasn't fair—what was *fair?* What had ever been *fair?* "You make a thousand promises and you break them all. I stopped depending on you when I was a child. Talk to me or don't talk to me. What is it to me?"

Ivan's face was dark with that same complicated fury—his guilt that he'd left Nikolai years before to fight, his frustrated anger that Nikolai had turned out so relentlessly feral despite the fact he'd rescued him, eventually; even his sadness that this was who they were, these two hard and dangerous men—and Nikolai was still enough his younger brother to read every nuance of that. And to take a kind of pleasure in the fact that despite the passage of all this time, Ivan was not indifferent.

Which, he was aware, meant he wasn't, either.

"One of these days, little brother, we're going to fight this out," Ivan warned him, shoving his hands through his dark hair the way he'd no doubt like to shove them around Nikolai's neck and would have, had this conversation taken place in person. Nikolai felt himself shift into high alert, readying for battle automatically. "No holds barred, the way we should have done two years ago. And when I crush you into the ground, and I will, this conversation will be one of the many things you'll apologize for."

"Is that another promise?" Nikolai asked pointedly, and was rewarded when Ivan winced. "I understand this is your pet fantasy and always has been. And you could no doubt win a fight in any ring, to entertain a crowd. But outside the ring? In real life with real stakes?" Nikolai shook his head. "You'd be lucky to stay alive long enough to beg for mercy."

"Why don't you fly to California and test that theory?" Ivan suggested, his expression turning thunderous. "Or is it easier to say these things when there are computer screens and whole continents to hide behind?"

"You would follow the rules, Vanya," Nikolai said with a certain grim impatience. "You would fight fair, show mercy. This is who you are." He shrugged, everything inside of him feeling too sharp, too jagged. "It will be your downfall."

"Mercy isn't weakness," Ivan growled.

"Only good men, decent men, have the luxury of

dispensing it," Nikolai retorted, ignoring the way his brother stared at him. "I wouldn't make that kind of mistake. You might put me on the ground, but I'd sink a knife in you on my way back up. You should remember that while you're issuing threats. I don't fight fair. I fight to survive."

They stared at each other for an uncomfortable moment. Ivan settled back in his chair, crossing his strong arms over his massive chest, and Nikolai sat still and watchful, like the sentry he'd once been.

"Is this about your new woman?" Ivan asked. Nikolai didn't betray his surprise by so much as a twitch of his eyelid, much less a reply. Ivan sighed. "I've seen the papers."

"So I gather."

Ivan studied him for another moment. "She's not your usual type."

"By which you mean vapid and/or mercenary, I presume," Nikolai said coldly. He almost laughed. "No, she's not. But you of all people should know better than to believe the things you read."

Ivan's gaze on his became curiously intent.

"Tabloid games don't always lead where you think they will, brother. You know that."

It was Nikolai's turn to sigh. "And how is your favorite tabloid game gone wrong?" he asked. "Your wife now, if I'm not mistaken. Or so I read in the company newsletter."

"Miranda is fine," Ivan said shortly, and then looked uncomfortable, that guilty look flashing through his dark eyes again. "It was a very private ceremony. No one but the man who married us."

"I understand completely," Nikolai murmured smoothly. "It might have been awkward to have to ex plain why your only living family member, the acting CEO of your foundation, was not invited to a larger wedding. It might have tarnished your image, which, of course, would cost us all money. Can't have that."

"She's my family, Kolya." Ivan's voice was a hard rumble, his jaw set in that belligerent way of his that meant he was ready to fight. Here and now.

And that really shouldn't have felt like one of his brother's trademark punches, a sledgehammer to the side of the head. It shouldn't have surprised him that Ivan considered that woman his family when he'd so easily turned his back on his only actual blood relation. Or that he was prepared to fight Nikolai—again—to defend her.

And yet he felt leveled. Laid out flat, no air in his lungs.

"Congratulations," he ground out. Dark and bitter. Painful. "I hope your new family proves less disappointing than the original version you were so happy to discard."

Ivan wasn't the only one who could land a blow.

Nikolai watched him look away from the screen, and rub one of his big hands over his hard face. He even heard the breath that Ivan took, then blew out, and knew his brother was struggling to remain calm. That should have felt like a victory.

"I know you feel that I abandoned you," Ivan said after a moment, in his own, painful way. "That everyone did, but in my case, over and over, when you were the most vulnerable. I will always wish I could change that."

Nikolai couldn't take any more of this. Ice floes were cracking apart inside of him, turning into so much water and flooding him, drowning him—and he couldn't allow this to happen. He didn't know where it was heading, or what would be left of him when he melted completely.

He only knew it wouldn't be pretty. For anyone. He'd always known that. The closest he'd ever been to *melted* was drunk, and that had only ever ended in blood and regret.

"It's only been two years, Ivan." He tried to pull himself back together, to remember who he was, or at least pretend well enough to end this conversation. "I haven't suddenly developed a host of tender emotions you need to concern yourself with trampling."

"You have emotions, Nikolai. You just can't handle them," Ivan corrected him curtly, a knife sliding in neat and hard. Deep enough to hit bone. His eyes were black and intense, and they slammed into Nikolai from across the globe with all of his considerable power. "You never learned how to have them, much less process them, so your first response when you feel something is to attack. Always."

"Apparently things *have* changed," Nikolai shot back with icy fury. "I wasn't aware you'd followed your wife's example and become no better than a tabloid reporter, making up little fantasies and selling them as fact. I hope the tips of the trade you get in bed are worth the loss of self-respect."

"Yes, Nikolai," Ivan bit out, short and hard. "Exactly like that."

Nikolai muttered dark things under his breath, fighting to keep that flood inside of him under control. Not wanting to think about what his brother had said, or why it seemed to echo in him, louder and louder. Why he had Alicia's voice in his head again, talking about sex and comfort in that maddeningly intuitive way of hers, as if she knew, too, the ways he reacted when he didn't know how to feel.

Did he ever know how to feel?

And Ivan only settled back in his chair, crossing his arms over his chest, and watched Nikolai fall apart.

"I'm the thing that goes bump in the night," Nikolai said through his teeth after a moment or two. "You know this. I've never pretended to be anything else."

"Because our uncle told you so?" Ivan scoffed. "Surely you must realize by now that he was in love with our mother in his own sick way. He hated us both for representing the choice she made, but you—" He shook his head. "Your only sin was in resembling her more than I did."

Nikolai couldn't let that in. He couldn't let it land. Because it was nothing but misdirection and psychological inference when he knew the truth. He'd learned it the hard way, hadn't he?

"I know what I am," he gritted out.

"You like it." Ivan's gaze was hard. No traces of any guilt now. "I think it comforts you to imagine you're an irredeemable monster, unfit for any kind of decent life."

You make it true, Alicia had told him, her dark eyes filled with soft, clear things he hadn't known how to define. *It's a self-fulfilling prophecy.*

"You think it yourself," Nikolai reminded Ivan tightly. "Or did I misunderstand your parting words two years ago?"

"If I thought that," Ivan rumbled at him, "I wouldn't think you could do better than this, would I? But you don't want to accept that, Nikolai, because if you did, you'd have to take responsibility for your actions." He held Nikolai's gaze. "Like a man."

I only see a man, Alicia had told him, her dark gaze serious. *I see you.*

But that wasn't what Nikolai saw. Not in the mirror,

not in Alicia's pretty eyes, not in his brother's face now. He saw the past.

He saw the truth.

He'd been nine years old. Ivan had been off winning martial arts tournaments already, and Nikolai had borne the brunt of one of his uncle's drunken rages, as usual.

He'd been lucky the teeth he'd lost were only the last of his milk teeth.

"I can see it in you," his uncle had shouted at him, over and over again, fists flying. "It looks out of your eyes."

He'd towered over Nikolai's bed, Nikolai's blood on his hands and splattered across his graying white shirt. That was the part Nikolai always remembered so vividly, even now—that spray of red that air and time had turned brown, set deep in the grungy shirt that his uncle had never bothered to throw out. That he'd worn for years afterward, like a promise.

His uncle had always kept his promises. Every last one, every time, until his nephews grew big enough to make a few of their own.

"Soon there'll be nothing left," his uncle had warned him, his blue eyes, so much like Nikolai's, glittering. "That thing in you will be all you are."

Ivan hadn't come home for days. Nikolai had thought that his uncle had finally succeeded in killing him, that he'd been dying. By the time Ivan returned and had quietly, furiously, cleaned him up, Nikolai had changed.

He'd understood.

There was nothing good in him. If there had been, his uncle wouldn't have had to beat him so viciously, so consistently, the way he had since Nikolai had come to live with him at five years old.

It was his fault his uncle had no choice but to beat the bad things out.

It was his fault, or someone would have rescued him.

It was his fault, or it would stop. But it wouldn't stop, because that thing inside of him was a monster and eventually, he'd understood then, it would take him over. Wholly and completely.

And it had.

"Nikolai."

Maybe Ivan had been right to sever this connection, he thought now. What did they have between them besides terrible memories of those dark, bloody years? Of course Ivan hadn't protected him, no matter how Nikolai had prayed he might—he'd barely managed to protect himself.

And now he'd made himself a real family, without these shadows. Without all of that blood between them.

"Kolya—"

"I can't tell you how much I appreciate this brotherly talk," Nikolai said, his tone arctic. Because it was the only way he knew to protect Ivan. And if Nikolai could give that to him, he would, for every bruise and cut and broken bone that Ivan had stoically tended to across the years. "I've missed this. Truly."

And then he reached out and cut off the video connection before his brother could say another word. But not before he saw that same, familiar sadness in Ivan's eyes. He'd seen it all his life.

He knew it hurt Ivan that this was who Nikolai was. That nothing had changed, and nothing ever would.

Ivan was wrong. Nikolai *was* changing, and it wasn't for the better. It was a terrible thing, that flood inside him swelling and rising by the second, making all of that ice he'd wrapped himself in melt down much too quickly.

He was changing far more than he should.

Far more than was safe for anyone.

He knew he needed to stop it, he knew how, and yet he couldn't bring himself to do it. At his core, he was nothing but that twisted, evil thing who had earned his uncle's fists.

Because he wasn't ready to give her up. He had a week left, a week of that marvelous smile and the way she frowned at him without a scrap of fear, a week of that wild heat he needed to sample one more time before he went without it forever. He wanted every last second of it.

Even if it damned them both.

Alicia stood in a stunning hotel suite high above the city of Prague, watching it glow in the last of the late-December afternoon, a storybook kingdom brought to life before her. Snow covered the picturesque red rooftops and clung to the spires atop churches and castles, while the ancient River Vltava curved like a sweet silver ribbon through the heart of it. She listened as bells tolled out joyful melodies from every side, and reminded herself—again—that she wasn't the princess in this particular fairy tale, despite appearances to the contrary.

That Nikolai had told her the night he'd met her that it would end in teeth. And tears.

The charity Christmas ball was the following night, where he would have that conversation with his ex-wife at last, and after that it wouldn't matter how perfect Prague looked, how achingly lovely its cobbled streets or its famous bridges bristling with Gothic saints. It didn't matter how golden it seemed in the winter sunset, how fanciful, as if it belonged on a gilded page in an ancient manuscript. She would leave this city as she'd found it, and this agonizing charade would end. Nikolai would get what he wanted and she would get her life back.

She should want that, she knew. She should be thrilled.

If she stuck her head out her door she could hear the low rumble of Nikolai's voice from somewhere else in the great, ornate hotel suite he'd chosen, all golds and reds and plush Bohemian extravagance. He was on a call, taking care of business in that ruthless way of his. Because he didn't allow distractions—he'd told her so himself.

Not foreign cities that looked too enchanted to be real. Certainly not her.

And Alicia was in a room that was twice the size of her flat and a hundred times more lush, one deep breath away from losing herself completely to the things she was still afraid to let herself feel lest she simply explode across the floor like that bottle of wine, practicing her prettiest smile against the coming dark.

None of this was real, she reminded herself, tracing her finger across the cold glass of the window. None of this was hers.

In the end, none of it would matter.

The only thing that would remain of these strange weeks were the pictures in the tabloids, stuck on the internet forever like her very own scarlet letter. There would be no record of the way she ached for him. There would be no evidence that she'd ever felt her heart tear open, or that long after he'd left that night, she'd cried into her mountain of frilly pillows for a scared little boy with bright blue eyes who'd never been lucky or safe. And for the girl she'd been eight years ago, who only Nikolai had ever tried to defend from an attack she couldn't even remember. No one would know if she healed or not, because no one would know she'd been hurt.

There would only be those pictures and the nonexistent relationship Nikolai had made sure they showed to the world, that she'd decided she no longer cared if her father knew about.

Let him think what he likes, she'd thought.

Alicia had taken the train out for his birthday dinner the previous week, and had sat with her sisters around the table in his favorite local restaurant, pretending everything was all right. The way she always pretended it was.

But not because she'd still been racked with shame, as she'd been for all those years. Instead, she'd realized as she'd watched her father *not* look at her and *not* acknowledge her and she understood at last what had actually happened to her, she'd been a great deal closer to furious.

"Will you have another drink, love?" her mother had asked her innocuously enough, but Alicia had been watching her father. She'd seen him wince at the very idea, as if another glass of wine would have Alicia doffing her clothes in the middle of the King's Arms. And all of that fury and pain and all of those terrible years fused inside of her. She'd been as unable to keep quiet as she'd been when she'd told Nikolai about this mess in the first place.

"No need to worry, Dad," she'd said brusquely. "I haven't been anywhere close to drunk in years. Eight years to be precise. And would you like to know why?"

He'd stared at her, then looked around at the rest of the family, all of them gaping from him to Alicia and back.

"No need," he'd said sharply. "I'm already aware."

"I was so drunk I couldn't walk," she'd told him, finally. "I take full responsibility for that. My friends poured me into a taxi and it took me ages to make it up to the house from the lane. I didn't want to wake anyone, so I went into the garden and lay down to sleep beneath the stars."

"For God's sake, Alicia!" her father had rumbled. "This isn't the time or place to bring up this kind of—"

"I passed out," she'd retorted, and she'd been perfectly calm. Focused. "I can't remember a single thing about it because I was *unconscious*. And yet when you saw Mr. Reddick helping himself to your comatose daughter, the conclusion you reached was that I was a whore."

There'd been a long, highly charged silence.

"He tried it on with me, too," her older sister had declared at last, thumping her drink down on the tabletop. "Vile pervert."

"I always thought he wasn't right," her other sister had chimed in at almost the same moment. "Always staring up at our windows, peering through the hedge."

"I had no idea," her mother had said urgently then, reaching over and taking hold of Alicia's hand, squeezing it tightly in hers. Then she'd frowned at her husband. "Bernard, you should be ashamed of yourself! Douglas Reddick was a menace to every woman in the village!"

And much later, after they'd all talked themselves blue and teary while her father had sat there quietly, and Douglas Reddick's sins had been thoroughly documented, her father had hugged her goodbye for the first time in nearly a decade. His form of an apology, she supposed.

And much as she'd wanted to rail at him further, she hadn't. Alicia had felt that great big knot she'd carried around inside of her begin to loosen, and she'd let it, because she'd wanted her father back more than she'd wanted to be angry.

She'd have that to carry with her out of her fake relationship. And surely that was something. Only she would know who had helped her stand up for herself eight years later. Only she would remember the things he'd changed in her when this was over. When the smoke cleared.

That was, if the smoke didn't choke her first.

"It's not even real," Alicia had blurted out one night, after a quarter hour of listening to Rosie rhapsodize about what a wedding to a man like Nikolai Korovin might entail, all while sitting on the couch surrounded by her favorite romance novels and the remains of a box of chocolates.

"What do you mean?"

"I mean, it's not real, Rosie. It's for show."

Alicia had regretted that she'd said anything the instant she'd said it. There'd been an odd, twisting thing inside of her that wanted to keep the sordid facts to herself. That hadn't wanted anyone else to know that when it came down to it, Nikolai Korovin needed an ulterior motive and a list of requirements to consider taking her out on a fake date.

Not that she was bitter.

"You're so cynical," Rosie had said with a sigh. "But I'll have you know I'm optimistic enough for the both of us." She'd handed Alicia a particularly well-worn romance novel, with a pointed look. "I know you sneak this off my shelf all the time. I also know that this tough, skeptical little shell of yours is an act."

"It's not an act," Alicia had retorted.

But she'd also taken the book.

If she'd stayed up too late some nights, crouched over her laptop with her door locked tight, looking through all the photos of the two of them together online, she'd never admit it. If she'd paused to marvel over the way the tabloids managed to find pictures that told outright lies—that showed Nikolai gazing down at her with something that looked like his own, rusty version of affection, for example, or showed him scowling with what looked like bristling protectiveness at a photographer who ventured too close, she'd kept that to herself, too. Because if she'd dared speak of it, she might betray herself—she might show how very much she preferred the tabloid romance she read about to what she knew to be the reality.

And then there was Nikolai.

"Kiss me," he'd ordered her a few days before they'd had to leave for Prague, in that commanding tone better suited to tense corporate negotiations than a bright little café in his posh neighborhood on a Tuesday morning. She'd frowned at him and he'd stared back at her, ruthless and severe. "It will set the scene."

He'd been different these past few days, she'd thought as she'd looked at him over their coffees. Less approachable than he'd been before, which beggared belief, given his usual level of aloofness. He'd been much tenser. Darker. The fact that she'd been capable of discerning the differences between the various gradations of his glacial cold might have worried her, if she'd had any further to fall where this man was concerned.

"What scene?" she'd asked calmly, as if the idea of kissing him hadn't made her whole body tremble with that ever-present longing, that thrill of heat and flame. "There's a wall between us and the street. No one can see us, much less photograph us."

"We live in a digital age, Alicia," he'd said icily. "There are mobile phones everywhere."

Alicia had looked very pointedly at the people at the

two other tables in their hidden nook, neither of whom had been wielding a mobile. Then she'd returned her attention to her steaming latte and sipped at it, pretending not to notice that Nikolai had continued to stare at her in that brooding, almost-fierce way.

"They took pictures of us walking here," she'd pointed out when the silence stretched too thin, his gaze was burning into her like hot coals and she'd worried she might break, into too many pieces to repair. "Mission accomplished."

Because nothing screamed *contented domesticity* like an early-morning stroll to a coffee place from Nikolai's penthouse, presumably after another long and intimate night. That was the story the tabloids would run with, he'd informed her in his clipped, matter-of-fact way, and it was guaranteed to drive his ex-wife crazy. Most of Nikolai's women, it went without saying—though her coworkers lined up to say the like daily—were there to pose silently beside him at events and disappear afterward, not stroll anywhere with him as if he *liked* them.

She'd been surprised to discover she was scowling. And then again when he'd stood up abruptly, smoothing down his suit jacket despite the fact it was far too well made to require smoothing of any kind. He'd stared at her, hard, then jerked his head toward the front of the café in a clear and peremptory command before storming that way himself.

Alicia had hated herself for it, but she'd smiled sheepishly at the other patrons in the tiny alcove, who'd eyed Nikolai's little display askance, and then she'd followed him.

He stood in the biting cold outside, muttering darkly into his mobile. Alicia had walked to stand next to him, wondering if she'd lost her spine when she'd felt that giant ripping thing move through her in her flat that night, as if she'd traded it for some clarity about what had happened to her eight years ago. Because she certainly hadn't used it since. She hadn't been using it that morning, certainly. The old, spined Alicia would have let Nikolai storm off as he chose, while she'd sat and merrily finished her latte.

Or so she'd wanted to believe.

Nikolai had slid his phone into a pocket and then turned that winter gaze on her, and Alicia had done her best to show him the effortlessly polite—if tough and slightly cynical—mask she'd tried so hard to wear during what he'd called *the public phase of this arrangement*. Yet something in the way he'd stared down at her that gray morning, that grim mouth of his a flat line, had made it impossible.

"Nikolai…" But she hadn't known what she'd meant to say.

He'd reached over to take her chin in his leather-gloved hand, and she'd shivered though she wasn't cold at all.

"There are paparazzi halfway down the block," he'd muttered. "We must bait the trap, *solnyshka*."

And then he'd leaned down and pressed a very hard, very serious, shockingly swift kiss against her lips.

Bold and hot. As devastating as it was a clear and deliberate brand of his ownership. His possession.

It had blown her up. Made a mockery of any attempts she'd thought she'd been making toward politeness, because that kiss had been anything but, surging through her like lightning. Burning her into nothing but smoldering need, right there on the street in the cold.

She'd have fallen down, had he not had those hard fingers on her chin. He'd looked at her for a long moment that had felt far too intimate for a public street so early in the morning, and then he'd released her.

And she'd had the sinking feeling that he knew exactly what he'd done to her. Exactly how she felt. That this was all a part of his game. His plan.

"Let me guess what that word means," she'd said after a moment, trying to sound tough but failing, miserably. She'd been stripped down to nothing, achingly vulnerable, and she'd heard it clear as day in her voice. There'd been every reason to suppose he'd read it as easily on her face. "Is it Russian for gullible little fool, quick to leap into bed with a convenient stranger and happy to sell out her principles and her self-respect for any old photo opportunity—"

"Little sun," he'd bit out, his own gaze haunted. Tormented. He'd stared at her so hard she'd been afraid she'd bear the marks of it. She'd only been distantly aware that she trembled, that it had nothing to do with the temperature. He'd raised his hand again, brushed his fingers across her lips, and she'd had to bite back something she'd been terribly afraid was a sob. "Your smile could light up this city like a nuclear reactor. It's a weapon. And yet you throw it around as if it's nothing more dangerous than candy."

Here, now, staring out at the loveliest city she'd ever seen, as night fell and the lights blazed golden against the dark, Alicia could still feel those words as if he'd seared them into her skin.

And she knew it would be one more thing that she'd carry with her on the other side of this. One more thing only she would ever know had happened. Had been real. Had mattered, it seemed, if only for a moment.

She blinked back that prickly heat behind her eyes, and when they cleared, saw Nikolai in the entrance to her room. No more than a dark shape behind her in the window's reflection. As if he, too, was already disappearing, turning into another memory right before her eyes.

She didn't turn. She didn't dare. She didn't know what she'd do.

"We leave in an hour," he said.

Alicia didn't trust herself to speak, and so merely nodded.

And she could feel that harshly beautiful kiss against her mouth again, like all the things she couldn't allow herself to say, all the things she knew she'd never forget as long as she lived.

Nikolai hesitated in the doorway, and she held her breath, but then he simply turned and melted away, gone as silently as he'd come.

She dressed efficiently and quickly in a sleek sheath made of a shimmery green that made her feel like a mermaid. It was strapless with a V between her breasts, slicked down to her waist, then ended in a breezy swell at her knees. It had been hanging in her room when she'd arrived, next to a floor-length sweep of sequined royal blue that was clearly for the more formal ball tomorrow night. And accessories for both laid out on a nearby bureau. She slid her feet into the appropriate shoes, each one a delicate, sensual triumph. Then she picked up the cunning little evening bag, the green of the dress with blues mixed in.

He's bought and paid for you, hasn't he? she asked herself as she walked down the long hall toward the suite's main room, trying to summon her temper. Her sense of outrage. Any of that motivating almost-hate she'd tried to feel for him back in the beginning. *There are words to describe arrangements like this, aren't there? Especially if you're foolish enough to sleep with him....*

But she knew that the sad truth was that she was going to do this, whether she managed to work herself into a state or not. She was going to wear the fine clothes he'd bought her and dance to his tune, quite literally, because she no longer had the strength to fight it. To fight him.

To fight her own traitorous heart.

And time was running out. By Monday it would be as if she'd dreamed all of this. She imagined that in two months' time or so, when she was living her normal life and was done sorting out whatever Nikolai fallout there might be, she'd feel as if she had.

A thought that should have made her happy and instead was like a huge, black hole inside of her, yawning and deep. She ignored it, because she didn't know what else to do as she walked into the lounge. Nikolai stood in front of the flat-screen television, frowning at the financial report, but turned almost before she cleared the entryway, as if he'd sensed her.

She told herself she hardly noticed anymore how beautiful he was. How gorgeously lethal in another fine suit.

Nikolai roamed toward her, his long strides eating up the luxurious carpet beneath his feet, the tall, dark, brooding perfection of him bold and elegant in the middle of so much overstated opulence. Columns wrapped in gold. Frescoed ceilings. And his gaze was as bright as the winter sky, as if he made it daylight again when he looked at her.

There was no possibility that she would survive this in anything like one piece. None at all.

You can fall to pieces next week, she told herself

firmly. It would be Christmas. She'd hole up in her parents' house as planned, stuff herself with holiday treats and too much mulled wine, and pretend none of this had ever happened. That *he* hadn't happened to her.

That she hadn't done this to herself.

"Are you ready?" he asked.

"Define ready." She tried to keep her voice light. Amused. Because anything else would lead them to places she didn't want to go, because she doubted she'd come back from them intact. "Ready to attend your exciting whirl of corporate events? Certainly. Ready to be used in my capacity as weapon of choice, aimed directly at your ex-wife's face?" She even smiled then, and it felt almost like the real thing. "I find I'm as ready for *that* as I ever was."

"Then I suppose we should both be grateful that there will be no need for weaponry tonight," he said, in that way of his that insinuated itself down the length of her back, like a sliver of ice. The rest of her body heated at once, inside and out, his brand of winter like a fire in her, still. "This is only a tedious dinner. An opportunity to make the donors feel especially appreciated before we ask them for more money tomorrow."

When he drew close, he reached over to a nearby incidental table and picked up a long, flat box. He held it out to her without a word, his expression serious. She stared at it until he grew impatient, and then he simply cracked open the box himself and pulled out a shimmering necklace. It was asymmetrical and bold, featuring unusually shaped clusters of blue and green gems set in a thick rope that nonetheless managed to appear light. Fun. As fanciful, in its way, as this golden city they stood in.

The very things this man was not.

"I would have taken you for the black diamond sort,"

Alicia said, her eyes on the necklace instead of him, because it was the prettiest thing she'd seen and yet she knew it would pale next to his stark beauty. "Or other very, very dark jewels. Heavy chunks of hematite. Brooding rubies the color of burgundy wine."

"That would be predictable," he said, a reproving note in his low voice, the hint of that dark humor mixed in with it, making her wish. *Want.*

He slid the necklace into place, cool against her heated skin, his fingers like naked flame. She couldn't help the sigh that escaped her lips, and her eyes flew to his, finally, to find him watching her with that lazy, knowing intensity in his gaze that had been her undoing from the start.

He reached around to the nape of her neck, taking his time fastening the necklace, letting his fingertips dance and tease her skin beneath the cloud of her curls, then smoothing over her collarbone. He adjusted it on her neck, making sure it fell as he wanted it, one end stretched down toward the upper swell of one breast.

Alicia didn't know if he was teasing her or tearing her apart. She could no longer tell the difference.

When he caught her gaze again, neither one of them was breathing normally, and the room around them felt hot and close.

"Come," he said, and she could hear it in his voice. That fire. That need. That tornado that spiraled between them, more and more out of control the longer this went on, and more likely to wreck them both with every second.

And it would, she thought. *Soon.*

Just as he'd warned her.

CHAPTER EIGHT

A GOLD-MIRRORED LIFT delivered them with hushed and elegant efficiency into the brightly lit foyer of the presidential suite in one of Prague's finest hotels, filled with the kind of people who were not required to announce their wealth and consequence because everything they did, said and wore did it for them. Emphatically.

These were Nikolai's people. Alicia kept her polite smile at the ready as Nikolai steered her through the crowd. This was his world, no matter how he looked at her when they were in private. No matter what stories she'd told herself, she was no more than a tourist, due to turn straight back into a pumpkin the moment the weekend was over. And then stay that way, this strange interlude nothing more than a gilt-edged memory.

She could almost feel the heavy stalk beginning to form, like a brand-new knot in her stomach.

Nikolai pulled her aside after they'd made a slow circuit through the monied clusters of guests, into a small seating area near the farthest windows. Outside, in the dark, she could see the magnificence of Prague Castle, thrusting bright and proud against the night. And inside, Nikolai looked down at her, unsmiling, in that way of his that made everything inside of her squeeze tight, then melt.

"I told you this would be remarkably boring, did I not?"

"Perhaps for you," she replied, smiling. "I keep wondering if the American cattle baron is going to break into song at the piano, and if so, if that very angry-looking German banker will haul off and hit him."

His blue eyes gleamed, and she felt the warmth of it all over, even deep inside where that knot curled tight in her gut, a warning she couldn't seem to heed.

"These are not the sort of people who fight with their hands," Nikolai said, the suggestion of laughter in his gaze, on his mouth, lurking in that rough velvet voice of his. "They prefer to go to war with their checkbooks."

"That sounds a bit dry." She pressed her wineglass to her lips and sipped, but was aware of nothing but Nikolai. "Surely throwing a few punches is more exciting than writing checks?"

"Not at all." His lips tugged in one corner. "A fistfight can only be so satisfying. Bruises heal. Fight with money, and whole companies can be leveled, thousands of lives ruined, entire fortunes destroyed in the course of an afternoon." That smile deepened, became slightly mocking. "This also requires a much longer recovery period than a couple of bruises."

Alicia searched his face, wondering if she was seeing what she wanted to see—or if there really was a softening there, a kind of warmth, that made that wide rip in her feel like a vast canyon and her heart beat hard like a drum.

He reached over and traced one of the clever shapes that made up the necklace he'd given her, almost lazily, but Alicia felt the burn of it as if he was touching her directly. His gaze found hers, and she knew they both wished he was.

It swelled between them, bright and hot and more complicated now, that electric connection that had shocked her in that club. It was so much deeper tonight. It poured into every part of her, changing her as it went, making her realize she didn't care what the consequences were any longer. They'd be worth it. Anything would be worth it if it meant she could touch him again.

She couldn't find the words to tell him that, so she smiled instead, letting it all flow out of her. Like a weapon, he'd said. Like candy.

Like love.

Nikolai jerked almost imperceptibly, as if he saw what she thought, what she felt, written all over her. As if she'd said it out loud when she hardly dared think it.

"Alicia—" he began, his tone deeper than usual, urgent and thick, and all of her confusion and wariness rolled into the place where she'd torn in two, then swelled into that ache, making it bloom, making her realize she finally knew what it was....

But then the energy in the suite all around them shifted. Dramatically. There was a moment of shocked silence, then an excited buzz of whispering.

Nikolai's gaze left hers and cut to the entryway, and then, without seeming to move at all, he froze solid. She watched him do it, saw him turn from flesh and blood to ice in a single breath.

It was the first time he'd scared her.

Alicia turned to see the crowd parting before a graceful woman in a deceptively simple black dress, flanked by two security guards. She was cool and aristocratic as she walked into the room, smiling and exchanging greetings with the people she passed. Her dark red hair was swept back into an elegant chignon, she wore no adornment besides a hint of diamonds at her ears and

the sparkle of the ring on her hand, and still, she captivated the room.

And had turned Nikolai to stone.

Alicia recognized her at once, of course.

"Isn't that…?"

"My brother's wife. Yes."

Nikolai's tone was brutal. Alicia flicked a worried
glance at him, then looked back to the party.

Miranda Sweet, wife of the legendary Ivan Korovin
and easily identifiable to anyone with access to Rosie's
unapologetic subscription to celebrity magazines, swept
through the assembled collection of donors with ease.
She said a word or two here, laughed there and only fal-
tered when her gaze fell on Nikolai. But she recovered
almost instantly, squaring her shoulders and waving off
her security detail, and made her way toward him.

She stopped when she was a few feet away. Keeping
a safe distance, Alicia thought, her eyes narrowing. Miranda Sweet was prettier in person, and taller, and the
way she looked at Nikolai was painful.

While Nikolai might as well have been a glacier.

Alicia could have choked on the thick, black tension
that rose between the two of them, so harsh it made her
ears ring. So intense she glanced around to see if anyone else had noticed, but Miranda's security guards had
blocked them off from prying eyes.

When she looked back, Nikolai and his brother's
wife were still locked in their silent battle. Alicia moved
closer to Nikolai's side, battling the urge to step in front
of him and protect him from this threat, however unlikely the source.

Then, very deliberately, Nikolai dropped his gaze.
Alicia followed it to the small swell of Miranda's belly,
almost entirely concealed by her dress. Alicia never

would have seen it. She doubted anyone was supposed to see it.

When Nikolai raised his gaze to his sister-in-law's again, his eyes were raw and cold. Alicia saw Miranda swallow. Hard. Nervously, even.

Another terrible moment passed.

Then Miranda inclined her head slightly. "Nikolai."

"Miranda," he replied, in the same tone, so crisp and hard and civil it hurt.

Miranda glanced at Alicia, then back at Nikolai, and something moved across her face.

Fear, Alicia thought, confused. *She's* afraid *of him.*

Miranda hid it almost immediately, though her hand moved to brush against her belly, her ring catching the light. She dropped her hand when she saw Nikolai glance at it.

"He misses you," she said after a moment, obvious conflict and a deep sadness Alicia didn't understand in her voice. "You broke his heart."

"Are you his emissary?"

"Hardly." Miranda looked at Nikolai as if she expected a reply, but he was nothing but ice. "He would never admit that. He'd hate that I said anything."

"Then why did you?" Cold and hard, and Alicia thought it must hurt him to sound like that. To be that terribly frigid.

Miranda nodded again, a sharp jerk of her head. Her gaze moved to Alicia for a moment, as if she wanted to say something, but thought better of it. And then she turned and walked away without another word, her smile in place as if it had never left her.

While Alicia stood next to Nikolai and hurt for him, hard and deep, and all the things he didn't—couldn't—say.

"I take it you weren't expecting her," she said after

a while, still watching Miranda Sweet work the party, marveling at how carefree she looked when she'd left a wind chill and subzero temperatures in her wake.

"I should have." Nikolai's gaze was trained on the crowd, dark and stormy. "She often makes appearances at high-level donor events when Ivan is held up somewhere else. It helps bring that little bit of Hollywood sparkle."

He sounded as if he was reporting on something he'd read a long time ago, distant and emotionless, but Alicia knew better. She felt the waves of that bitter chill coming off him, like arctic winds. This was Nikolai in pain. She could feel it inside her own chest, like a vise.

"A bit of a chilly reunion, I couldn't help but notice."

Nikolai shifted. "She believes I tried to ruin her relationship with Ivan."

Alicia frowned up at him. "Why would she think that?"

It took Nikolai a breath to look down, to meet her eyes. When he did, his gaze was the coldest she'd ever seen it, and her heart lurched in her chest.

"Because I did."

She blinked, but didn't otherwise move. "Why?"

A great black shadow fell over him then, leaving him hollow at the eyes and that hard mouth of his too grim. *Grief,* she thought. And something very much like shame, only sharper. Colder.

"Why do I do anything?" he asked softly. Terribly. "Because happiness looks like the enemy to me. When I see it I try to kill it."

Alicia only stared at him, stricken. Nikolai's mouth tugged in one corner, a self-deprecating almost smile that this time was nothing but dark and painful. Total devastation in that one small curve.

"You should be afraid of me, Alicia," he said, and the bleak finality in his voice broke her in two. "I keep warning you."

He turned back to the crowd.

And Alicia followed an instinct she didn't fully understand, that had something to do with that deep ache, that wide-open canyon in her chest she didn't think would ever go away, and the proud, still way he stood next to her, ruthlessly rigid and straight, as if bracing himself for another blow.

Like that brave boy he must have been a lifetime ago, who was never safe. Or lucky. Who had given up all hope.

She couldn't bear it.

Alicia reached over and slid her hand into his, as if it belonged there. As if they fitted together like a puzzle, and she was clicking the last piece into place.

She felt him flinch, but then, slowly—almost cautiously—his long fingers closed over hers.

And then she held on to him with all of her might.

Nikolai hadn't expected Alicia to be quite so good at this, to fill her role so seamlessly tonight, as if she'd been born to play the part of his hostess. As if she belonged right there at his side, the limb he hadn't realized he'd been missing all along, instead of merely the tool he'd planned to use and then discard.

He stood across the room, watching from a distance as she charmed the two men she'd thought might break into a fight earlier. She was like a brilliant sunbeam in the middle of this dark and cold winter's night, outshining his wealthiest donors in all their finery even here, in a luxurious hotel suite in a city renowned for its gleaming, golden, incomparable light.

Nikolai had never seen her equal. He never would again.

She'd held on to his hand. *To him.* Almost ferociously, as if she'd sensed how close he'd been to disappearing right where he stood and had been determined to stand as his anchor. And so she had.

Nikolai couldn't concentrate on his duties tonight the way he usually did, with that single-minded focus that was his trademark. He couldn't think too much about the fact that Ivan had a child on the way, no matter the vows they'd made as angry young men that they would never inflict the uncertain Korovin temper on more innocent children.

He couldn't think of anything but that press of Alicia's palm against his, the tangling of their fingers as if they belonged fused together like that, the surprising strength of her grip.

As if they were a united front no matter the approaching threat—Miranda, the pregnancy Ivan had failed to mention, the donors who wanted to be celebrated and catered to no matter what quiet heartbreaks might occur in their midst, even the ravaged wastes of his own frigid remains of a soul.

She'd held his hand as if she was ready to fight at his side however she could and that simple gesture had humbled him so profoundly that he didn't know how he'd remained upright. How he hadn't sunk to his knees and promised her anything she wanted, anything at all, if she would only do that again.

If she would choose him, support him. Defend him. Protect him.

If she would treat him like a man, not a wild animal in need of a cage. If she would keep treating him like that. Like he really could be redeemed.

As if she hadn't the smallest doubt.

Because if he wasn't the irredeemable monster he'd always believed—if both she and Ivan had been right all along—then he could choose. He could choose the press of her slender fingers against his, a shining bright light to cut through a lifetime of dark. Warmth instead of cold. Sun instead of ice. *He could choose.*

Nikolai had never imagined that was possible. He'd stopped wanting what he couldn't have. He'd stopped *wanting.*

Alicia made him believe he could be the man he might have been, if only for a moment. She made him regret, more deeply than he ever had before, that he was so empty. That he couldn't give her anything in return.

Except, a voice inside him whispered, *her freedom from this.*

From him. From this dirty little war he'd forced her to fight.

Nikolai nearly shuddered where he stood. He kept his eyes trained on Alicia, who looked over her shoulder as if she felt the weight of his stare and then smiled at him as if he really was that man.

As if she'd never seen anything else.

That swift taste of her on a gray and frigid London street had led only to cold showers and a gnawing need inside of him these past few days, much too close to pain. Nikolai didn't care anymore that he hardly recognized himself. That he was drowning in this flood she'd let loose in him. That he was almost thawed through and beyond control, the very thing he'd feared the most for the whole of his life.

He wanted Alicia more. There was only this one last weekend before everything went back to normal. Before he had his answer from Veronika. And then there was absolutely no rational reason he should ever spend another moment in her company.

He'd intended to have her here, in every way he could. To glut himself on her as if that could take the place of all her mysteries he'd failed to solve, the sweet intoxication that was Alicia that he'd never quite sobered up from. He'd intended to make this weekend count.

But she'd let him imagine that he was a better man, or could be. He'd glimpsed himself as she saw him for a brief, brilliant moment, and that changed everything.

You have to let her go, that voice told him, more forcefully. *Now, before it's too late.*

He imagined that was his conscience talking. No wonder he didn't recognize it.

Nikolai took her back to their hotel when the dinner finally ground to a halt not long after midnight. They stood outside her bedroom and he studied her lovely face, committing it to memory.

Letting her go.

"Nikolai?" Even her voice was pretty. Husky and sweet. "What's the matter?"

He kissed her softly, once, on that very hand that had held his with such surprising strength and incapacitating kindness. It wasn't what he wanted. It wasn't enough. But it would be something to take with him, like a single match against the night.

"You don't need to be here," he said quietly, quickly, because he wasn't sure he'd do it at all if he didn't do it fast. "Veronika will seek me out whether you're with me or not. I'll have the plane ready for you in the morning."

"What are you talking about?" Her voice was small. It shook. "I thought we had a very specific plan. Didn't we?"

"You're free, Alicia." He ground out the words. "Of this game, this blackmail. Of me."

"But—" She reached out to him, but he caught her hand before she could touch him, because he couldn't trust himself. Not with her. "What if I don't particularly want to be free?"

Under any other circumstances, he wouldn't have hesitated. But this was Alicia. She'd comforted him, protected him, when anyone else would have walked away.

When everyone else had.

It wasn't a small gesture to him, the way she'd held his hand like that. It was everything. He had to honor that, if nothing else.

"I know you don't," Nikolai said. He released her hand, and she curled it into a fist. Fierce and fearless until the end. That was his Alicia. "But you deserve it. You deserve better."

And then he'd left her there outside her room without another word, because a good man never would have put her in this position in the first place, blackmailed her and threatened her, forced her into this charade for his own sordid ends.

Because he knew it was the right thing to do, and for her, he'd make himself do it, no matter how little he liked it.

"But I love you," Alicia whispered, knowing he was already gone.

That he'd already melted into the shadows, disappeared down the hall, and that chances were, he wouldn't want to hear that anyway.

She stood there in that hall for a long time, outside the door to her bedroom in a mermaid dress and lovely,

precarious heels he'd chosen for her, and told herself she
wasn't falling apart.

She was fine.

She was in love with a man who had walked away
from her, leaving her with nothing but a teasing hint of
heat on the back of her hand and that awful finality in
his rough, dark voice, but Alicia told herself she was
absolutely, perfectly *fine.*

Eventually, she moved inside her room and dutifully
shut the door. She pulled off the dress he'd chosen for
her and the necklace he'd put around her neck himself,
taking extra care with both of them as she put them back
with the rest of the things she'd leave behind her here.

And maybe her heart along with them.

She tried not to think about that stunned, almost-shat-
tered look in his beautiful eyes when she'd grabbed his
hand. The way his strong fingers had wrapped around
hers, then held her tight, as if he'd never wanted to let
her go. She tried not to torture herself with the way he'd
looked at her across the dinner table afterward, over the
sounds of merriment and too much wine, that faint smile
in the corner of his austere mouth.

But she couldn't think of anything else.

Alicia changed into the old T-shirt she wore to sleep
in, washed soft and cozy over the years, and then she
methodically washed her face and cleaned her teeth.
She climbed into the palatial bed set high on a dais that
made her feel she was perched on a stage, and then she
glared fiercely at that book Rosie had given her without
seeing a single well-loved sentence.

The truth was, she'd fallen in love when she'd fallen
into him at that club.

It had been that sudden, that irrevocable. That deeply,
utterly mad. The long, hot, darkly exciting and surpris-

ingly emotional night that had followed had only cemented it. And when he'd let her see those glimpses of his vulnerable side, even hidden away in all that ice and bitter snow, she'd felt it like a deep tear inside of her because she hadn't wanted to accept what she already knew somewhere inside.

Alicia let out a sigh and tossed the paperback aside, sinking back against the soft feather pillows and scowling at the billowing canopy far above her.

She wasn't the too-drunk girl she'd been at twenty-one any longer—and in fact, she'd never been the shameful creature she'd thought she was. Had she tripped and fallen into any other man on that dance floor that night, she would have offered him her embarrassed apologies and then gone straight home to sort out her laundry and carry on living her quiet little life.

But it had been Nikolai.

The fact was, she'd kicked and screamed and moaned about the way he'd forced her into this—but he hadn't. She could have complained. Daniel was a CEO with grand plans for the charity, but he wasn't an ogre. He wouldn't have simply let her go without a discussion; he might not have let her go at all. And when it came down to it, she hadn't even fought too hard against this mad little plan of Nikolai's, had she?

On some level, she'd wanted all of those tabloid pictures with their suggestive captions, because her fascination with him outweighed her shame. And more, because they proved it was real. That the night no one knew about, that she'd tried so hard to make disappear, had really, truly happened.

She'd tasted him in that shiny black SUV, and she'd loved every moment of his bold possession. She'd explored every inch of his beautiful body in that wide bed of his. She'd kissed his scars and even the monster he wore on his chest like a warning. And he'd made her sob and moan and surge against him as if she'd never get enough of him, and then they'd collapsed against each other to sleep in a great tangle, as if they weren't two separate people at all.

All of that had happened. All of it was real.

All of this is real, she thought.

Alicia picked up the paperback romance again, flipping through the well-worn pages to her favorite scene, which she'd read so many times before she was sure she could quote it. She scanned it again now.

Love can't hinge on an outcome. If it does, it isn't love at all, the heroine said directly to the man she loved when all was lost. When he had already given up, and she loved him too much to let him. When she was willing to fight for him in the only way she could, even if that meant she had to fight every last demon in his head herself. *Love is risk and hope and a terrible vulnerability. And it's worth it. I promise.*

"You either love him or you don't, Alicia," she told herself then, a hushed whisper in her quiet room.

And she did.

Then she took a deep breath to gather her courage, swung out of the high bed and went to prove it.

Nikolai sat by the fire in the crimson master bedroom that dominated the far corner of the hotel suite, staring at the flames as they crackled and danced along the grate.

He wished this wasn't the longest night of the year, with all of that extra darkness to lead him into temptation, like one more cosmic joke at his expense. He wished he could take some kind of pride in the uncharacteristic decision he'd made instead of sitting here like he needed to act as his own guard, as if a single moment of inattention would have him clawing at her door like an animal.

He wished most of all that this terrible thaw inside of him wasn't an open invitation for his demons to crawl out and fill every extra, elongated hour with their same old familiar poison.

He shifted in the plush velvet armchair and let the heat of the fire play over his skin, wishing it could warm him inside, where too many dark things lurked tonight, with their sharp teeth and too many scenes from his past.

He hated Prague, happy little jewel of a city that it was, filled to the top of every last spire with all the joyful promises of a better life even the Iron Curtain had failed to stamp out. Anywhere east of Zurich he began to feel the bitter chill of Mother Russia breathing down his neck, her snow-covered nails digging into his back as if she might drag him back home at any moment.

It was far too easy to imagine himself there, struggling to make it through another vicious winter with no end, dreamless and broken and half-mad. Feral to the bone. In his uncle's bleak home in Nizhny Novgorod. In corrupt, polluted, snowbound Moscow with the equally corrupt and polluted Veronika, when he'd been in the military and had thought, for a time, it might save him from himself.

Or, even sadder in retrospect, that Veronika might.

Being in Prague was too much like being back there. Nikolai was too close to the raw and out-of-control creature he'd been then, careening between the intense extremes that were all he'd ever known. Either losing himself in violence or numbing himself however he could. One or the other, since the age of five.

He could feel that old version of him right beneath his skin, making him restless. On edge.

Then again, perhaps it wasn't Prague at all. Perhaps it was the woman on the other side of this hotel suite even now, with her dark eyes that saw more of him than anyone else ever had and that carnal distraction of a mouth.

He was in trouble. He knew it.

This was the kind of night that called for a bottle of something deliberately incapacitating, but he couldn't allow himself the escape. He couldn't numb this away. He couldn't slam it into oblivion. He had to sit in it and wait for morning.

Nikolai scowled at the fire while his demons danced on, bold and sickening and much too close, tugging him back into his dirty past as if he'd never left it behind.

As if he never would.

A scant second before Alicia appeared in his door, he sensed her approach, his gaze snapping to meet hers as she paused on the threshold.

He almost thought she was another one of his demons, but even as it crossed his mind, he knew better. Alicia was too alive, that light of hers beaming into his room as if she'd switched on the lamps, sending all of those things that tortured him in the dark diving for the shadows.

She'd changed out of her formal attire and was standing there in nothing but an oversized wide-necked T-shirt—a pink color, of course—that slid down her arm to bare her shoulder and the upper slope of one breast. Her curls stood around her head in abandon, and her feet were bare.

Nikolai's throat went dry. The rest of him went hard.

"It's below zero tonight," he barked at her, rude and belligerent. *Desperate.* "You shouldn't be walking around like that unless you've decided to court your own death, in which case, I can tell you that there are far quicker ways to go."

The last time he'd used a tone like that on a woman, she'd turned and run from him, sobbing. But this was Alicia. His strong, fearless Alicia, and she only laughed that laugh of hers that made him want to believe in magic.

When he looked at her, he thought he might.

"I've come to your room wearing almost nothing and your first reaction is to talk about the weather and death," she said in that dry way of hers, and God help him, this woman was worse than all his demons put together. More powerful by far. "Very romantic, indeed. My heart is aglow."

Nikolai stood up then, as if that would ward her off. He didn't know which was worse. That she was standing there with so much of her lush brown skin on display, her lithe and supple legs, that shoulder, even the hint of her thighs—naked and smooth and far too tempting. Or that teasing tone she used, so dry and amused, that set off brushfires inside him.

His body felt as if it was someone else's, unwieldy and strange. He wished he hadn't stripped down to no more than his exercise trousers, low on his hips, the better to while away a sleepless night at war with himself.

There was too much bare flesh in the room now. Too many possibilities. He could only deny himself so much....

He scowled at her, and she laughed again.

"Relax," she said, in that calm, easy way that simultaneously soothed and inflamed him. "*I'm* seducing *you*, Nikolai. You don't have to do anything but surrender."

"You are not seducing me," he told her, all cold com-

mand, and she ignored it completely and started toward
him as if he hadn't spoken. As if he hadn't said something similar to her what seemed like a lifetime ago.
"And I am certainly not surrendering."

"Not yet, no," she agreed, smiling. "But the night is
young."

"Alicia." He didn't back away when she roamed even
closer, not even when he could see her nipples poking
against the thin material of her shirt and had to fight to
keep himself from leaning down and sucking them into
his mouth, right then and there. "This is the first time in
my life I've ever done the right thing deliberately. Some
respect, I beg you."

Her smile changed, making his chest feel tight though
he didn't know what it meant.

"Tell me what the right thing is," she said softly, not
teasing him any longer, and she was within arm's reach
now. Warm and soft. *Right there.* "Because I think you
and I are using different definitions."

"It's leaving you alone," he said, feeling the stirrings
of a kind of panic he thought he'd excised from himself
when he was still a child. "The way I should have done
from the start."

She eased closer, her scent teasing his nose, cocoa
butter and a hint of sugar, sweet and rich and *Alicia*.
He was so hard it bordered on agony, and the way she
looked up at him made his heart begin to hit at him, er-
ratic and intense, like it wanted to knock him down.
Like it wouldn't take much to succeed.

"You vowed you didn't want to sleep with me again,"
he reminded her, almost savagely. "Repeatedly."

"I'm a woman possessed," she told him, her voice
husky and low, washing over him and into him. "Infatuated, even."

He remembered when he'd said those same words to her in that far-off stairwell, when her scent had had much the same effect on him. Her dark eyes had been so wide and anxious, and yet all of that heat had been there behind it, electric and captivating. Impossible to ignore. Just as she was.

Tonight, there was only heat, so much of it he burned at the sight. And he wanted her so badly he was afraid he shook with it. So badly he cared less and less with every passing second if he did.

"I've never had the slightest inclination to behave the way a good man might," he began, throwing the words at her.

"That simply isn't true."

"Of course it is. I keep telling you, I—"

"You've dedicated your life to doing good, Nikolai," she said, cutting him off, her voice firm. "You run a foundation that funds a tremendous amount of charity work. Specifically, children's charities."

"I'm certain bands of activists would occupy me personally if they could pin me down to a single residence or office." He glared at her, his voice so derisive it almost hurt, but he knew he wasn't talking to her so much as the demons in all the corners of the room, dancing there in his peripheral vision. "I take money from the rich and make it into more money. I am the problem."

"Like Robin Hood, then? Who was, as everyone knows, a great villain. Evil to the very core."

"If Robin Hood were a soulless venture capitalist, perhaps," Nikolai retorted, but there was that brilliant heat inside of him, that terrible thaw, and he was on the verge of something he didn't want to face. He wasn't sure he could.

Alicia shook her head, frowning at him as if he was

hurting her. He didn't understand that—this was him *not* hurting her. This was him *trying.* Why was he not surprised that he couldn't do that right, either?

"You help people," she said in that same firm, deliberate way, her gaze holding his. "The things you do and the choices you make *help people.* Nikolai, you do the right thing *every single day.*"

He didn't know what that iron band was that crushed his chest, holding him tight, making everything seem to contract around him.

"You say that," he growled at her, or possibly it was even a howl, torn from that heart he'd abandoned years ago, "but there is blood on my hands, Alicia. More blood than you can possibly imagine."

She stepped even closer, then picked up his much larger hands in hers. He felt a kind of rumbling, a far-off quake, and even though he knew there was nothing but disaster heading toward him, even though he suspected it would destroy him and her and possibly the whole of the city they stood in, the world, the stars above, he let her.

And he watched, fascinated beyond measure and something like terrified, that tight, hard circle around him pulling tighter and tighter, as she turned each hand over, one by one, and pressed a kiss into the center of each.

The way she'd done for the creature on his chest, that she'd called *pretty.*

She looked up at him again, and her dark eyes were different. Warm in a way he'd never seen before. Sweet and something like admiring. Filled with that light that made him feel simultaneously scraped hollow and carved new.

Shining as if whatever she saw was beautiful.

"I don't see any blood," she said, distinct and direct,

her gaze fast to his. "I only see you. I've never seen anything but you."

And everything simply...ended.

Nikolai shattered. He broke. All of that ice, every last glacier, swept away in the flood, the heat, the roaring inferno stretching high into the night, until he was nothing but raw and wild and *that look* she gave him took up the world.

And replaced it with fire. Fire and heat and all of the things he'd locked away for all those bleak and terrible reasons. Color and light, flesh and blood. Rage and need and all of that hunger, all of that pain, all of that sorrow and grief, loss and tragedy. His parents, taken so young. His brother, who should never have had to fight so hard. The uncle who should have cared for them. The army that had broken him down and then built him into his own worst nightmare. Veronika's lies and Stefan's sweet, infant body cradled in his arms, like hope. Every emotion he'd vowed he didn't have, roaring back into him, filling him up, tearing him into something new and unrecognizable.

"You have to stop this," he said, but when it left his mouth it was near to a shout, furious and loud and she didn't even flinch. "You can't be *kind* to a man like me! You don't know what you've done!"

"Nikolai," she said, without looking away from him, without hiding from the catastrophic storm that was happening right there in front of her, without letting go of his hands for an instant or dropping her warm gaze, "I can't be anything else. That's what *you* deserve."

And he surrendered.

For the first time in his life, Nikolai Korovin stopped fighting.

CHAPTER NINE

NIKOLAI DROPPED TO his knees, right there in front of her

For a moment he looked ravaged. Untethered and lost, and then he slid his arms around her hips, making Alicia's heart fall out of her chest, her breath deserting her in a rush. She could feel the storm all around them, pouring out of him, enveloping them both. His hard face became stark, sensual. Fierce.

It all led here. Now. To that look in his beautiful eyes that made her own fill with tears. A fledging kind of joy, pale and fragile.

Hope.

And she loved him. She thought she understood him. So when that light in his eyes turned to need, she was with him. It roared in her too, setting them both alight.

He pulled up the hem of her T-shirt with a strong, urgent hand that shook slightly, baring her to his view, making her quiver in return. And that fire that was always in her, always his, turned molten and rolled through her, making her heavy and needy and almost scared by the intensity of this. Of him. Of these things she felt, storming inside of her.

Her legs shook, and he kissed her once, high on her thigh. She could feel the curve of his lips, that rare smile, and it went through her like a lightning bolt, burning her straight down to the soles of her feet where they pressed into the thick carpet.

And then slowly, so slowly, he peeled her panties down her legs, then tossed them aside.

Alicia heard a harsh sort of panting, and realized it was her.

"Solnyshka," he said, in that marvelous voice of his, darker and harsher than ever, and it thrilled her, making her feel like the sun he thought she was, too bright and hot to bear. "I think you'd better hold on."

He wrapped one strong arm around her bottom and the back of her thighs, and then, using his shoulder to knock her leg up and out of his way, he leaned forward and pressed his mouth against her heat.

And then he licked into her.

It was white-hot ecstasy. Carnal lightning. It seared through her, almost like pain, making her shudder against him and cry out his name. She fisted her hands in his hair, his arms were tight around her to keep her from falling, and she simply went limp against his mouth.

His wicked, fascinating, demanding mouth.

She detonated. Her licked her straight over the edge, and she thought she screamed, lost in a searingly hot, shuddering place where there was nothing left but him and these things he did to her, this wild magic that was only his. *Theirs.*

"Too fast," he rumbled, from far away, but everything was dizzy, confused, and it took her a long breath, then another, to remember who she was. And where.

And then another to understand that he'd flipped them around to spread her out on the deep rug in front of the fire.

"Nikolai," she said, or thought she did, but she lost

whatever half-formed thought that might have been, because he was taking up where he'd left off.

He used his mouth again, and his hands. He stroked deep into her core, throwing her straight back into that inferno as if she'd never found release. Soon she was writhing against him, exulting in how he held her so easily, with such confident mastery, and used his tongue, his teeth, even that smile again, like sensual weapons.

Alicia arched up against him, into him. Her hands dug at the carpet below her, and his mouth was an impossible fire, driving her wild all over again, driving her higher and higher, until he sucked hard on the very center of her heat and she exploded all around him once again.

When she came back to herself this time, he was helping her up, letting her stumble against him and laughing as he pulled her T-shirt over her head, then muttering something as he took her breasts in his hands. He tested their weight, groaned out his approval, and then pulled each hard, dark nipple into his mouth.

Lighting the fire in her all over again. Making her burn.

He picked her up and carried her to the bed, following her down and stretching out beside her, sleek and powerful, tattooed and dangerous. He'd rid himself of his trousers at some point and there was nothing between them then.

Only skin and heat. Only the two of them, at last.

For a while, it was enough. They explored each other as if this was the first time, this taut delight, this delicious heat. Alicia traced the bright-colored shapes and lines that made up his monster with her tongue, pressed kisses over his heart, hearing it thunder beneath her. Nikolai stroked his big hands down the length of her back, testing each and every one of her curves as he worshipped every part of her equally.

He didn't speak. And Alicia kissed him, again and again, as if that could say it for her, the word she dared not say, but could show him. With her mouth, her hands. Her kiss, her smile.

They teased the flames, built them slowly, making up for all those lost weeks since the last time they'd touched like this. Until suddenly, it was too much. They were both out of breath and the fire had turned into something darker, more desperate. Hotter by far.

Nikolai reached for the table near his bed and then rolled a condom down his hard length, his eyes glittering on hers, and Alicia almost felt as if he was stroking her that way, so determined and sure. She could feel his touch inside of her, stoking those flames. Making her wild with smoke and heat and need.

Alicia couldn't wait, as desperate to have him inside her again as if she hadn't already found her own pleasure, twice. As if this was new.

Because it felt that way, she thought. It felt completely different from what had gone before, and she knew why. She might have fallen hard for him the night she met him, but she loved the man she knew. The man who had saved her from a prison of shame. This man, who looked at her as if she was a miracle. This man, who she believed might be one himself.

"Kiss me," she ordered him, straddling his lap, pressing herself against his delicious hardness, torturing them both.

He took her face in his hands and then her mouth with a dark, thrilling kiss, making her moan against him. He tasted like the winter night and a little bit like her, and the kick of it rocketed through her, sensations building and burning and boiling her down until she was nothing but his.

His.

The world was his powerful body, his masterful kiss, his strong arms around her that anchored her to him. And she loved him. She loved him with every kiss, every taste. She couldn't get close enough. She knew she never would.

He lifted her higher, up on her knees so she knelt astride him, then held her there. He took her nipple into his mouth again, the sharp pull of it like an electric charge directly into her sex, while his wicked fingers played with the other. Alicia shuddered uncontrollably in his arms, but he held her still, taking his time.

And all the while the hardest part of him was just beneath her, just out of reach.

"Please..." she whispered frantically. "Nikolai, *please*..."

"Unlike you," he said in a voice she hardly recognized, it was so thick with desire, with need, with this mighty storm that had taken hold of them both, "I occasionally obey."

He shifted then, taking her hips in his hands, and then he thrust up into her in a single deep stroke, possessive and sure.

At last.

And for a moment, they simply stared at each other. Marveling in that slick, sweet, perfect fit. Nikolai smiled, and she'd never seen his blue eyes so clear. So warm.

Alicia moved her hips, and his breath hissed out into a curse. And then she simply pleased them both.

She moved on him sinuously, sweetly. She bent forward to taste the strong line of his neck, salt and fire. She made love to him with every part of her, worshipping him with everything she had. She couldn't say the words, not to a man like Nikolai, not yet, but she could show him.

And she did.

Until they were both shuddering and desperate.

Until he'd stopped speaking English.

Until he rolled her over and drove into her with all of his dark intensity, all of that battle-charged skill and precision. She exulted beneath him, meeting every thrust, filled with that ache, that wide-open rift he'd torn into her, that only this—only he—could ever soothe.

And when he sent her spinning off into that wild magic for the third time, he came with her, holding her as if he loved her too, that miraculous smile all over his beautiful face.

At last, she thought.

"You're in love with him, aren't you?"

Alicia had been so lost in her own head, in Nikolai, that she hadn't heard the door to the women's lounge open. It took her a moment to realize that the woman standing next to her at the long counter was speaking to her.

And another moment for what she'd said to penetrate. *Veronika.*

The moment stretched out, silent and tense.

Alicia could hear the sounds of the ball, muffled through the lounge's walls. The music from the band and the dull roar of all those well-dressed, elegant people, dancing and eating and making merry in their polite way. She'd almost forgotten that *this* was the reason she was here at all. This woman watching her with that calculating gleam in her eyes, as if she knew things about Alicia that Alicia did not.

There was nothing hard or evil-looking about Veron-

ika, as Alicia had half expected from what little Nikolai had said of her. Her hair cascaded down her back in
a tumble of platinum waves. She wore a copper gown
that made her slender figure look lithe and supple. Aside
from the way she looked at Alicia, she was the picture
of a certain kind of smooth, curated, very nearly age-
less beauty. The kind that, amongst other things, cost a
tremendous amount to maintain and was therefore an
advertising campaign in itself.

Alicia told herself there was no need for anxiety. She
was wearing that bold, gorgeous blue dress, alive with
sequins, that had been waiting for her in her room. It
clung to her from the top of one shoulder to the floor,
highlighting all of her curves, sparkling with every
breath, and until this moment she'd felt beautiful in it.
Nikolai had smiled that sexy wolf's smile when he saw
her in it, and they'd been late coming here tonight. Very
late.

Standing with him in this castle-turned-hotel, dressed
for a ball in a gorgeous gown with the man she loved,
she'd felt as if she might be the princess in their odd little fairy tale after all.

She'd let herself forget.

"Tell me that you're not so foolish," Veronika said
then, breaking the uncomfortable silence. She sounded
almost…sympathetic? It put Alicia's teeth on edge. "Tell
me you're smart enough to see his little games for what
they are."

It was amazing how closely this woman's voice resembled the ones in her head, Alicia thought then. It was
almost funny, though she was terribly afraid that if she
tried to laugh, she'd sob instead. She was still too raw
from last night's intensity. A bit too fragile from a day
spent in the aftermath of such a great storm.

She wasn't ready for this—whatever this was.

"If you want to speak to Nikolai," she said when she was certain her tone would be perfectly even, almost blandly polite, "he's in the ballroom. Would you like me to show you?"

"You must have asked yourself why he chose you," Veronika said conversationally, as if this was a chat between friends. She leaned closer to the mirror to inspect her lipstick, then turned to face Alicia. "Look at you. So wholesome. So *real*. A charity worker, of all things. Not his usual type, are you?"

She didn't actually *tell* Alicia to compare the two of them. She didn't have to, as Alicia was well aware that all of Nikolai's previous women had been some version of the one who stood in front of her now. Slender like whippets, ruthlessly so. Immaculately and almost uniformly manicured in precisely the same way, from their perfect hair to their tiny bodies and their extremely expensive clothes. The kind of women rich men always had on their arms, like interchangeable trophies, which was precisely how Nikolai treated them.

Hadn't Alicia told him no one would believe he was interested in her after that kind of parade?

"I can't say I have the slightest idea what his 'type' is," she lied to Veronika. "I've never paid it as much attention as you've seemed to do."

Veronika sighed, as if Alicia made her sad. "He's using you to tell a very specific story in the tabloids. You must know this."

Alicia told herself she didn't feel a chill trickle down her spine, that something raw didn't bloom deep within at that neat little synopsis of the past few weeks of her life. She told herself that while Veronika was partly right, she couldn't know about the rest of it. She couldn't have any idea about the things that truly mattered. The things that were only theirs.

"Or," she said, trying desperately not to sound defensive, not to give any of herself away, "Nikolai is a famous man, and the tabloids take pictures of him wherever he goes. No great conspiracy, no 'story.' I'm sorry to disappoint you."

But she was lying, of course, and Veronika shook her head.

"Who do you think was the mastermind behind Ivan Korovin's numerous career changes—from fighter to Hollywood leading man to philanthropist?" she asked, a razor's edge beneath her seemingly casual tone, the trace of Russian in her voice not nearly as appealing as Nikolai's. "What about Nikolai himself? A soldier, then a security specialist, now a CEO—how do you think he manages to sell these new versions of himself, one after the next?"

"I don't see—"

"Nikolai is a very talented manipulator," Veronika said, with that sympathetic note in her voice that grated more each time Alicia heard it. "He can make you believe anything he wants you to believe." Her gaze moved over Alicia, and then she smiled. Sadly. "He can make you fall in love, if that's what he needs from you."

Alicia stared back at her, at this woman who *smiled* as she listed off all of Alicia's worst fears, and knew that she should have walked away from this conversation the moment it started. The moment she'd realized who Veronika was. Nothing good could come of this. She could already feel that dark hopelessness curling inside of her, ready to suck her in....

But her pride wouldn't let her leave without putting

up some kind of fight—without making it clear, somehow, that Veronika hadn't got to her. Even if she had.

"You'll forgive me," she said, holding the other woman's gaze, "if I don't rush to take your advice to heart. I'm afraid the spiteful ex makes for a bit of a questionable source, don't you think?"

She was congratulating herself as she turned for the door. What mattered was that she loved Nikolai, and what she'd seen in him last night and today. What she knew to be true. Not the doubts and fears and possible outright lies this woman—

"Do you even know what this is about?"

Alicia told herself not to turn back around. Not to cede her tiny little bit of higher ground—

But her feet wouldn't listen. They stopped moving of their own accord. She stood there, her hand on the door, and ordered herself to walk through it.

Instead, like a fool, she turned around.

"I try not to involve myself in other people's relationships, past or present," she said pointedly, as if the fact she hadn't left wasn't evidence of surrender. As if the other woman wasn't aware of it. "As it's none of my affair."

"He didn't tell you."

Veronika was enjoying herself now, clearly. She'd dropped the sympathy routine and was now watching Alicia the way a cobra might, when it was poised to strike.

Leave, Alicia ordered herself desperately. *Now.*

Because she knew that whatever Veronika was about to say, she didn't want to hear it.

"Of course he didn't tell you." Veronika picked up her jeweled clutch and sauntered toward Alicia. "I told you, he's very manipulative. This is how he operates."

Alicia felt much too hot, her pulse was so frantic it was almost distracting, and there was a weight in her stomach that felt like concrete, pinning her to the ground where she stood. Making it impossible to move, to run, to escape whatever blow she could feel coming.

She could only stare at Veronika, and wait.

The other woman drew close, never taking her intent gaze from Alicia's.

"Nikolai wants to know if my son is his," she said.

It was like the ground had been taken out from under her, Alicia thought. Like she'd been dropped into a deep, black hole. She almost couldn't grasp all the things that swirled in her then, each more painful than the next.

Not here, she thought, fighting to keep her reaction to herself, and failing, if that malicious gleam in Veronika's eyes was any indication. *You can't deal with this here!*

She would have given anything not to ask the next question, not to give this woman that satisfaction, but she couldn't help herself. She couldn't stop. None of this had ever been real, and she needed to accept that, once and for all. None of this had ever been—nor ever would be—hers.

No matter how badly she wished otherwise. No matter how deeply, how terribly, how irrevocably she loved him.

"Is he?" she asked, hating herself. Betraying herself. "Is your son Nikolai's?"

And Veronika smiled.

Nikolai saw Alicia from the other side of the ballroom, a flash of shimmering blue and that particular walk of hers that he would know across whole cities.

He felt it like a touch. Like she could reach him simply by entering the same room.

Mine, he thought, and that band around his chest clutched hard, but he was almost used to it now. It meant this woman and her smile were his. It meant that odd sensation, almost a dizziness, that he found he didn't mind at all when he looked at her.

It meant this strange new springtime inside of him, this odd thaw.

At some point last night, it had occurred to him that he might survive this, after all.

Nikolai had lost track of how many times they'd come together in the night, the storm in him howling itself out with each touch, each taste of her impossible sweetness. All of her light, his. To bathe in as he pleased.

And in the morning, she'd still been there. He couldn't remember the last time any woman had slept in his bed, and he remembered too well that the first time, Alicia had sneaked away with the dawn.

Daylight was a different animal. Hushed, he thought. Something like sacred. He'd washed every inch of her delectable body in the steamy shower, learning her with his eyes as well as his greedy hands. Then he'd slowly lost his mind when she'd knelt before him on the thick rug outside the glass enclosure, taking him into her mouth until he'd groaned out his pleasure to the fogged-up mirrors.

He didn't think he'd ever get enough of her.

She curled her feet beneath her when she sat on the sofa beside him. Her favorite television program was so embarrassing, she'd claimed, that she refused to name it. She was addicted to cinnamon and licked up every last bit of it from the pastries they'd had at breakfast, surreptitiously wetting her fingertip and pressing it against the crumbs until they were gone. She read a great many books, preferred tea first thing in the morning but coffee later, and could talk, at length, about architecture and why she thought that if she had it to do over again, she might study it at university.

And that was only today. One day of learning her, and he'd barely scratched the surface. Nikolai thought that maybe, this time, he wouldn't have to settle for what he could get. This time, he might let himself want...everything. Especially the things he'd thought for so long he couldn't have, that she handed him so sweetly, so unreservedly, as if they were already his.

Mine, he thought again, in a kind of astonishment that it might be true. That it was even possible. *She's mine.*

Alicia disappeared in the jostling crowd, and when she reappeared she'd almost reached him. Nikolai frowned. She was holding herself strangely, and there was a certain fullness in her eyes, as if she were about—

But then he saw the woman who walked behind her, that vicious little smile on her cold lips and victory in her gaze, and his blood ran cold.

Like ice in his veins and this time, it hurt. It burned as he froze.

"*Privyet,* Nikolai," Veronika purred triumphantly when the two of them finally reached him. As sure of herself as she'd ever been. And as callous. "Look who I discovered. Such a coincidence, no?"

This, he thought, was why he had no business anywhere near a bright creature like Alicia. He'd destroy her without even meaning to do it. He'd already started.

This is who you are, he reminded himself bitterly, and it was worse because he'd let himself believe otherwise. He'd fallen for the lie that he could ever be anything but the monster he was. It only took a glance at Veronika, that emblem of the bad choices he'd made and with whom, to make him see that painful truth.

"Alicia. Look at me."

And when she did, when she finally raised her gaze to his, he understood. It went off inside him like a grenade, shredding him into strips, and that was only the tiniest fraction of the pain, the torment, he saw in Alicia's lovely brown eyes.

Dulled with the pain of whatever Veronika had said to her.

He'd done this. He'd put her in harm's way. He was responsible.

Nikolai had been tested last night. He'd had the opportunity to do the right thing, to imagine himself a good man and then act like one, and he'd failed. Utterly.

All of his demons were right.

Nikolai moved swiftly then, a cold clarity sweeping through him like a wind. He ordered Veronika to make herself scarce, told her he'd come find her later and that she'd better have the answer he wanted, and he did it in Russian so Alicia wouldn't hear the particularly descriptive words he used to get his point across.

"No need," Veronika said, also in Russian, looking satisfied and cruel. He wanted to wring her neck. "I had the test done long ago. You're not the father. Do you want to know who is?" She'd smiled at Nikolai's frigid glare. "I'll have the paperwork sent to your attorney."

"Do that," Nikolai growled, and if there was a flash of pain at another small hope snuffed out, he ignored it. He'd see to it that Stefan was taken care of no matter what, and right now, he had other things to worry about.

He forgot Veronika the moment he looked away. He took Alicia's arm and he led her toward the door, amazed that she let him touch her. When they got to the great foyer, he let her go so he could pull his mobile from his tuxedo jacket and send a quick, terse text to his personal assistant.

"Whatever you're about to say, don't," he told her when she started to speak, not sure he could keep the riot of self-hatred at bay just then. She pressed her lips together and scowled fiercely at the floor, and his self-loathing turned black.

Your first response when you feel something is to attack, Ivan had said. But Nikolai had no idea how to stop. And for the first time since he was a boy, he realized that that sinking feeling in him was fear.

He slipped his mobile back in his pocket, and guided her toward the front of the hotel, not stopping until they'd reached the glass doors that led out through the colonnaded entrance into the December night. Above them, the palatial stairs soared toward the former palace's grand facade, but this entranceway was more private. And it was where his people would meet them and take her away from him. Take her somewhere—anywhere she was safe.

Finally, he let himself look at her again.

She was hugging herself, her arms bare and tight over her body. There was misery in her dark eyes, her full lips trembled, and he'd done this. He'd hurt her. Veronika had hurt *him,* and he'd been well nigh indestructible. Why had he imagined she wouldn't do her damage to something as bright and clean as Alicia, simply to prove she could? She'd probably been sharpening her talons since the first picture hit the tabloids.

This was entirely his fault.

"Your ex-wife is an interesting woman," Alicia said.

"She's malicious and cruel, and those are her better qualities," Nikolai bit out. "What did she say to you?"

"It doesn't matter what she said." There was a torn,

thick sound in her voice, and she tilted back her chin as if she was trying to be brave. He hated himself. "Everyone has secrets. God knows, I kept mine for long enough."

"Alicia—"

"I know what it's like to disappoint people, Nikolai," she said fiercely. "I know what it's like to become someone the people you love won't look at anymore, whether you've earned it or not."

He almost laughed. "You can't possibly understand the kind of life I've led. I dreamed about a father who would care about me at all, even one who shunned me for imagined sins."

"Congratulations," she threw at him. "Your pain wins. But a secret is still a—"

"Secrets?" He frowned at her, but then he understood, and the sound he let out then was far too painful to be a laugh. "She told you about Stefan."

And it killed him that Alicia smiled then, for all it was a pale shadow of her usual brightness. That she gave him that kind of gift when he could see how much she hurt.

"Is that his name?"

"He's not mine," he said harshly. "That's what she told me back there. And it's not a surprise. I wanted to be sure."

"But you wanted him to be yours," Alicia said, reading him as she always did, and he felt that band around his chest pull so tight it hurt to breathe, nearly cutting him in half.

"You want to make me a better man than I am," he told her then, losing his grip on that darkness inside of him. "And I want to believe it more than you can imagine. But it's a lie."

"Nikolai—"

"The truth is, even if Stefan was my son, he'd be better off without me." It was almost as if he was angry—as if this was his temper. But he knew it was worse than that. It was that twisted, charred, leftover thing she'd coaxed out of its cave. It was what remained of his heart, and she had to *see*. She had to *know*. "I was drunk most of the five years I thought I was his father. And now I'm—" He shook his head. *"This."*

"You're what?" Her dark eyes were glassy. "Sober?"

He felt that hard and low, like a kick to the gut. He didn't know what was happening to him, what she'd done. He only knew he had to remove her from this—get her to a minimum safe distance where he could never hurt her again, not even by mistake.

"Seeing Veronika made things perfectly clear to me," he told her. "All I will ever do is drag you down until I've stolen everything. Until I've ruined you. I can promise you that." He wanted to touch her, but he wouldn't. He couldn't risk it. "I would rather be without you than subject you to this—this sick, twisted horror show."

He was too close to her, so close he could hear that quick, indrawn breath, so close he could smell that scent of hers that drove him wild, even now.

He was no better than an animal.

Alicia looked at him for a long moment. "Are you still in love with her?" she asked.

"Do I *love* her?" Nikolai echoed in disbelief. "What the hell is *love,* Alicia?"

His voice was too loud. He heard it bouncing back at him from the polished marble floors, saw Alicia straighten her back as if she needed to stand tall against it. He hated public scenes and yet he couldn't stop. He rubbed his hands over his face to keep himself from punching the hard stone wall. It would only be pain, and it would fade. And he would still be right here. He would still be him.

"Veronika made me feel numb," he said instead, not realizing the truth of it until he said it out loud. Something seemed to break open in him then, some kind of painful knotted box he'd been holding on to for much too long. "She was an anesthetic. And I thought that was better than being alone." He glared at her. "And she didn't love me either, if that's your next question. I was her way out of a dead-end life, and she took it."

"I think that however she's capable of it, she does love you," Alicia argued softly. "Or she wouldn't want so badly to hurt you."

"Yes," he said, his voice grim. "Exactly. That is the kind of love I inspire. A vile loathing that time only exacerbates. A hatred so great she needed to hunt you down and take it out on you. Such are my gifts." He prowled toward Alicia then, not even knowing what he did until she'd backed up against one of the marble columns.

But he didn't stop. He couldn't stop.

"I was told I loved my parents," he said, the words flooding from him, as dark and harsh as the place they'd lived inside him all this time. "But I can't remember them, so how would I know? And I love my brother, if that's what it's called." He looked around, but he didn't see anything but the past. And the demons who jeered at him from all of those old, familiar shadows. "Ivan feels a sense of guilt and obligation to me because he got out first, and I let him feel it because I envy him for escaping so quickly while I stayed there and rotted. And then I made it my singular goal to ruin the only happiness he'd ever known."

He'd thought he was empty before, but now he knew.

This was even worse. This was unbearable, and yet he had no choice but to bear it.

"That's a great brotherly love, isn't it?"

"Nikolai," she said thickly, and she'd lost the battle with her tears. They streaked down her pretty face, each one an accusation, each one another knife in his side. "You aren't responsible for what happened to you as a child. With all the work you do, you can't truly believe otherwise. You *survived,* Nikolai. That's what matters."

And once again, he wanted to believe her. He wanted to be that man she was called to defend. He wanted to be anything other than *this*.

"I've never felt anything like these things I feel for you," he told her then, raw and harsh, so harsh it hurt him, too, and then she started to shake, and that hurt him even more. "That light of yours. The way you look at me—the way you *see* me." He reached out as if to touch her face, but dropped his hand back to his side. "I knew it that first night. I was *happy* when you walked into that conference room, and it terrified me, because do you know what I do with *happy?*"

"You do not kill it," she told him fiercely. "You try, and you fail. Happiness isn't an enemy, Nikolai. You can't beat it up. It won't fight back, and eventually, if you let it, it wins."

"I will suck you dry, tear you down, take everything until nothing remains." He moved closer, so outside himself that he was almost glad that he was so loud, that he was acting like this so she could see with her own eyes what kind of man he was. "Do I love you, Alicia? Is that what this is? This charred and twisted thing that will only bring you pain?"

"I love you," she said quietly. Clearly and distinctly, her eyes on his. Without a single quaver in her voice.

Without so much as a blink. Then she shifted, moved closer. "I love you, Nikolai."

Nikolai stilled. Inside and out. And those words hung in him like stained glass, that light of hers making them glow and shine in a cascade of colors he'd never known existed before.

He thought he almost hated her for that. He told himself he'd rather not know.

He leaned in until her mouth was close enough to kiss, and his voice dropped low. Savage. "Why would you do something so appallingly self-destructive?"

"Because, you idiot," she said calmly, not backing away from him, not looking even slightly intimidated. "*I love you.* There's always a risk when you give someone your heart. They might crush it. But that's no reason not to do it."

He felt as if he was falling, though he wasn't. He only wished he was. He leaned toward her, propping his hands on either side of her head as he had once before, then lowering his forehead until he rested it against hers.

And for a moment he simply breathed her in, letting his eyes fall shut, letting her scent and her warmth surround him.

He felt her hands come up to hold on to him, digging in at his hips with that strong grip that had already undone him once before, and he felt a long shudder work through him.

"This is the part where you run for cover, Alicia," he whispered fiercely. "I told you why I couldn't lose control. Now you know."

He heard her sigh. She tipped back her head, then lifted her hands up to take his face between them. When he opened his eyes, what he saw in her gaze made him shake.

"This is where you save yourself," he ground out at her.

She smiled at him, though more tears spilled from her eyes. She held him as if she had no intention of letting him go. She looked at him as if he was precious. Even now. "And then who saves you?"

CHAPTER TEN

NIKOLAI'S HANDS SLIPPED from the marble column behind her, his arms came around her, and he held her so tightly, so closely, that Alicia wasn't sure she could breathe.

And she didn't care.

He held her like that for a long time.

A member of the hotel staff came over to quietly inquire if all was well, and she waved him away. A trio of black-suited people who could only be part of Nikolai's pack of assistants appeared, and she frowned at them until they backed off.

And outside, in the courtyard of the former palace, it began to snow.

Nikolai let out a long, shaky breath and lifted his head. He kissed her, so soft and so sweet it made her smile.

"If I had a heart, I would give it to you," he said then, very seriously. "But I don't."

She shook her head at him, and kissed him back, losing herself in that for a long time. His eyes were haunted, and she loved him so much she didn't know if she wanted to laugh or cry or scream—it seemed too big to contain.

And he loved her, too. He'd as much as said so. He just didn't know what that meant.

So Alicia would have to show him. Step by step, smile by smile, laugh by laugh, until he got it. Starting now.

"You have a heart, Nikolai," she told him gently, smiling up at that beautifully hard face, that perfectly austere mouth, her would-be Tin Man. "It's just been broken into so many pieces, and so long ago, you never learned how to use it properly."

"You're the only one who thinks so," he said softly.

She reached out and laid her hand on his chest, never looking away from him.

"I can feel it. It's right here. I promise."

"And I suppose you happen to know how one goes about putting back together a critically underused heart, no doubt fallen into disrepair after all these years," he muttered, but his hands were moving slow and sweet up her back and then down her arms to take her hands in his.

"I have a few ideas," she agreed. "And your heart is not a junked-out car left by the side of a road somewhere, Nikolai. It's real and it's beating and you've been using it all along."

He looked over his shoulder then, as if he'd only then remembered where they were. One of his assistants appeared from around the corner as if she'd been watching all along, and he nodded at her, but didn't move. Then he looked out the glass doors, at the snow falling into the golden-lit courtyard and starting to gather on the ground.

"I hate snow," he said.

"Merry Christmas to you, too, Ebenezer Scrooge," Alicia said dryly. She slid an arm around his waist and looked outside. "It's beautiful. A fairy tale," she said, smiling at him, "just as you promised me in the beginning."

"I think you're confused." But she saw that smile of

his. It started in his eyes, made them gleam. "I promised you fangs. And tears. Both of which I've delivered, in spades."

"There are no wolves in a story involving ball gowns, Nikolai. I believe that's a rule."

"Which fairy tale is this again? The ones I remember involved very few ball gowns, and far more darkness." His mouth moved into that crooked curve she adored, but his eyes were serious when they met hers. "I don't know how to be a normal man, Alicia. Much less a good one." His smile faded. "And I certainly don't know how to be anything like good for you."

Alicia smiled at him again, wondering how she'd never known that the point of a heart was to break. Because only then could it grow. And swell big enough to hold the things she felt for Nikolai.

"Let's start with normal and work from there," she managed to say. "Come to Christmas at my parents' house. Sit down. Eat a huge Christmas dinner. Make small talk with my family." She grinned. "I think you'll do fine."

He looked at her, that fine mouth of his close again to grim.

"I don't know if I can be what you want," he said. "I don't know—"

"I want you," she said. She shook her head when he started to speak. "And all you have to do is love me. As best you can, Nikolai. For as long as you're able. And I'll promise to do the same."

It was like a vow. It hung there between them, hushed and huge, with only the falling snow and the dark Prague night as witness.

He looked at her for a long time, and then he leaned

down and kissed her the way he had on that London street. Hard and demanding, hot and sure, making her his.

"I can do that," he said, when he lifted his head, a thousand brand-new promises in his eyes, and she believed every one. "I can try."

Nikolai stood facing his brother on a deep blue July afternoon. The California sky arched above them, cloudless and clear, while out beyond them the Pacific Ocean rolled smooth and gleaming all the way to the horizon.

"Are you ready?" Ivan barked in gruff Russian. He wore his game face, the one he'd used in the ring, fierce and focused and meant to be terrifying.

Nikolai only smiled.

"Is this the intimidating trash talk portion of the afternoon?" he asked coolly. "Because I didn't sign up to be bored to death, Vanya. I thought this was a fight."

Ivan eyed him.

"You insist on writing checks you can't cash, little brother," he said. "And sadly for you, I am the bank."

They both crouched down into position, studying each other, looking for tells—

Until a sharp wail cut through the air, and Ivan broke his stance to look back toward his Malibu house and the figures who'd walked out from the great glass doors and were heading their way.

Nikolai did a leg sweep without pausing to think about it, and had the great satisfaction of taking Ivan down to the ground.

"You must never break your concentration, brother," he drawled, patronizingly, while Ivan lay sprawled out before him. "Surely, as an undefeated world champion you should know this."

Ivan's dark eyes promised retribution even as he jack-knifed up and onto his feet.

"Enjoy that, Kolya. It will be your last and only victory."

And then he grinned and slapped Nikolai on the back, throwing an arm over his shoulders as they started toward the house and the two women who walked to meet them.

Nikolai watched Alicia, that smile of hers brighter even than a California summer and her lovely voice on the wind, that kick of laughter and cleverness audible even when he couldn't hear the words.

"You owe him an apology," she'd told him. It had been January, and they'd been tucked up in that frilly pink bedroom of hers that he found equal parts absurd and endearing. Though he did enjoy her four-poster bed. "He's your brother. Miranda is afraid of you, and she still risked telling you how hurt he was."

He'd taken her advice, stilted and uncertain.

And now, Nikolai thought as he drew close to her with his brother at his side, he was learning how to build things, not destroy them. He was learning how to trust.

The baby in Miranda's arm wailed again, and both women immediately made a cooing sort of sound that Nikolai had never heard Alicia make before his plane had landed in Los Angeles. Beside him, Ivan shook his head. And then reached over to pluck the baby from his wife's arms.

"Naturally, Ivan has the magic touch," Miranda said to Alicia with a roll of her eyes, as the crying miraculously stopped.

"How annoying," Alicia replied, her lips twitching.

Nikolai stared down at the tiny pink thing that looked even smaller and more delicate in Ivan's big grip.

"Another generation of Korovins," he said. He caught Miranda looking at him as he spoke, and thought her smile was slightly warmer than the last time. Progress. He returned his attention to Ivan and the baby. "I don't think you thought this through, brother."

"It's terrible, I know," Ivan agreed. He leaned close and kissed his daughter's soft forehead, contentment radiating from him. "A disaster waiting to happen."

Nikolai smiled. "Only if she fights like you."

Later, after he and Ivan spent a happy few hours throwing each other around and each claiming victory, he found Alicia out on the balcony that wrapped around their suite of rooms. He walked up behind her silently, watching the breeze dance through the cloud of her black curls, admiring the short and flirty dress she wore in a bright shade of canary yellow, showing off all of those toned brown limbs he wanted wrapped around him.

Now. Always.

She gasped when he picked her up, but she was already smiling when he turned her in his arms. As if she could read his mind—and he often believed she could—she hooked her legs around his waist and let him hold her there, both of them smiling at the immediate burst of heat. The fire that only grew higher and hotter between them.

"Move in with me," he said, and her smile widened. "Live with me."

"Here in Malibu in this stunning house?" she asked, teasing him. "I accept. I've always wanted to be a Hollywood star. Or at least adjacent to one."

"The offer is for rain and cold, London and me," he said. He shifted her higher, held her closer.

"This is a very difficult decision," she said, but her eyes were dancing. "Are you sure you don't want to come live with me and Rosie instead? She's stopped shrieking and dropping things when you walk in rooms. And she did predict that the night we met would be momentous. She's a prophet, really."

"Move in with me," he said again, and nipped at her neck, her perfect mouth. He thought of that look on his brother's face, that deep pleasure, that peace. "Marry me, someday. When it's right. Make babies with me. I want to live this life of yours, where everything is multicolored and happiness wins."

And then he said the words, because he finally knew what they meant. She'd promised him he had a heart, and she'd taught it how to beat. He could feel it now, pounding hard.

"I love you, Alicia."

She smiled at him then as if he'd given her the world, when Nikolai knew it was the other way around. She'd lit him up, set him free. She'd given him back his brother, broke him out of that cold, dark prison that had been his life. She was so bright she'd nearly blinded him, all those beautiful colors and all of them his to share, if he liked. If he let her.

"Is that a yes?" He pulled back to look at her. "It's okay if you don't—"

"Yes," she said through her smile. "Yes to everything. Always yes."

She'd loved him when he was nothing more than a monster, and she'd made him a man.

Love hardly covered it. But it was a start.

"Look at you," she whispered, her dark eyes shining. She smoothed her hands over his shoulder, plucking at the T-shirt she'd bought him and made him wear. He'd enjoyed the negotiation. "Put the man in a blue shirt and he changes his whole life."

She laughed, and as ever, it stopped the world.

"No, *solnyshka,*" Nikolai murmured, his mouth against hers so he could feel that smile, taste the magic of her laughter, the miracle of the heart she'd made beat again in him, hot and alive and real. "That was you."

* * * * *

A Devil in Disguise

To Michelle Tadros Eidson for a few high finance clues, Jane Porter for two key backstory points that changed everything, and to Jeff Johnson for being the perfect husband to a crazed writer on deadline. Again.

CHAPTER ONE

"OF COURSE YOU are not resigning your position," Cayo Vila said impatiently, not even glancing up from the wide expanse of his granite-and-steel desk. The desk loomed in front of a glorious floor-to-ceiling view over a gleaming wet stretch of the City of London, not that he had ever been observed enjoying it. The working theory was that he simply liked knowing that it was widely desired by others, that this pleased him more than the view itself. That was what Cayo Vila loved above all else, after all: owning things others coveted.

It gave Drusilla Bennett tremendous satisfaction that she would no longer be one of them.

He made a low, scoffing sound. "Don't be dramatic."

Dru forced herself to smile at the man who had dominated every aspect of her life, waking and sleeping and everything in between, for the past five years. Night and day. Across all time zones and into every little corner of the globe where his vast empire extended. She'd been at his beck and call around the clock as his personal assistant, dealing with anything and everything he needed dealt with, from a variety of his personal needs to the vagaries of his wide-ranging business concerns.

And she hated him. Oh, how she hated him. *She did.* It surged in her, thick and hot and black and deep, making her skin seem to shimmer over her bones with the force of it. It was hard to imagine, now, knowing the truth, that she'd harbored softer feelings for this man for so long—but it didn't matter, she told herself sternly. It was all gone now. *Of course it was.* He'd seen to that, hadn't he?

She felt a fierce rush of that hard sort of grief that had flooded her at the strangest times in these odd few months since her twin brother Dominic had died. Life, she had come to understand all too keenly, was intense and often far too complicated to bear, but she'd soldiered on anyway. What choice was there? She'd been the only one left to handle Dominic's disease—his addictions. His care. His mountain of medical bills, the last of which she'd finally paid in full this week. And she'd been the only one left to sort through the complexities of his death, his cremation, his sad end. *That* had been hard. It still was.

But this? This was simple. This was the end of her treating herself as the person who mattered least in her life. Dru was doing her best to ignore the swirling sense of humiliation that went along with what she'd discovered in the files this morning. She assured herself that she would have resigned anyway, eventually, *soon*—that finding out what Cayo had done was only a secondary reason to leave his employ.

"This is my notice," she said calmly, in that serene and unflappable professional voice that was second nature to her—and that she resolved she would never again utilize the moment she stepped out of this office building and walked away from this man. She would cast aside the necessarily icy exterior that had seen her through these years, that had protected her from herself as well as from him. She would be as chaotic and emotional and yes, *dramatic* as she wished, whenever she wished. She would be *flappable* unto her very bones. She could already feel that shell she'd wrapped around her for so long begin to crack. "Effective immediately."

Slowly, incredulously, a kind of menace and that disconcerting pulse of power that was uniquely his emanating from him like a new kind of electricity, Cayo Vila, much-celebrated founder and CEO of the Vila Group and its impressive collection of hotels, airlines, businesses and whatever else took his fancy, richer than all manner of sins and a hundred times as ruthless, raised his head.

Dru caught her breath. His jet-black brows were low over the dark gold heat of his eyes. That fierce, uncompromising face made almost brutally sensual by his remarkable mouth that any number of pneumatic celebutantes swooned over daily was drawn into a thunderous expression that boded only ill. The shock of his full attention, the hit of it, that all these years of proximity had failed to temper or dissipate, ricocheted through her, as always.

She hated that most of all. Her damnable weakness.

The air seemed to sizzle, making the vast expanse of his office, all cold contemporary lines and sweeping glass that seemed to invite the English weather inside, seem small and tight around her.

"I beg your pardon?"

She could hear the lilt of Spanish flavor behind his words, hinting at his past and betraying the volatile temper he usually kept under tight control. Dru restrained a small ripple of sensation, very near a shiver, that snaked along her spine. They called him the Spanish Satan for a reason. *She* would like to call him far worse.

"You heard me." The bravado felt good. Almost cleansing.

He shook his head, dismissing her. "I don't have time for this," he said. "Whatever this is. Send me an email outlining your concerns and—"

"You do," she interrupted him. They both paused; perhaps both noting the fact that she had never dared interrupt him before. She smiled coolly at him as if she were unaware of his amazement at her temerity. "You do have time," she assured him. "I cleared this quarter-hour on your schedule especially."

A very tense moment passed much too slowly between them then, and he did not appear to so much as blink. And she felt the force of that attention, as if his gaze were a gas fire, burning hot and wild and charring her where she stood.

"Is this your version of a negotiation, Miss Bennett?" His tone was as cool as hers, his midnight amber gaze far hotter. "Have I neglected your performance review this year? Have you taken it upon yourself to demand more money? Better benefits?"

His voice was curt, clipped. That edge of sardonic displeasure with something darker, smokier, beneath. Behind her professional armor, Dru felt something catch. As if he could sense it, he smiled.

"This is not a negotiation and I do not want a raise or anything else," she said, matter-of-factly, wishing that after all this time, and what she now knew he'd done, she was immune to him and the wild pounding of her heart that particular smile elicited. "I don't even want a reference. This conversation is merely a courtesy."

"If you imagine that you will be taking my secrets to any one of my competitors," he said in a casual, conversational tone that Dru knew him far too well to believe, "you should understand that if you try, I will dedicate my life to destroying you. In and out of the courts. Believe this, if nothing else."

"I love nothing more than a good threat," she replied in the same tone, though she doubted very much that it made *his* stomach knot in reaction. "But it's quite unnecessary. I have no interest in the corporate world."

His mouth moved into something too cynical to be another smile.

"Name your price, Miss Bennett," he suggested, his voice like smoke and sin, and it was no wonder at all that so many hapless rivals went over all wide-eyed and entranced and gave him whatever it was he wanted almost the very moment he demanded it. He was like some kind of corporate snake charmer.

But she wasn't one of his snakes, and she refused to dance to his tune, no matter how seductive. She'd been dancing for far too long, and this was where it ended. It had to. It would.

"I have no price," she said with perfect honesty. Once—yesterday—he could have smiled at her and she'd have found a way to storm heaven for him. But that was yesterday. Today she could only marvel, if that was the word, at how naive and gullible she'd been. At how well he'd played her.

"Everyone has a price." And in his world, she knew, this was always true. Always. One more reason she wanted to escape it. Him.

"I'm sorry, Mr. Vila," she said. She even shrugged. "I don't."

Not anymore. Dominic was gone. She was no longer his sole support. And the invisible chains of emotion and longing that had ruled her for so long could no longer keep her here. Not now she'd discovered, entirely by accident, what Cayo truly thought of her.

He only watched her now, those dark amber eyes moving over her like the touch of his hands, all fire and demand. She knew what he saw. She had crafted her corporate image specifically to appeal to his particular tastes, to acquiesce, as ever, to his preferences. She stood tall before his scrutiny, resisting the urge to fuss with her pencil skirt or the silk blouse she wore, both in the muted colors he preferred. She knew the deceptively simple twist that held her dark brown hair up was elegant, perfect. There was no bold jewelry that he might find "distracting." Her cosmetics were carefully applied, as always, to keep her looking fresh and neat and as if she hardly needed any at all, as if she simply possessed a perfect skin tone, attractively shaded lips and bright eyes without effort. She had become so good at playing this role, at being precisely what he wanted. She'd done it for so long. She could do it in her sleep. She had.

Dru could see the precise moment he realized that she was serious, that this wasn't merely a bargaining tactic she was trotting out as some kind of strategic attempt to get something from him. That she meant what she was saying, however impossible he found it to fathom. The impatience faded from his clever gaze and turned to something far more calculating—almost brooding. He lounged back against his massive, deliberately intimidating chair, propped his jaw on his hand, and treated her to the full force of that brilliant, impossible focus of his that made him such a devastating opponent. *No* was never a final answer, not to Cayo Vila. It was where he began. Where he came alive.

And where she got off, this time. For good. She couldn't help the little flare of satisfaction she got from knowing that she would be the one thing he couldn't *mogul* his way into winning. Not anymore. Not ever again.

"What is this?" he asked quietly, sounding perfectly reasonable, having obviously concluded that he could manipulate her better with a show of interest in what she might be feeling than the sort of offensive strategy he might otherwise employ. "Are you unhappy?"

What a preposterous question. Dru let out a short laugh that clearly hit him the wrong way. In truth, she'd known it would. His eyes narrowed, seeming almost to glow with the temper that would show only there, she was well aware. He so rarely unleashed the full force of it. It normally only lurked, beneath everything, like a dark promise no one wanted him to keep.

"Of course I'm unhappy," she replied, keeping herself from rolling her eyes by the barest remaining shred of her once iron control. "I have no personal life. I have no life at all, in point of fact, and haven't for five years. I manage yours instead."

"For which you are extraordinarily well paid," he pointed out. With bite.

"I know you won't believe me," she said, almost pityingly, which made his eyes narrow even further, "and you will certainly never discover this on your own, God knows, but there is more to life than money."

Again, that shrewd amber stare.

"Is this about a man?" he asked in a voice she might have called something like disgruntled had it belonged to someone else. She laughed again, and told herself she couldn't hear the edge in it, that he should hit so close to a bitter truth she had no intention of acknowledging.

"When do you imagine I would have the time to meet men?" she asked. "In between assignments and business trips? While busy sending farewell gifts to all of *your* ex-lovers?"

"Ah," he said, in a tone that put her back right up, so condescending was it. "I understand now." His smile then was both patronizing and razor-sharp. Dru felt it drag across her, clawing deep. "I suggest you take a week's holiday, Miss Bennett. Perhaps two. Find a beach and some warm bodies. Drink something potent and scratch the itch. As many times as necessary. You are of no use to me at all in this state."

"That is a charming idea," Dru said, something dark and destructive churning inside her, through lips that felt pale with rage, "and I appreciate the offer, naturally. But I am not you, Mr. Vila." She let everything she felt about him—all these years of longing and sacrifice, all the things she'd thought and hoped, all the foolish dreams she'd had no idea he'd crushed in their infancy until today, even that one complicated and emotional night in Cadiz three years ago they never discussed and never would—burn through her as she stared at him. "I do not 'scratch the itch' with indiscriminate abandon, leaving masses in my wake, like some kind of over-sexed Godzilla. I have standards."

He blinked. He did not move a single other muscle and yet Dru had to order herself to stay in place, so powerfully did she *feel* the lash of his temper, the kick of those amber eyes as they bored into her.

"Are you unwell?" he asked with soft menace, only the granite set of his jaw and the deepening of his accent hinting at his mounting fury. But Dru knew him. She knew the danger signs when she saw them. "Or have you taken complete leave of your senses?"

"This is called *honesty*, Mr. Vila," she replied with a crispness that completely belied the alarms ringing wildly inside her, screaming at her to run, to leave at once, to stop *taunting* him, for God's sake, as if that would prod him into being who she'd imagined he was! "I understand dat it's not something you're familiar with, particularly not from me. But that's what happens when one is as carelessly domineering and impossible as you pride yourself on being. You are surrounded by an obsequious echo chamber of minions and acolytes, too afraid of you to speak the truth. I should know. I've been pretending to be one among them for years."

He went terrifyingly still. She could feel his temper expand to fill the room, all but rattling the windows. She could see that lean, muscled body of his seem to hum with the effort she imagined it took him to keep from exploding along with it. His gaze locked on hers, dark and furious. Infinitely more lethal than she wanted to admit to herself.

Or maybe it was that she was simply too susceptible to him. Still. *Always,* something inside her whispered, making her despair of herself anew.

"I suggest you think very carefully about the next thing that comes out of your mouth," he said in that deceptively measured way, the cruelty he was famous for rich in his voice then, casting his fierce face into iron. "You may otherwise live to regret it."

This time, Dru's laugh was real. If, she could admit to herself, a little bit nervous.

"That's what you don't understand," she said, grief and satisfaction and too many other things stampeding through her, making her feel wild and dangerously close to a certain kind of fierce, possibly unhinged joy. That she was defying him? That she was actually getting to him, for once? She had no idea anymore. "I don't care. I'm essentially bulletproof. What are you going to do?

Sack me? Blacklist me? Refuse me a reference? Go right
ahead. I've already quit."

And then, at long last, fulfilling the dream she'd
cherished in one form or another since she'd taken this
horribly all-consuming job in the first place purely to
pay for Dominic's assorted bills—because she couldn't
help but love her brother, despite everything and because she was all he'd had, and that had meant something to her even when she'd wished it didn't—Dru
turned her back on Cayo Vila, her own personal demon
and the greatest bane of her existence, and walked out
of his life forever.

Just as she'd originally planned she would someday.

There really should have been trumpets, at the very
least. And certainly no trace of that hard sort of anguish
that swam in her and made this much, much more difficult than it should have been.

She was almost to the far door of the outer office,
where her desk sat as guardian of this most inner sanc-
tum, when he snapped out her name. It was a stark command, and she had been too well trained to ignore it.
She stopped, hating herself for obeying him, but it was
only this last time, she told herself. What could it hurt?

When she looked over her shoulder, she felt a chill
of surprise that he was so close behind her without her
having heard him move, but she couldn't think about
that—it was that look on his face that struck her, all
thunder and warning, and her heart began to pound,
hard.

"If memory serves," he said in a cool tone that was at
complete odds with that dark savagery in his burnished
gold gaze, "your contract states that you must give me
two weeks following the tendering of your notice."

It was Dru's turn to blink. "You're not serious."

"I may be an 'oversexed Godzilla,' Miss Bennett…"
He bit out each word like a bullet she shouldn't have
been able to feel, and yet it hurt—it *hurt*—and all the
while the gold in his gaze seemed to sear into her, making her remember all the things she'd rather forget. "But
that has yet to impede my ability to read a contract.
Two weeks, which, if I am not mistaken, includes the
investor dinner in Milan we've spent months planning."

"Why would you want that?" Dru found she'd turned
to face him without meaning to move, and her hands
had become fists at her sides. "Are you that perverse?"

"I'm surprised you haven't already found the answer
to that from my ex-lovers, with whom you are so close,
apparently," he threw at her, his voice a sardonic lash.
"Didn't you spend all of those hours of your wasted life
placating them?"

He folded his arms over his chest, and Dru found herself noticing, as always, the sheer, lean perfection of his
athletic form. It was part of what made him so deadly.
So dizzyingly unmanageable. Every inch of him was
a finely honed weapon, and he was not averse to using
whatever part of that weapon would best serve him.
That was why, she understood, he was standing over
her like this, intimidating her with the fact of his height,
the breadth of his shoulders, the inexorable force and
power of his relentless masculinity. Even in a bespoke
suit which should have made him look like some kind
of dandy, he looked capable of anything. There was that
hint of wildness about him, that constant, underlying
threat he wore proudly. Deliberately.

She didn't want to see him as a man. She didn't want
to remember the heat of his hands against her skin, his
mouth so demanding on hers. She would die before she

gave him the satisfaction of seeing that he got to her now. Even if she still felt the burn of it, the searing fire.

"You know what they say," she murmured, sounding almost entirely calm to her own ears. Almost blasé. "Those who sleep with someone for the money earn every penny."

He didn't appear to react to that at all, and yet she felt something hard and hot flare between them, almost making her step back, almost making her show him exactly how nervous he made her. But she was done with that. With him. She refused to cower before him. And she was finished with quiet obedience, too. Look what it had got her.

"Take the rest of the day off," he suggested then, a certain hoarseness in his voice the only hint of the fury she couldn't quite see but had no doubt was close to liquefying them both. And perhaps the whole of the office building they stood in as well, if not the entire City of London besides. "I suggest you do something to curb your newfound urge toward candid commentary. I'll see you tomorrow morning. Half-seven, as usual, Miss Bennett."

And it was suddenly as if a new sun dawned, bathing Dru in a bright, impossible light. Everything became stark and clear. He loomed there, not three feet away from her, taking up too much space, dark and impossible and faintly terrifying even when quiet and watchful. And he would never stop. She understood that about him; she understood it the way she comprehended her own ability to breathe. His entire life was a testament to his inability to take no for an answer, to not accept what others told him if it wasn't something he wanted to hear. He had never encountered a rule he didn't break, a wall he couldn't climb, a barrier he wouldn't slap down simply because it dared to stand in his way.

He *took*. That was what he did. At the most basic level, that was who Cayo Vila was.

He'd taken from her and she hadn't even known it until today, had she? Some part of her—even now—wished she'd never opened that file drawer, never discovered how easily he'd derailed her career three years ago without her ever the wiser. But she had.

She could see the whole rest of her life flash before her eyes in a sickening, infinitely depressing cascade of images. If she agreed to his two weeks, she might as well die on the spot. Right here, right now. Because he would take possession of her life the way he'd done of her last five years, and there would be no end to it. Ever. Dru knew perfectly well that she was the best personal assistant he'd ever had. That wasn't any immodesty on her part—she'd had to be, because she'd needed the money he'd paid her and the cachet his name had afforded her when it came time to wrangle Dominic into the best drug-treatment clinics and programs in the States, for all the good it had done. And she still believed it had all been worth it, no matter how little she had to show for it now, no matter how empty and battered she felt. Dominic had not died alone, on a lonely street corner in some desperate city neighborhood, never to be identified or mourned or missed. That was what mattered.

But Dominic had only been the first, original reason. Her pathetic feelings for Cayo had been the second—and far more appalling—reason she'd made herself so indispensable to Cayo. She'd taken pride in her ability to serve him so well. It left a bitter taste in her mouth today, but it was true. She was that much of a masochist, and she'd have to live with that. If she stayed even one day more, any chance she had left to reclaim her life, to do something for herself, to *live,* to crawl out of this terrible hole she'd lowered herself into all on her own, would disappear into the big black smoke-filled vortex that was Cayo Vila.

He would buy more things and sell others, make millions and destroy lives at a whim, hers included. And she would carry on catering to him, jumping to do his bidding and smoothing the path before him, anticipating his every need and losing herself, bit by bit and inch by inch, until she was nothing more than a pleasant-looking, serene-voiced husk. A robot under his command. Slave to feelings he would never, could never return, despite small glimmers to the contrary in far-off cities on complicated evenings never spoken of aloud when they were done.

Worse, she would *want* to do all of it. She would *want* to be whatever she could be for him, just so long as she could stay near him. Just as she had since that night she'd seen such a different side of him in Cadiz. She would cling to anything, wouldn't she? She would even pretend she didn't know that he'd crushed her dreams of advancement with a single, brutal email. She was, she knew, exactly that pathetic. Exactly that stupid. Hadn't she proved it every single day of these past three years?

"No," she said.

It was, of course, a word he rarely heard.

His black brows lowered. His hard gold eyes shone with amazement. That impossibly lush mouth, the one that made his parade of lovers fantasize that there could be some softness to him, only to discover too late that it was no more than a mirage, flattened ominously.

"What do you mean, no?"

The lilt of his native Spanish cadence made the words sound almost musical, but Dru knew that the thicker his accent, the more trouble she was in—and the closer that volcanic temper of his was to eruption. She should have turned on her heel and run for safety. She should have heeded the knot in her belly and the heat that moved over her skin, the panic that flooded through her.

"I understand that you might not be familiar with the word," she said, sounding perhaps more empowered, more sure of herself, than was wise. Or true. "It indicates dissent. Refusal. Both concepts you have difficulty with, I know. But that is, I am happy to say, no longer my problem."

"It will become your problem," he told her, a note she'd never heard before in his voice. His gaze narrowed further, into two outraged slits of gold, as if he'd never actually seen her until this moment. Something about that particular way he looked at her made her feel lightheaded. "I will—"

"Go ahead and take me to court," she said, interrupting him again with a careless wave of her hand that, she could see, visibly infuriated him. "What do you think you'll win?"

For the first time in as long as she'd known him, Cayo Vila was rendered speechless. The silence was taut and breathless between them, and, still, was somehow as loud as a siren. It seemed to *hum*. And he simply stared at her, thunderstruck, an expression she had never seen before on his ruthless face.

Good.

"Will you take my flat from me?" she continued, warming to the topic. Emboldened, perhaps, by his unprecedented silence. By the chaos inside of her that was

all his fault. "It's only a leased bedsit. You're welcome
to it. I'll write you a check right now, if you like, for
the entire contents of my current account. Is that what
it will take?" She laughed, and could hear it bouncing
back at her from the glass wall, the tidy expanse of her
desk, even the polished floor that made even the outer
office seem glossy and that much more intimidating to
the unwary. "I've already given you five years. I'm not
giving you two more weeks. I'm not giving you another
second. I'd rather die."

Cayo stared at his assistant as if he'd never seen her
before.

There was something about the way she tilted that
perfect, pretty oval of her face, the way her usually
calm gray eyes sparkled with the force of her temper,
and something about that mouth of hers. He couldn't
seem to look away from it.

Unbidden, a memory teased through his head, of her
hand on his cheek, her gray eyes warm and something
like affectionate, her lips—but no. There was no need
to revisit *that* insanity. He'd worked much too hard to
strike it from his consciousness. It was one regrettable
evening in five smooth, issue-free years. Why think
of it at all?

"I would rather die," she said again, as if she was
under the misapprehension that he had not heard her
the first time.

"That can always be arranged," he said, searching
that face he knew so well and yet, apparently, so little—looking for some clue as to what had brought this
on. Here, now, today. "Have you forgotten? I am a very
formidable man."

"If you are going to make threats, Mr. Vila," she

replied in that crisp way of hers, "at least pay me the compliment of making them credible. You are many things, but you are not a thug. As such."

For the first time in longer than he could remember—since, perhaps, he had been the fatherless child whose mother, all the village had known too well, had been so disgraced that she had taken to the convent after his birth rather than face the wages of her sin in its ever-growing flesh—Cayo was at a loss. It might have amused him that it was his personal assistant who had wrought this level of incapacity in him, his glorified secretary for God's sake, when nothing else had managed it. Not another multimillion-pound deal, not one more scandalous affair reported breathlessly and inaccurately in the tabloids, not one of his new and—dare he say it—visionary business enterprises. Nothing got beneath his skin. Nothing threw him off balance.

Only this woman. As she had once before.

It was funny. It was. He was certain he would laugh about it at some point, and at great length, but first? He needed her. Back in line where she belonged, back securely in the role he preferred her to play, and he ignored the small whisper inside him that suggested that there would be no repairing this. That she would never again be as comfortably invisible as she'd been before, that it was too late, that he'd been operating on borrowed time since the incident in Cadiz three years ago and this was only the delayed fallout—

"I am leaving," she told him, meeting his gaze as if he were a naughty child in the midst of a tiresome strop, and enunciating each word as if she suspected he was too busy tantruming to hear her otherwise. "You will have to come to terms with that and if you feel it necessary to file suit against me, have at it. I booked a ticket to Bora Bora this morning. I'm sorted."

And then, finally, his brain started working again. It was one thing for her to take herself off to wherever she lived in London, or even off on a week's holiday to, say, Ibiza, as he'd suggested. But French Polynesia, a world away? Unacceptable.

Because he could not let her go. He refused. And he wanted to examine that as little as he had the last time he'd discovered that she wanted to leave him. Three years ago, only a week after that night in Cadiz he'd seen—and still saw—no point in dredging forth.

It wasn't personal, of course, then or now; she was an asset. In many ways, the most valuable asset he had. She knew too much about him. Everything, in fact, from his inseam to his favorite breakfast to his preferred concierge service in all the major cities around the globe, to say nothing of the ins and outs of the way he handled his business affairs. He couldn't imagine how long it would take to train up her replacement, and he had no intention of finding out. He would do as he always did—whatever was necessary to protect his assets. Whatever it took.

"I apologize for my behavior," he said then, almost formally. He shifted his stance and thrust his hands into the pockets of his trousers, rocking back on his heels in a manner he knew was the very opposite of aggressive. "You took me by surprise." Her gray eyes narrowed suspiciously, and he wished that he had taken the time to learn how to read her as thoroughly as he knew she could read him. It put him at a disadvantage, another unfamiliar sensation.

"Of course I will not sue you," he continued, forcing himself to keep an even, civil tone, and the rest of himself in check. "I was simply reacting badly, as anyone would. You are the best personal assistant I've ever had. Perhaps the best in all of London. I am quite sure you know this."

"Well," she said, dropping her gaze, which he found unaccountably fascinating. She said something almost under her breath then, something that sounded very much like *that's nothing to be proud of, is it?*

Cayo wanted to pursue that, but didn't. He had every intention of cracking her wide open and figuring out every last one of her mysteries until he was sure that none remained, that she could never take him by surprise again, but not now. Not here. Not until he'd dealt with this situation the only way he knew how.

Which was to dominate it and contain it and make it his, by whatever means necessary.

"As you must be aware, however," he continued, "there will be a great number of papers to sign before you can leave the company. Confidentiality agreements being the least of it." He checked the watch on his wrist with a quick snap of his arm. "It's still early. We can leave immediately."

"Leave?" she echoed, openly frowning now, which was when it occurred to him that he'd never seen her do that before—she was always so very serene, with only the odd flash in her eyes to hint at what went on in her head. He'd never wanted to know. But this was a full frown, brows drawn and that mouth of hers tight, and he was riveted. Why could he not tear his attention away from her mouth? The lines he'd never seen before, making the smooth expanse of her forehead more interesting somehow? It made him much too close to uncomfortable. As if she was a real person instead of merely his most prized possession, exhibiting brand-new traits. Worse, as if she was a woman.

But he didn't want to think about that. He certainly didn't want to remember the only other time he'd seen her as anything more than his assistant. He didn't want this woman in his bed. Of course he didn't. She was too clever, too good at what she did. He wanted her at his beck and call, at his side, where she belonged.

"My entire legal team is in Zurich," he reminded her gently. "Surely you have not forgotten that already in your haste to leave?"

He watched her stiffen, and thought she would balk at the idea of a quick trip to Switzerland, but instead, she swallowed. Visibly. And then squared her shoulders as if a not-quite-two-hour trip on the private jet was akin to a trial by fire. One that she was reluctantly willing to suffer through, if it would rid her of him.

"Fine," she said, with an impatient sort of sigh that he did not care for in the least. "If you want me to sign something, anything, I'll sign it. Even in bloody Zurich, if you insist. I want this over with."

And Cayo smiled, because he had her.

CHAPTER TWO

By the time the helicopter touched down on the helipad on the foredeck of the gently moving luxury yacht, Dru had worked herself into what she could only call a state.

She climbed out of the sleek little machine only when she realized she had no other choice, that the pilot was shutting it down and preparing to stay on board the great yacht himself—and Dru did not fancy spending who knew how long sitting in a helicopter simply to prove a point. She was quite certain that Cayo would leave her there.

On some level, she was bitterly aware she really should have expected he'd pull a stunt like this. Unabashed abduction. Simply because he could.

So, in spite of the fact that she wanted to put whole worlds between them, she found herself following Cayo's determined, athletic stride across the deck, too upset to really take in the sparkling blue sea on all sides and what she was afraid was the Croatian mainland in the distance. The sea air teased tendrils of her hair out of the twist that had been carefully calibrated to withstand the London drizzle, and she actually had a familiar moment of panic, out of habit, as if it should still matter to her what she looked like. As if she should still be concerned that he might find her professional appearance wanting in some way. It appalled her how deep it went in her, this knee-jerk need to please him. It was going to take her a whole lot longer to quit the Cayo Vila habit than she'd like.

And the fact that he had spirited her away to the wrong country didn't help.

"You do realize this is kidnapping, don't you?" she demanded. Not for the first time. The difference was that this time, Cayo actually stopped and looked at her, turning his dark head slowly so that his hard gaze made every hair on her body prickle to attention. She sucked in a breath.

"What on earth are you talking about?" he asked silkily. At his most dangerous, but she couldn't let that intimidate her. She wouldn't. "Nobody forced you to come on this trip. There was no gun to your back. You agreed."

"This is not Switzerland," she pointed out, trying to keep her rising panic at bay. "It doesn't even resemble Switzerland. The sea is a dead giveaway and unless I am very much mistaken, that is Dubrovnik."

She stabbed a finger in the general direction of the red-roofed, whitewashed city that clung to the rugged coastline off the side of the yacht, and the walls and fortress that encircled it so protectively. The blue waters of the Adriatic—because she knew where she was, she didn't need him to confirm it so much as explain it—were as gorgeous and inviting as ever. She wanted to throw him overboard and watch those same waters consume him, inch by aggravating inch. Only the fact that he was so much bigger than she—and all of it sleek and smooth muscle she did not trust herself near enough to touch—prevented her trying. And only barely prevented her, at that.

He didn't glance toward the shore. Why should he? He had undoubtedly known where they were going the moment he'd mentioned Zurich back in London. He'd certainly known when they'd landed in a mysterious airfield somewhere in Europe and he'd hurried her onto the helicopter before she could get her bearings. This was only a surprise for *her*.

"Did I say Switzerland?" he asked, that voice of his deceptively soft and all the more lethal for it, while his gaze remained hard. "You must have misheard me."

"Exactly what is your plan?' she threw at him, temper and fear and something else she couldn't quite identify sloshing around inside her, making her feel like a bomb about to detonate. "Am I your prisoner now?"

"How theatrical you are," he said, and she had the impression that he was choosing his words carefully. That much harsher words lurked behind that quiet tone that she knew meant he was furious. "How did you manage to hide that so long and so well?"

"You must have mistaken me for someone else," Dru hurled at him. "I'm not going to mindlessly obey your commands—"

"Are you certain?" That black gold gaze of his turned darker, harder as he cut her off. It made her feel oddly hollow, and much too hot. She assured herself it was anger, nothing more. "If memory serves, obedience is one of your strengths."

"Obedience was my job," she said with some remnant of her former iciness. "But I quit."

He looked at her for a long, simmering moment.

"Your resignation has not been accepted, Miss Bennett," he snapped out, fierce and commanding. As if she should not dare mention the matter again. And then he turned his back on her and strode off across the gleaming, sun-kissed deck as if it was settled.

Dru stood where he'd left her, feeling a little bit silly and more than a little off balance in her smart office clothes and delicate heels that were completely inappropriate for a boat. She stepped out of her stilettos and scooped them up in her hand, trying to breathe in the crisp sea air. Trying to curl her now-bare toes against the cool deck as if that might ground her.

Trying to breathe.

She moved over to the polished rail and leaned her elbows against it, frowning at the rolling waves, the gorgeously craggy coastline beckoning in the distance, rich dark greens and weathered reds basking in the sun. She felt it all twist and shift inside her then, all of the struggle and agony, the sacrifice and frustrated yearning. The grief. The hope. The brutal truth some part of her wished she'd never learned. It all seemed to swell within her as if it might crack her open and rip her apart—as if, having finally opened the door to all the things she'd repressed all this time, the lies she'd told herself, she couldn't lock it back up. She couldn't pretend any longer.

Misery rose inside her, thick and black and suffocating. And fast. And for a moment, she could do nothing but let it claim her. There was so much she couldn't change, couldn't help. She couldn't go back in time and keep her father from dying when she and Dominic had still been toddlers. She couldn't keep her mother from her string of lovers, each more vicious and abusive than the last. She couldn't keep sweet, sensitive Dominic from choosing oblivion, and then courting it, his life and his drugs getting harder every year, until it was no more than a waiting game for his inevitable and tragic end.

The long, hard breath she took felt ragged. Too close to painful.

And she was free of those obligations now, it was true, but she was also irrevocably and impossibly alone. She hardly remembered her father and her mother hadn't acknowledged her existence in years. She'd built her life around handling Dominic's disease, and with him gone, there was nothing but…emptiness. She would fill it, she promised herself. She would build a life based finally on what she wanted, not as some kind of response to people and things that were forever out of her control. Not a life in opposition to her mother's choices. Not a life contingent on Dominic's problems. A life that was only hers, whatever that looked like.

All she had to do was escape Cayo Vila first.

Another fresh wave of pain crashed through her then, just as hard to fight off. Sharper, somehow. Wrenching and dark. *Cayo.* Three years ago she'd thought she'd seen something in him, some glimmer of humanity, an indication that he was so much more than the man he pretended to be in public. And she'd taken that night, some intimate conversation and a single, ill-conceived, far too passionate kiss, and built herself a whole imaginary world of possibility. Oh, the ways she'd wanted him, the ways she'd believed in him—and all the while he'd thought so very little of her that he'd blocked her chances for another position in the Vila Group and, in so doing, any kind of independent career. Without a word to her. Without any conversation at all.

With three careless sentences.

Miss Bennett is an assistant, he'd emailed Human Resources not long after that night she'd so foolishly believed had changed everything between them. She'd applied for the job in marketing, thinking it was high time she spread her wings in the company, took charge of her own career rather than merely supported his. *She is certainly no vice president. Look elsewhere.*

He hadn't hidden the fact he'd done it, either. Why should he have? It was right there in Dru's file, had she ever bothered to look. She hadn't, until today, while doing a bit of housecleaning about the office. She'd been so sure everything was different after Cadiz, if unspoken, unaddressed. She hadn't minded that she hadn't got that job; she'd thought she and Cayo had an understanding—she'd believed they were a team—

So help her, she thought now, forcing back the angry, humiliated tears she was determined not to cry, she would never again be so foolish.

She'd known exactly who he was when he'd hired her, and she knew exactly who he was now. She'd spend the rest of her life working out how she'd managed to lose sight of that for so long, how she'd betrayed herself so completely for a fantasy life in her head, built around a single kiss that still made her flush hot to recall, but she wouldn't forget herself again. It was cold comfort, perhaps, but it was all she had.

She found him in one of the yacht's many salons, a sleek celebration of marble and glass down an ostentatious spiral stair that was as gloriously luxe as everything else on this floating castle he'd won in a late-night card game from a Russian oligarch.

"It was easy to take," he'd said with a small shrug when she'd asked why he'd wanted another yacht to add to his collection. "So I took it."

He sat now in the sunken seating area with one of his interchangeable and well-nigh-anonymous companions melting all over him, all plumped-up breasts and sheaves of wheat-blond hair cascading here and there. He had discarded his jacket somewhere and now looked deliciously rumpled, white shirt open at the collar and his olive skin seeming to gleam. The girl pouted and whined something in what sounded like Czech when she saw Dru walk in, as if it was Dru's presence that was keeping Cayo's attention on the flat-screen television on the inner wall rather than on the assets she had on display. As if, were Dru not there, he might actually pay her some mind.

You are fast approaching your expiration date, Dru seethed uncharitably at the other woman, but then caught herself. This was not a cat fight. It wasn't even a competition.

Dru had spent entirely too long telling herself that it was all perfectly fine with her, that she didn't mind at all that this man who had kissed her with so much heat and longing in an ancient city, and who had looked at her as if she were the only person in the world who could ever matter to him, slaked his various lusts with all of these anonymous women. *Why should it matter?* she'd argued with herself a thousand times in the middle of the night while she lay alone and he was off tending to his companion du jour. *What we have is so much deeper than sex...*

It was all so desperate. So delusional and terribly, gut-wrenchingly pathetic.

She held a shoe in each hand now, like potential weapons, and she allowed herself a grim moment of amusement as she watched Cayo's ever-calculating gaze move to the sharp stiletto heels immediately, as if he joined her in imagining her sinking them deep into his jugular. He smirked and returned his attention to

the television and the almighty scroll of the New York
Stock Exchange across the bottom of the screen, as if
he'd assessed the threat that quickly and dismissed it
that easily.

And her. Again. As ever.

"Have you finished having your little fit?" he asked.
She felt her heart race, that same anger—at him and,
worse, at herself—shaking through her, making her
very nearly tremble.

"I want to know what you think is going to happen
now that you've stranded me on this boat," Dru replied,
biting the words out. "Will you simply keep me impris-
oned here forever? That seems impractical, at the very
least. Boats eventually dock, and I can swim."

"I suggest you take a deep breath, Miss Bennett,"
he said in that obnoxiously patronizing tone, not even
bothering to glance at her again, his entire lean body insulting in its disinterest. "You are becoming hysterical."

It was too much, finally. She didn't even think.

She cocked one arm back in a moment of searing,
possibly insane, mind-numbing rage and threw a shoe.

At his head.

It sliced through the air, the wicked heel seeming almost to glow, and she pictured it spearing him directly
between the mocking, impossible eyes—

But then he reached up and snatched it out of its
flight at the last moment, his hand too large and masculine against the delicate point of the heel.

When he looked at her then, his dark golden stare
burned with outrage. And something else—something
that seemed to echo in her, hard and loud. Anticipation?
The shared memory of an old street, that explosive kiss?
But no, that was impossible. Nothing more than her desperate fantasies in action yet again.

Dru panted slightly, as if that had been her in vicious flight. As if he now held her like that, captured against his hard palm. That same current of wild, hot heat that she wished was simple fury seemed to coil within her and then pulse low, the way it always did when he was near.

"Next time," she told him from between her teeth, her other hand clenching her remaining shoe, heel first, "I won't miss."

Once again, she'd surprised him. And he liked it as little as he had in London.

Her gray gaze was alert and intent and he didn't like all the things he could see in it, none of which he understood or wanted to try to understand. He didn't like the faint flush on her cheeks, or the way she looked with her feet bare and her hair something other than perfect for the first time in as long as he'd known her. *Sexy.*

He had to jerk his gaze from hers and when he did, he found himself looking down at the vicious little stiletto she'd flung at his throat. It was a weapon, certainly, but it was also one of those delicate, wickedly feminine shoes that he did not want to think about in reference to his personal assistant. He did not want to imagine her slipping the sleek little shoe on over those elegant feet of hers that he'd never noticed before, or think about what the saucy height of the heel would do to her hips as she walked—

Damn her.

Cayo rose to his feet slowly, not taking his eyes from hers.

"What am I going to do with you?" he asked, impatient with her defiance. And equally impatient with his own failure to end this distracting and disruptive situation that was already well out of hand. But those errant strands of silky dark hair teased at the curve of her lips, her chin, and he could not seem to look away.

"You have had a number of options of things to do with me over the years," she pointed out, in something less than her usual crisp tone. As if she was boiling over with fury, which he should not find as compelling as he did. "You could have let me move to a different position in your company, for example. You could have let me go today. You opted to kidnap me instead."

Abruptly, Cayo remembered that they were not alone. He dismissed the clingy blonde with a careless wave of his hand and ignored the sulky expression that followed it. The woman huffed and muttered as she exited the salon, irritating him far more than she should have. Could not one female in his usually carefully controlled existence do as he wished today? Must everything be a trial?

He tossed Drusilla's stiletto down on the seat where the blonde had been, and wondered why he was even having this conversation in the first place. Why was he encouraging Drusilla further by allowing her to speak to him in that decidedly disrespectful tone?

And why on earth did he have the wholly uncharacteristic urge to explain the reasons he'd shot down her bid for that promotion three years ago? What was the matter with him? The last time he'd defended or justified his behavior was…never.

"I don't share my things," he said then, coolly, purely to put her in her place. She stiffened, and then what could only be hurt washed through her gray eyes. And for the first time in years, Cayo felt the faintest hint of something that might have been shame move through him. He ignored it.

"I'd ask you what kind of man you are to say something so deliberately insulting and borderline sociopathic, but please." Drusilla sniffed, her eyes still wounded, which he hated more than he should have. "We both already know exactly what kind of man you are, don't we?"

"The papers call me a force of nature," he replied, his voice light if cold, and it was a reminder. The last one he planned to give her. He was not a man who suffered insubordination, and yet he'd been tolerating hers for hours, up to and including an attempted attack on his person. Had she been a man, he would have responded in kind.

Basta ya! he thought, impatiently. Enough was enough.

He found himself moving toward her, tracking the nervous swallow she took as he came closer, as if she was neither as disgusted nor as impassive as she appeared. That same, seductive memory rolled over then inside him, and shook itself awake. Dangerously awake.

She shifted her weight from one bare foot to the other, reminding him as she did so that she was, in fact, a woman. Not a perfect robot built only to serve his needs as any good assistant should. That she was made of smooth, soft flesh and that her legs were perfectly formed beneath that sleek skirt. That she was not the ice sculpture of his imagination, nor a shadow. And that he'd tasted her heat himself.

He didn't like that, either. But he let his gaze fall over her anyway, noting as if for the first time that her trim figure boasted lush curves in all the right places, had he only let himself pay closer attention to them. Something about her disheveled hair, the temper in her gaze, the complete lack of her usual calm expression

was getting under his skin. His heart began to beat in
a rhythm that boded only ill, and made him think of
things he knew he shouldn't. Those sleek legs wrapped
around his waist as he held her against a wall in the old
city. That mouth of hers hot and wet beneath his. That
cool competence of hers he'd depended upon all these
years, melting all around him...

Unacceptable. There was a reason he never let himself think of that night, damn it. Damn *her*.

"Calling you a force of nature rather takes away from
your responsibility, doesn't it?" she asked, as if she
didn't notice or care that he was bearing down on her,
though he saw her fingers tighten around the shoe she
still clutched in one hand. "You're not a deadly hurri-
cane or an earthquake, Mr. Vila. You're an insulated,
selfish man with too much money and too few social
skills."

"I believe I preferred you the way you were before,"
he observed then, his voice like a blade, though she
didn't flinch.

"Subservient?"

"Quiet."

Her lips crooked into something much too cold to be
a smile. "If you don't wish to hear my voice or my opin-
ions, you need only let me go," she reminded him. "You
are so good at dismissing people, aren't you? Didn't I
watch you do it to that poor girl not five minutes ago?"

He took advantage of his superior height and leaned
over her, putting his face entirely too close to hers. He
could smell the faintest hint of something sweet—soap
or perfume, he couldn't tell. But desire curled through
him, kicking up flames. He remembered burying his
face in her neck, and the need to do it again, *now,* howled

through him, shocking in its intensity. And he didn't know if he admired her or wanted to throttle her when she didn't move so much as an inch. When she showed no regard at all for her own safety. When, instead, she all but *bristled* in further defiance.

He had the strangest feeling—he wouldn't call it a premonition—that this woman might very well be the death of him. He shook it off, annoyed at himself and the kind of superstitious silliness he thought he'd left behind in his unhappy childhood.

"Why are you so concerned with the fate of 'that poor girl'?" he asked, his voice dipping lower the more furious he became. "Do you even know her name?"

"Do you?" she threw back at him, even angling closer in outraged emphasis, as if she was seconds away from poking at him with something more than her words. "I'm sure I drew up the usual nondisclosure agreement whenever and wherever you picked her up—"

"Why do you care how I treat my women, Miss Bennett?" he asked icily. Dangerously. In a tone that should have silenced her for days.

"Why don't you?" she countered, scowling at him, notably unsilenced.

And suddenly, he understood what was happening. It was all too obvious, and what concerned him was that he hadn't seen this boiling in her, as it must have done for years. He hadn't let a single meaningless night, deliberately ignored almost as soon as it had happened, haunt him or affect their working relationship. He'd thought she hadn't, either.

"Perhaps," he suggested in a tone that brooked no more of her nonsense, "when I asked you if there was a man and you denied it, you were not being entirely forthcoming, were you?"

For a moment she only stared back at him, blankly. Then she sucked in a breath as shocked, incredulous understanding flooded her gaze—followed by a sudden flare of awareness, hot and unmistakable. She jerked back. But he had already seen it.

"You are joking," she breathed. She sounded horrified. Appalled. Perhaps a bit too horrified and appalled, come to that. "You actually think… *You?*"

"Me," he agreed, all of that simmering fury shifting inside him, rolling over into something else, something he remembered all too well, despite his claims to the contrary. "You would hardly be the first secretary in history to have a bit of a sad crush on her boss, would you?" He inclined his head, feeling magnanimous. "And I will take responsibility for it, of course. I should not have let Cadiz happen. It was my fault. I allowed you to entertain…ideas."

She seemed to pale before him, and despite himself, despite what he said and what he wanted, all he could think about was that long-ago night, the Spanish air soft around him as they'd walked back to their hotel from the bodega, the world pleasantly blurry and her arm around his waist as if he'd needed help. Support. And then her mouth beneath his, her tongue, her taste, far more intoxicating than the *manzanilla* he'd drunk in some kind of twisted tribute to the grandfather whose death that same day he'd refused to mourn. He'd kissed her instead. There'd been the wall. The sweet darkness. His hands against her curves, his mouth on her neck… All these years later, he could taste her still.

He'd been lying to himself. This was not just annoyance, anger, that moved in him, making him hard and ready, making his blood race through his veins. This was *want*.

"I would be more likely to have a 'crush' on the Grim Reaper," she was saying furiously, her words tripping over each other as if she couldn't say them fast enough. "That sounds infinitely preferable, in fact, scythe and all. And I was your personal assistant, not your secretary—"

"You're whatever I say you are." His tone was silken and vicious, as if that could banish the memory, or put it where it belonged. And her and this driving *want* of her with it. "Something you seem to have forgot completely today, along with your place."

She sucked in a breath, and he saw it again—that flash of sizzling awareness, of sexual heat. Of memory. That light in her gray eyes that he'd seen once before and had not forgotten at all, much as he'd told himself he'd done. Much as he'd wanted to do.

More lies, he knew now, as his body hummed with the need to taste her. Possess her.

"I haven't wasted a single second 'entertaining ideas' about your drunken boorishness in Cadiz," she hissed at him, but her voice caught and he knew she was as much a liar as he was. "About one little kiss. Have you? Is that why you blocked me from that promotion? Some kind of jealousy?"

He wasn't jealous, of course, it was a laughable idea—but he wanted that taste of her and he wanted her quiet, and there was only one way he could think of to achieve both of those things at once. He told himself it was strategy.

His heart pounded. He wanted his hands on her. *He wanted.*

Strategy, he thought again.

And he didn't quite believe his own story, but he bent his head anyway, and kissed her.

It was as if the air between them simply burst into flame.

Or perhaps that was her.

This cannot be happening again—

But Dru had no time to think anything further. His mouth was on hers, *his beautiful mouth,* hard and cruel and impossible, and he closed the distance between them as ruthlessly as he did anything else. Just as he'd done years ago on a dark street, in the deep shadows of a Spanish night. One hand slid over her hip to the small of her back, hauling her against the wall of his chest, even as his lips took control of hers, demanding she let him in, insisting she kiss him back.

And, God help her, she did.

She dropped her other shoe, she lost her mind, and she did.

It was so *hot. Finally,* a small voice whispered, insistent and jubilant. He tasted of lust and command and she was dizzy, so dizzy, she forgot herself.

She forgot everything but the heat of that mouth, the way he angled his head to kiss her more deeply, the way his palm on the small of her back pressed into her and in turn pressed her into the hard granite expanse of his lean chest. Her breasts felt too full and almost sore as they flattened against him, into him, and everywhere they touched felt like a fever, and she was kissing him back because he tasted like sorcery and for one brief, searing, shocking moment she wanted nothing more than to lose herself in an incantation she could hardly understand.

But she *wanted*. She *wanted* almost more than she had ever wanted anything else, the inexorable pull of his mouth, his taste, *him,* roaring through her, altering her, changing everything—

He broke the kiss to mutter something harsh in Spanish, and reality slammed back into Dru. So hard she was distantly amazed her bones hadn't shattered from the impact.

She shoved against his chest blindly, and was entirely too aware not only that he chose to let her go, but that it was as if her very blood sang out to stay exactly where she was, plastered against him, just as she'd done once before and to her own detriment.

She staggered back a foot, then another. She was breathing too hard, teetering on the edge of a terrible panic, and she was afraid it would take no more than the faintest brush of wind to toss her right over into its grip. She could see nothing through the haze that seemed to cover her vision but that hooded, dangerous, dark amber gaze of his and that mouth—*that mouth*—

She should know better. She *did* know better. She could feel hysteria swell in her, indistinguishable from the lump in her throat and the clamoring of her pulse. Her stomach twisted and for a terrifying moment she didn't know if she was going to be sick or faint or some horrifying combination thereof.

But she sucked in another breath, and that particular crisis passed, somehow. He still only watched her. As if he knew exactly how hard her blood pumped through her body and where it seemed to pool. As if he knew exactly how much her breasts ached, and where they'd hardened. As if he knew how she burned for him, and always had.

Dru couldn't stand it. She couldn't stand *here*. So

she turned on her bare heel, and bolted from the salon. She picked up speed as she moved, aware as she began to run up the grand stairway toward the deck that she was breathing so heavily she might as well be sobbing. Maybe she was.

You little fool, some voice kept intoning in her head. *You're nothing but a latter-day Miss Havisham and twice as sad—*

She blinked in the bright slap of sunshine when she burst out onto the deck, momentarily blinded. She looked over her shoulder when she could see and he was right there, as she knew he would be, lean and dark and those hot, demanding eyes that looked almost gold in the Adriatic sunshine.

"Where are you going?" He was taunting her, those wicked brows of his raised. That mouth—*God, that mouth—* "I thought you didn't care about a little kiss?"

It's the devil or the deep blue sea, she thought, aware that she was almost certainly hysterical now. But her heart was already broken. She couldn't take anything more. She couldn't survive this again. She wasn't sure she'd survived it the first time, come to that.

Dru simply turned back around, took a running start toward the side of the yacht one story up from the sea, and jumped.

CHAPTER THREE

SHE HAD ACTUALLY thrown herself off the side of the damned boat.

Cayo stood at the rail and scowled down at her as she surfaced in the water below and started swimming for the far-off shore, fighting to keep his temper under control. Fighting to shove all of that need and lust back where it belonged, shut down and locked away in the deepest recesses of his memory.

How had this happened? *Again?*

And yet he was all too aware there was no one to blame but himself. Which only made it worse.

"Is that *Dru?*" The voice that came from slightly behind him was shocked.

"'*Dru?*'" Cayo echoed icily.

He didn't want to know she had a casual nickname. He didn't want to think of her as a person. He didn't want this intoxicating taste of her in his mouth again, or this insane longing for her that stormed through him, making him so hard it bordered on the painful and, moreover, a stranger to himself. *He didn't want any of this.* But that dark drum that he told himself was only temper beat ever hotter inside of him, making him a liar yet again.

"I mean Miss Bennett, of course," the crew member

beside him, the head steward if Cayo was not mistaken, all but stammered. "Forgive me, sir, but has she…fallen? Shouldn't we go and help her?"

"That is an excellent question," Cayo muttered.

He watched her for a long, tense moment, out there in the blue sweep of water, her strokes long and sure. He was very nearly forced to admire the willfulness and sheer bloody-mindedness she'd displayed today. Was still displaying, in fact. To say nothing of her grace and skill in the water, even fully dressed. He had to fight with himself to get his body under control, to force away the thick, near-liquid desire that still pumped through him and *that thing* in him that was far too alert now and would not have stopped at that kiss. Oh, no. That had been the sort of kiss that started scorching affairs, and had it not been Drusilla, he would not even have thought twice—he would have taken her there and then, on the floor of the salon if necessary.

And up against the wall. And down among the soft pillows in the seating area. And again and again, just to test all that shocking chemistry that had blown up around them—that he had told himself he'd forgotten entirely until it was all he could think of all over again. Just to see what they could make of it.

But it *was* Drusilla.

Cayo had always been a practical man. Deliberate and focused in all he did. He had never varied from the path he'd set himself; he'd never been tempted to try. Except for one unfortunate slip in Cadiz that night, and a repeat here on this yacht today.

That was two slips too many. And it was quite enough. He had to get himself back under control and stay there.

He watched as she flipped over to her back in the

water, no doubt checking for any potential pursuit, and fought with that part of him that suggested he simply leave her there. She had already wasted too much of his time. His schedule had been packed full today, and he'd shoved it all aside so he could try to keep her from leaving. Why had he done any of this? And then kissed her?

It didn't matter, he told himself ruthlessly. She was too valuable to him as his assistant to risk her drowning, of course. Or to become his lover, as his body was still enthusiastically demanding. He'd decided the same thing three years ago when she'd applied for that promotion. He'd determined that she should stay exactly where she was and everything should remain exactly as it had been before they'd gone to Spain. He still didn't see why anything should change, when it had all been so perfect for so long, save two kisses that shouldn't have happened in the first place.

He didn't understand why she wanted to leave his employ so desperately, or why she was so furious with him all of a sudden. But he felt certain that if he threw enough money at the problem, whatever it was and especially if it was no more than her hurt feelings, she would find that it went away. His mouth twisted. People always did.

"Sir? Perhaps one of the motorboats? Only she's got a bit far out, now…?" the steward asked again, sounding simultaneously more subservient and more worried than he had before, a feat that might have amused Cayo had he not still been so at odds with his own temper.

He did not care for the feeling—uncertain and off balance. He did not like the fact that Drusilla made him feel at all, much less like that. She was the perfect personal assistant, competent and reliable. And impersonal. It was when he saw her as a woman that he ran into trouble. He started to feel the way he imagined other, lesser men felt. Unsure. Even needy. Wholly unlike himself and all he stood for. It horrified him unto his very bones.

Never again, he'd vowed when he was still so young. *No more feelings.* He'd felt far too much in the first eighteen years of his life, and done nothing but suffer for it. He'd decided he was finished with it—that succumbing to such things was for the kind of man he had no intention of ever becoming. Weak. Malleable. Common. He refused to be any of those things, ever again.

And he'd let that drive him for nearly two decades. If something was out of his reach, he simply extended his reach and then took it anyway. If it was not for sale, he applied pressure until it turned out it was after all— and often at a lesser price thanks to his machinations. If a woman did not want him, he simply took pains to shower her with her heart's desire, whatever that might be, until she decided that perhaps she'd been too hasty in her initial rejection. If a bloody assistant wanted to leave his employ, he simply replaced her, and if he felt she should stay, he gave her whatever she wanted so that she did. He bought whatever he desired, because he could. Because he would never again be that little boy, marked with his mother's shame, expected to amount to little more than the sin that had made him. Because he did not, could not, and would not *care.*

Not that he did now, he assured himself. Not really. But whatever this was inside him—with its deep claws and driving lust, with its mad obsession over a woman who had tried to leave him twice today already—it was too close. Much closer than it should have been. It pumped in his blood. It made him hard. It made him *want.*

It was outrageous. He refused to allow it any more traction. *He refused.*

"Ready one of the motorboats," he said in a low voice, and heard a burst of action behind him, as if the yacht's entire staff had been poised on a knife's edge, waiting to hear the order. "I will fetch her myself."

He detected a note of surprise in the immediate affirmative answer he received, because, of course, he was Cayo Vila. Something he had clearly lost sight of today. He did not collect women or employees, they were delivered to him, like any other package. And yet here he was, chasing after this woman. Again. It was impossible, inconceivable—and even so, he was doing it.

So there was really only one question. Was he going out to drag her back onto the yacht and continue to tolerate this ridiculous little bit of theater until he got what he wanted? Or was he going out there to drown her with his bare hands, thereby solving the problem once and for all?

At the moment, he thought, his narrowed gaze on her determined figure as it made its stubborn way through the sea, away from him, he had no idea.

"Are you going to get in the boat? Or are you so enjoying your swim that you plan to make a night of it?" Cayo snapped from the comfortable bench seat in the chic little motorboat where he lounged, all dark and dangerous above her.

Dru ignored him. Or tried, anyway.

"It is further to the shore than it looks," he continued in that same clipped tone. That mouth of his crooked in one corner, though there was nothing at all like a smile about it. "Not to mention the current. If you are not careful, you might very well find yourself swept all the way to Egypt."

Dru kept swimming, feeling entirely too close to grim. Or was that *defeated?* Had she truly kissed him like that? *Again?* Cadiz had been one thing. He had been so different that night, and it had seemed so organic, so excusable, given the circumstances. But there was no excuse for what had happened today. She knew how little he thought of her. *She knew.* And still, she'd kissed him *like that.* Wanton and wild. Aching and demanding and hot—

She would never forgive herself.

"Egypt would be far preferable to another moment spent in your company—" she threw at him, but he cut her off simply by clicking his fingers at the steward who operated the sleek little vessel for him. The engine roared to life, drowning out whatever she might have said next.

Dru stopped swimming then and trod water, watching in consternation and no little annoyance as the small craft looped around her, leaving her to bob helplessly in a converging circle of its wake. She got a slap of seawater in the face, and had to scrub at her eyes to clear them. When she opened them again, the engine had gone quiet once more and the boat was much too close. Again. Which in turn meant that *he* was much too close. How could she be in the middle of the sea and still feel so trapped? So hemmed in?

"You look like a raccoon," he said in his blunt, rude way. As if he was personally offended by it.

"Oh," she replied, her voice brittle. "Did you expect that I would maintain a perfectly made-up face while swimming for my life? Of course you did. I doubt you even know what mascara *is.* That it requires application and does not, in fact, magically appear to adorn the eyelashes of whatever woman happens to gaze upon you."

It took far more strength than it should have to keep from rubbing at her eyes again, at the mascara that had no doubt slid off her own lashes to coat her cheeks. *It doesn't matter,* she snapped at herself, and found she was surprised and faintly appalled at the force of her own vanity.

"I don't want to think about your mascara or your made-up face," he replied in that deceptively smooth voice of his, the one that made her bones seem to go soft inside her skin. "I want to pretend this day never happened and that I never had to see beyond the perfectly serene mask you normally wear."

"Whilst I, Mr. Vila, could not possibly care less about what you want."

That amused him. She could see his version of laughter move across that fierce, fascinating face, a kind of light over darkness. She had to swallow against her own reaction, and told herself it was the sea. The salt. The exertion. Not him. Not the aftereffects of a kiss that the water should have long since washed away.

God, she was such a terrible liar.

"What you do and do not care about," he replied in a voice gone smooth and sharp, like finely honed steel, "are among the great many things I do not want to know about you." His hard mouth crooked into a cold, predatory version of a smile. Dru would have preferred to come face-to-face with a shark, frankly. She reckoned she would have had far more of a chance. "I know you are perfectly capable of discerning my meaning, Miss Bennett. I'll wait."

Dru was treading water again, and while the words she wanted to hurl at him crowded on her tongue, she gulped them back down, a bit painfully, and reviewed her situation. The truth was, she was tired. Exhausted. She had used up all her energy surviving these last years; she had precious little of it left, and what she did have she'd wasted on this contest of wills with Cayo today.

As if to underscore that thought, another wave crashed into her face, making her choke slightly and then duck down beneath the water. Where, for just a second, she could float beneath the surface and let herself feel how broken she was. How battered. Torn apart by this confusing day. By the long years that had preceded it. By kisses that never should have happened and the brother who never should have left her like this. She felt her body convulse as if she was sobbing there, underwater. As if she was finally giving in to it all.

It had been too much. Five long years of worrying and working and imagining bright futures that she'd never quite believed in. Not fully. But she'd tried. When Dominic was free of his addictions, she'd told herself. When she worked so hard because she wanted to, not because she had to. She'd dreamed hard, and convinced herself it could happen if she only worked hard enough. She'd dreamed her way out of her rotten childhood into something brighter, hadn't she? Why not this, too?

And then had come that terrible day when she'd received the news that Dominic was dead. She'd had to trail Cayo through a manufacturing plant in Belgium, acting as if her heart hadn't been ripped from her body and stamped into oblivion half the world away, not that Cayo had noticed any difference. Not that she'd let him see it. She'd made certain that all of Dominic's bills and debts were paid, while a squat and encompassing grief hunkered down on her, waiting. Just waiting. She'd ignored that, too. She'd reasoned it was her *job* to ignore it, to pretend she was perfectly fine. She'd taken pride in her ability to be perfect for Cayo. To fulfill his needs no matter what was happening to her.

Reading that email early this morning in London and seeing her years with Cayo for the sham they really were had landed the killing blow. It was the final straw. And part of her wanted simply to sink like a stone now, deep into the embrace of the Adriatic, and be done with all of this. Just let it all go. Hadn't Dominic done the same, at the end of the day? Why shouldn't she? What was she holding on to, anyway?

But Cayo would think it was all about him, wouldn't he? She knew he would. And she couldn't allow that. She simply couldn't.

She kicked, hard, and shot back up to the surface and the sun, pulling in a ragged breath as her gaze focused on Cayo. He still sat there, noticeably irritated, as if it was no matter to him whether she sank or swam, only that she was disrupting his afternoon.

Somehow, that was galvanizing.

She would not go under again, she understood then, as she stared up at him, at this man to whom she'd sacrificed herself, day in and day out, thanks to her own rich fantasy life. She would not break, not for Cayo, not for anything.

How could she? She was already broken.

And there was a strength in that, she thought, wiping the water from her face and pretending she didn't feel a heat beneath her eyes that indicated it was not entirely the sea she was scrubbing away.

I promise you, Dominic, she thought fiercely, her own little prayer, *I will walk away from this man at long last and I will take you to Bora Bora the way you always wanted. I'll give you to the wind and the water the way I swore I would. And then we'll both be free.*

So she swallowed back the bitter words she would have liked to throw out to make herself feel better about just how much of a fool she'd been and swam over to the side of the boat. She reached up to grip the edge of it. Cayo shifted, moving that taut, tense body of his even closer. He was more furious than she'd ever seen him. She could feel it as easily as she felt the sun far above, the sea all around.

"Fine," she said, tilting her head to look up at him as if none of that bothered her in the least. "I'll get in the boat."

"I know you will," he agreed silkily. *Furiously,* she thought. "But while I have you here, Miss Bennett, let's talk terms, shall we?"

Dru let go of the gunwale with one hand and used it to slick her hair back from her face. The twist she'd carefully created this morning in London was long gone now, and she imagined that the dark mass of her hair hung about her like seaweed. Happily, she was certain that Cayo would deeply disapprove of it. That little kick of pleasure allowed her to simply raise her brows at him and wait. As if none of this hurt her. As if *he* didn't hurt her at all.

"I imagine that this entire display was a calculated effort to get me to recognize that you are, in fact, a person," he said in that insufferable way of his, so very patronizing, that Dru would not have been at all surprised if it had left marks.

"How good of you to ignore almost everything I actually said," she murmured in a similar tone, even as she eyed him warily.

"I will double your salary," he told her as if he hadn't heard her.

Dru was forced to calculate how very much money it was that he was offering her, and wonder, for the briefest treacherous second, if it was truly necessary to escape him... But of course it was. She could stay with him, or she could have her self-respect, whatever was left of it. She couldn't have both. Today had certainly proved that.

There were so many things she wanted to say, but the way he looked at her made Dru suspect that if she said any of them, he would leave her in the water. She knew exactly how ruthless he could be. So she only held on to the side of the small motorboat, bobbing gently along with it in the rise and fall of the waves, and watched him.

"I'm cold," she said crisply, because there were minefields in every other thing she might have thought to say. "Are you going to help me into the boat?"

There was a brief, intense sort of moment, and then he leaned over, slid his hands beneath her arms, and hoisted her up and out of the water as if she weighed no more than a child. Water sluiced from her wet clothes as her feet came down against the slippery bottom of the small boat, and she was suddenly aware of too many things. The sodden fabric of her skirt, ten times heavier than it should have been, wrapped much too tightly around her hips and thighs. The slick wetness of her blouse as it flattened against her skin in the sea breeze. The heavy tangle of her wet hair, tumbling this way and that in a disastrous mess. All of which made her feel much too cold, and, oddly, something very much like vulnerable.

But then she looked up, and the air seemed to empty

out of her lungs. And she did not have to see his eyes to know that he was staring at the way her soaking-wet clothes molded to her curves, and, a quick glance down confirmed, left nothing at all to the imagination. Her blouse had been a soft gray when dry, but wet it was nearly translucent, and showed off the bright magenta bra she'd worn beneath.

Dru couldn't process the kaleidoscope of emotion that shifted through her then: chagrin, embarrassment, that horrible vulnerability, those underwater sobs threatening to spill out once again. She looked longingly at the sea once more, and if she hadn't been so cold she might well have tossed herself right back into it.

"Don't even think about it," he gritted out, and then several things happened simultaneously.

The boat lurched forward, no doubt in response to some signal of Cayo's, and Dru would have toppled against him had he not grabbed her around the waist and deposited her on the pristine white cushions next to him. She had the impression of his strength and heat, and there was that wild, desperate surge of desire inside of her that made her hate herself anew, and then she was sitting beside him as the boat headed toward the boarding deck of the great yacht, wet skirt itchy and awful against her and her hair flying madly in the wind.

Cayo did not speak again until they were safely back on board, and one of his silent and expressionless crew members had draped a very warm, very large towel over her shoulders. She aimed a grateful smile at the head steward as she wrapped the soft towel tight around her, and then felt very much like the poster child for *Les Misérables* when she directed her attention back toward her former employer. Pathetic and bedraggled whilst Cayo, naturally, gazed down at her like some kind of untouchable Spanish god, all of his dangerous beauty gleaming in the last of the day's sun.

The crew members disappeared as if they could see the coming storm closing in on them. If she had had any sense at all, she would have done the same. Instead she stood there and waited, her back straight as a ruler and her expression, she hoped, as serene as possible when she was still so wet and wrecked. Cayo slid his sunglasses down his haughty blade of a nose and regarded her with a glint in those dark gold eyes that should have cowed her at fifty paces—and he was much closer than that.

"I'm sure you know precisely where there are extra clothes on this yacht," he said quietly. She didn't trust that tone. It suggested great horrors lurking beneath it. "I suggest you avail yourself of them. Then come find me. We will behave like civilized, professional people. We will discuss the terms of your continued employment in more detail. And we will pretend that the rest of this day never happened."

Dru forced a smile. She told herself she was entirely uncowed.

"I was cold and wanted to get out of the water," she said. "I'm still quitting." She shrugged at his incredulous expression. "I can either tell you what you want to hear and then disappear at the first available opportunity, or I can be honest about it and hope you'll let me leave with some dignity. Your choice."

He was looking at her as if he had long since destroyed her with the force of that incinerating gaze alone, and was looking at some ash remnant where she'd once stood. She gazed back at him, and told herself the goose bumps were only from the cold.

"Surely we left dignity far behind today, you and

I," he said in a very low voice that seemed to shiver through her, or maybe she simply shivered in response, she couldn't tell.

"Your choice remains the same," she managed to say as if she hadn't noticed. As if it didn't matter. As if this was easy for her and she didn't feel something far too much like a sob, like despair, clogging the back of her throat. "Dignity or no."

For a moment, there was no sound but the ocean breeze, and the waves against the hull of the yacht.

"Go clean yourself up, Miss Bennett," Cayo said then, so softly, dark and menacing and his accent too intense to be anything but furious, and it all should have scared her. It really should have, had there been any part of her left unbattered. Unbroken. "And we'll talk."

But when Dru walked into the luxurious, dark-wood-paneled and chandeliered study that was part of his expansive master suite some time later, she was not, she knew very well, "cleaned up" in the way that he'd expected. He was standing at his desk with his mobile phone clamped to his ear, talking in the brusque tone that indicated he was tending to some or other facet of his business. She could probably have figured out which facet, had she wanted to, had she listened attentively as she would have done automatically before— but she didn't want to do any of the things she'd done before, did she? They'd all led her here. So instead, she simply waited.

And she wasn't surprised when he turned to look at her and paused. Then scowled.

"I must go," he said into the phone and ended the call with a jerk of his hand, all without taking his eyes from her.

A stark, strained moment passed, then another.

"What the hell are you wearing?" he asked.

"I was unaware there was a dress code I was expected to follow," she replied as if she didn't understand him. "The last woman I saw on this boat, only an hour or so ago, appeared to be wearing dental floss as a fashion statement."

"She is no longer with us," he said, his eyes narrow and hostile, "but that does not explain why you are dressed as if you are…" His voice actually trailed away.

"A normal person?" she asked. She'd known he would not like what she wore, hadn't she? She'd chosen these clothes deliberately. She could admit that much. "Come now, Mr. Vila. This is the twenty-first century. This can't be the first time you've seen a woman in jeans."

"It is the first time I have seen *you* in jeans." His voice was hard then, as hard as the way he was looking at her. As hard as the way her pulse seemed to jump beneath her skin. It made goose bumps rise on her arms. "But I had no idea your hair was so…" Whatever flared in his gaze then made Dru's skin seem to stretch tight and then shrink into her. "Long."

Dru shrugged as if she was completely unfazed by him and moved farther into the room, settling herself on one of the plush armchairs that was angled for the best sea view through the broad windows. He had been right—she knew where all the extra clothes were stored. All the items that Cayo kept stocked for any unexpected female guests as well as the skeleton wardrobe he kept for both her and him should his business bring them here by surprise.

And by "Cayo kept stocked" she meant, of course, that she did.

After she'd washed away the sea and her own self-destructive reaction to him throughout this long day, particularly that mind-numbing kiss, she had toweled off and then opened up the little emergency suitcase that she'd had installed in the offices and residences he visited most often, scattered here and there across the globe.

Inside the case, a conservative gray suit was pressed in plastic, with two blouses to choose from, one in a pale pink and one in an understated taupe, and a change of underthings in non-racy, uninteresting beige. She'd packed pins for her hair and the proper tools to tame the wavy mess of it into professional sleekness. There was a small bag of her preferred toiletries and another of her basic cosmetics. There were sensible shoes that would go with anything and a black cashmere cardigan in case she'd felt called to appear "casual." She'd even packed away an assortment of accessories, all conservatively stylish, so she could look as pulled together as she always did even if she'd found herself on board thanks to one of Cayo's last-minute whims. She'd packed everything, in other words, that she could possibly need to climb right back into her role as his handy robot without so much as an unsightly wrinkle.

And she hadn't been able to bring herself to do it.

Instead, she'd let her hair dry naturally as she'd taken her time dressing, and now it hung in dark waves down her back. She'd found a pair of white denim jeans in one closet, much more snug than she liked, which was only to be expected given the gazelle-like proportions of most of his usual female guests, and a lovely palazzo top in a vibrant blue-and-white pattern in another, which was loose and flowy and balanced out the jeans. She'd tossed on a slate-gray wrap to guard against the sea air now that evening was upon them and the temperature had dropped, and had left her feet and her face entirely bare.

She looked like...herself. At last. Yet Cayo stared at her as if she were a ghost.

"Is this another version of throwing yourself overboard, Miss Bennett?" he asked, his voice a lash across the quiet room. It made her heart leap into a wild gallop in her chest. "Another desperate bid for my attention?"

"You are the one who wanted to talk, not me," she replied, summoning a cold smile from somewhere though she didn't feel cold at all. Not when she was near him. No matter what he did. "I would have been perfectly happy to remove myself from the glare of your attention. For good."

That muscle in his lean jaw moved, but nothing else did. He was like a stone carving of simmering rage.

"What if I triple your salary?" His voice was cold and yet grim, his dark eyes flat and considering. "Did you say you lived in a leased bedsit? I'll buy you a flat. A penthouse, if you like. Pick the London neighborhood you prefer."

So much of her longed to do it. Who wouldn't? He was offering her an entirely different life. A very, very good life, at the price of a job she'd always liked well enough, until today.

But...then what? she asked herself. Wasn't what he suggested really no more than a sterile form of prostitution, when all was said and done? Give herself over to him, and he would pay for it. And she would do it, she knew with a hollow, painful sort of certainty, not because it made financial sense, not because she stood to gain so much—but because she longed for him. Because he would be using her skills and she would be dreaming about *one more night* like the one in Cadiz. *One more kiss* like the one today. What would become of her after five more years of this? Ten? She'd put Miss Havisham to shame in her bought-and-paid-for London flat, tarting herself up every day in her corporate costume to better please him, his favorite little automaton....

She could see it all too clearly and it made her feel sick. It would be easier if she could simply do it for the money, the way she had when this had started. But she was too far gone. At least, she thought now, she knew it. Surely that was something. A first step.

"I don't want to live in London," she told him. She lifted a shoulder and then dropped it. She ignored the way her stomach twisted, and that howling, broken-hearted part of her that wanted him any way she could have him. Even now. Even like this. "I don't want a flat."

"Where, then?" He raised a brow. "Are you angling for a house? An estate? A private island? I think I have all of the above."

"Indeed you do," she replied. It was almost comforting to pull up all of that information she knew about him and his many and varied assets—until she remembered how deeply proud she'd always been that she so rarely had to consult the computer to access Cayo's details. It was yet more evidence of how deeply pathetic she was. "You have sixteen residential properties, some of which are also estates. You also own three private islands, as well as a modest collection of atolls. That's at last count. You do always seem to acquire more, don't you?"

Cayo leaned back against the wide desk that stretched across the center of the room as if it were a throne he expected to be worshipped upon and crossed his arms over his chest, and she couldn't deny the intensity of that midnight stare. She felt it like fire, down to the bar soles of her feet. Her toes curled slightly in response, and she flexed her feet to stop it. And still he merely watched her, that gaze of his dark and stirring, and she had no idea what he saw.

"Pick one." It was a command.

"You can't buy me back," she said, her own voice just as quiet as his. Just as deliberate. "I don't want your money."

"Everyone has a price, Miss Bennett." He rubbed at his jaw with one hand, a considering light in his unnerving eyes. "Especially those who claim they do not, I usually find."

"Yes," she said, shifting in her chair as a kind of restlessness swirled through her. She wanted to fast forward through this, desperately. She wanted to be on the other side of it, when she'd already found the strength to defy him, had walked away and was living without him. She wanted this done already; she didn't want to *do* it. "I know how you operate. But I have no family left to threaten or save. No outstanding debts you can leverage to your advantage. No deep, dark secrets you can threaten to expose or offer to hide more deeply. Nothing at all that can force me to take a job I don't want, I'm afraid."

He only watched her in that way of his, as if it made no difference what she said to him. Because, she realized, it didn't. Not to him. He was immoveable. A wall. And maybe he even enjoyed watching her batter herself against the sheer iron of his will. She wouldn't put anything past him. Desperation coursed through her then, a hectic surge of electricity, and Dru couldn't sit still any longer. She got to her feet and then eased away from him, as if by standing she'd ceded ground to him.

"Miss Bennett," he began in a voice she recognized.

It was the voice he used to mollify his victims before he felled them with a killing blow. She knew it all too well. She'd heard it in a hundred board rooms. In a thousand conference calls.

She couldn't take it here, now. Aimed directly at her.

"Just stop!" she heard herself cry out. There was an inexorable force moving through her, despair and desperation swelling large, and she couldn't seem to do anything but obey it. She faced him again, her hands balling into fists while a scalding heat threatened the back of her eyes. "Why are you doing this?"

"I told you," he said impatiently, so cold and forbidding and *annoyed* while she fell into so many pieces before him. "You are the best personal assistant I've ever had. That is not a compliment. It is a statement of fact."

"That might be true," she managed to say, fighting to keep the swirl of emotion inside her to herself. "But it doesn't explain this." When he shifted his weight as if he meant to argue, because of course he did, he always did, she threw up her hands as if she could hold him off. "You could replace me with fifteen perfect assistants, a fleet of them trained and ready to serve you within the hour. You could replace me with anyone in the entire world if you chose. There is absolutely no reason for any of this—not three years ago and not now!"

"Apparently," he said coldly, "your price is higher than most."

"It's insane." She shook her hair back from her face, ordered herself not to burst into tears. "You don't need me."

"But I want you." Harsh. Uncompromising.

And not at all in the way she wanted him. That was perfectly plain.

It was as if something burst inside of her.

"You will never understand!" She stopped trying to hold herself back, to keep herself in check. What was the point? "There was someone I *loved*. Someone I lost. Years I can never get back." She didn't care that her voice was as shaky as it was loud, that her eyes were wet. She didn't care what he might see when he looked at her, or worry that he might suspect she was talking about more than her brother. She had given herself permission to do this, hadn't she? This was what *flappable* looked like. "There is no amount of money you can offer me that can fix the things that are broken. Nothing that can give me back what I lost—what was taken from me. *Nothing.*" Nor, worse, what she'd given him, fool that she was. She heaved a ragged breath and kept on. "I want to disappear into a world where Cayo Vila doesn't matter, to me or anyone else."

She wanted that last bit most of all.

And in a cutting bit of unwelcome self-awareness, she accepted the sad truth of things. He didn't have to offer her flats or estates or islands. He didn't have to throw his money at her.

If he'd said he wanted her and meant, for once, that he wanted *her*...

If, even now, he'd pulled her close and told her that he simply couldn't imagine his life without her...

There was that little masochist within, Dru knew all too well, who would work for him for free, if only he wanted her like that.

But Cayo didn't want anyone like that. Especially not her. She could tell herself he was incapable of it, that he'd never known love and never would—but that was no more than a pretty gloss on the same ugly truth. She understood all of that.

And still, she yearned for him.

"You have made your point," he said, after a strained moment.

"Then, please. Let me go." It was harder to choke out than it should have been. She hated herself for that, too.

For a moment she thought he might, and her stomach dropped. *Disbelief,* she lied to herself.

There was that odd light in his fascinating eyes—but then his face seemed to shutter itself and darken, and he straightened to his full height, the better to look down at her. And she reminded herself that this was Cayo Vila, and he let nothing go. He never bent. He never compromised. He simply kept on going until he won.

She couldn't understand why she couldn't seem to breathe.

"You owe me two weeks," he said, as if he were rendering a prison sentence. "I intend to have them. You can do your job for those two weeks and fulfill your contractual obligations to me, or I'll simply keep you with me like a dog on a leash, purely out of spite."

But he didn't look spiteful. He looked something far closer to sad, and it made her stomach twist. Again. And that terrible longing swelled again inside her, making her ache. Making her wish—but her wishes were dangerous, and they tore her into tatters every time. She shoved them aside.

Cayo smiled, as if from far away, hard and wintry.

"Your choice, Miss Bennett."

CHAPTER FOUR

HE SHOULD HAVE been happy—or at the very least, satisfied.

Cayo lounged back against his chair and gazed around the white-linen-draped table that stretched the length of the formal dining room in the Presidential Suite of the Hotel Principe di Savoia in Milan, surveying the small dinner he'd had Drusilla throw here in one of Europe's most prestigious spaces. The rooms of the vast suite gave the impression of belonging to royalty perhaps, so stunning were they, all high ceilings, carefully selected antiques and the finest Italian craftsmanship on display at every turn. Wealth and elegance seemed to shimmer up from the very floors to dance in the air around them.

The investors were duly impressed, as expected. They smoked cigars and let out loud belly laughs over the remains of the last of the seven courses they'd enjoyed. Their pleasure seemed to ricochet off the paneled mahogany walls and gleam forth from the impressive Murano glass chandeliers that hung above them, in resplendent reds and blues, and would no doubt be reflected in the size of their investments, as planned. This would be another success, Cayo knew without the smallest doubt. More money, more power for the Vila Group.

And yet all he could seem to concentrate on tonight was Drusilla.

"Fine," she had thrown at him on the yacht, those gray eyes of hers both furious and something far darker, her mouth very nearly trembling in a way that had made him feel restless. Unsettled. "I'm not going to play this game with you any longer. If you want your two weeks, you'll have them—but that's the end of it."

"Two weeks as my assistant or my pet," he'd reiterated. "I don't care which."

She'd laughed, and it was a hollow sound. "I hate you."

"That bores me," he'd replied, his gaze hard on hers. "And furthermore, makes you but one among a great many."

"By that you mean, I imagine, the entire world?" she'd sniped at him. Her tone, the way she was standing there with her hands in fists—it had made him suspicious.

"I'd suggest you think twice before you attempt to sabotage me in some passive-aggressive display in your last days with me, Miss Bennett," he'd cautioned her, and the look she'd turned on him then should have flayed him alive. Perhaps it had. "You won't like the result."

"Don't worry, *Mr. Vila,*" she'd said, his name a low, dark curse, hitting him in ways he didn't fully understand. "When I decide to sabotage you, there will be nothing in the least bit passive about it."

She'd stalked away from him that afternoon, and he hadn't seen her again until the following morning, when she'd presented herself in his suite at breakfast, dressed in the perfectly unremarkable sort of professional clothes she usually wore. No skintight white jeans licking over her long legs to taunt him and remind him how they'd once clenched over his hips. No wild gypsy hair to shatter his concentration and invade his dreams. She'd sat herself in a chair with her tablet on her lap, and had asked him, as she'd done a thousand times before, with no particular inflection or agenda, if his plans for the day deviated from his written schedule.

As if the previous day had never happened.

If he didn't know better, he thought now, watching her through narrowed eyes, he could almost imagine that nothing had changed between them at all. That she had never quit, that he had never forced her into giving him her contracted two weeks.

That they had never kissed like that, nor let their tempers flare, revealing too many things he found he did not wish to think about, and too much heat besides.

Almost.

Tonight she looked as professional and cool as ever, with the prettiness he could no longer seem to ignore an enviable accent to her quiet competence. She wore a simple blue sheath dress with a tailored jacket that trumpeted her restrained and capable form of elegance, her trademark. She operated as his right hand in situations like this, his secret weapon, making it seem as if he was not giving a presentation designed to result in lavish investments so much as sharing a fascinating opportunity with would-be friends.

She made him seem far more engaging and charming than he was, he'd concluded over the course of the long evening, and wondered how he'd never seen that quite so clearly before. She gave him that human touch that so many furious and defeated rivals claimed he lacked.

He'd watched her do it tonight—lighting up the carefully selected group of ten investors with her attention, making them talk about themselves, letting them each feel interesting and important. *Valued.* She hung on their words, anticipated their questions, soothed them and laughed with them in turn, all of it in that cool, intelligent way of hers that seemed wholly authentic instead of cloying. They ate her up.

And because of her, Cayo could simply be his ruthless, focused self, and no one felt overly intimidated or defensive.

She sat at the far end of the lavishly appointed table now, her tablet in her hand as always, periodically tapping into it as she fielded questions and tended to the various needs of everyone around her. She made it look so easy. She was smooth and matter-of-fact, as if it was only natural that the French businessman should demand a Reiki massage at two in the morning and it *delighted* her to be able to contact the concierge on his behalf. She was his walking computer, his butler, and, if Cayo was honest, his true second-in-command. Smart, dependable, even trustworthy. He should have encouraged her to leave him three years ago when she'd wanted that promotion. She could have been running companies for him by now. She was that good.

Which was, of course, why he'd been so loath to let her do it.

Or one reason, anyway, he thought now, darkly impatient with himself. He idly fingered his wineglass as he half pretended to pay attention to the conversation that swelled around him. Not that anyone expected him to charm them, of course. Or even be particularly polite, for that matter. That was Drusilla's job.

She is magnificent, he thought, and ignored the sud-

den pang that followed as he considered how soon she
would be gone. How soon he would have to think up a
new approach, a new game to get what he wanted from
investors like this without her deft touch, her quiet, almost invisible support.

And how soon he would have to face this stubborn
thing in him he didn't want to acknowledge: how little
he wanted her to leave, and his growing suspicion that
it was far less about business than he was comfortable
admitting. Even to himself.

"Trust me, Mr. Peck," he heard her say to the self-
satisfied gentleman on her left, heir to what remained
of a steel fortune in one of those smaller, ugly-named
American cities, making the man puff up as if she was
sharing a great confidence, "this is the sort of meal that
will change your life. Three Michelin stars, naturally.
I've made you a reservation for tomorrow at nine."

She straightened then, and her gaze met his down the
length of the table, with all of the investors and cigar
smoke and concentrated wealth in between them. It was
as if the rest of the room was plunged into darkness, as
if it ceased to exist entirely, and there was nothing but
Drusilla. Nothing but the searing impact of their connection. And he saw the truth on that pretty face of hers
he could now read far too well. He felt it kick in him, as
if she'd reached across the table, over the remnants of
the feast they'd all shared and the money they'd won,
and landed a vicious blow with the nearest blunt object.
A hard one, directly into his solar plexus.

She hated him. He hadn't thought much of it when
she'd said it, as so many people had said the same over
the years that it was like so much white noise. But he
was beginning to believe she actually meant it. And
more, that she thought he was a monster.

None of that was new. None of it was surprising. But this was: he knew full well he'd acted like one.

He'd do well to remember that.

Much later that night, the investors were finally gone, off to their own debaucheries or beds or both, and Cayo found he couldn't sleep.

He prowled through the suite's great room, hardly noticing the opulence surrounding him, from the paintings that graced the walls of the vast, airy space to the hand-blown light fixtures at every turn and breathtaking antiques littered about. He pushed his way out onto the terrace that wrapped around the suite, offering commanding views across Milan. The spires of the famous Duomo in the city center pierced the night, lit up against the wet, faintly chilly dark. On a clear day the Alps would be there in the distance, snowcapped and beautiful, and he had the fanciful notion he could sense them out there, looming and watchful. But he could see nothing at all but Drusilla. As if she haunted him, and she hadn't even left him yet.

Monster, he thought again, the word on a bitter loop in his head. *She thinks you are a monster.*

He didn't know why it mattered to him. Why it interfered with his rest. But here he was, scowling out at a sleeping city in the dead of night.

He couldn't stop running through the events of the past days in his head, and he hardly recognized himself in his own recollections. Where was his famous control, which made titans of industry cower before him? Where was the cool head that had always guided him so unerringly and that had caused more than one competitor to accuse him of being more machine than man? Why did he care so much about one assistant's resignation that he'd turned into…this creature who roared and threatened, and abducted her across the whole of Europe?

It was just as his grandfather had predicted so long ago, he thought, the long-forgotten memory surfacing against his will, still filled with all of the misery and pain of his youth. He moved to the edge of the terrace and stood there, unmindful of the wet air, the cold, the city spread out before him. And then he found himself thrust back in time and into the place in the world he liked the very least: his home. Or more precisely, the place he'd been born, and had left eighteen years later. For good.

The entire village had predicted he would come to nothing. He was born of sin and made of shame, they'd sneered, as often to his face as behind his back. Look at his mother! Look how she'd turned out! A whore abandoned and forced to spend the rest of her days locked away in a convent as penance. No one would have been at all surprised if his own life had followed the same path. No one would have thought twice if he'd ended up as disgraced and shunned as she had been before she'd disappeared behind the convent walls.

No one had expected Cayo Vila to be anything more than the stain he already was on his family's name.

In fact, that was all they expected of him. That was, the whole of the small village and his grandfather agreed, his destiny. His fate. That was what became of children like him, made in disgrace and summarily discarded by both his parents.

And yet, despite this, he had tried so hard. His lips curled now, remembering those empty, fruitless years. He'd wanted so badly to *belong,* since he'd first understood, as a small boy, that he did not. He'd obeyed his grandfather in all things. He'd excelled at school. He'd worked tirelessly in the family's small cobbler's shop, and he'd never complained, while other boys his age played *fútbol* and roamed about, carefree. He'd never fought with those who threw slurs and insults his way— at least, he'd never been caught. He'd tried his best to prove with his every breath and word and deed that he was not deserving of the scorn and contempt that had been his birthright. He'd tried to show that he was blameless. That he belonged to the village, to his family, despite how he'd come to be there.

He'd really believed he could sway them. That old current of frustration moved through him then, as if it still had the power to hurt him. It didn't, he told himself. Of course it didn't. That would require a heart, for one thing, and he had done without his for more than twenty years. Deliberately.

"I have done my duty," his grandfather had said to him on the morning of his eighteenth birthday, almost before Cayo had been fully awake. As if he'd been unable to wait any longer, so great was the burden he'd carried all these years. "But you are now a man, and you must bear the weight of your mother's shame on your own."

Cayo remembered the look on his grandfather's stern face, so much like his own, the light in the dark eyes as they met his. It had been the first time in his life he'd ever seen the old man look anything close to happy.

"But, *abuelo*—" he had begun, thinking he could argue his case.

"You are not my grandson," the old man had said, that terrible note of finality in his voice. His grizzled old chin had risen with some kind of awful pride. "I have done what I must for you, and now I wash my hands of it. Never call me *abuelo* again."

And Cayo never had. Not when he'd made his first million. Not when he'd bought every piece of property in that godforsaken village, every house and every field, every shop and every building, by the time he was twenty-seven. Not even when he'd stood over the old man's bed in the hospital, and watched impassively as the man who had raised him—if that was what it could be called—breathed his last.

There had been no reconciliation. There had been no hint of regret, no last-moment reversals before death had come to claim the old man three years ago. Cayo had been thirty-three then, and a millionaire several times over. He had owned more things than he could count. A small Spanish village tucked away in the hills of Andalusia hardly registered.

He had not seen himself as any kind of stain on the village's heralded white walls as he'd been driven through the streets in the back of a Lexus, and he very much doubted that any of the villagers mistook him for one. They'd hardly dare, would they, given that he'd held their lives and livelihoods in his hand. He had not seen himself as having anything to do with the place, with the Cadiz province, Andalusia, or even Spain itself, for that matter. He had hardly been able to recall that he had ever lived there, much less felt anything at all for the small-minded people who had so disdained him—and were now compelled to call him landlord.

"Not you!" his grandfather had wheezed, surfacing from his final illness only briefly, only once, to stare at Cayo in horror. It had been some fifteen years. *"Ay dios mio!"*

"Me," Cayo had confirmed coldly, standing at the foot of the hospital bed.

The old man had crossed himself, his hands knotted with arthritis, frail and shaking. Cayo had been unmoved.

"The devil is in you," this man who shared his blood had croaked out, his voice a faint thread of sound in the quiet room. "It has always been in you."

"My apologies," Cayo had said. His voice had been dry. Almost careless. What could such a small, shriveled husk of a man do to him now? It had seemed almost like a dream that he had ever had the power to hurt Cayo. Much less that he had succeeded. "I was your duty then, and it seems I am now your curse."

As if he'd agreed entirely, the old man had not spoken another word. He'd only crossed himself again, and had soon thereafter slipped away.

And Cayo had felt absolutely nothing.

He hadn't let himself feel much of anything since he'd walked out of that village on his eighteenth birthday. On that day, he'd looked back. He'd mourned what he'd believed he'd lost. He'd *felt*. Betrayed. Discarded. All the many things a weak man—a boy—felt. And when he'd finally pulled himself together and accepted the fact that he was alone, that he'd never been anything but alone and never would be again, he'd brushed himself off and shut down the pathetic part of him that still clung to all those counterproductive *feelings*. He'd left his heart in the hill town of his youth, and he'd never had cause to regret that. Or, for that matter, notice its lack.

So he had felt nothing when he'd walked into the hall where Drusilla had waited, her expression carefully neutral as befitted a personal assistant well paid to have no reaction at all to anything in her boss's life. He'd felt nothing on the long drive back to his hotel in Cadiz City, down from the mountains with their Moorish villages and out toward the Costa de la Luz, like a trip through his own memories. He'd felt nothing throughout the rest of that long night, though the *manzanilla* had first loosened his tongue and then, later, had him kissing Drusilla against a wall in a narrow walkway in the old city, lifting her high against him so her legs wrapped around his hips, drowning himself in the honeyed heat of her mouth, her kiss.

Nothing at all.

Her lips had enchanted him, full and slick against his. And that lithe body, those sensual curves, the spellbinding slide of her against him. He was hard again, remembering it, as if he was still on that dark city street three years ago instead of in a chilly Milan night, here, now. And that treacherous heart he'd thought he'd trained to know better beat out a rhythm that made him question things he shouldn't. Made him *want* so hard, so deep, it began to feel more like *need*. He bit out a blistering Spanish curse that had no discernible effect at all, and rubbed his hands over his face.

Whatever this was, whatever terrible madness that was taking him over against his will and beyond his control, it had to stop.

Madre de Dios, but it had to.

Dru shivered as the cold air hit her, pulling her wrap tighter around her and wishing she'd dressed for bed in something more substantial than the champagne-colored silk pajamas the presidential suite's dedicated butler had produced along with the outfit she'd worn at the dinner. She'd been trying to sleep for hours. She'd been lying in her bedroom, glowering at all its opulence as if the gold-and-cream Empire-style chairs or gilt-edged scarlet chaise were to blame for her predicament.

Why had she given in to him? Why had she agreed to work through the two weeks he'd demanded? It had been two days since she'd backed down and she still couldn't answer herself. Not satisfactorily. Not in any way that didn't make her hate herself more. Finally, she'd given up, and decided to take in some fresh air.

Outside, the night was damp. The overcast sky made the darkness feel fuller, somehow, while the city lights twinkled softly all around. It was beautiful. Like everything Cayo touched, everything he did. Like Cayo himself. And as cold.

She'd stayed because it was the quickest, easiest solution, or so she'd spent the past two days telling herself. Escape from Cayo meant subjecting herself to this and really, what was two more weeks? It had been five years. Two weeks would fly by, and that would be the end of it. Done and dusted.

The problem was, she knew better. On some level, she was relieved. As if this was a reprieve. As if Cayo might come to his senses and redeem himself—

She despaired of herself and this faith she had in him, so desperately misplaced. She truly did. How could she trust herself to be strong enough to walk away from him again when it had been so hard the first time? What made her think she could really do it in two weeks' time when she'd failed so spectacularly now?

"If you throw yourself from a height like this, I think you'll find the Piazza della Repubblica will provide somewhat less of a cushion than the Adriatic," he said from the shadows, making Dru jump. She clapped her hands to her chest as if she could force her heart to stop its panicked clamoring, whirling around to gape at him as he bore down upon her. "All the king's horses and all the king's men, and so on."

He looked dark and brooding, and, as if to taunt her, distractingly, impossibly sexy. He wore a luxurious-looking navy silk robe he hadn't bothered to pull closed over the sort of male underclothes that clung black and tight to acres of his taut thighs, making him look like a heart-stopping combination of an underwear model and a king. Dru's mouth went dry. It was one thing when he swanned about in his five-thousand-pound suits. It was another when he wore what passed for casual attire, all of which seemed to emphasize his athleticism, his masculine grace. But this… This was something else.

This was a fantasy come to life. *Her* fantasy, in fact. Suddenly, she was acutely aware that she was hardly dressed, that the silk pajamas caressed her skin with every breath, that she felt more naked than if she'd actually been unclothed, somehow. She felt heat wash over her, then spread, the flush of it rolling all through her body, like his touch.

And it didn't matter how angry she was at him, how foolish she felt or how betrayed. In the middle of the night, on a terrace in Italy, Dru was forced to admit the fact that she had never truly got a handle on just how devastatingly attractive Cayo was, or how much it had always affected her. Even before that night in Cadiz City.

"I didn't know you were out here," she said, and she could hear it in her voice, that slight quaver that gave her away. That all but shouted the things she didn't want to admit to herself and certainly didn't want him to know. How she melted for him, even now. How she ached in all the places she wished he would touch her with those capable hands, that difficult, addicting mouth. Her lips, her breasts. And that hunger between her thighs.

It was as if the dark, or the late hour, made it impossible to lie to herself any longer.

He tilted his head very slightly to the side as he drew close, studying her face. He'd been even colder and more distant than usual at dinner, prompting Dru to truly question her sanity and self-respect when she'd found herself *worrying* about him. What did that say about her, that even now, abducted and threatened and coerced, she took time out from her righteous indignation to worry about the man who'd done all of those things? *To her?*

Nothing good, she knew. Nothing healthy. No wonder she couldn't sleep.

"Here we are again in the dark," he said, a curious note in that deep voice of his. His face was even fiercer in the shadows, hardly lit up at all by the light spilling out from within, but still the dark amber of his eyes seemed to sear into her.

She didn't know what he meant. She felt his words resonate in her, and the exquisite ache that followed in their wake made her despair of ever really leaving this man, ever really surviving him.

"I didn't mean to disturb you, Mr. Vila." But her voice was a jagged rasp of sound, and it gave her away. It told him everything, she was sure of it. Angry, exhausted tears flooded her eyes, shaming her as much as they infuriated her. She blinked them back, glad for the excuse to look away from him.

He reached over and touched her, his hand hard and warm on her upper arm. Dru froze; afraid, suddenly, to meet his gaze. Afraid he would see all of the confusion and attraction and hurt she so desperately wanted to hide. Instead, she pretended to be vastly interested in her hair, of all things, in the ponytail she'd pulled it into and then drawn to the side and over her shoulder. She ran her hands over it, nervously. But he only moved his hand to wrap his fingers around the length of it himself, pulling gently on the silken length, tilting her head up to face him before letting go.

Something sharp and near enough to sweet pierced through her then, taking her breath. Maybe this was only a dream. Maybe this was nothing but another one of those Cayo dreams she'd wake from in such a panic in her tiny bedsit, gasping out loud while her body ached, alone and frustrated and wild with so much emotion she could never release.

But she knew better.

"Tell me," he said, his voice low and still so powerful, filling her up, making her resolve and determination feel far too flimsy, far too malleable. Making her wish she could simply be angry with him, and stay that way. "Why do you really want to leave me?"

He didn't throw it at her. He asked. That and the damp night surrounding them made it different, somehow. Made her look at him as if here, in the deepest part of the night, he might be close enough to the man she'd believed him to be that she could actually tell him a part of the truth.

But she blinked again, and the heat in her eyes reminded her who he really was.

"Why are you so determined I should stay?" she asked quietly. "You think so little of me. You believe I am good for nothing but a position as your assistant forever."

His hard mouth moved, though it was not a smile. "There are those who would kill for that privilege."

He was so close, the sheer masculine poetry of his beautiful torso *right there* and seemingly impervious to the chill, and it was astonishingly hard for Dru to keep her attention where it belonged.

And the fact that she still couldn't control her response to him—that it was as powerful now as it had been all along, as it had been three years ago—made her shiver, as if her body could no longer pretend it was unaffected. How else would she destroy herself, she wondered then in a kind of anguish, before this was done? How else would she sacrifice what mattered to her, her very self, on the altar of this man?

"I assume it was a punishment?" She searched his face, her heart plummeting as she saw what she always saw and nothing more. That implacable ruthlessness of his, that fierce beauty. As unreachable as the stars above her, concealed tonight by the clouds.

He frowned. "Why would I punish you?"

She felt her brows rise in disbelief. "Cadiz. Of course."

He made an impatient noise.

"Surely we have enough to discuss without beckoning in every last ghost," he said, but there was that odd note in his voice again. As if he did not believe himself, either.

"Just the one ghost." Her eyes never left his. "It was one little kiss, didn't we agree? And yet you punished me for it."

"Don't be absurd."

"You punished me," she repeated, firmly, despite the scratchiness she could hear in her voice. "And you were the one who started it."

He had done more than start it. He had ignited them both, set them afire. He'd had his arm thrown around her, and she'd been pleasantly full of *tortitas de camarones* and *calamares en su tinta,* Spanish sherry, and the heady knowledge that after the two years she'd been working for him, Cayo had finally shown her that there was more to him than his ruthless demands, his take-no-prisoners style of doing business. She'd smelled the hint of his expensive scent, like leather and spice, felt the incredible, hard heat that emanated from his skin beneath his clothes, and the combination had made her light-headed. She'd felt for him, and that heartbreaking scene with his grandfather. She'd ached for what he'd been through, what it had done to him. He'd *talked* to her that night, really talked to her, as if they were both simply people. As if there was more to them than the roles they played, the duties they performed.

It had been magical.

And then Cayo had swung her around, backing her up against the nearest wall. She'd seemed to *explode* into him, as if she'd been waiting for exactly that moment. He'd muttered words she didn't understand and then his mouth had been on hers, as uncompromising as anything else he did. All of that fire, all of that need, had rolled through her like a tempest, and she'd lost herself. She'd lost her head. It had been slick and dizzy and terrifyingly right and she'd found herself wrapped around him, her legs around his hips as he pressed that marvelous body of his against hers, his mouth plundering hers, taking and taking and taking—

It kept her up at night. Still.

"There was no punishment." Cayo's low voice snapped Dru back into the present.

His clever eyes probed hers in the dark, as if he could see straight into her memory, as if he knew exactly what it did to her even at three years' distance. As if he felt the same heat, the same longing.

As if he, too, wished they hadn't been interrupted three years ago.

The laughing group of strangers further down the walkway had drawn near. He'd set her down on her feet, gently. Almost too gently. They'd stared at each other, both breathing hard, both dazed, before continuing on to their hotel, where they'd parted in the hall outside their rooms without a word.

And they'd never discussed it again.

"Then why...?"

He raked a hand through his hair. "I didn't want you to leave," he said, his voice gruff. "There was no hidden agenda. I told you, I don't like to share." He blew out a breath, and when he spoke again, it was with an edge. "You are an integral part of what I do. Surely you know it."

She shook her head, unable to process that. The layers of it. What she knew he meant and, harder to bear, what she so desperately wanted him to mean instead. He was talking about work, she reminded herself fiercely, even as he looked at her with that fire in his dark amber eyes. He was always talking about work. For Cayo, there was nothing else. Why couldn't she accept it?

It was too much. It hurt.

"What are you so afraid of?" she asked before she could think better of it. Before she could question whether she wanted to hear the answer. "Why can't you just admit what you did?"

He scowled at her, and she thought he might snap something back at her, but he didn't. For a moment he looked torn, almost tortured, however little sense that made. The city was so quiet around them, as if they were the only people alive in the world, and Dru found herself biting down on her lower lip as if that smallest hint of pain could keep her anchored—and keep her from saying the things she knew she shouldn't.

This time, when he reached for her, he used the back of his hand and brushed it with aching gentleness over her cheek, soft and impossibly light, sending the hint of fire searing through her like the faintest kiss, until Dru's next breath felt like a sob.

"You're cold," he said, again in that gruff voice. That stranger's voice that nevertheless made her feel weak.

And she was chilly, it was true. She was trembling slightly. Uncontrollably.

If he wanted to think that was the cold, she wouldn't argue.

"Get some sleep," he ordered her, his eyes too dark, his mouth too grim.

And when he left her there, shaky and on the verge of more tears she hardly understood, her mind spinning as wildly as it had so long ago in Cadiz, it almost felt as if she'd dreamed it, after all.

Almost.

CHAPTER FIVE

CAYO WAS IN A FOUL temper. He sipped his espresso, as harsh and black as his current mood, and eyed Drusilla over the top of it when she appeared at breakfast the next morning.

He had spent what was left of the night chasing the ghosts of his past out of his head, and failing miserably. Now, in the bright morning light, the opulence of the suite's great room like a halo all around her, Drusilla looked her usual, sleekly professional self—and he found it profoundly irritating. Gone was the woman he'd been unable to keep from touching on the terrace in the dark, her hair out of that ubiquitous twist she favored and so soft across her shoulder, wrapped up like a sweet-smelling gift in silk and soft cashmere. Gone as if she had been no more than a particularly haunting dream.

And still, he wanted her. Then. Now. In whatever incarnation she happened to present him with.

"We are going to Bora Bora," Cayo announced without preamble. "Have the butler order you the appropriate wardrobe."

He might have panicked, he thought with something like black humor, if he knew how. If he'd ever experienced something this confounding before. As it was, he only watched her walk toward him, and told himself that the pounding desire that poured through him was nothing more than resentment. Lack of sleep. Anything but what he knew it was.

She paused before dropping gracefully into the seat opposite him at the small table near the windows where he'd taken his breakfast, and he saw a host of emotions he couldn't quite identify chase across her face in a single instant before she smoothed it out into her customary neutrality.

That annoyed him, too.

"Has something happened with the Vila Resort there which requires your personal attention?" she asked, her voice as calm and unruffled as the rest of her—as if last night she hadn't sounded so uneven, so breakable. As if she hadn't spoken to him the way she would to the architect of her despair. As if he hadn't touched her like that, as though she were fragile. Precious, even.

What are you so afraid of? he heard her ask again, and it made something inside him seem to tear itself in half.

"It is a part of the Vila Group," he replied, in a voice far short of civility. "It all requires my personal attention."

Her too-knowing gray eyes met his, held for a moment, then dropped to the tablet she'd placed on the table before her. She smiled when the hovering staff placed a large silver pot of tea before her, and waved away the offer of food. And for some reason, her silence felt like a rebuke.

"We leave tonight," he said, his tone still clipped, though markedly more polite than it had been. He didn't know why he was responding meekly instead of as he'd prefer, which involved hauling her up and into his arms and dealing with all of this sexual tension once and for all. No matter what she thought of him—or what he thought of himself, for that matter. "Consider it my gift to you for your years of service, if you must."

Something flared in her gaze again, then disappeared behind that smooth, calm wall of hers he found he liked less and less the longer he looked at it. He wondered if it was as hard for her to maintain that courteous, professional veneer as it was becoming for him to keep his hands off her.

He rather doubted it.

"Will this 'gift' count as part of my final two weeks?" she asked lightly, though when her gaze met his, it hinted of steel. "Because that's all the time you have left, Mr. Vila. No matter what you choose to do with it."

"You said it was where you wanted to go," he reminded her, furious—at her for not accepting what he was reluctant to admit was an olive branch, and at himself for offering it in the first place. But something in the way she'd looked at him last night had burrowed deep beneath his skin. He could feel it now, like an impossible itch.

"Yes," she agreed softly. "I want to go to Bora Bora." She raised one delicate shoulder and then let it fall. "I never said I wanted to go with you."

That sat there between them.

There was no reason at all, Cayo reasoned, that it should feel like a slap when he could see clearly that she was only being frank. He already knew what she thought of him. Hadn't she been at such great pains to make sure of it? No matter how different it might have appeared in the dark last night? He shouldn't be surprised, if that was what this odd feeling was. He wasn't.

"Life," he said after a moment, his accent thicker than it should have been, almost as if his temper was high, which wasn't in the least bit rational, "is all about compromise."

"Really?" she asked. Her eyes searched his, and she looked somewhere between amused and genuinely baffled, which somehow made it worse. "How would you know?"

Cayo tossed back the rest of his espresso and decided he was tired, that was all. There was no deeper reason for any of this. How could there be? He hadn't slept. That was why his head was so muddled. Why he could not seem to sort through his own thoughts, his own motivations. Nor even his own reactions.

"I am finding it difficult to track all of your accusations," he said after a moment, his tone dry. Almost conversational. "You believe I am a sociopath, yet last night you told me I am also afraid. Today I am unfamiliar with compromise. Before, I was Godzilla, was I not?" He was fascinated by the color that rose in her cheeks, and then equally intrigued by the way she squared her shoulders, as if withstanding an attack. "I believe I take your meaning, Miss Bennett. I am a monster without equal."

Monster. It was only a word, he told himself then, as it seemed to echo hard in him, recalling that whitewashed village high in the Spanish mountains, his grandfather's harsh pleasure on his eighteenth birthday. *It is just a word. It means nothing.*

"You are a man who assumes that his will is sufficient permission to do anything he likes," Drusilla said slowly, as if she were considering each word carefully. "There are no consequences for the things you do." She reached for her tea, and poured a stream of the hot liquid into the delicate cup before her. Her gaze flicked to his, then away. "It would never occur to you to care."

He wanted to touch her with a new kind of fury, so intense was his desire to feel her skin against his. To take that mouth of hers and learn it, own it, make it his. To follow her down onto the nearest flat surface and lose himself inside her, at last.

But he did nothing of the kind. He held on to his control by the faintest, thinnest thread. Again.

"Of course not," he said coldly, as if there was nothing steaming up the air between them, as if there were no tension at all, no desire, no *need.* He reached for the *Financial Times* folded beside his plate and told himself he was dismissing her as he'd always done before, without thought. Without a single care, as accused. "That's what I pay you for."

It was a remarkably long trip.

I didn't want you to leave, he'd said.

Dru couldn't stop replaying it in her head, again and again. She handled the packing, the delivery of appropriate clothes for Cayo from the Milan ateliers he preferred and her own hurried selections from La Rinascente, the city's premier department store hardly a stone's throw from the Duomo. She sent out a flurry of emails, made the day's series of phone calls, and carried out the usual duties of her job, accustomed as she was to performing it wherever she happened to find herself.

But she couldn't seem to get last night out of her mind. The chill of the air, the inky dark and his hand so soft against her cheek. That storm in his midnight gaze that had crashed through her, too. That still did. Why should a few quiet words and a couple of touches affect her so? Why should she feel as if everything was different, when nothing seemed to have changed at all?

They boarded one of Cayo's jets in Milan late that evening, and Dru made her way to her usual bedchamber. She stretched out on the bed and dared not let herself succumb to the turmoil inside herself, not when there was still the rest of her two weeks to live through. She couldn't let herself crack so soon. She'd never survive.

When she woke hours later, they simply went to work as if they were in the Vila Group's London headquarters rather than on a plane headed across the planet. She sat right there at his side in the area set apart for business. She queued up his calls, handling the many details of each, presenting him with the necessary documents and background materials he needed, and reminding him of anything he might have forgot or overlooked as the calls wore on. She prepped the various people who rang in, alerting them to Cayo's shifting moods and often suggesting ways to combat them. Between calls, they discussed various strategies to employ or different approaches to take to tackle each new issue or person.

"I'm tired of his games," Cayo said of one mutinous board member at one point, raking his hands through his hair in agitation. "I want to end him."

"That's one approach." Dru removed a stack of documents from in front of him and replaced them with another, larger stack. "Another might be to simply work around him the way you did with the Argentina project last year. Isolate him. Who will he play his games with then?"

Cayo eyed her for a moment, an approving gleam in his dark gaze that should not have given her so much pleasure.

"Who indeed?" he asked softly.

Dru made sure his coffee was always hot and fixed to his taste, and insisted that he eat something substantial after a certain span of time, simply serving him a meal if he refused to step away from the work at hand. When his voice took on that particularly icy edge that boded only ill, she calmly suggested he repair to the master suite to either rest or work out his temper on the exercise equipment that flew with him everywhere. She was on top of their travel plans, too; making certain that there was not the smallest chance that Cayo Vila should find himself inconvenienced in any small way, no matter where he was in the world or what he had to do. All of which she'd done a million times before.

But it wasn't the same.

Something really had changed last night, and it permeated even their most simple exchanges. The very air between them seemed electric, charged. Her hand brushed his and they both froze. She looked up from her tablet to find him watching her, a brooding sort of expression in those dark eyes of his, the gold in them gleaming in a way she didn't recognize. But she *felt* it. In her breasts, deep in her belly. In her limbs that were too heavy today, her breath that she couldn't quite catch.

It made her wonder. It made her too hot, too shivery, *too aware.* It made her want—again, anew—what she could never have.

Some seventeen hours into the almost twenty-four-hour trip, plus refueling stops, and they had worked roughly nine of them. Hardly half a day's work in Cayo's book, Dru knew. They took a break, sitting in the common area of the plane. Dru sipped at her water and knew better than to ask why Cayo was watching her with that new, disconcerting light in his eyes. Dark

and considering, as if he had never seen her before.
As if that strange, dream-like conversation on the terrace in Milan really had shifted something fundamen-
tal between them. That, she was sure, was why she felt
almost watery, insubstantial. Needy and breathless. Unable to think about anything but Cayo, in all the ways
she shouldn't.

"Why Bora Bora?" he asked. "When I suggested
you take a holiday, I assumed you'd go to Spain. Por-
tugal, perhaps. This seems like something of a reach."

Dru rolled the water bottle between her palms, letting the cold glass soothe her, letting the sound of the
engines wash over her like white noise.

"Why *not* Bora Bora?" she asked lightly. "If working for you has taught me nothing else, it's to demand
the best in all things."

"Indeed." Some fire flared there, in that golden topaz
gaze, and for a moment she couldn't look away. Then
his lips quirked into a hard sort of smile, sardonic and
faintly amused. "I'm delighted to discover you take indolence as seriously as you take everything else."

"Perhaps all I want from life is to sit under a palm
tree and stare at the sea," she said, though the very
thought was faintly unnerving, somehow.

"And be waited upon hand and foot?" he asked, a
note in his voice she couldn't decipher.

She thought of Dominic's ashes, packed away in the
tin that functioned as an urn and sat in the center of her
bookshelf back in London. And of the promises she'd
made, to him and to herself. That she would let him go
into the wind, the water. The least she could do was
honor the man he might have been, had he made different choices, or been stronger against his own demons.

And she knew that she needed it, too. The closure. The ceremony. A way to let go, once and for all.

"Something like that," she said now, not quite meeting Cayo's eyes.

He didn't believe her. She could see it in the way he shifted in his deep leather seat, as he scraped that thick, black hair back from his brow.

"How debaucherous." It was a taunt. And it hit hard, though she should have been impervious to him.

"I leave that kind of thing to you, Mr. Vila," she snapped.

Unwisely.

Everything seemed to pull taut. There was no air, no sound. Dru had the panicked sense that the plane had dropped from the sky—but no, Cayo did not move a muscle, it was only in her head. She felt her heart thud hard against her chest, then slow, and she could not seem to look away from him, from that hard mouth of his that she could not pretend she didn't crave. From that dangerous light in his eyes as he stared back at her.

"Is that a challenge, Miss Bennett?" he asked softly, that voice rolling through her, turning all of that need into an ache, insistent and sweet, burning her from the inside out. His cruel mouth moved into a hard smile, and she felt it like a caress. "I will endeavor to live up to your fantasies."

Did he know? Dru felt herself flush. Did he know what kept her awake—what tormented her, what she could see all too clearly even now—that delicious fusion of what had happened in Cadiz and on the yacht and what she imagined came next—

"But first," he continued in that silky, supremely dangerous tone, his gaze narrow on hers even as he gestured toward his phone again, "let's close this deal in Taiwan."

Dru felt hollowed out and more than a little light-headed with jet lag, not to mention her own much too vivid imagination, when they finally made it to what she assumed was Bora Bora, but which could have been anywhere for all she was able to discern in the thick, heavy dark.

The helicopter they'd taken after their landing in Tahiti set down in a small field lit with tall tiki torches. The night was close and warm, sultry against her skin. She could smell the sea and the deep green of wild, fragrant growing things. The sweetness of flowers hung heavy, like perfume against the dark, and when she tipped her head back to watch the helicopter fly away again, she had to stifle a gasp at the brilliance of the stars that crowded the night sky. The roar of the helicopter faded, leaving only a deep tropical hush behind. It seemed to arrow into her soul.

"Come," Cayo ordered her impatiently, and strode off.

Porters appeared from the darkness to handle the bags, and Dru followed Cayo over a wooden walkway, lit with more torches and hemmed in on all sides with lush greenery. Even in the dark, Dru could all but taste the burst of *jungle* all around her. Cayo was ahead of her, his long legs eating up the distance and before she knew it, she was hurrying—matching her stride to his, just as she'd always done.

Just like the dog on a leash he'd threatened to make her, a small voice inside of her pointed out. She shook it off.

Cayo stopped walking before a large Polynesian-style house with high, arched rooftops and wide, open

windows that stretched the length and width of the
walls, featuring pulled-back sliding shutters and un-
obstructed views.

And on the other side of the walkway was water.
Nothing but dark water, lapping gently against the
shore, and off in the distance, a smattering of low lights.
Dawn was coming, bluing the inky night. Dru could
make out a mountain in front of her, off on its own island across the water, black and high.

"This is the villa," Cayo said.

He looked down at her as she drew closer to him,
his ruthless face softened, somehow, by the soft tropical dark. Or perhaps she was only being fanciful. The
torch lights surrounded them in a halo of golden light,
and somehow made it seem as if they were standing
even closer together than they were. As if there was
nothing else in the world but the two of them, adrift in
all this lushness.

"I don't know why you would ever leave a place
like this," she said, trying to shift the focus back to
the place. Away from the two of them. She smiled, but
suspected it looked as nervous, as unsettled, as she felt.
Still, she pushed on. "But perhaps it takes a different
kind of imagination to conquer the world from this far-
off little corner of it."

And suddenly he was too close, though she hadn't
seen him move. He loomed above her, his shoulders
wider than they should have been and his chest too
broad, and he was too close for Dru to breathe, too close
for her to do anything but lose herself in the dangerous
amber of his gaze.

Her pulse went crazy beneath her skin. Her mouth
went dry. And she felt that long, low ache between
her legs.

His hard gaze slammed into hers, as if he meant to hold her there with the force of it. And sure enough, Dru found she couldn't move.

"Don't speak to me like I'm another one of those investors," he said fiercely. Almost angrily. "Don't expect me to dance to your tune simply because you make a bit of cocktail conversation."

He was right, she had been doing exactly that—and she hated that he'd seen it so clearly. That he'd seen *her*. She'd always thought she'd wanted that but the truth of it terrified her. It was her job to read him, not the other way around. Never the other way around!

"My apologies," she bit out. "I won't point out your lack of imagination again."

He didn't speak. He only reached over and dragged his thumb across her lips, testing their shape, and it wasn't a soft touch, a lover's caress. It was starkly, undeniably sexual. If she hadn't known better, if it hadn't been impossible and unthinkable, Dru would have said he was staking his claim. Imprinting her with his touch, as he might brand cattle or stamp a logo onto a product. Leaving his mark.

She should have slapped his hand away. Instead, she burned. Long and slow and deep.

The way she always had. The way she always would.

"Believe me," he said, and his voice was so soft and still so demanding. So consuming. A thread of sound in the sultry night, surrounded by flickering golden light and the wild, incapacitating staccato of her own heartbeat. "My imagination grows more vivid by the hour."

Dru's lips felt as if they were on fire, and she could feel his touch all through her body, coursing through her veins, even after he dropped his hand and eased away. Her heart didn't stop its frantic beating. Her mouth was

still so dry, her stomach in a knot. She felt him everywhere. And for a long moment, he only looked at her,
his dark eyes hot and shrewd and that cruel mouth impassive.

And even that felt like a touch, and with the same
result.

Cayo turned then to greet the smiling man who approached them, from inside the villa Dru realized she'd
forgot about entirely. When he looked back at her, his
gaze was too dark to read.

I didn't want you to leave, he'd said on the terrace in
Milan, half a world away now. And still it rang in her,
through her, like a bell. *I still don't.*

She wanted that to mean something. She *wanted.*
And she could still feel his touch moving through her,
making her his as surely as if he'd tattooed his name
on her skin in the blackest ink.

You're tired and overwrought, she told herself, fighting back another surge of heat behind her eyes. *Nothing
will feel like this in the morning. It can't.*

"You look exhausted," Cayo said, his gaze moving
over her face, making her imagine he could read her
every thought that easily. He nodded, as if coming to
some kind of decision, and the way his mouth curved
then looked self-mocking. "Frederic will show you to
your rooms."

And then he walked away, disappearing into the
thick night.

Leaving her to make sense of what was happening
to her—to them—on her own.

Fighting off emotions she couldn't understand, much
less process, Dru obediently followed Frederic through
the villa. There were tall, vaulted ceilings and the same
rich, dark wood she'd seen outside. Airy, spacious

rooms without proper windows, simply cut-out spaces in the walls to let in paradise on all sides. Bright-colored wall hangings, low and inviting sofas in magentas and creams. Polynesian artifacts on built-in shelves in the walls, and glorious flowers scattered across ornamental tables. She followed Frederic down a level and then outside again. They walked along another, far shorter path that delivered her to a private bungalow splayed out over its own private pier. Here, too, the walls were open to the night, letting the softest of breezes into the expansive suite. Dru couldn't seem to breathe deeply enough to take it all in.

And again—still—all she wanted to do was dissolve into the tears she knew were waiting for her and cry herself dry. Cry until she couldn't feel this anymore, whatever this was: Cayo and the dark and that touch, imprinted on her skin. Claiming her.

With a smile, Frederic showed her the glass floor hidden away beneath a rug in the sitting area.

"In the day," he promised, "you will see many fish. Even turtles."

"Thank you," she whispered, summoning her smile from somewhere.

"Sleep now," the man said kindly. "It will be better when you sleep."

And she wanted to believe him. She did.

Everything felt too huge, too unwieldy, she thought when he left. Her own head. This place. Cayo, of course. Cayo most of all. It all felt impossible, and painful. It hurt from the inside out. She moved over to the opening across from the four-poster bed draped in filmy mosquito netting from high above, and looked out at the water and the smudge of orange light behind the mountain in the distance. Daybreak was coming. And she was in paradise with the devil, and she burned for him as if she'd already fallen. Perhaps she had. Perhaps that was why this had hurt so much from the start.

There was no reason at all she should cry now. She wiped away the tear that tracked its way down her cheek. And then all the ones that followed. She felt her face crumple in on itself, and had to pull on reserves she hadn't known she had to breathe through it—to fight back the sobs that she knew lurked *just there* and would be the end of her.

She must not give in. *She must not start.* It was only two weeks, and less than that now. She needed to be strong only a little while longer.

Oh, Dominic, she thought as she crawled on to the bed, not even bothering to change out of the clothes she'd been wearing across several continents and more time zones than she could count. *I wish you could see this place. It's even better than you dreamed.*

Her last thought as she drifted off into blessed unconsciousness was of Cayo. That mesmerizing curve of his hard, impossible mouth. The touch of his hand in the cold, wet dark, so hot against her chilled skin. That unquenchable fire that burned ever hotter, ever brighter by the day, no matter how she tried to deny it. No matter how hard she fought. He would destroy her. She knew it. She'd always known it—it was one of the foremost reasons she had to leave him.

So there was no reason at all that she should be smiling against the soft white pillows as she drifted off into oblivion.

CHAPTER SIX

DRU WOKE TO sunshine on all sides. It streamed in the open windows of her room, bathing her in light and the sweet, fragrant breeze. It felt like some kind of blessing, chasing away what shadows remained from the long night before. She stretched luxuriously on the soft mattress and told herself she was fine now. Fully restored. Cayo's touch, his talk of debauchery, that fire that only seemed to build between them—it was all part of a darkness dispelled. She was sure of it.

She rose from her bed and dressed slowly, in deference to the sultry weather. She pulled on a loose and flowing pair of linen trousers and paired them with a strappy black vest. Then she swept all of her hair up into as sleek a ponytail as was possible in this climate. The result, she thought, frowning at herself in the mirror, was as close to tropical and yet professional as she was likely to get. She slipped on a pair of thonged sandals and stepped outside, where it appeared to be well into a perfect afternoon.

Dru blinked in the brightness and took in her surroundings. There was another pier down from her bungalow with a selection of small watercraft drawn up to it and on the shore nearby. She could see water in all directions, a darker blue on the far side of the island and

that stunning turquoise beneath her bungalow in what
must be the famous Bora Bora Lagoon.

She walked back into the villa and was struck anew
by the beauty she'd only partially registered last night.
The dark wood, the high ceilings to draw up the day's
heat, all of it exposed to the tropical paradise and thus
a part of it, too. The jungle pressed in on all sides, with
the sea just beyond. It felt as wild as it did welcoming,
and made something in her seem to ease as she stood
there.

When she finished eating a simple meal of toast and
tea out on one of the many terraces overlooking the
water, she felt restless. Cayo typically did not expect her
to rush to work after a long-haul flight unless he had
explicitly stated otherwise, so she didn't feel she had to
seek him out at once. She assured herself any employee
would feel the same—that it had nothing to do with all
the churning emotion he'd stirred in her the night before. *Nothing at all.* Instead, she wandered down to the
wooden path and followed it. It ran down to the pier,
then on, making its lazy way down to the farthest point
of the island and then looping back around.

Palm trees rustled over her head and bright flowers
bloomed jubilantly on either side of the tidy boardwalk.
She could hear birds up above and the waves against the
shore. It made perfect sense to her that Dominic would
have wanted this to be his final resting place. The sun
was warm on her face, the breeze a caress against her
skin. She felt serene. At peace.

All you needed was a good night's sleep, she told
herself firmly.

As the villa came into view again, perched up over its
own gleaming white beach, she saw there was a whole
section of it she'd yet to explore. It was not until she

left the path and climbed up for a closer look that she realized that what looked like a separate wing was, in fact, Cayo's master suite.

The wide-open walls meant she could step inside too easily and so, giving in to an urge she didn't recognize, she stepped into the first of the rooms, and then sucked in a sharp breath. It was an airy space appointed with deft masculine touches, bold colors and clean lines, but the centerpiece was the massive bed that dominated the room. *Cayo slept here last night,* a little voice whispered. Or perhaps more recently, as it was still unmade, the snowy white coverlet tossed to one side, the pillows dented.

And suddenly, Dru went hot all over. Then cold. Almost as if she was feverish.

She reached over and traced the indentation in the nearest pillow with a fingertip. She imagined him naked and dark against the crisp sheets, that perfect, impossible body on display, her own body softening and melting at the pictures in her head—

It was clearly time to find the man—her boss, she reminded herself sharply—and concentrate on what remained of her time in this job, not on her incurable madness where he was concerned. Not on the way she burned.

She glanced at the art and small collections of statues and carvings as she made her way down the hall, peering into each room as she passed. There was a library fitted with a wall of books, a seating area within and a covered lanai outside with a plush loveseat and two armchairs—perfect for a read in the shade. There was a private lounge with a flat-screen television on one wall and a fire pit with a dramatic chimney on the other, and what looked like a built-in bar in the corner.

And then an office suite, kitted out with computers and other equipment, sleek modern furniture—and Cayo.

Dru stopped in the doorway, watching him as he frowned down at his laptop with his mobile clamped to his ear, as usual. His hair looked unruly, as if he'd spent hours raking it back with his fingers, and he'd neglected to shave. It made him look even more dark and sexy than usual. Unpredictable, somehow. Edgy.

"You misunderstand me," he was saying in cold, deadly French into his mobile. "It is no matter to me whether we ever open a plant in Singapore. But I suspect it is of great importance to you. Perhaps you'd like to rethink your tactics?"

He looked absurdly beautiful, as if someone had carved him into being from the finest stone and set him among lesser statues. He fairly gleamed in the golden sunlight streaming in behind him. He looked terrible and great the way the old gods might have, dangerous and mighty, and if he'd announced that he could command the weather at his whim, she would have believed it. The storm within her howled into being anew, the fever and the yearning, and he was to blame.

He raised his head then and met her gaze. Her stomach dropped and she stopped kidding herself about *serenity* and *a good night's sleep*. It was as if he was inside her, provoking her, making her ache and burn.

He looked at her as if she were naked and beneath him. And Dru couldn't help but wish she was, no matter how much she hated herself for her own eternal weakness.

Cayo sat back in his chair, his eyes on her as he finished the call with an abruptness that she knew must have made the man on the other end wince. He tossed his mobile on to the desktop in front of him and then regarded her, his golden eyes narrow and much too shrewd. His olive skin seemed darker against the loose white shirt he wore, making it impossible not to notice his lean, muscled arms and that perfect chest. Her breasts swelled against her vest. Her palms felt damp. And there was that same familiar ache, blooming into life so low in her belly.

Sleep or no sleep, she was doomed.

"Henri is still giving you trouble?" she asked, determined to ignore what was happening to her, what she felt. Desperate to concentrate on business instead.

"He remains unclear on the chain of command," Cayo replied, though the way he looked at her made her think he was not thinking of Henri or the Singapore project at all. "I think he has already convinced himself that I am not, in fact, the majority shareholder now."

"You expected that," Dru reminded him. She reached out a hand and touched the door frame next to her, running her finger over the dark wooden beam. The slightly rough texture made her feel even warmer, somehow, as if she was touching him instead. "You felt his personal connection with the employees and his decades of company loyalty far outweighed any tussles over authority you might have to have."

"So I did." He leaned against the arm of his chair and propped up his jaw in his hand, eyeing her in a way that made her keenly aware that he was one of the most powerful men in the world and she was…the only person she knew who had tried to defy him. "How do you find Bora Bora? Is it living up to your expectations?"

Dru couldn't seem to hold his gaze for more than a second at a time, and had no idea why. She felt…fluttery. It was as if he really had branded her last night with that odd, small touch in the dark, and she didn't know how to regain her equilibrium. Not when he was in front of her like this. Her lips seemed to tingle all over again, as if remembering. *Yearning.*

"I don't understand you," she said.

"That is hardly a breaking news item," he said dryly. "What is it you feel you need to understand? I am a simple man, when all is said and done. I like what I like." His hard mouth curved, his dark eyes gleamed gold. "I want what I want."

She ignored the way his voice lowered so suggestively, the images that it conjured before her and the wildfires it sent spinning over her skin. She dropped her hand to her side and nodded at the view behind him. An infinity pool lay on the far side of the patio, the water as smooth as glass, surrounded by more of the smooth dark wood, and beyond it, the endless sea. Yet Cayo sat with his back to it, more interested in his laptop computer, the documents spread out before him on the desk, the television on the wall tuned, as ever, to the financial news.

"You haven't been here in years." She knew she should walk to the desk, sit down, act appropriately and do her job, but she couldn't bring herself to move that close to him. Not so soon after the last two nights of all that savage intensity. Not yet. "Not in as long as I've worked for you."

"It was eight years ago, I believe," he agreed, that lean body much too still, as if he was deliberately leashing all of his power as he sat and watched her. As he *waited.* "When I bought the place from some Saudi prince or another."

Dru bit at her lip, that fluttery feeling twisting and suddenly too close to another surge of what felt like tears. As if it was impossible to be around him without all of this emotion welling up in her. She was afraid she might simply burst.

"I don't understand the point of owning beautiful things you never see." Her voice should have sounded casual. Easy. Not…raw. Wounded. She was supposed to be so good at this kind of thing! "And now that you're here for the first time in almost a decade, you're sitting inside in an office, working. Moving all your money and power about like an endless game of chess. Why bother collecting all these little pieces of paradise if you never plan to let yourself enjoy them?"

He looked at her for a beat, then another. And then that same look she'd seen the night before, as if he'd come to some kind of decision, gleamed in his eyes. A little chill snaked down Dru's back. Cayo moved from his chair, rising to his feet and prowling toward her.

Dru had to fight to stand still—not to break and run. He stopped when he was a foot or so away, and that cruel mouth of his, brutally sensual and entirely too dangerous, quirked slightly in the corner. Dru felt it like another touch, like the hand he'd pressed against her cheek in Milan, like his thumb across her mouth last night. Her blood seemed too hot in her veins, her skin felt too tight across her body, and when she reached over to grab the doorjamb again, it was because her legs were too weak to hold her upright.

And still, he only looked at her. Through her. Making the fire inside her leap high, burn white.

"I appreciate your concern," he said in that silky voice that teased along her oversensitive skin, moved like a shiver down her spine, and then made even her bones ache. "It's too bad you insist upon leaving me. We could play chess with my properties together."

"What a lovely idea," she said with a great insincer-

ity she took no pains to conceal, and which made him
look something close enough to amused. "But I am terrible at chess."

"I find that hard to believe." She thought he nearly
smiled then, gazing down at her. "You are always at
least six moves ahead. You'd excel at it."

She had the oddest sense of déjà vu for a moment and
then it came to her—he was talking to her like a person. Not as his employee, but as another human being.
Someone he actually knew. The last time he'd done this,
he'd teased her in just this way. They'd smiled. They'd
told stories, shared parts of themselves over small dishes
of food and large glasses of wine. Or she'd thought they
had. That had been that long dinner in Cadiz, before
their fateful walk home, and Dru couldn't stand her own
treacherous heart, the way it softened for him anew, as
if she didn't know exactly where moments like this led.
Precisely nowhere, with a three-year detour through infatuated subservience.

She could not let him reel her in. Not again.

"I'm not here to play games," she said quietly, hoping
he couldn't hear the unevenness in her voice, that clash
between what was good for her and what she wanted.
"I'm here to be your personal assistant. The only other
offer on the table was to be your dog. On a leash. Isn't
that what you said? Is that what you'd prefer?"

His gaze heated, becoming so molten she could
hardly bear it, though she didn't look away. His mouth
twisted. She remembered belatedly that he was much
too close, his potent masculinity and all of that restless, brilliant power of his bright and brilliant between
them, making her swallow hard. Making her feel too
hot, too weak, all at once.

"If you want to be my pet you must sit," he growled at her. Daring her. Commanding her. "Stay. *Surrender.*"

And the worst part was, she very nearly obeyed.

"I do appreciate the offer," Dru whispered when she could speak, but she hardly heard her own voice, lost as it was in the thunder of her heartbeat, the shriek and clamor of the storm only gaining strength inside her. "But I think I'll pass."

She should have moved—but she didn't. She only stood there, paralyzed, as Cayo closed the distance between them and stretched an arm up, over his head, to brace himself against the doorjamb and look down directly into her face.

She thought of old gods again, stunning and unpredictable, implacable and fierce. Something deep inside her seemed to go very, very still. He leaned there, propped up in the doorway, dark eyes and that sinful body, exuding the ruthlessness and command that made him who he was.

Worse than that, he looked at her as if he knew her at least as well as she knew him. As if he could read her as easily as she'd learned to read him. And the very notion was as terrifying—as impossible—as it had been before.

"Tell me," he said, his voice even lower, his golden amber eyes so hot she worried they might blister her skin or consume her whole. "What are *you* hiding from?"

For a moment, she looked almost as if he'd punched her in the stomach. But then she blinked, the mask Cayo had come to hate descended, and she even produced a strained sort of smile.

That might have irritated him, but he was done with this. He'd decided he would have her no matter what games she played, and he would lick that wall away if he had to. He looked forward to it.

"The only thing I've been hiding from today is our workload," she said brightly. Hiding, he knew. Right there in front of him. "Perhaps we should get to it."

"Forget about work," he growled, a sentence that had never crossed his lips before, perhaps not ever. And he didn't allow himself to consider the ramifications of that—all he could seem to concentrate on was the confusing woman in front of him. And how very much he wanted her, despite all the reasons he knew that was a bad idea. "We're in Bora Bora. Work can wait."

"I beg your pardon?" She looked unduly horrified.

"What's the point of being the boss if I can't decree a holiday on a whim?" he asked, striving for a lighter tone and, if that look on her face was any indication, failing. "Didn't you suggest I enjoy myself in paradise not five minutes ago?"

"To hell with the consequences, is that it?" she asked, throwing that back at him, and her eyes flashed as if she was angry with him. Which grated.

He didn't understand any of this. He didn't understand what was happening to him, and he certainly didn't understand why everything he said made her so unhappy, or so furious. Or both at once. Why she leaped from boats to escape him, then looked at him on a dark Italian terrace with all the world in her eyes and spoke of *punishment,* making him feel small three years later.

He was not a man who dealt well in uncertainties.

But what he did know was passion. Sex and desire. He had built his life around what he wanted. He knew *want.* And much as she claimed to hate him, much as she threw words or shoes at his head, he knew she wanted him as much as he wanted her. He could see it.

He'd always seen it, if he was honest with himself. And he was tired of fighting off the only thing that made sense in all of this.

"Consequences are for lesser men," he said.

He'd already decided. When he'd walked away from her last night despite the way he burned to take her, when he'd found himself handling his own brutal need alone in his shower, he'd known he was done with this. She was leaving him anyway. There was only so much complication that could occur in the time she had left. Why was he denying himself? He was not the kind of man who did without the things he wanted.

She blinked at his arrogance, but that was better. He didn't want the threat of tears, the sting of her temper. And he certainly didn't want that neutral wall of hers, designed to keep the world at an icy remove. He wanted heat. He wanted that fire again, and who cared anymore what burned?

"Come," he said. It was an order. He didn't pretend otherwise. "Kiss me."

Drusilla's eyes flew wide. One hand went to her throat. He imagined he could feel her pulse there, imagined it kicking against his own hand instead of hers. He wanted to press his mouth to her skin and taste her excitement for himself.

"What did you say?" Her voice was no more than a whisper.

"You heard me."

"I am not going to kiss you," she said, coming over all flustered and something like prim then, her gray eyes brimming with outrage.

Yet behind it, mixed in with it, that consuming, distracting heat that matched his. That called to him. That meant, he knew, that he already had her. It was only a matter of time.

"But you will, Drusilla," he promised her. "Trust me."

Dru didn't know why she wasn't running away from him.

Her heart pounded so hard it made her feel faint, everything inside her seemed to be in revolt, and yet she only stood there. Gazing back at him, while uncertainty and longing howled and fought and pooled between her legs in a hot pulse of desire.

"Don't call me that," she said instead of all the other things she could have said—*should* have said. What was the matter with her? Why couldn't she seem to summon the will to protect herself the way she should?

"Your name?" His eyes gleamed like gold. He was so close, so arrogant and sure, and it was harder and harder to remember all the reasons she shouldn't let herself fall over this particular cliff. All the reasons she shouldn't jump headfirst, for that matter.

"My mother is the only person who ever called me Drusilla," she found herself telling him as if she were not standing in this doorway torn apart by tension, while her body clamored for things she was afraid to look at too closely. And far more afraid to do. Or not do. She wasn't sure which scared her more. "And I have not laid eyes on that woman in at least ten years."

"Dru, then," he said, and it moved through her like honey, her name in his mouth. It set fires in her in places she hardly knew existed. It felt like a lock falling open, but she knew better than to give in to that. She knew better than to trust herself around this man. Look at what a kiss had wrought! "And I think you want to be on my leash, after all. Don't you?"

There was no denying the sensual intent behind that question. Or the frank appraisal in his eyes.

Or what it did to her.

The hall fell away. The world with it. There was only him. Only Cayo. Nothing but the exquisite tautness that wound around them, stealing her breath, making his eyes seem to glow. There were scarcely two feet between them and yet all she could focus on was his mouth and that carnal knowledge, that masculine certainty, in the way he looked at her.

She should have said something. Anything.

When she only gazed at him, fighting for breath, unable to speak, his eyes went dark with a need she was afraid she recognized all too well.

"Then come." Another order, which should have enraged her. His mouth curved into something sardonic—and impossibly sexy. Those wicked brows rose in challenge. "Heel."

She felt the words sizzle through her, white-hot and life-altering, and that was when she knew with a sharp burst of clarity that there was only one way this would end. She knew him, didn't she? Cayo's attention span when it came to the women who shared his bed was famously short. If she really wanted to leave him, if she really wanted to be free of this hold he seemed to have on her, then this was the way to do it. This was a one-way street. No turning back.

No matter what it cost her.

"Well?" he asked softly, taunting her.

Dru swallowed, hard. She held his gaze for a long moment, understanding that this was a line she could never uncross. That she had no idea, really, what giving in to this kind of inferno might do to her—the damage it might cause. She'd spent three years recovering from a kiss, after all. She couldn't imagine what this would do.

But it didn't matter now. He looked at her with that certainty in his eyes, that sheer male confidence and stark carnal promise, and she knew that she didn't have it in her to walk away from this. Not when she'd spent so long imagining it, fantasizing about it. Yearning for it with everything she had.

Who cares how you have him, so long as you do? a greedy voice inside her asked, and she didn't have it in her to disagree. She'd lost her will to fight somewhere high above the Pacific Ocean. She didn't have to lose herself, too. She wouldn't, she promised herself. This was a strategy, not a surrender.

She closed the distance between them, watching the light in his fascinating eyes burn ever brighter the closer she came. She slid her hands over the taut planes of his chest, reveling in his heat, his bold strength. There was no going back—but there was no way forward, either, without this. And the truth was that she wanted him. She always had. This way she could have everything— she could have Cayo in the way she'd dreamed of since Cadiz, and then her freedom in a little over a week. In every way that mattered, this was a victory.

It was, she assured herself, her gaze searching his. *It was.* But what she felt was that wild flame searing into her, burning through her, making all these things she clung to, all these things she told herself, so much ash.

"Please do not tell me that you intend to do all of this in tedious slow motion," Cayo said, that curve in his mouth telling her he was teasing her again and connecting hard to all the places that longed for him like this, for his touch, turning her fever for him ever higher. "I believe that is far more entertaining in films than in real life."

"For God's sake," she said, no longer his assistant, not in a moment like this. Not when they were changing everything, no doubt for the worse, and she couldn't even pretend to care about that as she should. "Shut up."

And then Dru stretched up onto her toes, plastered herself against the length of him, and doomed herself forever by pressing her mouth to his.

CHAPTER SEVEN

SHE TASTED THE way he remembered. Better. So hot and good and *his*.

Cayo's arms came around her, pulling her against him, into him, needing to feel the weight of her breasts against his chest, the softness of her belly against the thrust of his hardness, the gentle swell of her hips against his. He kissed her again and again, reveling in the punch of it. The kick.

And she met him. Her arms wrapped around his neck, her mouth moved against his with the same urgency, the same demand. He thought she said his name. He wasn't sure he could speak or if he did, what language he might use, or if it would all come out as nonsense. He didn't care.

She was intoxicating, and he could finally let himself indulge in her as he wished.

At last, he sank his hands into her dark hair, exulting in the feel of it, the scent. Warm silk and the faint hint of vanilla. He pulled out the band that held her hair and let the mass of waves fall around her shoulders. He angled his mouth for a better fit, gathering her closer, taking what he wanted, at last.

He smoothed his hands down the sensual curve of her back, then tested her pert bottom, making them both groan when he moved her against the thrust of his arousal. It wasn't enough. It was barely a start. He took and he took until she was gasping his name, breathing hard, and he had to rein himself in. Or have her right there in the hallway—and he had no intention of going too quickly.

Not with this woman. Not with Dru. Not when it felt as if he'd waited lifetimes for this. For her.

He moved to taste, briefly, the freckles the sun had already raised across the bridge of her nose, then traced the line of her cheekbone, her satiny cheek, her stubborn jaw. She smelled of coconut and flowers, and tasted like magic, and he could not seem to get close enough.

She made a small noise in the back of her throat, like a purr, and it nearly undid him. *Mine,* he thought, with a surge of possessive triumph. *All mine.*

He took her hand in his, marveling at how delicate she was, how perfectly formed. He led her down the hall, the afternoon sun still golden and shining through the windows of the rooms they passed, and he couldn't pretend he didn't feel victory thump through him like a drumbeat when she simply followed him like this, those gray eyes dizzy with want—very much like the docile, biddable female she had pretended to be for so many years, but wasn't. The surrender of a strong woman, he thought with pure male satisfaction, was so much more exciting than that of a weak one. He intended to revel in hers.

Once in his bedroom, he pulled her to him again, luxuriating in the feel of her in his arms. *Finally.*

He took her mouth again, kissing her anew as he maneuvered her toward the bed. When the back of her knees hit the mattress she pulled away and looked up at him, her breath coming too fast, her fathomless gray

eyes dark now and dazed with need, her pretty face soft
and flushed and *his*.

She was his.

Cayo didn't speak. He didn't counter his own uncharacteristic possessiveness, or even try. Nothing about
Dru had made sense so far, not since that rainy morning
in London when she'd changed everything he took for
granted. Why should this? He tugged the vest up over
her head, sliding it over all of that long, dark hair, and
smiled when he saw her royal blue bra and the round
breasts he'd only glimpsed through her wet blouse before now.

"Perfecto," he murmured, and leaned down to press
his mouth against the crest of one breast, sucking on it
through the thin, glossy material. Dru gasped, and so
he did the same with the other, waiting until her head
was thrown back and her eyes closed before he reached
around and unhooked the bra. She reached to pull it
from her arms and he bent and licked the closest nipple,
pulling it into his mouth.

And Dru went wild.

Cayo got lost in it then, in her. In her heat, her softness, her beautiful cries. He stripped her trousers from
her long, sleek legs, then that other scrap of satin and
lace. He hardly noticed as he shrugged out of his own
clothes, because it wasn't fast enough, it meant he
wasn't touching her, and it took entirely too long before
he was naked and she was sprawled across his bed the
way he wanted her, the way he'd wanted her for longer
than he'd been aware of it. This was no new need that
roared in him, demanding he take her again and again
until they were both sated. What moved in him felt old
and complicated, as if he'd hidden it from himself. But
he wasn't hiding any longer. He stretched out beside

her, propping himself up on one arm, fiercely satisfied to see her nipples were hard and her tattletale English skin was pink and rosy.

His.

She rolled as if she meant to begin exploring him herself, but he pressed her back down.

"But I want—"

"Sit," he murmured, tracing a finger down to her breast and toying with its peak, making Dru arch from the bed with a moan.

He bent to replace his fingers with his lips, and she cried out again, writhing beneath him as he tugged her nipple into the heat of his mouth even as he cupped her other breast in his hand. Then he kissed his way down the gentle swell of her abdomen, licking over her navel and the gentle curve of her hips. He learned she had a trio of small birthmarks near her left hip bone, and that she couldn't keep her hips still, especially when he held them between his hands and then curved his fingers around to test the shape and sweet, silken perfection of her bottom.

And then he parted her thighs and kissed his way even lower.

"Cayo—" she started again, naked passion in that voice, so full of *want* it made his hardness ache in response.

"Stay," he ordered her, and licked his way into her molten core, exulting in the fresh, hot taste of her desire.

She arched from the bed again, her hips rising to meet his mouth as he took her, tasted her, made her his. Unequivocally. And then she exploded all around him, sobbing out his name as she fell off the side of the world.

And it was not nearly enough.

He moved back up the bed, and pulled her to him,

then rolled them both, sitting up and lifting her so she sat astride him. He wanted to see her. He wanted to see everything.

"Cayo…" She whispered his name, her eyes fluttering open, to gaze at him as he pressed against the core of her.

She was wet and hot and soft, and he wanted her so badly he nearly shook with it. He held her bottom in his hands, lifted her, and watched as she shivered in turn when he slid himself along the entrance to her core, teasing her. Her gray eyes darkened again. She pulled her perfect lower lip between her teeth. She lifted her arms and wrapped them around his shoulders, bringing her breasts flush against his chest.

"Surrender," he whispered, and then he drove into her, and there was nothing at all but fire.

That perfect, encompassing fire. It roared through him, into him. It incinerated everything he thought, everything he knew, until there was nothing at all but Dru. And she was supple and curvy and draped all around him. She began to move her hips and he groaned, too close to the edge.

He wrapped his hands around her hips to slow her down, then set his own pace. Slow. Deliberate. Torturing them both. Hot and endless strokes that made him grit his teeth and made her drop her head to his neck and sob out her pleasure. He moved her up and down as he thrust into her, again and again, wanting it never to end. Wanting to stay balanced in all this lush perfection forever. Wanting to breathe her in like this, so deep inside her he hardly knew which one of them was which.

She lifted her head then and her gaze locked with his. Held. He felt her breath on his face, her legs tight around him, and still he moved, building that fire into a raging blaze, making her moan even louder, watching those gray eyes of hers glaze over with the same incomparable passion that stormed through him. Taking him over. Making him want nothing more than to burn in it, over and over, too hot to bear, until there was nothing left of him.

This is Dru, he thought, unable to stop looking at her, touching her, feeling her in every part of him. *And this is mine.*

And he understood then that he had no intention of ever letting her go. Whatever that might mean.

She closed her eyes and threw back her head, her lovely back arching toward the setting sun through the windows behind her, the fading light casting her lush body in oranges and golds.

Like some kind of pagan goddess, and all of her his.

She started to shudder again, wild and untamed in his arms, and when she called out his name this time, he followed her over the edge. At last.

Dru lay tangled with him in the wide bed and watched the sun drip down toward the sea, then melt away.

She could not seem to form coherent thoughts. There was only the buzzing in her limbs and under her skin, like some kind of high-voltage live wire, still sending out sparks. She felt Cayo's hard shoulder beneath her cheek. She felt the heat of his skin and the way his chest rose and fell. She did not think. She wasn't sure she wanted to think. She watched the sky instead.

Cayo stirred beside her when the sun dropped below the horizon, as if roused by the twilight. He turned to face her, his eyes dark and once again unreadable in the deep shadows of his chamber.

He slid his hand up to hold her cheek and then

brought her face to his. For a moment he only gazed at
her, and she felt a great stillness inside her, a kind of
hush. As if she was waiting for something, poised on
the edge of another high cliff while all the rest of her
seemed to shiver.

The clock is already ticking, a voice whispered inside her head, ruthlessly practical when Dru felt anything but. *He's already gone.*

But as if he could hear her, he kissed her. Deep and
slow. Sweet. Addicting. And then the fire kicked in. As
if it could never be quenched. As if none of this would
ever be enough. She had been a terrible fool, she acknowledged as his hand moved over her face, angling
her mouth closer to his for a better fit, a deeper kick. She
should have known better than to think she could handle
this. She would leave him as planned, she understood
then in some deep, primitive way, but then she would
mourn him, and she might never stop. She had walked
right into this, and there was nothing for her but Miss
Havisham and regret on the other side of it. And still
she kissed him, unable to help herself. Unable to stop
what she'd already started, what she'd already done.

No sense borrowing trouble, she thought then, in
some desperation. It would come no matter what she
did. It would hurt. Maybe she'd always known that.

He rose over her in the bed and settled himself between her legs, and Dru let go of a future that seemed
far away from this moment, too far away to matter. He
settled his weight on his hands and looked down at her,
still watching her with those too-shrewd eyes of his.

"Dru," he said. Just her name. As if he was tasting it.

"Cayo," she replied in kind, feeling far too vulnerable. She didn't know what he saw when he looked down
at her like that. She didn't know how to prevent him

from seeing everything, all of her hopes and fears and terrors, not when she had abandoned herself so completely to be with him like this.

But he simply twisted his hips and thrust into her. Slick. Hot.

And she stopped caring what he saw. What he knew. She concentrated instead on the sleek perfection of this age old dance between them. As if she'd been made to fit him, just like this.

He moved slowly, hypnotically. As if he did not wish to build that fire between them this time so much as encourage it to burn high on its own. She matched his lazy rhythm, her hips rising to meet his, every part of her exulting in the way they fit together. In the way they moved together. Slow and easy and devastating.

She told herself it was the only thing that mattered.

This time, she could reach up and explore the sheer beauty of his lean, smooth torso. She ran her hands over his hard pectorals, then trailed her way down that mouthwatering abdomen. Smooth skin stretched across steel. Hard male beauty unlike any other. Ferocious and proud. Fierce and demanding. She pulled herself up from the bed to kiss his chest, to taste the bold heat of him, the incomparable strength. The delectable power.

The pace began to change, then, the fire burning ever hotter. Cayo's shoulders blocked out the world, and she forgot everything but this. Everything but him. Everything but the wildness they made here, and the way it stormed through her, tearing her apart from within.

He slid down to pull her close and she loved it. The full, hard weight of him against her, pressing her into the bed, making her feel somehow small and yet cherished, all at once. She could feel his breath in her ear, and then he began to murmur words she didn't know in

Spanish, crooning against the length of her neck while still he thrust into her, over and over and over again. She wrapped her legs around his hips and clung to him, mindless and wanton, entirely at his command. And when he reached between them and pressed his fingers against the heart of her need, she burst into a million pieces. Again.

He kept on as she shattered around him, until he shouted out her name and shuddered against her, burying his face into the crook between her neck and her shoulder. And even broken into too many pieces to count, even thrown as she was off the side of a very high cliff and still floating her way down to earth, Dru understood that nothing was ever going to be the same again. Especially not her.

Cayo's version of enjoying himself in paradise, Dru was not greatly surprised to learn, involved cutting down his business hours to something like six or eight hours per day instead of more than twice that.

"What a great sacrifice this must be," she murmured toward the end of one such "holiday" afternoon as she took more dictation, her fingers flying across the keyboard when she would have preferred to explore him instead, not that he had asked. "To abandon yourself so hedonistically into a normal person's version of a workday."

Cayo eyed her, his dark eyes as hot as they were amused. In deference to the fact he'd decreed this a vacation—and, perhaps, all that had changed between them—he wore a white shirt he had not bothered to button, displaying his mouthwatering physique and olive complexion and making Dru glad she was so adept at touch-typing. She could stare at him without missing a single word. His feet were even propped up on the desk in front of him, completing the picture. He would have looked like indolence incarnate had he not been sitting in his office suite, composing lists of commands for his fleet of vice presidents the world over to obey as soon as Dru pressed Send.

"You are always welcome to distract me," he said after a moment.

She opened her mouth to offer a knee-jerk sort of demurral, but stopped herself. What was there to lose? Cayo's business would storm ahead the way it always did when these strange days were over, when she was gone. But she would never get another chance to have him like this. She had the sense again, as she had repeatedly since that first day here, that she was gathering up all these white-hot, deliriously passionate moments to hoard later, when she was alone. When she was free. When she had nothing but memories to hold on to.

"If you insist, Mr. Vila," she said now, watching that fierce light blaze in his eyes. She slid out of the chair she'd pulled up next to his desk and onto the floor, smiling slightly as his hard face tightened with desire.

Slowly, holding his gaze, she crawled between his legs.

"Is this a new form of taking dictation, Miss Bennett?" he asked, that dark amusement in his low voice, though she could hear the faint rasp in it that hinted at the fire within him, and she smiled, running her hands over his hard thighs, his taut abdomen. His legs thudded down on either side of her, caging her right where she wanted to be. "I'm a fan."

Then she reached into his soft trousers, lifting out the hard, smooth length of him and taking him deep in her mouth.

He groaned. And Dru worshipped him, tasting the velvet smoothness of him, loving him with her mouth, her tongue, her hands and her lips, bringing him to a roaring finish with his hands gripped tight in her hair.

It was these moments she was collecting, she told herself as he lifted her into his lap and kissed her hungrily, his heartbeat pounding hard beneath her as he held her against his chest. These moments when she could kid herself and pretend that he was hers.

They fell into a kind of pattern as the days passed. Cayo was still her boss, despite the dramatic change in their relationship, and Dru did not dispute that. What might have been untenable if she hadn't already planned to leave him was really more like a game when it was only her heart, not her career, at stake. So she was happy enough to continue performing her duties, with only cosmetic alterations.

"Don't do that thing with your hair," Cayo said one morning as she stepped out of the massive, glass-enclosed shower, complete with a window overlooking the ocean, that was its own room in the master suite's bath.

He stood in the door that led out into his bedroom, his dark eyes burning as they tracked over her, watching as she wrapped herself in a towel. He'd pulled on another pair of the linen trousers he favored in the warm weather, but no shirt, and all of that muscled masculine perfection on display made her feel overheated. Again.

They'd woken at dawn and gone for a swim in the quiet lagoon. He'd lifted her against him where he stood, simply pulled her bikini bottoms to the side and slid inside her, rocking them both to mindlessness in the clear, warm water, as the sun began to light the perfect sky above them.

She was still trembling slightly from the aftereffects.

"Don't do what with my hair?" she asked. It couldn't be healthy, wanting someone like this. She'd imagined sleeping with him would be a single act, a fix, the end of all that yearning and infatuation.

But instead, you made it worse, that voice inside was quick to remind her. As if she didn't know.

He made a vague gesture toward the back of his head. "That twist," he said. A strange expression crossed his face then, something she might have called vulnerability on another man—but that was impossible. This was Cayo. "I like it down around your shoulders," he said gruffly. "I like my hands in it."

And he'd turned and disappeared, leaving Dru to make of that what she would.

She pulled on the cheerful, bright blue-and-yellow maxidress she'd adopted as her uniform here, and ran her fingers through her hair as it settled around her shoulders in damp waves. She stared at herself in the large mirror that dominated the nearest wall, and hardly recognized herself. The exposure to the sun had brought out her freckles, and that sheen to her skin. Her eyes were bright, her mouth soft, somehow. And her dark hair tumbled all around her, still wet from her shower, giving her a sensual and sultry sort of look. She was poles apart from the image of Dru Bennett she'd prided herself on embodying in her five years at the Vila Group: impeccably, quietly fashionable. Professional above all else.

She could lie and tell herself that it was the islands doing this to her, turning her into a different person, but she knew better. It was Cayo.

She just had to remember that it was temporary.

Back in London, Dru would never dress this way.

Just as she would never interrupt a dictation session as she had the other day, or wear her hair down because a man demanded it. Just as she would never sleep with her boss, no matter how much she might have wanted him, and then carry on working for him. But this was Bora Bora, and it was as if what she did here didn't count.

It's only a handful of days, she reminded herself now as she walked to meet him in the office. *It will be like none of this happened when I get back home.*

She told herself that the twisting feeling in her stomach was joy. That it was happiness that she was letting herself do this, experience this, live in the moment here, when it was so unlike her. She had her whole life in front of her to regret this, after all. There was no sense starting now.

But it was as if Cayo knew that there was something she wasn't telling him—or perhaps he felt the pressure of the temporary nature of this as well. Sometimes he merely picked her up and held her against the nearest wall when he wanted her, his expression so fierce as he thrust within her, as if he saw the same painful future before him. Or he woke her again and again in the night, to taste her, to touch her, to send her flying over the edge. As if to prove he could. As if to make sure it was real.

One afternoon, after he'd ended their workday, he found her on the lanai outside the library. He stood in the entryway for a long moment, watching her, until Dru set her crime novel aside and gave him her full attention.

"Did you need something?" she asked, and smiled at him, ready for another series of commands. Plans for the next day's business, perhaps.

"I don't know how you do it." His voice was dark

and low. It made a shiver of unease snake along the back of her neck.

"Read?" she asked mildly.

He ignored that.

"Your words, your smiles." He ran a hand along the jaw he shaved irregularly here, and looked not unlike a pirate as he gazed down at her, rakish and unapologetically lethal. But she didn't recognize that look in his eyes. "Even in my bed. There are a thousand places for you to hide, aren't there? And you do."

Her heart thudded hard against her ribs. And there was a kind of ringing in her ears, as if alarms were going off all around them. But she knew that wasn't true—there was only the sound of the waves as they crashed against the sand. The birds singing in the trees. The wind dancing through the chimes out on the terrace.

"I don't know what you mean."

"Do you know, I almost believe you."

He didn't look angry, or upset in any way. She could have handled either of those without blinking. He looked almost…resigned. All of that clever attention of his focused on her, and growing darker by the moment. And it was making her feel panicky. Desperate. Afraid, again, of what he might see.

"I'm not hiding." She stood, then opened up her arms, proving it. "I'm right here."

He smiled, and it had the usual effect of rendering her breathless, for all it was shaded as much with regret as with desire. She didn't want to know why.

"Are you, Dru?" he asked. But he closed the distance between them as if he found her as difficult to resist as she did him, and pulled her against him. "Are you really?"

Dru didn't answer. She kissed him instead. Hot. Desperate. With everything she was capable of giving him.

He didn't speak again.

He had her kneel on the small sofa, then took her from behind, his hands on her hips and his hard chest at her back as he thrust into her, making her sob out his name with only the glittering sea before them as witness.

And when he bent his head to her neck, spent in the aftermath of their passion, she murmured soothing words and told herself it was another victory. Another memory; hers to hoard.

CHAPTER EIGHT

THEY SAT OUT on one of the patios one evening, surrounded by softly flickering candles, with the canopy of stars bright and astonishing above them. Dru leaned back in her chair and stared up at them, aware on some level that time was passing even in moments like this one, when she felt outside of time altogether.

Don't forget what temporary means, she advised herself. *Don't pretend that any of this can last.*

Across from her, Cayo was finishing a call with a CFO at one of his New York companies. He frowned out toward the dark ocean as he talked, his voice growing increasingly more impatient. Dru sipped at her wine and watched him, imprinting that impossible face into her memory, making sure she had memories enough to spare. That blade of a nose, that granite jaw. Her boss become her lover. Now that it had happened, it felt inevitable. As if they had always been headed here. As if the three years in between Cadiz and now had been part of some grander plan.

Just as she had always intended to leave him, eventually. Lest she forget her own plans. Her promises.

Victory, she chanted quietly in her own head. *This is a victory. I'll go home the winner at the end, and do exactly as I planned to do two weeks ago.*

But she wasn't sure she believed her own cheering squad.

The staff brought out plates of tuna tartare to start, and Dru took a bite, sighing with pleasure at the burst of flavor, the excruciatingly fresh taste. She took a sip of her wine. She smiled when Cayo ended his call and ignored the way he looked at her, so dark and brooding.

"It's fantastic," she told him. "You should have some."

"Are you working tonight, Dru?" His tone was cold, brusque. It lanced into her, as no doubt he intended it to do. "I thought we agreed that business ended at half five today. When I want you to perform in your role as perfect assistant, capable of any measure of small talk under any and all circumstances, I will let you know."

"Or don't have any," she said blandly. "More for me."

His mouth moved into a hard kind of curve, too intense to be a smile.

More courses appeared before them. Parrotfish stuffed with crab. Mahi-mahi in a sweet coconut curry. A platter of grilled shrimp and scallops, and another of artfully arranged sushi. The table was bright with all the colors, and the food looked almost too pretty to eat. Almost.

"Tell me something about you," he said when their plates were full, and there had been no sound for some time save the clink of silver against china and the ever-present crash of the ocean against the shore. "Something I don't know." He shook his head impatiently when she opened her mouth. "I don't mean anything on your CV, which you trot out by rote and which I know is stellar or I wouldn't have hired you."

Dru put down her fork and regarded him calmly for a moment, while that same alarm inside her shrieked anew. There was no reason he should want to "know something" about her. She needed to change the subject, redirect his attention. He had enough weapons to use against her as it was. Why add to his arsenal?

"What is it you want to know?" she asked, warily. She picked up her wine, pressed the glass to her lips and then decided she already felt too unbalanced. There was no need to throw alcohol in the mix and make it that much worse. "Is this when we discuss our lists of past lovers? Mine is shorter than yours. Obviously."

His dark amber eyes gleamed, as if he appreciated her attempt to focus the conversation back on him, and what was, she was all too aware, an impressive and lengthy list indeed. But he didn't take the bait. He only smiled slightly, and speared a plump shrimp on the sharp tines of his fork.

"You personally witnessed the ignoble end of my family, such as it was," he said, his voice as low as his gaze was intent, and something about it shivered through her, making her ache for him in a different way. "What of yours? You never speak of them. I assume you did not spring full-grown from an office-supply warehouse, brandishing one of those gray suits of yours like a weapon."

The expression on his face said he wasn't entirely sure about that. Dru cleared her throat and recognized that she was stalling. She couldn't seem to help it. There had been a time when she would have been thrilled to encourage his interest in her—any interest at all. But not now. Not when she had a much greater sense of how hard it was going to be to leave him already. What would it be like if he really knew all of her? How would she survive losing him then?

"Did you encourage personal chatter about the office

all these years and I missed it?" she asked lightly. He inclined his head, awarding her the point, but he still waited expectantly. He was still not distracted from his question. *Damn him.* She set her wine back on the glass-topped table, feeling jerky and uneven. Unduly defensive. "We lived in Shropshire, in a village outside Shrewsbury, until my father died. Dominic and I were barely five years old." She saw his brows knit together and nodded. "Twins, yes. We moved around a good bit after that. In the end, it was a relief to go to university and stay in one place for a few years."

"Why did you move around so much?" he asked. If she didn't know better, she would think he was fascinated. That he really wanted to know the answer. And maybe that was why she told him—because, despite everything, she wanted to believe that he could want that, and that trumped even her heightened sense of self-preservation. To say nothing of her sense, full stop.

"My mum had a lot of boyfriends," she said, which was more than she usually told anyone. It was amazing how easy it was to strip all those hard, dark years of the fear and the tears and simply cram it all into one little sentence that barely hinted at either. "Some became stepfathers."

She had no intention of telling him anything further. But when she dared meet his gaze again, he was looking back at her the way he always did. Dark eyes in that warrior's face, brooding and *intent*. As if she was a mystery he wanted to puzzle out. And would.

"My mother also remarried, I suppose you could say," he said then, in that dry way of his that hinted at a dark humor she'd never imagined he could possess. Or had thought she'd only imagined lurked in him on that one night in Cadiz. She would miss it. She could tell. "But as she is now a bride of Christ we are not meant to complain."

Dru couldn't help but smile, and his eyes warmed in return, and she knew then that she was going to tell him things she'd never breathed to another soul. Because she still wanted him to know her, despite how temporary this was. Despite the very real fear that it would give him too much power over her. She wanted to imagine, when he was on to his next assistant, ensconced on one of his yachts with his next blonde supermodel, that he would remember her, too. And when he did—*if* he did—she wanted this to have mattered. And that meant sharing parts of herself she'd never let anyone else see.

"They were always violent." She was surprised how little her voice shook, and how easy it was to look at him and forget what she'd been through. How safe he made her feel, simply by not looking away. As if that simple act shared the burden of it, somehow. "To Mum, and then increasingly to Dominic. I was quite good at not being seen."

"I believe you," he said, an undercurrent in his voice. "You still are."

"But then I got older," she said. She was far too captivated by the way he watched her, as if he was supporting her that simply, that completely, to respond to the strange thing he said. She filed it away. "And they started to notice me more." She swallowed, then shook her head slightly, as if to shake away the memories. His gaze darkened. Hardened. "There was one named Harold who was the worst. Always trying to get me alone. Always quick to stick his hands where he shouldn't. But when I told Mum she slapped my face and called me a liar and a whore." Dru shrugged, almost as if that memory didn't still sting. Almost as if she was so tough it hardly registered, when the truth was, she'd never said that out loud before. Not like that. "So when I could, I left. The last time I saw her I was nineteen."

The only other person she'd shared her dark history with was Dominic, and they'd always used their own shorthand—never quite mentioning the facts of what had happened so much as the effects. She'd never told any of her mates at university, or even the small handful of boyfriends she'd had back when she'd still had time for a social life. It had seemed so private, and so terribly shameful, and her mates had all been about having a laugh, not dredging up the horrors of Dru's childhood. She'd enjoyed them precisely *because* they weren't the sort for intimate confidences or bared souls. It meant hers were safe.

She jerked her gaze away from Cayo's now, reaching blindly for her wine, no longer caring what it might do to her. It was better than what *he* was doing to her simply by listening. By making her feel safe when there was no such thing. She knew that better than most.

"And your brother?" Cayo asked after a moment. "Your twin? You're not close with him either?"

It shocked her. It felt like a kick in the stomach, an attack, and her first reaction was pure, unadulterated fury. And then, if she was honest, a lot of it was that same old, terrible guilt she always felt where Dominic was concerned.

"Not as such, thanks," she snapped at Cayo, not caring if she was being unfair. "As he's dead."

And then she hated herself. So deeply and so comprehensively it made her feel ill. She slid the wineglass back onto the table and wrapped her arms around her middle, certain she needed help to keep herself together.

Cayo didn't look away. He gave no indication that he minded that she'd snapped at him like that, out of nowhere. He simply sat much too still and much too close across the table, watching her fall apart.

"I'm sorry," he began after a moment, his voice calm.

"No," she interrupted him, her words feeling thick in her mouth. "I'm sorry. I shouldn't have said it like that. How would you know? Only it was rather recent and I've still not managed to figure out how to talk about it. About him."

"Recent?" Cayo frowned then. He looked as close to confused as she'd ever seen him. "What do you mean by recent? I don't recall you taking any time off."

In the past five years. He didn't have to say that part. It was understood.

"Time off?" She shook her head, then let out a hollow little sound, not really a laugh at all. "It's not as if you give out any personal time, Cayo. I can't imagine even having asked for time off. Look how you reacted to my resignation."

That muscle leapt in his jaw, betraying his temper. His eyes went black with something that looked again like pain. Tortured and grim, the way he'd looked that night in Milan. It made her want to reach over and touch him, soothe him. And once more, she deeply regretted her words the moment they hung in the sweet night air between them, but she couldn't seem to stop herself. And she couldn't take them back.

"Yes," he said after a moment in a deep, rough voice she hardly recognized. "Of course. I am such a heartless monster that I would keep you from your brother's funeral, purely out of spite."

Her own heart seemed to tighten at that, and she shook her head. "That's not what I meant."

"After all," he continued in the same dark and bitter tone that made her want to weep and to protect him, somehow, from whatever made him sound that way, even if it was her, "what do I know of family? You are the only person in the world who knows how little regard my own grandfather held for me. You heard him. You are also the only person in the world who has maintained any kind of close relationship with me for any length of time." His smile then hurt to see. "You would certainly know how little qualified I am to speak on the subject of families."

She felt awful, and it moved in her like heat. Like fear. And she couldn't stand it.

"Don't be an idiot," she said, almost crossly.

He froze. His dark eyes widened.

"I said I doubted you would give me time off," she said, very distinctly. "You are a demanding boss, Cayo. You insist on round-the-clock availability and access. I had no reason to think you would greet the news that I even *had* a personal life with anything but horror."

"You have no idea what I would do," he replied tightly.

"I know exactly what you would do," she retorted. "It's what you pay me for. What you offered me three times my salary and the private island of my choice for, if memory serves."

For a moment he only looked at her. The moment stretched out between them, and despite what she'd just told him, Dru had no idea how he would react. None at all.

And then, impossibly, proving how little she knew him after all, he threw back his head and laughed.

She'd never known he *could* laugh. It was an infectious sound. Joy moved across his hard, fierce face, the laughter lighting him up, changing him, changing *her*—

The truth slammed into her, stealing her breath, making her head spin. The scales fell from her eyes, and hard—so hard they seemed to bruise her on their way down.

She was in love with him.

And quite clearly, she had been for a very long time.

Once again, she'd been fooling herself. She'd called it an "infatuation," called it her "feelings for him." She'd minimized it in her own head, worrying only that this trip would take recovering from. She hadn't dared so much as think the truth. Meanwhile, she'd chosen to lose herself in his life. She'd never thought to ask why she'd been passed over for that other job three years ago even though she'd known perfectly well she'd been qualified for it. Worse, she'd chosen to keep her distance from her brother—when he'd died, but even before, if she was honest. It was easier to send money from afar than it was to roll around in the messes Dominic had made, though it hurt her to admit she'd done exactly that. She'd done all of it.

All to cater to and care for a man who would never love her back. Who hadn't the slightest idea what love *was*.

Then again, came that voice inside her, brutal and unflinching, *do you?*

The world seemed to tilt around her wildly, sickeningly, as if she'd found herself trapped on some carnival fun ride. She felt a terrible shame wash through her, scalding her. She'd wanted her damaged, selfish mother to love her as she should have done. She'd wanted all of those stepfathers to love her like a daughter. She'd wanted Dominic to love her more than his addictions.

And Cayo... He couldn't love anything, could he? So she'd settled for making him *need* her instead. And she'd thought he valued her for that, if nothing else.

Was that what she'd wanted, in his office that day that seemed so long ago now? Had some part of her believed she would fling her resignation at him, still smarting from the printed email she'd found, and he would leap to his feet and declare his love for her?

Of course he hadn't. No one ever had, and Cayo wouldn't know how, even if he did feel the things she did. Her entire life was a great and complicated monument to deeply pathetic, sadly epic, and wholly unrequited love.

She was such a fool.

And he was watching her now, that unexpected laughter still on his face, making him more than simply beautiful in that hard, fierce way—making him handsome, too. Almost approachable.

It broke what was left of her heart.

"Are you all right?" he asked, his eyes still bright as they searched hers, sharpening as they saw whatever must have been there—the truth, she feared. The terrible truth she could never, ever let him know.

She didn't know how she did it.

"I'm fine," she managed to say. He frowned, no doubt at that shaky note in her voice that made her sound anything at all but *fine,* so she gestured at her mouth, and lied. "I've bit my tongue, that's all."

Time, it turned out, was the one thing Cayo couldn't control.

It was the afternoon of her final day—which neither one of them had mentioned directly yet, though it hung there between them no matter how many times he'd taken her the night before, or this morning—and he could not bring himself to pay attention to the conference call that she was participating in as his representative. He sat next to her at the small table in the office, his legs stretched out before him, and found he could do nothing at all but watch her as she spoke into the speaker phone in the center of the table.

"I'll be certain to bring that to Mr. Vila's attention," she said, in that smooth and capable voice of hers that, now he knew what lay behind it, made him burn. "But in the meantime, I think we need to take another look at those figures before we jump to any conclusions."

Maybe it was that he could see her, when the rest of the people on the call could not. No doubt they pictured the usual Dru, in her sleek suits and dangerous heels, her hair tamed and twisted out of view. But he saw the real Dru. Wild hair and that hint of color on her pale skin, the dusting of freckles across her nose and shoulders. Bare feet and a turquoise sarong wrapped around a hot pink bikini. Not in the least bit professional, not that anyone could have told that from her cool voice.

She was magnificent. She was his. And she was going to leave him.

He didn't know what he was going to do about that, he only knew he couldn't allow it. He wouldn't.

But he also knew he'd run out of options.

She propped her head up with one hand as she listened to the call, the various executives talking over each other, all of them completely unaware that Cayo was listening to them dither and bicker. He'd found that it could be highly educational to use Dru in this way, to make them think they were talking to someone far more approachable than Cayo ever was. He'd found it helped ferret out all manner of truths.

He wished the same could be said of Dru herself.

"Mr. Vila prefers to be offered potential solutions when presented with problems, Barney," she said into the speaker. "I can certainly raise your concerns to him, but I suspect he's going to give you a similar reply. Only he won't be quite as polite."

There was some laughter, and she glanced over to smile at him, her gray eyes sparkling nearly silver. *Real,* he thought with satisfaction. Not one of her work smiles she trotted out to placate or soothe him from time to time, all of which he'd come to hate. But even so, he knew she was still hiding from him. He didn't know what, or why, but he could see the secrets in her eyes. Even now.

Perversely, it only made him want her more.

He'd told her that she was the only person he'd ever had any kind of close relationship with, and the stark truth of that haunted him. She was the only person alive that he had ever trusted. He had allowed her unparalleled access to all parts of his life. To him. No employee had ever been so entrenched in his personal life before and he had certainly never allowed one of his women anywhere near his business. Only Dru bridged those worlds. Only Dru.

And his time with her was almost up.

Giving in to an urge he hardly understood, as if it might ease the sudden heaviness in his chest, Cayo reached over and took her hand. Her eyes flew to his, but he concentrated on the slide of her fingers against his. The way they fitted together so well, even here. He brought her hand up to his lips and pressed a kiss to the back of it. She curved her palm to better fit against his mouth, his jaw, as if she was holding him too, and something shifted inside him. A wall he hadn't known was there tumbled down, and he knew, then, what he must do.

There was one way to keep her. One strategy he hadn't tried. It would keep her close. With him. And so what if it wouldn't be precisely as it had been? It was good enough. He might even like having her as his family, whatever that word really meant. She was the closest thing to it he'd ever known.

He just had to get her to say yes.

"The helicopter will be here in two hours," Dru said the following morning, careful to sound calm. Matter-of-fact. "The plane will be ready to go once we get to Tahiti."

Cayo stood at the end of the pier, with his back to her. He looked remote, forbidding and still, she wanted to lean into all of that broad strength, rest her head against his shoulder blade. She wanted to let the pure, male scent of him surround her. She wanted to soak in his heat like the sun. Her bare toes curled into the smooth, warm wood beneath her feet and she told herself she was fine. That she felt nothing but relief that it was all almost over, with only the long plane ride left to survive. *Perfectly fine.*

They had woken up at dawn, wrapped around each other in Cayo's huge bed. He had pulled her over him before she was wholly awake, sliding into her so smoothly she'd wondered whether it was real or a dream. *Or goodbye,* a harsher voice in her head had suggested. She'd ignored it, leaned down to him and kissed him.

Slowly, they'd explored each other. Long, drugging kisses and endless touches, building a different kind of flame. One that burned long and sweet. One that danced and seduced and drew out the perfection of each caress. One that made them both sigh out their pleasure when it turned white-hot and wild all around them.

Dru felt the glowing embers of that same fire inside her, even now. She'd almost been afraid to track Cayo down after she'd confirmed their arrangements—as if she thought he could see straight through her to that place that would never stop burning for him. That place he could ignite with so little effort—a look, a touch. Would that ever fade? Would time without him dim it? Somehow, she doubted it.

"I suppose no one can stay in paradise forever, can they?" she asked brightly when he didn't turn to face her, trying to make conversation—anything to cover her own nervousness. Anything to pretend it didn't hurt.

"Don't." It was hard. Fierce.

"It's so lovely here." She felt helpless. Unable to stop. "But it's not real, is it?"

He turned then, so dark and ruthless, dressed in no more than a pair of white loose trousers and still, so dangerous. She almost took a step back to keep him from looming over her, but she restrained herself. His eyes slammed into hers.

"But this is?" His accent was more pronounced than usual, and she felt it inside, like an echo. "Your deliberately inane chatter? Surely you know by now that it won't work on me."

That might have stung—it did—but Dru couldn't let herself fall into that trap. There would be no fighting that led to kissing, no explosions of temper or passion or anything else. No shoes. No jumping from the pier. She wouldn't let him sabotage her departure. More importantly, she wouldn't let herself do the same.

"You are far too busy to spend any more time hiding away from the world," she said, and that wasn't idle conversation or flattery. It was the simple truth. He was who he was. "Even here."

"As you pointed out to me only last night," he said gruffly, "the point of hiring the best people in the world is occasionally to delegate responsibilities to them."

"I did say that." She smiled, but it felt hollow. He didn't return it. And last night felt so far away now. As if it belonged to other people. "Cayo…"

She bit her lip and watched his dark amber eyes turn nearly black with a mixture of pain and passion, and her heart seemed to squeeze tight in her chest. If she started crying now, she worried she would never stop. She tried to shove that dangerous ache away.

"Don't make this harder than it has to be," she whispered.

Still, he only stared back at her, as if he were hewn from stone. He looked powerful beyond measure, ruthless and fierce and she thought it might kill her to leave him. That thing inside her that had no pride, no respect, no boundaries whatsoever, might physically take her down as she tried to walk away. Her little masochist within, who wanted him and only him, however she could have him. Whatever that meant.

However much it hurt.

"It doesn't have to be hard," he said then.

His voice was low, and there was an intense light deep in the dark of his gaze. He reached over and traced a lazy pattern just above the waistband of her linen trousers, where there was a gap between them and her top. She sucked in a breath, so attuned to him that even that faintest touch unleashed the fire in her, made her body ready itself for him, as if on command. When he looked at her again, there was gold in his eyes and the faintest curve on that cruel mouth of his.

"I think you should marry me," he said.

The world stopped.

No breath. No sound. No air.

But somehow, she didn't faint. She didn't fall. She only stood there, staring back at him. "What did you just say?"

"Don't play that game." He took her chin in his hand, his gaze piercing into her, seeing far too much—and she couldn't allow that. She wouldn't survive it if he knew she loved him. Dru jerked her head back, and he let go, but not without reminding them both, wordlessly, that he'd allowed it.

"You can't be serious," she said, her breath, her voice—all of her ragged. Uneven. Trembling as if what he'd said was some kind of earthquake and she was still swaying in the aftermath.

"I have never been more serious in my life," he grated out, his dark eyes flashing.

And this, she found, hurt worst of all. It was everything she'd ever wanted—more than she'd dreamed possible—but not like this. Never like this. Two weeks ago he'd tricked her onto that plane, claiming they were bound for Zurich. This was no different.

It just hurt more.

"No," she said, her voice barely a whisper. "I can't."

"Why not?" It was the voice he used to do business, to make deals. To convince whoever dared say no to him that they should change their answer—and they usually did.

Dru felt bruised. Battered. Torn apart by what she knew was the right thing to do, and that treacherous part of her that wanted him however she could get him. Why couldn't she simply jump at this chance, her masochistic side wondered. He might learn to love her. Maybe he already did, in as much as he was able. And wasn't *maybe* good enough?

But there was another voice in there now, a new one. Fragile and tiny, but hers.

"I deserve better," she heard herself say.

The effect on Cayo was immediate and dramatic, though he didn't seem to move. It was as if all that power, all that ferocity, was suddenly burning in his exotic eyes while the rest of him went terribly, alarmingly still. As if she'd wounded him beyond measure.

"'Better'?" he echoed.

Dru's hands shot out, as if to touch him, to hold him, but at the final moment she found she didn't dare. Her throat was thick with grief, her chest hurt, and there was nothing she could do. She couldn't make this better—and he was making it worse.

"I have a promise to keep to my brother," she whispered. "Nothing is more important than that."

Not even you, she thought miserably, while everything inside her revolted.

"Marry me." But it was less a command than a plea, wrapped up though it was in his ruthless delivery. "It's the only solution." When she only stared back at him through eyes that grew blurrier by the moment, he looked almost desperate. "I don't know how to lose you," he said, his voice near a whisper. "I can't."

"You'll have to learn," she managed to push out past the constriction in her throat.

"Dru—"

"I can't settle, Cayo." She threw that out, through the riot inside of her, through the tears that threatened. And it just kept hurting more. "Not even for you."

"Dru."

Even the way he said her name hurt. As if she was the one who'd mortally wounded him. He reached over and took her face in his hands, and that was when she noticed the tears wetting her cheeks, despite her best efforts.

But he didn't love her. He didn't even pretend. Not even now, to marry her. To keep her. *He didn't love her.* So she could tear herself into pieces by leaving now, or she could stay with him and marry him and fall apart by degrees, year by loveless year, until she really did hate him the way she'd only wished she could two weeks ago.

"I am not the monster you think I am," he said, soft and dark and straight into her heart, like a knife.

"Your two weeks are up, Cayo." It was the hardest thing she'd ever done. The greatest sacrifice she'd ever made. She stepped back, watched his hands drop away, and knew she would never be whole again. "You have to let me go."

CHAPTER NINE

IF THIS WAS what it was like to *care,* Cayo thought some weeks after he'd returned from Bora Bora and Dru had left him on the tarmac without a backward glance, he had been right to discourage the practice for the whole of his adult life.

When I decide to sabotage you, she had told him once, *there will be nothing the least bit passive about it.* He couldn't help but wonder if this was what she'd meant. This…aching sense of loss that colored everything a dull gray.

He hated it.

He glared at one of his many vice presidents across the wide expanse of his London desk, and managed, somehow, to refrain from wringing the man's neck.

"I don't understand why I'm having this conversation," he said coldly. The other man winced. Cayo drummed his fingers on the glossy expanse of his desktop. "Surely I hired you to make decisions at this level yourself."

He was being far kinder than he felt. Personable, even. But he knew he was measuring himself against the kind of results Dru could have wrung out of this man with a few smiles and a supportive word or two and, by that tally, he was a failure.

That was something he was getting used to, however gracelessly. And she still wasn't here. She had disappeared completely after his plane had touched down on British soil, just as she'd promised she would. He supposed he hadn't believed it would happen, that she would really do it. He still didn't.

"Of course, of course, I would be happy—" the vice president in front of him stammered out. "It's only that you always wanted to hear every detail of every potential negotiation before—"

"That was before," Cayo said, and sighed. He rubbed at his temples and tried to stop glaring. "If there's nothing else…?"

He sat back in his mighty chair behind his massive desk and watched the other man sprint for the safety of the outer office. And then, like clockwork, his new assistant appeared in the doorway to update him on his schedule and his messages.

Claire was everything anyone could want in a personal assistant, he thought then, eyeing her. The agency had placed her the day he'd arrived back from French Polynesia, and she'd acquitted herself beautifully in the weeks since. She was a quick learner. She was eager to please and yet didn't tremble every time he spoke, like so many of his executives. She was even pleasant enough to look at, in a very blond and vaguely Nordic sort of way, which he knew always put the potential investors and various clients at ease. She'd been with him a month now and he had yet to detect a single flaw.

Save one. She wasn't Dru. She hardly knew how he took his coffee, much less how to finesse his fractious and demanding board of directors with seeming ease and nonchalance. He didn't ask for her thoughts on delicate business negotiations. He would never trust

her to have his interests at heart while tending to long
calls filled with unhappy executives. Claire was, he supposed, a perfectly decent personal assistant.

Which forced him to consider the fact that Dru had
been far more than that. She'd been more like a partner.
And she was gone now, as if she'd never been at Vila
Group at all. As if she'd never been with him.

What had he expected? He kept asking himself the
same question, and there was never any answer. *Dru
hated him.* She'd told him so. Had he really believed that
sex could change that? Or that it might change who he
was—who he had always been? This monster who did
not even know when he was crushing the life out of the
only thing he'd ever really cared about?

"Mr. Vila?" Claire asked. A note in her voice suggested it was not the first time she'd said his name.
"Shall I get Mr. Young on the phone for you?"

He was not himself. He had not been for some weeks
now, and well did he know it.

"Yes," Cayo muttered. It wasn't her fault she wasn't
Dru. He had to keep reminding himself of this. Several
times a day. "Fine."

He dealt with the call with his usual lack of tact or
mercy and when it was done, found himself at the great
wall of windows that looked out over the City. He had
been scowling out at the depressingly typical British
rain for several minutes before it occurred to him that
he'd been doing too much of this lately. Brooding like
a moody adolescent.

He was disgusted with himself. Had he moped when
his grandfather had tossed him out? He had not. After
an initial moment to absorb what had happened, he had
walked off that mountain and built a life for himself. He
hadn't mourned. He hadn't *brooded*. He'd focused

and he'd worked hard, and in time, he'd come to think of his grandfather's betrayal as the best thing that had happened to him. Where would he be without it?

But, of course, he knew. He would have been a cobbler like his grandfather in that pretty little whitewashed town, living out a simple life beneath the red roofs, smiling at the tourists who snapped pictures and paid too much for their restaurant meals. Suffering through the whispers and the gossip that would never have subsided, no matter how diligently he worked to combat them, no matter what he did. Paying and paying for his mother's sins, forever and ever without end. He let out a derisive snort at the thought.

I am better off, he told himself. Then told himself he believed it. *Then and now.*

But even so, he stared out the window and saw Dru instead.

They'd sprawled on a blanket on the sandy beach together one night in Bora Bora, wearing nothing but the bright, full moon beaming down from above them. Dru had been nestled against his shoulder, her breath still uneven from the heady passion they'd indulged in, scattering their clothes across the beach in their haste. Their insatiable need.

"I'll admit it," Cayo had said. "I never had a pet quite like you before."

"No?" He'd heard laughter in her voice, though he could only see the top of her head. "Do I sit and stay better than all the rest?"

"I was thinking how much I enjoy it when you surrender," he'd murmured. Hadn't he had her sobbing out his name only a few moments before? He'd been teasing her—something he'd only just realized was reserved for her alone, but when she'd shifted position so she could look at him, her gaze had been serious.

"Careful what you wish for," she'd said softly, in a voice that didn't match the look in her eyes.

"I don't know what you mean," he'd said, reaching out to curl a dark wave of her hair behind her ear, reveling in the thick silk of it between his fingers. "There is nothing wrong with surrender. Particularly to me."

"Easy for you to say." Her voice had been wry. "You've never had the pleasure."

He'd smiled, but then the moment had seemed darker, somehow. Or more honest, perhaps.

"Is that what you're afraid of?" he'd asked quietly.

She'd let out a small sound, as if she'd almost laughed, and then looked away.

"My brother was an addict," she'd said, her voice small, but determined. "I don't know why it feels like I'm betraying him to tell you that. It's true."

Cayo had said nothing. He'd only stroked her back, held her close, and listened. She'd told him about Dominic's attempts at recovery, about his inevitable falls from grace. She'd told him about the way it had been before, when she'd worked in other jobs, and had dropped them to rush to Dominic's side, only to find herself heartbroken and lied to, again and again. And occasionally sacked, to boot. She'd told him about the good times peppered in with the bad. About how close she'd been to her twin once, how for a long time the only thing they'd had in the world had been each other.

"But that wasn't quite true, because he also had his addictions," she'd said. "And he always surrendered to them, eventually. No matter how much he claimed he didn't want to. And then one day he just couldn't come back."

He'd turned then, rolling her over to her back so he could gaze down at her, searching her face, her eyes. But she'd been as unreadable as ever. Still hiding in plain sight, her gray eyes shadowed tonight, and darker than they should have been.

She'd reached out, then, carefully, as if he was something precious to her. She'd traced the line of his jaw, his nose, even the shape of his brows with her fingertips, then run them over his lips, her mouth curving slightly when he'd nipped at her.

"I wonder what that's like?" she'd whispered then, and he'd seen something like agony in her eyes, there and then gone. "Unable to resist the very thing you know will destroy you. Drawn to it, despite yourself."

"Dru," he'd said, frowning down at her. "Surely you can't think—"

But she hadn't let him finish. She'd silenced him with a searingly hot kiss and then moved against him, seducing him that easily. He'd forgotten all about it, until now.

Had she been warning him? Had she known that she would get into his blood like this, poisoning him from the inside out, making him a stranger to himself? Cayo frowned out the window now, through the rain lashing across the glass. For the first time in almost twenty years, he wondered if it was worth it, this great empire he'd built and on which he focused to the exclusion of all else. Lately he wondered if, given the chance, he would trade it in. If he would take her instead.

Not that she'd offered him any such choice.

His intercom buzzed loudly behind him. He didn't move. He didn't know, anymore, if he was furious or if he was simply the wreckage of the man he'd been. And he didn't like it, either way.

It took everything he had not to sic his team of investigators on her, not to have her every move reported back to him, wherever she was now, like the jealous, obsessive fool she'd once accused him of being. He'd been fighting the same near-overwhelming urge for weeks. She'd told him he needed to learn how to lose her, and he'd found it was not a lesson he was at all interested in mastering. The truth was, Cayo had never been any good at losing.

You have to let me go, she'd said. And he had, though it had nearly killed him, kept him up at nights and ruined his days. She was the one thing he'd ever given up on. The one thing he'd let slip through his hands.

And that felt like the greatest failure of all.

Cayo couldn't forgive himself. For any of it. Or her, for doing this to him. For turning him into this weak, destroyed creature, not at all who he'd believed himself to be, before.

Worst of all, for making him *care*.

Dru hadn't had time to collapse into the fetal position under her duvet once she'd made it back to her tiny bedsit in Clapham from the rainy tarmac where she'd last seen Cayo, despite the fact that was all she wanted to do.

Her already-booked flight straight back to Bora Bora had been leaving in two days' time. She'd met with Cayo's studiously blank-faced attorneys on the morning before her flight, and she'd signed whatever they'd put in front of her, not caring if it took blood and her firstborn, so long as it ensured her freedom. Finally. It had been the last necessary step.

And more than that, it had meant he was letting her go.

Some part of her had imagined he might pull his Godzilla routine. Roar and smash, grab and hoard. Demand another two weeks. Trap her into that marriage he'd proposed. *Something.* But he'd let her walk away from him at the airport. There had been nothing but a look in his eyes that she'd never seen before, turning all of that dark amber nearly black and eating her alive inside. The cold, dull, gray English day around them had been so depressingly *real life* she'd almost wondered if Bora Bora, the yacht in the Adriatic, Milan, and everything that had happened between them had been no more than a fevered dream.

The attorneys had been real, however, sliding papers at her one after the next in the Costa Coffee near Clapham Junction. She'd signed the last five years of her life away with every pen stroke. At his command. With his blessing.

Cayo Vila, who never gave in, who had never heard the word *no,* had let her go, at last.

Just as she'd told him to do, she'd reminded herself. Just as she'd asked.

And then she'd gone back home, carefully taken the tin that held Dominic's ashes, taped it shut and wrapped it up, and packed it away in her checked bag.

The trip had been brutal. When she'd finally staggered into her hotel on the southern part of Bora Bora's main island, far away from Cayo's private island, it had been impossible not to notice the differences. She'd told herself she didn't care. That she'd come for a specific reason and to perform a specific task, and when had she become such a princess that she found her rather smallish room that faced a bit of garden *depressing?* It was still a garden in Bora Bora.

She'd been furious with herself—and with Cayo—for spoiling her so thoroughly. She'd become used to all of the luxury he surrounded himself with, apparently. It had only served to make her that much more appalled at herself and all the many ways she'd let herself down.

It had taken her a week to get up her nerve—and, if she was honest, to recover a little bit from those two intense weeks she'd spent with Cayo. But finally she'd been ready. One evening, at sunset, she'd taken one of the kayaks out and brought Dominic's ashes with her. As the sky exploded in oranges and pinks, she'd tipped his ashes out into the beautiful, peaceful lagoon.

And while she'd kept her promise to the first man she'd ever loved, and always would, she'd talked to him.

"I wish I could have saved you," she'd whispered to the water, the sky, the sea beyond. "I wish I'd tried harder."

She'd remembered her brother's delighted laughter that she'd never heard enough of. She'd thought of his wickedly amused gray eyes, so much brighter and more alive than hers—and then, sometimes, so much duller. She thought of his too-lean form, his shaggy dark hair, his poet's hands, and the tattoo on his shoulder of two hummingbirds that was, he'd once said with his cheeky grin, meant to represent the two of them. Free and in flight, forever.

"I wish I knew what happened to that picture of us as babies," she'd said, smiling at the memory of the old photograph. "I still don't know which one of us was which."

She'd mourned. She'd thought of their mother, so terrified of being on her own that any man had done, no matter how vicious. She'd thought of all those years when it had been Dominic and Dru against the world, and how much she'd miss that for the rest of her life. He'd taken something from her she could never get back, and as she floated out there with jagged Mount

Otemanu before her and the world she knew so far away she'd let herself weep for the family she'd lost, her potential children who would never know their uncle, the whole rest of her life stretching out before her with nothing of her twin in it except what she carried with her. In her.

Which wasn't enough, she'd thought then, bitterly. It would never be enough.

"You took part of me with you, Dominic," she'd told him as the inky darkness fell. "And I'll never forget you. I promise."

And when all his ashes were gone she'd made her way back to her hotel, where, finally, she'd curled up on the bed, pulled the duvet over her head, and fallen apart.

She'd stayed there for days. She'd cried until she'd felt blinded by her own tears, until she'd made herself retch from the force of her sobs. She'd let it all out, at last, the terrible storm she'd been carrying with her all this time. The grief of so many years, the pain and the fury and all the lies she'd told herself about her motivations. How much she'd loved Dominic and yes, to her shame, how much she'd sometimes hated him, too. His excuses and his promises, his grand plans that never amounted to anything and his pretty, pretty lies that she'd so desperately wanted to believe. She'd wept for everything she'd lost, and how alone she was, and how little she knew what to do with herself now that she had nothing left to survive, no purpose to fulfill, no great sacrifice remaining to build her life around.

But one day she sat up, and opened all the windows. She let the breeze in, sweet with flowers and the sea. She breathed in, deeply. She had her tea out on the hotel's pretty beach, and felt born again. Made new. As if she really had put Dominic to rest.

Which meant it was time to face the truth about her feelings for Cayo.

"Am I so scary?" he'd asked so long ago that night in Cadiz. The restaurant had been noisy and crowded, and his arm had brushed against hers as they sat so close together at the tiny table. His unforgettable eyes had still been so sad, but there was a curve to that cruel mouth of his, and Dru had felt giddy, somehow. As if they were both lit up with the magic of this night when everything, she'd been sure, was changing.

"I think you take pride in being as scary as possible," she'd replied, smiling. "You have a reputation to uphold, after all."

"I am certain that somewhere beneath it all, I am nothing but clay, waiting to be molded by whoever happens along," he'd said, that near-smile deepening at the absurdity of a man like him being swayed by anything at all save his own inclination.

"Metal that might, under certain circumstances, be welded, perhaps," she'd said, laughing. "Never clay."

"I bow to your superior knowledge," he'd said, swirling his sherry in his glass, his gaze oddly intent on hers. She'd felt herself flush with heat, and had felt out of control. Reckless. Yet it had felt right, even so. More right than she could remember anything else feeling, maybe ever. He'd leaned close, then murmured close to her ear. "What would I do without you?"

She knew what he'd do without her, Dru thought now, staring up at the perfect sky and the glorious lagoon, neither of which seemed to be as bright as they'd been before. Without Cayo. He was probably doing it right now—carrying on being Cayo Vila, scary by design, taking whatever he wanted and expanding his holdings on a whim.

But she was distorted by his absence. Disfigured. And it didn't seem to get any better, no matter how many days passed.

She sat in her cramped seat on an Air Vila flight from Los Angeles to London, staring at the picture of him on the back of the in-flight magazine, and she thought her heart might tear itself apart in her chest.

I can't do this, she thought then, scraping away the tears before they fell on her snoring seatmate. She couldn't live out whatever life it was she thought she ought to live, knowing that he was out there, knowing that she would only ever see him in these painful, far-away glimpses. On the telly, perhaps. In the magazines. But never again right in front of her. Never again close enough to touch, to taste, to tease.

She'd been in love with him for so long. She was still in love with him, however hard she wished it away. It hadn't changed. She was starting to believe it never would. She felt minimized. Diminished, somehow, without him. As if she'd depended on him just as much as he'd depended on her all this time.

Back in her bedsit in London, she tried to tell herself that her whole life was ahead of her. That she need only pick a path to follow and the world was hers. She woke the morning after her return and scanned the papers, looking for clues to her next chapter—but it all seemed cold and empty. Pointless.

She was haunted by Cayo even now, in a tiny flat he'd never visited, on a bright morning that shouldn't have had anything at all to do with him. Her eyes drifted shut as she stood at her small refrigerator, and she saw him. Dark amber eyes. That fierce, ruthless face, with that blade of a nose and his cruel, impossible mouth. She *felt* him. She couldn't breathe without imagining his hands on her skin, his smile, the sound of his voice as he said her name. And that same old fire still burned within her, stubborn and hot, even now.

Did it really matter how he wanted her, as long as he did? Dru found herself pacing the small space that was her kitchen in agitation. She wished he'd handled it differently back in Bora Bora. She wished he'd lied and told her he wanted her, needed her—and not only as his assistant. She might not have believed him, but she'd have wanted to. And maybe it would have been enough.

But she couldn't marry him when he couldn't even pretend to love her. It turned out that was her line in the sand. Her single remaining boundary.

"A girl has to have some standards," she said out loud, shaking her head at herself. At the things she'd clung to all her life, like her belief that she would never be like her mother—and here she was, alone in her flat, halfway to Miss Havisham, arguing her way back to a man who could never love her the way she deserved to be loved.

But that was the problem. Dru didn't simply want to be loved. She wanted to be loved *by Cayo*. And she couldn't see how it made any kind of sense to do without him entirely. Maybe a sliver of Cayo really was better than nothing at all—because nothing else would do. The thought of another man was laughable. What would be the point? Another man wouldn't be Cayo.

Why couldn't they continue as they'd been? She considered it now, scowling fiercely into her sink basin, and the truth was, she couldn't even remember why she'd been so angry with him. Or why she'd been so desperate to get away from him. These weeks were the longest she'd gone without seeing him since she'd started to work for him five years ago. And she hated it. She craved the simple solace of his dark gaze, his impatient voice. Him. She missed *him*.

He might not want her the way she wished he could. He might only have proposed to her as some last-ditch effort to hold on to something he didn't want to lose, the same way he might feel about a particularly limited-edition racecar, for example. Dru understood that. And it wasn't that it didn't hurt. It was that being without him hurt more.

She wanted him more than she wanted her self-respect, it turned out, whatever that made her. A fool. Her mother. A very sad woman destined for a sad life of *slivers*. She supposed she would spend the rest of her life dealing with the fallout of this choice she couldn't seem to help making today. One way or the other.

But in the meantime, she knew exactly what she had to do.

Dru strode back into his life, and into the center of his office, on an otherwise unremarkable Wednesday afternoon.

She looked casual and chic in tight black trousers tucked into high, gleaming boots with dangerous heels and a very complicated sort of burgundy jumper that tied like a scarf and was somehow carelessly elegant. Her glorious hair was swept back into a low ponytail. She'd clearly spent more time in the sun, and it suited her. She had a healthy glow about her, and her eyes were clear as they met his.

Mine, he thought, with a nearly vicious surge of desire.

He wanted his mouth on her. He wanted to be inside her. He wanted her with a savagery that should have taken him out at the knees. Instead, Cayo thrust his hands into his pockets and stood there behind his desk, watching her, as the fury he'd been tamping down began to boil.

"I know how little you like it when people drop in on you without appointments," Dru said in that calm, easy voice of hers that had been haunting him for weeks. "I apologize." She smiled that damned smile of hers. The one he hated. "Your new assistant seems lovely."

"She is perfect in every way," Cayo agreed, his voice all but a growl. "A paragon, in fact. Truly the best personal assistant I've ever had."

"I'm delighted to hear that," she said, so very pleasantly. As if he was just another rich man she had to placate. As if she was working. "Though, if memory serves, you are a bit free with that particular bit of praise. It does render it rather meaningless, I'd say."

He didn't say anything. He couldn't.

"I went back to Bora Bora, as planned," she told him quietly, her gaze searching his, though he didn't know for what.

"I hope your flight was pleasant." He couldn't help his sardonic tone, or the way his brow lifted. "Fly commercial, did you?"

"It took over forty hours." There was the hint of a rueful smile on her lips, which was closer, at least, to something real.

He was meant to respond to that, he knew. He should have. Her eyes met his as if she was encouraging him simply to talk to her, as he might have done before. But he couldn't do it. She'd wrecked him in ways he still didn't understand. She'd left him. He'd let her leave. He still couldn't comprehend either one of those things.

And beyond all that, he wanted her. Pure and simple. Despite knowing exactly how much wanting her destroyed him.

"Dru." He said her name with all the fury and betrayal and longing inside him, letting it pour out of him, not even caring how it hit her. "Why are you here?"

He watched her swallow, hard, as if she was nervous. It became physically painful that he still wasn't touching her.

"I've come to interview," she said, and her voice didn't quite shake but still, he heard emotion there beneath it. A better man might not have taken that as some kind of victory—but he had no such pretensions.

"Interview?" he echoed. He could hear the chill in his own voice. "For what?"

Her chin rose, those gray eyes of hers glittered, and once more, she was hiding from him. He could see it.

"My old position, of course."

He'd dreamed of this. Exactly this. He couldn't help but smile, and he didn't have to see her reaction to know it wasn't a very nice smile at all.

But she didn't break. Not his Dru.

"I'd like my old job back," she said, very distinctly. Politely. She folded her hands in front of her like the passive and obedient underling she had only ever pretended she was, and walked straight into his hands with her head held high. "I've come to beg for it, if necessary."

CHAPTER TEN

HE LOOKED AS though he wanted to take her apart with his teeth. Dru fought to control herself—her pounding heart, her galloping pulse, that heaviness in her stomach that couldn't decide if it was desire or anxiety. Or some combination of both.

"If you would like to beg, don't let me stop you," Cayo bit out after a long moment, though his midnight amber eyes gleamed. "You can begin on your knees."

She remembered that day in Bora Bora with picture-perfect clarity. She remembered crawling to him across the polished wood floor, smiling up at him from between his strong legs. Wanting him more than her next breath. She still did. Heat flashed over her, and she was afraid she turned bright red. His eyes were narrow and hot, and she knew beyond a shadow of a doubt that he was remembering the same thing.

"Sweet memories," he said, deliberately provoking her, but she couldn't seem to react the way she might have before. She couldn't seem to breathe past the sheer *force* of him. It was if she'd dulled the intensity of him in her memory, to protect herself. He was shocking and bold, dark gold eyes and jet-black hair, and all that mouthwatering muscle and masculine grace. His suit was perfectly tailored and made him look sleek. Predatory. But not at all tamed. Not Cayo.

And now she knew what he could do with every last inch of that beautiful body. She found she'd lost her voice completely.

His eyes gleamed even more molten gold than before. He stepped out from behind his desk and roamed around to the front, leaning back against it so he was only a foot or two away from her. She schooled herself not to react, not to step away or show anything on her face, even as the back of her neck prickled in warning. In desperate, mindless want.

"Tell me," he said in that soft, supremely dangerous voice of his. "What would possess you to reapply for this job you wanted so desperately to leave? What will it look like the next time you decide you hate me, do you think? What will you throw at me then?"

"Perhaps I was hasty," she managed to say, before she lost what remained of her sense and begged him to take her, however he wanted her. "I may have let my grief over the loss of my brother affect my better judgment."

He eyed her for a long, chilly moment.

"The position is already filled." Cold. Harsh. Absolute. "You were correct," he continued, and there was so much Spanish in his voice that her breath caught. "It was ridiculously easy to replace you. It took a single phone call."

"Oh, I see," she said then, pretending she was as strong as she made herself sound. "You feel I deserve you at your scariest. Vicious and cutting. Is this my latest punishment?"

"What would I possibly punish you for?" he demanded, his voice low and dark. It connected hard with her belly. "It seems that I was nothing more than a convenient way for you to scratch that itch. Just as I told you to do." His smile then should have drawn blood. "What happened, exactly, that I should feel you need punishing?"

Maybe he *had* drawn blood. Maybe this was her, unable to move, bleeding out where she stood and all too aware it was her own fault. She should have left well enough alone. She should have figured out how to survive it—after all, she'd known going into it that getting closer to Cayo would end like this. Exactly like this. Perhaps she shouldn't have been so cavalier.

"Nothing," she said, and it was just as well that she was already so close to numb, already so worn out from all the heartbreak and the grief, that it was only a quiet sort of storm that shook through her then. Only a little bit of rain and another gray sky. No need for any commotion. "Nothing happened at all."

She inclined her head at him and then she turned and started for the door. It had been a mistake to come here. Cayo was a bell that could never be unrung. She had to move on, no matter how much it hurt. In time, she'd recover sufficiently from all of this. Of course she would. She'd stop thinking about him. People recovered from heartbreak all the time, all the world over.

She would, too, she vowed. *She would.*

"There is still one position that remains open, however," he said from behind her, and the dark, almost satisfied tone he used made goose bumps break out all over her skin.

Dru stopped walking, and hated herself for it. *You are no better than a junkie,* her inner voice castigated. *No better than your brother—and just like your mother. You'd take any punishment he doled out.*

The masochist inside preened, and she did nothing to prove either one wrong.

"What position is that?" she asked, her voice cool. Disembodied, perhaps, as if she was somewhere else, far from here. Watching from a distance while people other than her were cut to pieces. "Your personal punching bag?"

"My wife."

It was another slap, just as it had been on his island, and this time, she was already so weak. She had already broken down enough to come here. This was just another blow. For a moment she thought she might succumb to the tears that threatened to spill from her eyes—but she blinked them away, furiously, and then turned back to him.

They stared at each other. His dark, wicked brows were raised high, challenge and command. All of the tension and pain, all of the hurt and longing, everything he was to her no matter how she fought against it seemed to hang there and draw tight between them. He looked like thunder. His eyes blazed. And she couldn't seem to summon the pride or self-preservation that might have let her laugh at his twisted version of a proposal. She could only endeavor to keep her tears at bay just a little while longer.

He didn't say that he needed her, that he wanted her. That he longed for *her*. He didn't say that this was hard for him. He looked the way he always looked. Untouchable. Impossibly ruthless. And the most dangerous man she'd ever met.

"Your wife," she said, as if she barely recognized the word. She could hardly speak past the lump in her throat. "And what would that position entail, exactly?"

That predatory gleam shone in his gaze, and his

lean body was so tense, rippling with tension, that she thought he really might pounce. Behind him, rain began to lash at the windows and the sky was dark, and there he stood in the middle of all that, more elemental by far.

"I'm sure we'll think of something," he said, in a voice that made her imagine him thrusting into her: that slick, perfect fit. The electricity. The wildness that made her forget herself completely.

"And when that fades?" she asked, her voice thick. "You are not known for your attention span, are you?"

He pushed away from the desk and started toward her, like a lethal weapon aimed directly at her, and Dru had to fight herself to stand still. Not to run in the opposite direction. Or toward him.

"I have thought of very little else but you since the day you walked in here and quit," he said, moving far too close, forcing her to look up at him. "I never wanted you to leave in the first place. It's not my attention span that's at issue here, is it?"

"I can't marry you." She bit that out, final and sure. Desperate.

His dark brows lowered. "Are you holding out for someone richer, Dru? More powerful?" He didn't laugh as he said it. He didn't have to. His voice dropped, even as his mouth curved into that cold, mocking facsimile of a smile. "Better in bed?"

"Love," she heard herself say, to her utter horror. But there was no unsaying it, even when he looked at her as if she'd thrown another shoe at his head—and had hit her target this time. "There's no point marrying without love."

"Of course," he breathed, and she had never seen that look on his face. Remote and terrible, and if he'd been someone else she'd think she'd ripped his heart from his chest. But this was Cayo. His mouth twisted. "You have already made clear your opinion on my character. Who indeed could marry a monster such as me?"

But though his words were the bitterest she'd ever heard, so much so they made her flinch in reaction, he still moved closer. He reached over and ran his hand down the sleek end of her ponytail, drawing it forward to drape over one shoulder, the gentle touch at odds with the way his gaze burned into hers, fierce and uncompromising. And she remembered, then, that night on the chilly terrace in Milan, when he'd done the same thing. When he'd made her heart ache. When he'd made her believe there was more to this than simply that wildfire.

She remembered treading water in the sea, how she'd ducked under the waves and felt, for a moment, that she might simply let herself sink. How that had seemed better than facing this man who cast such a shadow over her whole life. Who she could not seem to do without, however much she thought she should.

Who had accused her of hiding from him, time and again, and here she was, hiding the most important truth of all from him. When really, what was she protecting? She had nothing and no one. She was wholly alone. She had nothing to lose.

But it was still so hard, so overwhelming, that spots danced before her eyes.

"I don't think you're a monster, Cayo," she whispered. And maybe she had nothing to lose, but it still felt like leaping from a very high cliff into nothingness. "I love you."

He went terrifyingly still, his eyes turning to poured gold.

"And you like to collect things," she continued, not caring about how scratchy her voice sounded, or how many unshed tears pressed against her throat. "You're good at it. You obsess for a time and then you forget all about it while you chase your next obsession." She shook her head, and stepped back from him. "I can't even blame you for that. I saw what your grandfather was like. But how can I marry you when you don't love me back? When you can't?"

"Dru—" he started, but it was a stranger's voice, and he was looking at her as if she'd become a ghost again, right there in front of him, and she knew that it was time to leave. That she should never have come. That she had betrayed herself once again.

"You don't have to say anything," she said softly, and she meant it. She did. "I should have stayed away. I'm sorry."

And then she turned back around and walked away from him. For the last time.

He tracked her back to a converted townhouse in a part of Clapham that was a world away from his three-story penthouse at the top of an old Victorian ware-house perched at the edge of the Thames. This was what she preferred to him, he told himself as he caught the door from one of her neighbors and climbed the narrow, grimy stairs to her second-floor flat—this dingy little place and the dim little life that went with it.

He was so angry with her, Cayo thought it might actually burn off the top of his head.

He pounded on her door, not even pretending to be polite.

"I know you're in there," he growled through the door. "I saw you enter the building not five minutes ago."

He heard the rattle of her locks and then she swung the door open and stood there, scowling up at him, and his curse was that he felt her prettiness like a punch to his gut. Her cheeks were flushed with emotion, making her gray eyes gleam, and he was tired of playing nice. Or trying to. He'd let her go, hadn't he? What else was he meant to do? And she'd been the one to come back and make it perfectly clear that he'd been a fool to do so. That he should have ignored what she'd told him. That he shouldn't have let her go in the first place.

"You are not welcome here," she told him in that cold voice that only made him want her more. It made him think about what best melted all of that ice, and he was certain she could see it on his face when he saw her eyes widen. "Go away."

"I can't do that," he said. He stepped toward her and she leapt back, terrified, he suspected, that he might touch her and prove what a liar she was. He simply shouldered his way inside the flat and kicked the door shut behind him.

And then they were all alone. No brand-new personal assistant in the outer office. And he was blocking the only exit. Cayo could see precisely when that occurred to her, and he smiled.

It was a laughably tiny little place, a bedsit indeed, all in white with a few accent colors—a wooden headboard, the pop of scarlet pillows on her bed—to suggest the idea of space without actually having any. She kept it scrupulously neat, and that was why it seemed slightly bigger than it was—but only slightly.

To his right, a wardrobe and a double bed jutted out into the small, fitted kitchen. Her laptop lay there, on a café table next to what looked like an abandoned cup of tea, and something about the sight made his chest feel tight. He could imagine her there, dressed in whatever she slept in, her glorious hair knotted on the back of her head as she scrolled through the internet with her morning tea. To his left, when he wrenched his gaze away from her laptop and his imagination, was the smallest version of a living room he'd ever seen, featuring only a plush white armchair, a small trunk and a little shelf with a television sat on it.

This was where she slept. Dreamed. Imagined her life without him. Lived it. Even while claiming she was in love with him.

She would pay for that, too, he promised himself. And dearly.

"This is my space," she fumed at him. "It's not one of the many things that belong to you, that you can storm in and out of as you please. I get to decide what happens here, and I want you to leave."

"I'm not leaving." He leveled a dark look at her. "Nor am I planning to run away if things become intense, unlike some."

He moved farther into the room, grimly amused at the way she skittered away from him, or tried to, as there was nowhere left to go. He picked up one of the handful of framed photographs that sat on the narrow bookshelf at the top of her headboard. A younger Dru and a pale, skinny boy who looked just like her, the same dark hair, those same unfathomable gray eyes. Dru was staring into the camera, mischief in her eyes and a slight smile on her lips, while her brother slung an arm around her neck and laughed. They looked happy, he thought. Truly happy. The constriction in his chest pulled taut.

"I did not *run away*," she was protesting. She reached over and snatched the picture from his hand, holding it against her chest for a moment before replacing it. "There was no point continuing that conversation. There still isn't. It hurts too much."

"All you do is run away," he contradicted her, not even attempting to temper the harshness in his voice. "You jumped off the damned yacht. You demanded I let you go. You walked out of my office. And that's not counting the numerous ways you run away without ever leaving the room."

"That's not running away," she hissed at him. "That's called the survival instinct. I'll do whatever I have to do to survive, Cayo, including climb out this window and down the side of this—"

"I promise you that if you attempt to run away from me again," he cut her off, his gaze hard on hers, his voice brooking no argument, "I will lock you up in the nearest tower and throw away the key."

"Another excellent threat," she retorted, unfazed, if that glint in her eyes was any indication. "With shades of Rapunzel, no less. Sadly, not a single one of your sixteen properties features a tower."

"Then I'll buy one that does."

They glared at each other for a long moment, while everything inside him rioted. What was it about this woman? How did she do this to him? Even now, all he wanted was to sling her over his shoulder and then onto the bed, and who cared what she thought about that? He knew how she'd *feel,* and it was rapidly becoming the only thing that mattered to him. She stood in her small living area, her arms crossed over her chest, her sleek boots kicked off next to the armchair so it was only Dru in her stocking feet with too much color in her cheeks.

And he wanted her so badly it was painful.

"What do you want, Cayo?" she asked then, her voice soft, as if it really did hurt her. And he hated that, but there was no other way.

"I want you," he said, gravely. Deliberately holding

her gaze. "That hasn't changed, Dru. I don't believe it will."

She held herself even tighter, while her cheeks paled and she bit down on her lower lip. And he wanted his hands on her. He wanted to bury his face in her hair and inhale the sweet fragrance of it. He wanted to hold her slender shoulders in his hands. He wanted to be what chased her pain away, not what caused it. But he had never known how to do such things. He'd never tried. He didn't know how to start, and all she ever did was leave.

But she loved him. And that was like a bright light where there had never been anything but dark. It was everything.

"I meant what I said in your office," she whispered. "I shouldn't have come back. I should have stayed gone. If you leave now, you'll never see me again."

"I believe you." He kept himself from touching her, but barely. "But I'm not prepared to watch you martyr yourself. Not for me."

Dru felt as if he'd kicked her.

"I'm no martyr," she said in a low voice, her mind reeling.

"Are you certain?" His voice was like silk, danger and demand. And he didn't back down so much as an inch. "I can almost see the flames dance around you as you burn yourself at the stake of your choosing."

She couldn't handle this. He was so much larger than life and standing in the middle of her tiny flat, taking it over, as if the space could not contain him. As if it groaned around him, near enough to bursting at the seams with the effort of holding the force of him within these walls. She couldn't seem to make sense of it. Or breathe past the knot in her stomach.

"I have no idea what you're talking about," she said, but she hardly sounded like herself.

He started toward her, backing her up against the cold windows on the far side of the room. It took all of three steps, and then the cold glass was at her back and Cayo was a wall in front of her, big and tempting and more dangerous to her than anything else in the world.

"What have you told yourself?" he asked in that smooth way that made her look around wildly for some escape route. "Have you cried over me, Dru? The man who cannot love you back? Have you forgotten I know you, too?"

"Are you mocking me?" She was incredulous. Not sure if that was anger or agony that surged inside of her, she focused on that fiercely cruel face of his and asked herself why she'd expected anything else. "Are you really that much of a monster, after all?"

His dark amber eyes glowed with something that was not quite malice—something that shivered through her and made her catch her breath. Temper. Fury. And that simmering, unquenchable desire that had ensnared them in this in the first place.

"How convenient for you," he said, his voice no less deadly for all it was so soft, like a lover's. "To find yourself someone else you can love so bravely, and from afar."

His words slammed into her like blows. Dru heard herself make some kind of horrible squeaking sound, and thought her legs would give out. She staggered back against the windowsill, while Cayo only stood there, pitiless, and watched.

"You only love what can never love you back," he

told her in that same way, so calmly, as if he didn't know how devastating it was. As if he couldn't see what it was doing to her—or more likely, didn't care. "You arrange your life around distant objects that you can circle but never approach. You thrive on it."

"You…" She could hardly speak. She felt winded. "You don't know what you're talking about."

"Don't I?" She saw the shadows in his eyes, the darkness that lurked there. "Do you love me, Dru? Or do you only think you do because you imagine there's no danger I could ever return it? No chance you might risk yourself, not really. You get to pretend to suffer for your great love while remaining, as ever, completely and utterly alone. Hermetically sealed away. The perfect bloody martyr." He paused, his eyes flashed, and his voice dropped. "Just as you did with your brother."

She lifted a hand as if to stave him off, unable to keep herself from trembling, and sank down against the wall, her legs no longer capable of holding her upright. But he was relentless—he was ruthless down into his bones, and he squatted down before her, his coat flaring around him like a cape, his suit clinging to the hard muscles of his thighs. A perfect and pitiless god, rendering his terrible judgment.

"You," he said, as if she had missed his point, "have no idea what love is."

For what felt like a long time—whole ages, perhaps centuries—Dru could only stare at him, stricken, too deeply shaken even to weep. She felt cracked open, as if she yawned wide and he was the brash, bright light exposing all of her darkness to the air.

And it hurt so much and so deeply that she dimly suspected she hadn't yet got to the real pain—that this was only the shock that preceded it.

"And you do?" she asked eventually. Belligerently, though her voice quaked.

Cayo's eyes were brilliant. Dark and gold and molten fire, burning her alive. He reached over and took her hands in his, and she should have jerked away. But instead, she exulted in the feel of his skin against hers after all this time. It pumped through her like heat, as though her own blood betrayed her, as though there was no part of her that wasn't his no matter what she told herself. Or told him.

"Let me tell you what I know," he told her, his voice low, intense. Urgent. His accent was thick and melodic then, wrapping around her, caressing her. "I want you. I want you in ways that I don't understand. I can live without you, but I don't want to. I don't see the point."

"Cayo—"

"*Callate,*" he ordered her. He shifted back on his heels, dropping her hands though she still felt as if he touched her, as if he surrounded her. She folded her hands over what was left of his heat. "I tried. I let you go. *You came back.*" His fierce face looked almost harsh. Stark and serious. "You only love what you cannot have, and I have never been anything but a monster. I've never wanted to be anything but what I am." His cruel mouth moved slightly, hinting at that curve. "Until now."

Something swelled up in the space between them, precarious and new. Dru felt the tears trickle down her cheeks but made no move to wipe them away. She could only see Cayo. And like one of those hummingbirds that Dominic had inked into his skin, she felt something flutter up and hover, skittish and shy, like some kind of gift. *Hope,* she thought, and that great cavern inside her, that terrible emptiness that had eaten her alive for so long, began at last to shrink.

She didn't want pain. She didn't want that masochistic streak. She wanted him. She always had. And she was tired of hiding. It was time to stop. Past time.

This time she was the one who reached out. She sat forward and ran her hands along his severe jaw, then held his fierce, impossible face between her hands. She felt the heat of him moving through her, warming her from the inside out.

"If I am not a martyr," she said, her voice small but strong, "and you are not a monster, then who do you suppose we are?"

"That's the point," he said, his hands coming up to cover hers, his gaze melting into hers, the world shifting all around them and the fire that always burned between them bright and hot and true. Making them something more than they were before. Soldering them together. Welding them, finally, into one. Not clay, but tempered steel. "I want to find out. With you."

"I think we can do that," she whispered, and then she tipped forward and kissed him, like a vow.

He found her sprawled out on one of the loungers on the private deck off the owner's suite on the great yacht, her lovely curves displayed to mouthwatering perfection in a wickedly simple bikini.

She smiled as he approached, but did not set aside her tablet until he lifted her bodily into the air and captured her mouth with his. He had not seen her in almost a full twenty-four hours and felt as desperate as if it had been years.

He set her to her feet carefully, enjoying the slide of her against him.

"What is it?" she asked, her clever eyes moving over his face.

He reached into his pocket and pulled out a long, narrow white box and handed it to her. She looked up at him for a moment, then looked down and opened the box. She gasped. And Cayo tensed, not certain this had been the right thing to do.

Dru pulled the pendant into the air and stared at it, her eyes filling with tears.

"Hummingbirds..." she whispered. Two birds nestled together on the silver chain, in the bright and bold colors that could only be Murano glass. They sparkled in the golden sunlight, looking very nearly alive. And when she looked at him again, her eyes were wet, but she was smiling.

"You won't forget him," Cayo said, his voice rough. "And neither will I."

She threw her arms around him and kissed him then. For a long time. Soft and sweet. Making both of them sigh.

It had been eight months now since that scene in her cramped Clapham bedsit. Eight months of Dru in his life, testing him and changing him, making him wonder how he'd lived without her for so long. He could no longer imagine any possible scenario that did not include this woman, who had somehow made him the man he'd never believed he could be. Flesh and blood. Alive. Not a monster, after all. Not as long as she loved him.

"When are you going to marry me?" he demanded when they were both breathless and she was boneless against him.

"When you deserve it," she said, pulling away from him. She wiped at her eyes and then she looked at him as if she thought that eventuality was highly unlikely, and he laughed.

"Must I bribe you into it?" he asked. "You won't take a house. Land. Atolls or islands."

He waved a hand and she followed the gesture, looking out over the deep blue of the Aegean Sea toward the sunny, green little island that stretched there off the side of the yacht. Private and uninhabited. And his. She had insisted that he visit all of his properties or sell them, and so he had, leaving the minutiae of his affairs more and more in the capable hands of his fleet of vice presidents. *Delegating.* This Greek island, one of the Cyclades not far from Mykonos, was the last on the list. He found he liked it. And the process of exploring them all, with her.

"No," she agreed. "I don't want your property. But..."

"Yes?" She amused him. Fascinated him.

"Perhaps a company." Her gray eyes gleamed as she fastened the pendant around her neck. The hummingbirds seemed to dance and shimmer against her skin. "Just a small one."

"Why am I unsurprised that the life of leisure bores you?"

She only smiled. "You have that boutique advertising agency in New York, don't you, that is currently in dire need of leadership?"

He was aware she knew full well that he did.

"What do you know about managing an advertising agency?" But his tone was indulgent and in any case, he had no doubt that this woman could do anything she chose to do, and well.

"I managed you for five years," she said dryly. "I imagine a company filled with artistic Americans could only be a breeze in comparison. A bit of holiday, really."

"I love you," he said, because he did, and because he could think of nothing that pleased him more than the idea of her doing this *with* him. Building all of this *with* him. Making it their empire, not his. Making it matter. "You can run whatever you want, *mi amor*. But I will have to insist that you marry me."

She only watched him, her gray eyes clear and sparkling, and he reached over to take her hands in his, pulling her to him. The sun spilled all over her, bathing her in light, and still she shone brighter.

"There is a little-known clause in all my contracts," he said softly, pressing kisses to her cheek, to the freckles across her nose, to her sweet mouth. "All Vila Group subsidiaries must be run by a Vila. So you see how it is. My hands are tied."

Dru laughed and threaded her arms around his neck.

"You know how I love a sacrifice," she teased him. "I suppose it's a good thing, then, that I love you enough to make such a huge one."

"It is," he said gruffly, but he smiled, and then kissed her again, sealing it.

And it would be, he thought. A very good thing, and they would spend their whole lives making it better. He had no doubts.

He was Cayo Vila. He didn't take no for an answer, and he didn't know how to fail.

* * * * *

#3205 THE TYCOON'S DELICIOUS DISTRACTION
Maggie Cox

Forced to rely on physio Kit after a skiing accident confines him to a wheelchair, Hal Treverne has no escape from her intoxicating presence. But unleashing the simmering desire beneath her ever-so-professional facade is a challenge this tycoon will relish!

#3206 HIS TEMPORARY MISTRESS
Cathy Williams

Damian Carver wants revenge on the woman who stole from him, and her sister Violet won't change his mind...until he needs a temporary mistress, and Violet's perfect! But sweet-natured Violet soon turns the tables on his sensuous brand of blackmail....

#3207 THE MOST EXPENSIVE LIE OF ALL
Michelle Conder

Champion horse breeder Aspen has never forgotten Cruz Rodriguez, so when he reappears with a multimillion-dollar investment offer, Aspen's torn. She may crave his touch, but his glittering black eyes hide a deception that could prove more costly than ever before!

#3208 A DEAL WITH BENEFITS
One Night with Consequences
Susanna Carr

Sebastian Cruz has no intention of giving Ashley Jones's family's island back, but he does want her. He'll agree to her deal, but with a few clauses of his own—a month at his beck and call... and in his bed!

HPCNM1121

REQUEST YOUR FREE BOOKS!

¿ FREE NOVELS PLUS
2 FREE GIFTS!

YES! Please send me 2 FREE Harlequin Presents® novels and my 2 FREE gifts (gifts are worth about $10). After receiving them, if I don't wish to receive any more books, I can return the shipping statement marked "cancel." If I don't cancel, I will receive 6 brand-new novels every month and be billed just $4.30 per book in the U.S. or $4.99 per book in Canada. That's a saving of at least 14% off the cover price! It's quite a bargain! Shipping and handling is just 50¢ per book in the U.S. and 75¢ per book in Canada.* I understand that accepting the 2 free books and gifts places me under no obligation to buy anything. I can always return a shipment and cancel at any time. Even if I never buy another book, the two free books and gifts are mine to keep forever.

106/306 HDN FVRK

Name	(PLEASE PRINT)	

Address		Apt. #

City	State/Prov.	Zip/Postal Code

Signature (if under 18, a parent or guardian must sign)

Mail to the **Harlequin® Reader Service:**
IN U.S.A.: P.O. Box 1867, Buffalo, NY 14240-1867
IN CANADA: P.O. Box 609, Fort Erie, Ontario L2A 5X3

**Are you a current subscriber to Harlequin Presents books
and want to receive the larger-print edition?
Call 1-800-873-8635 or visit www.ReaderService.com.**

* Terms and prices subject to change without notice. Prices do not include applicable taxes. Sales tax applicable in N.Y. Canadian residents will be charged applicable taxes. Offer not valid in Quebec. This offer is limited to one order per household. Not valid for current subscribers to Harlequin Presents books. All orders subject to credit approval. Credit or debit balances in a customer's account(s) may be offset by any other outstanding balance owed by or to the customer. Please allow 4 to 6 weeks for delivery. Offer available while quantities last.

Your Privacy—The Harlequin® Reader Service is committed to protecting your privacy. Our Privacy Policy is available online at www.ReaderService.com or upon request from the Harlequin Reader Service.

We make a portion of our mailing list available to reputable third parties that offer products we believe may interest you. If you prefer that we not exchange your name with third parties, or if you wish to clarify or modify your communication preferences, please visit us at www.ReaderService.com/consumerschoice or write to us at Harlequin Reader Service Preference Service, P.O. Box 9062, Buffalo, NY 14269. Include your complete name and address.

TABBY looked up at him and froze, literally not dari[ng]
to breathe. That close his eyes were no longer dark [but]
a downright amazing and glorious swirl of honey, g[old]
and caramel tones, enhanced by the spiky black lash[es]
she envied.

His fingers were feathering over hers with a gentleness s[he]
had not expected from so big and powerful a man, and lit[tle]
tremors of response were filtering through her, undermini[ng]
her self-control. She knew she wanted those expert hands [on]
her body, exploring much more secret places, and color ro[se]
in her cheeks, because she also knew she was out of her dep[th]
and drowning. In an abrupt movement, she wrenched h[er]
hands free and turned away, momentarily shutting her eyes [in]
a gesture of angry self-loathing.

"Try on the rest of the clothes," Acheron instructed cool[ly,]
not a flicker of lingering awareness in his dark deep voice.

Tension seethed through Acheron. What the hell was t[he]
matter with him? He had been on the edge of crushing th[at]
soft, luscious mouth beneath his, close to wrecking the no[n-]
sexual relationship he envisaged between them. Imperson[al]
would work the best and it shouldn't be that difficult, [he]
reasoned impatiently, for they had nothing in common. S[he]
cleaned up incredibly well, he acknowledged grudging[ly]

ritting his teeth together as his gaze instinctively dropped
the sweet pouting swell of her small breasts beneath the
ingy top.

He had done what he had to do, he reminded himself
imly. She was perfect for his purposes, for she had as much
ding on the success of their arrangement as he had. Thank-
lly nothing in his life was going to change in the slightest:
had found the perfect wife, a nonwife....

Two hours later, Acheron opened the safe in his bed-
om wall to remove a ring case he hadn't touched in years.
he fabled emerald, which had reputedly once adorned a
aharajah's crown, had belonged to his late mother and
ould do duty as an engagement ring. The very thought of
utting the priceless jewel on Tabby's finger chilled Acheron's
nticommitment gene to the marrow, and he squared his
road shoulders, grateful that the engagement and the
arriage that would follow would be 100 percent fake.

* * *

*Will sharp-tongued, independent firestorm Tabby Glover
ccept Greek billionaire Acheron Dimitrakos's outrageous
marriage proposal?*

Find out in January 2014!

HARLEQUIN®
Presents®

Revenge and seduction intertwine…

Miranda Lee brings you her stunning novel, packed with power, temptation and excitemen

Don't miss
A MAN WITHOUT MERCY
January 2014

His out-of-hours invitation…

Dumped by her fiancé *via text,* Vivienne Swan wants to nurse her shattered heart privately…until an intriguing offer from Jack Stone tempts her from her shell. But is Vivienne playing with fire? Jack's a man used to taking what he wants, and now she's at his mercy!

HP13